I0730571

PRAISE FOR

"A western-dystopian filled with the kind of angst, drama, and swoonworthy romance that readers will wish every sequel delivered."
-Independent Book Review

"Sevier and Smith are masters of their craft, queens of writing concise beautiful prose that manages to weave plotlines together without feeling jumbled or confusing."
-Emily S Hurricane, Author

"A genre-bending take on the classic western, this wonderfully satisfying, superbly crafted tale is hard to beat."
-Prairies Book Review

THE FOOL'S ADVENTURE SERIES

Guns & Smoke
Leather & Lace
Chains & Reckoning

CHAINS & RECKONING

The Fool's Adventure Series
Volume 3

LAUREN SEVIER
ABBIE LYNN SMITH

This is a work of fiction. Similarities to real people, places, or events are entirely coincidental.

CHAINS & RECKONING

First Edition

Copyright © 2025 by Lauren Sevier & Abbie Lynn Smith

Written by Lauren Sevier & Abbie Lynn Smith

TRIGGER WARNING

Please be aware that *Chains & Reckoning* contains dark and possibly triggering themes including graphic violence, language, depictions of child abuse, depictions of human trafficking, implied cannibalism, intimate partner violence, cigarette play, mild erotic asphyxiation, depictions of torture, depictions of castration, and implied sexual abuse of a minor.

Remember that your mental health matters.

This one is for our readers. Thank you for allowing us to tell you this story and becoming part of our crew.

CHAPTER ONE

SAVANNAH

DARKNESS HAS NEVER BEEN a friend of mine, but for *him*, I'd march into the depths of hell.

An opaque fog rolled over the banks of the Mississippi River, blanketing the city of New Orleans in an oppressive silence. Little more than the flicker of oil lamps and the clop of hooves sounded through the confining air, except for the occasional slam of doors and windows.

That, and my thundering heart as William Ellis led his stallion through the barren streets. Though more than an hour had passed since our tryst in the cemetery, my skin buzzed, nerves unsettled.

Will's body heat surrounded me, staving off the early autumn chill.

The few wandering souls brave enough to venture through the late night caught a glimpse of us and slunk into the shadows, fearing that the *Beast* had come to reap their souls, no doubt. I caught sight of Will's eyes as we passed beneath an oil lamp. The orange glow gave his skin a dark pallor, bringing forth the legend that haunted the city's streets.

His arms tightened around me, and his lips pursed into a thin line, all hints of the man I'd slept with left behind in the cemetery.

The momentary disgust that'd flashed in his eyes when I'd revealed he was my first burned into my brain. Whether his disgust was at himself or me, I didn't know, and I wouldn't ask. Confirmation either way wouldn't make me feel better.

Spanish moss on the low-hanging branches of the oak trees in Lee Square swayed on the breeze. Dread coiled like a pit viper in my stomach. No one had seen me leave Lee Manor earlier, save a stable hand. Audrey and Lucas's engagement party had captured everyone's attention at the time.

If there were guards on duty, however, I had no doubt rumors would continue to swirl through the household staff, heavy as the fog that masked our approach.

Will guided his mount around to the side alley, his fingers flexing against the reins.

Was he thinking of my admission about Sebastian's cruelty? Or was the memory of what happened between us in the graveyard heavy in his mind? His eyes were unreadable as he swung off of his stallion at the entrance to the stable and reached up to me. His broad hands grasped my waist as I slipped from the saddle. I took in a sharp breath as I slid along the length of him.

Our eyes met as my feet hit the cobblestones. His arms tightened around me, his lips parting as he seemed to duck his head toward mine, but then he stopped as though thinking better of it.

"Come, *mi sol*, I'll see you to your room." With one hand, he led his stallion into its stall, and the other gripped mine tight.

Silence as heavy as the New Orleans fog fell between us. Up the back staircase, past the back house, and into the front. He held me tight the entire time, until we arrived at my door. I tugged my hand from his, twisting the knob to my room and shoving the door open.

"Savvy—" Will's brows were pinched together, pain written in his eyes. His fingers twitched at his sides. Something seemed to steel him, and he settled back on his feet and ran a hand through his long hair. "Goodnight."

I let out a dark laugh. "Oh no, William Ellis," I said. "You just tried to blow your brains out. You're staying with me." His mouth opened as if to protest, but I fixed him with a hard stare. "I'm keeping an eye on you. Come on." I didn't wait for him. I knew he would follow me. He always did.

The door snicked shut behind him as I kicked my shoes off. I crossed to the far corner and kicked up the rug, then used my fingernails to pry up the loose floorboard. When I rose to my full height, I fixed him with a heavy look.

"Weapons," I said, pointing to the hole in the floor. "All of them." He opened his mouth in protest but instead released a weary sigh as he started rifling through his pockets.

The gun he nearly killed himself with was the first to go. He removed a couple of knives from one pocket, and another gun. Then a smaller knife. He motioned to his jacket in my hands. I passed it over, silently balking as he removed even more weapons.

How had I not felt *any* of those when we were in the cemetery?

"Is that all?" I asked as he tossed his jacket to my vanity bench.

A sheepish look crossed his face. "There's a blade in my boot."

I glared, extending a hand and snapping my fingers at him. He removed a small switchblade and tossed it in with the rest of the weapons. I leaned down, replacing the floorboard and rug.

"I'll give them back when I'm sure you aren't going to hurt yourself," I said simply.

I'd been horrified when I caught up to him in that graveyard, listening to him talking to a dead man about why he wasn't meant for this world. When he'd danced with me at the party, I knew something was wrong, but I could never have imagined his wounds ran this deep. I'd known Will for three years. In all of that time, I didn't think he was that bad off. I did what I could to help him, but it wasn't enough.

I wasn't enough.

I loosed a breath as I reached for the ties of my dress. I couldn't very well call for the maids who'd helped me into it earlier. There were already enough rumors flying around. The last thing I needed was for the staff to confirm I'd slept with Will. Not because I was ashamed of it. In fact, in the moment before Will's repulsion was laid bare before me, I'd been . . . euphoric. I'd never felt so close to someone before, so vulnerable, but, also, so *seen*. I thought he understood me . . . that he *cared*. And maybe he did.

Still, it left me cold, empty, whereas before I'd been so full of hope, of light.

Warm fingertips trailed along my back, working the laces of my gown. I dropped my hands to my sides as Will brushed my hair over my shoulder. I took in a sharp breath at the unexpected contact.

"You know what?" he said, stopping just short of loosening the laces enough for me to breathe. He gripped my hand and tugged me toward the bathroom, swinging the door open and pulling me inside. My eyes widened as he turned on the faucet to the tub.

"What are you doing?"

Will glanced over his shoulder, a glint in his eye. "Aftercare."

As he rifled through the copious bottles of oils and salts, pouring one in after another, I said, "You don't want to mix all of that. You'll smell like a brothel." He set down the colored bottle in his hand. I turned to head back to my room to give him some privacy.

"This isn't for me," he said. I froze. If it wasn't for him, then—

Will took my hand gently, brushing a calloused thumb across my skin. Goosebumps erupted along my arm. "I promised you that I would give you so much more than that graveyard.

"Starting with"—he moved toward the linen cabinet and tugged a large, puffy white towel from within—"taking care of you."

I couldn't stop my mouth from dropping open at his suggestion. He wanted me to—to let him give me a bath?

Will stared at my horrified expression with a look of confusion. "What?"

"I—I'm fine. You don't have to do this." My cheeks heated and I averted my gaze, unable to watch as amusement filled his eyes.

"I know. I want to," he said with such sincerity that my chest ached. "Savvy, we've already slept together."

"So?"

"So you'll fuck me fully clothed but you won't let me see you naked?" he asked, a teasing edge to his voice.

It was familiar, his playfulness. Some of the tension eased from my shoulders, but I still couldn't look at him. "We—you—" I blew out a breath, eyes heating beneath my discomfort.

When I finally lifted my gaze to his, Will's features softened. The teasing grin had slipped from his face. "You've never let anyone see you naked, have you?"

My jaw clenched and I crossed my arms over my chest.

Will said, "Which means you've never *seen* a naked man."

"What? Of course I have—"

"Who?"

"What?" I asked, back straightening beneath his sudden question.

"Who have you seen naked?"

"Name any of Audrey's bedmates," I said, rolling my eyes and waving a hand.

Will made a sound that clearly said he didn't believe me. "How about this..." He lifted his hands, deft fingers unbuttoning the front of his shirt. "I'll get naked with you."

"No."

A spark lit his eyes once more, and I could sense the taunt before he spoke. My stomach plummeted and skin heated as I remembered how our bodies came together in the cemetery. How it'd felt to be joined to him in a way I'd never experienced before.

I wanted to do it again. Jesus Christ, this was a bad idea.

"C'mon, you've got dirt everywhere." He slid the fabric from his shoulders, baring his chest to me. I mapped the broad lines of his shoulders, catching on an oblong scar just beneath his collarbone. "It's just a bath."

Will closed the distance between us and placed gentle hands on my shoulders, brushing his calluses across my bare skin. I forced the tension from them, eyes fluttering shut at his touch.

"Let me take care of you." He cupped my cheek, and my eyes opened to find stark sincerity reflected back in his.

I knew this man. Trusted him in a way I'd never trusted another.

A sigh heaved from between my lips. "Fine," I said, turning my back to him. "But you're *not* getting in with me." I flattened my palms against my breasts. "Undo me."

I felt Will's answering grin when he pressed his lips to my cheek. My heart felt like it would pound right out of my chest as his fingers worked quickly over the laces. I held the fabric upright as he loosened them. Without a word, I walked past him, holding the dress as best I could, and grabbed the towel he'd retrieved.

"Turn around." I didn't miss the smirk that lit up his features as he complied. I turned my back to him then, focusing far too intently on wrapping the towel around my chest. The white fabric of my dress whooshed as it fell to the floor.

What the hell was I doing? This was insane.

I stepped out from the pile of fabric, knuckles blanched as I gripped the towel. Keeping my eyes low, I moved toward the tub. Blessedly, the bath oils had bubbled up. I turned off the faucet, keenly aware of Will's gaze on my skin as I stepped into the hot water. After taking a steely breath, I slid the towel from my body and sank into the heated depths. I tucked my knees up to my chest, wrapping my arms tightly around them.

Without a word, Will retrieved a clip and secured my hair out of the way. Then, he grabbed a bar of soap and lathered my skin. I rested my chin on my knees, keeping my eyes shut tight as he washed away the dirt from my back and shoulders.

"You're so tense, Savvy." He kept his touches feather light. I scowled, opening my eyes and shifting to see him from my periphery. A grin crossed his face. "I can help with that."

"I'm not having sex with you," I said, rolling my eyes.

He let out a breathy chuckle and deposited the soap in its dish. Then he worked his fingers into my shoulders, rubbing them and forcing the tension from my muscles. Sweet relief spread along my body. I relaxed into his hands, my head tilting to one side as he worked his fingers against my neck, and I let out a moan.

Jesus Christ. I *was* tense.

Will's hands slid down my spine. I leaned into the movement. I'd never let anyone touch me like this. Why the hell not? My limbs loosened as he worked. Eventually, I leaned back against the cool porcelain of the tub. He turned his attention to the muscles of my arms.

"See, this is what a good lover does." He leaned close to reach my other arm, his breath sending goosebumps across my skin.

I scoffed. "Someone thinks mighty high of themselves."

"I distinctly remember someone calling me *God*."

"I was drunk."

"No, you weren't," he said. He was right, of course. I'd only ever been drunk once: the night with him in the stable.

A hint of regret made me wish I'd let Will into the bathtub with me. I imagined folding against his chest. Even so, as he rinsed away the soap and pressed his lips to my forehead, there was something so tender in the moment, something I couldn't describe. Something unexpected.

"You don't have to be embarrassed," Will whispered, brushing his lips across my cheek. "Not with me."

A smile found its way to my mouth. Logically, I knew that. I knew that no matter what I did or said, I was safe with Will. I always had been. I feathered a kiss across his mouth. He cupped my cheek and tipped my head up, parting my lips with his. I turned toward him, water sloshing over the side of the tub as my slickened hands slid along his bare shoulders. I tugged him hard toward me.

A door slammed nearby. I tensed, sitting up suddenly, skin heated and chilled at the same time. The last thing I needed was anyone seeing *this*. The doorknob jiggled.

"Wait!" I shouted, recoiling from Will and the heated kiss. "Who is it?"

"Savannah?"

My shoulders relaxed slightly. "Jesse?"

"Could you hurry up?" His muffled voice held an edge of panic. I glanced over my shoulder at Will, who shrugged. I climbed from the bathtub, yanking my forgotten towel from the floor and wrapping it around myself.

"Just a minute!"

My heart pounded as I ushered Will toward the door. A breath, then he disappeared into my room.

"Savannah?" Jesse asked again.

"Jesus Christ, if you need to pee so bad, you should have gone to your own room," I said, scowling as I entered my room and slammed the bathroom door behind me, heart pounding wildly.

Will stood before me, his black slacks slung low across his hips. I rested my shoulders back against the bathroom door, my eyes fluttering shut as I let out a long breath. Why did he have to look so damn tempting? When I dared peek at him, a familiar grin shone back at me. My heart stuttered and skin heated.

"Something wrong, Savvy?"

Through the door, Jesse's movements were muffled. I crossed to my wardrobe, gripping the front of my towel tight as I tossed it open and rifled through the neatly folded stack of nightgowns on the bottom. I shoved one over my head, relinquishing my towel to the floor. When I turned, Will still stood there, tempting as ever.

My tongue darted out to wet my lips as my eyes grazed the dips of his lean muscles, the definition directing my eyes to the outline of his cock straining against his pants.

"My eyes are up here."

The teasing lilt in his voice made my cheeks heat once more. I groaned beneath my breath, shaking my head as I unclipped my hair and let it fall in soft curls around my shoulders. I brushed past him, turning the lamp on my bedside table low and tossing back the covers of the bed.

"What are you doing?" he asked.

"I'm exhausted." I slid beneath the covers and to the far side of the bed. Will glanced toward the door. "Don't even think about it."

As I settled beneath the plush covers, I rolled onto my side to put an end to any arguments he could have given me. A breath passed before the mattress dipped beneath his weight. His heat crept across the sheets toward me. I fought against the temptation to melt into him. I needed to keep my distance.

The room plunged into darkness as Will extinguished the lamp. He tossed an arm over his head. Silence settled heavily over us. So much had happened in a matter of a few hours, but I couldn't go to sleep without making one thing clear.

"You don't get to die on me, William Ellis," I said into the silence.

I thought I heard a sharp intake of breath, but I couldn't be sure.

CHAPTER TWO

BONNIE

I WAS DROWNING.

Or at least, that was how it felt in my head. Memories pressed down, suffocating me until I couldn't breathe anymore. My thoughts were sluggish and heavy, unable to put the memories in the right order or compartmentalize them. They floated around me in a haze until I couldn't make sense of them anymore.

Who was I?

Audrey, the rich daughter of a powerful criminal hiding in her gilded cage of privilege.

Bonnie, former slave turned rebel outlaw, ready to watch the world burn.

Or was I some strange amalgamation of them both?

I kept reaching for a way out, but as if there were water closing over my head, I just sank deeper until nothing remained but blackness.

When my eyes cracked open what felt like a million years later, the room spun and wobbled away from me, and I shut them again. The smell of smoke lingered in my nostrils, my skin tight and a little chapped from the heat of the blaze. That was right. A fire. I set a fire last night.

"Good morning, gorgeous." Jesse's deep whisper in my ear made my muscles relax instantly. He was here. Safe and alive and with *me*. Hard hands clenched against the small of my back, and I groaned as the early morning light pierced my slitted eyes.

"Mornin', sunshine," I breathed out, nuzzling my face closer to the heat of his skin. Blinking into wakefulness was painful and disorienting.

"What happened last night?" he asked, pressing his lips to the top of my head.

Last night.

Snippets of memories come back to me bit by bit. Clear images crawling through the sticky molasses of my mind. My father, a man who was supposed to love me, turned out to be a liar and worse . . . so much worse. I didn't know the details, but not only was he using me the way almost every other man had done, but he was responsible for the end of the world. The Culling. Millions dead. Society crumbling. The rise of gang life, outlaw crews, and slavery.

All of it.

I sat up quickly, my head sloshing inside my skull. Although I lacked the specifics, one thing was certain: Jesse's parents and my father were somehow connected. Somehow linked in a dark secret that'd changed the fabric of the world and caused untold suffering. As their children, could we escape the lines they'd drawn between our families?

"After I told you to leave me in the study, guards came in, then my father and Lucas. I started smashing things and pretending I was looking for glowroot—"

"Another brilliant con," he said, with a small, tense chuckle. I finally looked at him; worry hid in the stern set of his brows, and his smile didn't quite reach his eyes. He'd never looked at me like that before. I tried to shake off the discomfort of his scrutiny. Of course he was worried.

Once an addict, always an addict.

"They sedated me," I explained, climbing from the bed to see he'd changed my clothes sometime in the night. Gone was the silk gown from my engagement party. Instead, I was wrapped in soft pajamas, a short white cotton nightgown. His moment of hesitation shouldn't bother me. Of course Jesse would worry about my sobriety. He loved me. I wobbled on my feet, and he reached a hand out to steady me.

I didn't know why I did it. Instinct. Reflex. But, I *flinched*.

Our eyes met and held, his hand falling away as his worry intensified. What was going on with me this morning? Why did everything seem the wrong side up? Jesse was—*is*—the love of my life. I trusted him more than anyone . . . didn't I?

Taking a few steadying breaths, I tried to calm the chaos inside my mind. Unease settled in the pit of my stomach, and I swallowed down the fear that all those walls I'd broken down to allow him into my heart were building themselves up again. I couldn't allow that.

I *wouldn't*.

"Bon—"

"It's fine. I'm *fine*. Just hungover from the drugs. Once I have some food, it should soak right up." I lied so easily to myself, but I was resolved to push through this strangeness between us until we found solid ground once more.

He rose from the mattress, the movement as slick and graceful as a mountain lion, his chest bared to my hungry attention. Jesse's body, now covered in ink, always made me weak. His arm snaked around my waist, and he crushed me against his hard frame. He was so tall, so overwhelming. His broad shoulders and trim hips dwarfed me, making me small against him. I'd always thought he looked as if some otherworldly force had chiseled him from stone, but I'd never thought that he was cold. No. Jesse was the embodiment of warm, sun-bleached, desert stone. Burning me up with every touch.

Today was no different.

I melted against him, pliant and relieved by the feel of his strong arms encircling my waist. This was what I needed to focus on, to remember. How safe and precious he made me feel. Or that being in his arms was the only place I'd ever felt fully myself. Whatever was happening in my muddled thoughts this morning would surely pass.

"Bon, we should *talk*—"

Talk. Honestly, nothing sounded worse. I was struggling to make sense of the memories in my head and my reaction to them. There was no way I'd be able to have a coherent conversation. At least, not yet. Not until I'd had time to process. I tried twisting out of his arms, resisting the pull my body had to him, but it was useless.

His head dipped, lips seeking mine. At the last second, I turned my mouth away, letting his fall on my neck instead. There was no escaping him, there had never been any escaping him. He folded against me, as naturally as breathing. His lips ran down the column of my throat, tracing my pulse and forcing my heart into a gallop.

This was never our problem. Sex was one of the things we *always* did right. The strap of my nightgown slipped off my shoulder, and a moan fell unbidden from my mouth, breathless and eager. Always so *fucking* weak for him.

"There's my girl," he whispered into the shell of my ear before tugging the lobe between his teeth. My eyes rolled back and fluttered shut, muscles warming and turning to liquid beneath his wandering hands.

"Jesse—" I swallowed hard, attempting to dampen my rising passion. "We have so much to do this morning."

Even to my ears the argument sounded weak. I couldn't see his lascivious smile of victory, but I felt it curl against my collarbone. His hard hands slipped down the curve of my spine, artist's hands, warrior's hands, hands that could create beauty or destroy it at his whim. Grasping both of my ass cheeks roughly, he yanked my hips forward until I was forced onto the tips of my toes with a gasp, his hard erection nestled between my thighs.

"Fuck, Bon," he groaned into the crook of my neck, the sound rumbling like thunder from deep inside his chest and rattling my bones. "I *missed* you."

Tears stung my eyes at the admission. I'd missed me too. I'd missed *us.* Even when I didn't remember, I'd ached for this. A part of me still did. Maybe it was the part that was still so hesitant and confused this morning. Or maybe it was because *this man* wasn't the noble farm boy I had fallen in love with all those years ago. He'd fallen in love with me all over again, a man obsessed, endlessly searching for me until finally, *finally* he'd found me.

Now, I had to fall in love with this new, ruthless version of *him.*

"*Please,*" I begged, my fingers tangling in his hair and tugging hard. His eyes clashed with mine, the blue a dark, tumultuous sea of longing.

Then his hard lips were on mine and he stole my breath. Drowning me in him. Devouring me. His teeth were merciless against my lips, nibbling and biting, his tongue claiming me as his control snapped.

He always did love it when I begged.

"Lay on the bed," he demanded, relenting his crushing embrace. I backed up a step, then another, never breaking eye contact. Not making any sudden movements. As if I were facing down a dangerous animal, poised and ready to attack at the slightest provocation. His chest heaved, lips parted, as he luxuriated in my obedience. The backs of my knees hit the mattress, and with careful slowness I sat down, taking a second too long and watching the muscle in Jesse's jaw twitch. Then I laid back, shivering as his oppressive heat assaulted me as he came near.

"Spread your legs."

I didn't hesitate. Didn't question. Didn't argue.

I spread them wide, the soft fabric of my nightgown bunching up my thighs with the motion. I wasn't wearing underwear. Not since he'd ripped them off of me the night before. Fucking me senseless in a linen closet during my engagement party, all while my fiancé socialized, oblivious outside. It was ridiculous that I'd ever thought marriage to someone else would release me from the hold Jesse always had on my heart. I would have to break myself into pieces and dig out the shards of him that pulsed through my blood, nestled into my bones, filled my every thought.

His jaw was tight as his hard hands wrapped around my thighs, and he stared at me, slick for him.

"*Please, Jesse,*" I whispered, desperate to feel close to him. Desperate to bridge that distance. That insidious disconnect I couldn't quite explain. "*I need you.*"

He yanked me toward him on the bed, throwing my legs over his shoulders as he dropped heavily onto his knees, all semblance of control evaporating in an instant. "You beg *so fucking* pretty for me."

Then he was feasting on me like a man possessed. With every buck and roll of my hips, he yanked me harder against his face or took that sensitive little bundle of nerves between his teeth. I raked my nails against his scalp as wave after wave of pleasure crashed into me. As orgasm after orgasm was wrenched from my body, leaving me limp and sobbing with the exquisiteness of it. I trembled involuntarily by the time he finally released me from the onslaught of his mouth. And the dark hunger in his blue eyes had only grown sharper.

He towered over me, engulfed me, his hands making quick work of pulling my rumpled nightgown off my body to rake his eyes over every inch of pale skin. Every raised scar. Like a map he loved to memorize. As he pushed his boxers down and settled between my thighs, I reached up to him, chin tilted in lusty defiance, my nails digging into his hips.

"Tell me what you want, Bonnie," he said softly into my mouth. He wanted me to beg again. I knew it with every fiber in my being. Only now the time for games had come to an end. Reaching between our bodies, I stroked him as his shuddered breath fell into my open mouth. His hand, each individual finger, gripped my jaw so carefully. Sliding down until it wrapped around my throat. The pads of his fingers covered my pulse points, feeling the rapid beat of my heart. He didn't squeeze, didn't threaten to take away my air. Trust, the kind of trust that spanned the edges of life and death, shimmered between us with this new kind of touch.

He anchored me to the mattress, and I arched my neck, pressing it into his palm and giving him the power to pin me down. His nostrils flared and his teeth ground together, a rumble of pleasure vibrating between our bodies, soaking into my skin.

"*Everything.*"

It wasn't a plea, but a command, falling confident from my lips. I knew what I wanted. What I *needed*. And though Jesse was a changed man after our years apart, he would never leave me unsatisfied. Never balk in the face of a challenge. With a hard thrust he joined us together, filling me, destroying me, making me *his*.

He wasn't careful with me; he set a pounding rhythm, murmured praises falling from his mouth hot on my skin. My eyes rolled back in my head, eyelids fluttering shut as the clench of his fingers on my throat made me dizzy with a pleasure I'd never known before. The clap of our bodies filled the room with nothing but the sounds of us. Until the world faded away into nothing. Until the distance between us was ripped away.

"Open. Your. *Fucking.* Eyes," Jesse ground between clenched teeth, each word punctuated with a hard thrust of his hips into mine. His hand tightened on my throat, and like lightning, pleasure spiked through my veins, gasping at the sensation, my eyes flew open at his demand. Until I was tumbling into the brightest blue of his. Seeing down into every part of him. His soul on clear display as I shattered, tears streaming down my cheeks as I came apart again and again and again. Breaking into pieces that he had put together. Cursing, he spilled himself deep inside me, his body trembling and his hands desperately cradling my face as if worried he'd broken me.

He wiped the tears from my skin, chest heaving as he struggled to regain his breath. I wrapped my exhausted arms around him, pulling him down onto my chest, his cheek nestled between my breasts as we both recovered from the exertion. We stayed that way until our hearts slowed and the sweat cooled on our skin, breathing even.

"Are you okay?" he asked, nuzzling into me until his lips found my skin and kissed me softly wherever he could reach.

"Yeah," I said, but something rang false in my head.

"Was it too much? Did I hurt you?" A note of concern laced his voice, and I absentmindedly ran my fingers through his hair.

That was when it came together in my mind. I realized why I'd felt so strange all morning since waking up in his arms. I should have felt whole. Complete. Happy. All those gaps in my memories filled, the pieces of my personality returned. Even the trauma that'd shaped much of my life now had new context for me to gain more perspective.

But Jesse *had* hurt me.

Getting my memories back should have brought us closer together. Instead, I remembered *everything* over the last few months. I could see so clearly every single lie he told to manipulate his way into my heart. Every insecurity he designed. Every time he broke my heart, it'd all been part of *his plan*. Each opportunity to be honest with me, to tell me the truth, to confide in me, he ignored. I was an outlaw. My word was my bond. When I made a promise, I kept it. I knew Jesse was a good liar. Had always known he had a natural talent for deception. In fact, that hint of outlaw had been one of the many things that'd attracted me to him all those years ago.

I never imagined he would use that talent against me.

I shook my head, giving him a shaky smile. "No."

I could be a good liar too.

Even though Jesse tried to tug me back into bed several times, I managed to escape him to clean up in the bathroom, my nightgown thrown back on haphazardly. Splashing cold water over my face, I pushed my haunted thoughts to the back of my mind. This was *Jesse*. He loved me. He loved me obsessively. Desperately. I just needed to push through these intrusive thoughts. After all, we'd been through worse.

Instead, I needed to focus on something I could control.

By the time I returned to the bedroom, Jesse had thrown on his jeans. Thank God, because I didn't know that I'd be able to keep my resolve if he was still naked in my bed.

"There's only *two weeks* until Lee and Lucas plan to marry me off, and that's not a lot of time for me to devise and execute a plan." Jesse stepped away, letting out a weary sigh at the resignation in my voice.

"Why does it have to be you?"

My mind went blank at his question.

"What?" I asked, confused.

"Why does it *always* have to be you?" he asked, hands falling helplessly to his sides.

Before, Jesse wouldn't have questioned me like this, and I wasn't really sure how to respond. I opened my mouth to make my case, but the words didn't come. *Why did it always have to be me?* Was it possible for me to just walk away? To pretend I knew nothing as my father seized the control he'd always wanted?

I could, I realized, do just that. We could leave, find somewhere to make a life and finally just . . . live it. This fight wasn't like the others. I'd been dragged into those. Hunted. Deceived. Manipulated.

This fight only had to be mine if I chose it.

"It doesn't *have* to be me. But if not me, then who?"

He sighed, running frustrated hands through his hair. "Anyone."

"If I'm right, then *my father* is responsible for the Culling. Which is bad enough, but I know, *for sure*, that he sold me into slavery as a child. Is the reason my mother was raped and murdered. That he sent Sixgun to your hometown and burned it down. Killed your parents. Orphaned *The Kid*—"

Jesse grabbed my hands, anchoring me as my voice rose. Thinking about The Kid, after being apart from him for so long, missing the feel of him next to me on our bedrolls or sharing the saddle of my horse . . . it broke something inside me. Helpless tears welled in my eyes, but I refused to let them fall.

"We can't change what's happened, Bon," he said softly, squeezing my hands tight. I shook my head.

"No, we can't. But we can stop it from happening again." My voice was firm and determined as I sucked in a steadying breath. "There's something I didn't tell you last night. Something I remembered. When Sixgun was talking to my father about Montana, my dad was *pissed* at him for killing your mom. He wasn't supposed to. '*You had clear orders to keep Anna alive so she could tell us where she hid them.*'"

I searched his eyes for any hint of what he might be thinking, but he'd gotten too good at perfecting his poker face. I hated it. Not being able to tell what was going through his mind. Feeling this destructive chasm growing between us.

"*Hid them*, Jesse. Your parents hid something from him. Something he's been looking for our entire lives. I can't stand by and do nothing. Maybe the girl you met in Vegas could, and maybe you wish I was her again right now—"

"Hey, that's not—"

"I know we need to talk, but I'm not ready for those conversations yet. Getting my memories back has been *complicated* and confusing. What I *do* know is that this fight is mine. I'm done being a pawn, and I'm done making decisions from a place of fear. I'm ready to take my life back."

I squeezed his hands before letting them fall. Padding on bare feet, I crossed to my desk and began clearing it off, keeping a few large pieces of paper on top. I sat, one leg crossed beneath me as I pulled the map of the manor into focus and picked up a pencil to take notes on it. I'd made this when I was tracking the guards keeping us apart, noting every rotation and shift change. I'd been furious then, locked up like I was in some gilded cage. Now, I was grateful I'd gathered the intel.

All I heard, even over the cacophony of my own thoughts, was the rustling of Jesse's shirt as he pulled it on and buttoned it. All I felt was the unsettling heat of him as he approached, looming behind my left shoulder. It was maddening.

Damn me to hell, but part of me wanted to just disappear with him. Beyond a border somewhere where my father, Jones, no one would ever find us. It ached within me, warring with the fuckin' moral compass that Jesse was, in part, responsible for installing near my heart.

"Alright then, where do we start?"

His words were deep, full of conviction, and they washed over me like a purifying rain. Reminding me that I wasn't alone anymore. I glanced at him over my shoulder, offering him a smile that softened the creases at the edges of his eyes.

"We?"

He buried his nose in my hair and kissed the crown of my head before pulling back and staring straight down into my soul.

"Together. Always."

And just like that, Jesse James made me fall in love with him all over again. He dragged a velvet-lined chair over to see the crude maps I'd drawn and the markings of the guard rotations. One of his eyebrows rose as he noted the attention to detail. I smirked. He was always so easily impressed.

"I'd like to start with figuring out what your parents hid from my father that he wants so badly, but that's not realistic. I don't know where to even begin trying to figure that out." My mind whirled as I thought about all the players on the board, their possible motivations, and tested each in my mind to seek out a weak link. "Lucas. This whole marriage plot feels off. That seems like a thread we could pull on."

"Another reason for me to hate the fucker," Jesse said, his arm slung across the back of my chair possessively.

"The ledger," I said, as memories clicked together like puzzle pieces. My father closing the front of the large red leather book as soon as I passed the door or called a greeting from the hallway. Late nights I'd seen him scribbling into it. "Not his official ones. There's another he keeps that he records everything in. All the underhanded businesses and the unofficial debts. It's like a map of his entire empire. But he keeps it locked up somewhere. I've never seen where he hides it."

"How are we supposed to get it then?" Jesse asked. I turned to him, a wicked smile curling over my mouth and a wild glint in my eyes. One he recognized immediately. He groaned, leaning his head back against his chair.

"Don't say it," he pleaded with me.

"C'mon, farm boy. You know how much I love a good con."

Chapter Three

WILL

I COULD WATCH SAVANNAH sleep for hours. I had, in fact, done just that. After sleeping off most of the alcohol from the night before, I'd woken before the sun, surrounded by her wild hair and the scent of her soap. She'd tangled herself around me in the night, and I'd trapped her in my long limbs.

You don't get to die on me, William Ellis.

A month ago, she'd scowl when I darkened her doorstep. She hadn't known about my obsession with her, how I got drunk on her goodness. Used it to stave off the monster inside me.

Last night, that monster almost won.

I still tasted the cold steel and bitter grief on my tongue, left behind by the barrel of my gun. The one she'd yanked from my hand, battering away all the demons in my head like she was swatting away mosquitos on a hot summer night. The demons were still there today, biding their time and waiting for me to be alone with my thoughts. So I clutched her tighter, silently praying that whatever worthiness she saw inside me would help me feel less hopeless. Less numb.

I knew when she stirred, the pattern of her breathing shifting as her body stretched long in my arms. Burying my head in the crook of her neck and holding on for dear life, I pretended to sleep. Her fingers buried in my hair a moment later.

"Oh, William," she sighed, wriggling gently to extricate herself from the cocoon of my body.

"Don't."

She stilled, and my heart pounded in my chest. The word fell hot on her neck, over her racing pulse. My lips came down on it, feather-light, until she released a small, sultry sound from the back of her throat.

I shouldn't fucking do this.

"Not yet," I whispered against her skin. Falling into her again like this would only hurt her. I wasn't a good man. But the self-control I'd clung to all these years snapped last night as I had her in the soft graveyard dirt I'd been prepared to die on. There was no control now. Only the pieces of me that yearned for her even more starkly than before. Writhing beneath me as all her rules faded away beneath the pleasure of us.

Shifting on top of her, I lifted my head and drank in the sight of her golden eyes. I was drunk on them, glazed by sleep and passion. Her lips parted. To do what, I didn't know. Talk us out of it, curse me for my callousness last night, moan my name in ecstasy. It wasn't a chance I wanted to take.

So I parted them with my tongue, swallowing her reluctant eagerness like it was medicine that could save me. Her hands in my hair moved lower, down the back of my neck, clutching at my sides and shoulders between haggard breaths.

"It wasn't a dream," I confirmed against her mouth, cupping her jaw and tilting her eyes back up to mine. "It wasn't a dream."

Then I kissed her deeper, more desperately. Her hips wriggled beneath me, our bodies begging for just another taste of before. Pushing back, she stared up at me like she was signing away her soul to the devil. Enticed but wary.

A wicked smile curled on my lips as I parted her knees and settled myself between her hot thighs. Her nightgown rose up her hips, and she licked her lips as her eyes traveled down the middle of my bare chest.

I shouldn't fucking do this.

But I would enjoy every second of her shattering beneath me. I'd keep her trapped here, in this room, corrupt every inch of naivete from her, until I could make her come with just a look. Until all that goodness I craved so much tangled with the darkness inside me. It wasn't right and I didn't fucking care. Not as long as she was here with me.

My hands slid along the soft skin of her thigh, pulled her hips into mine until she felt how hard my cock was; it strained against the fabric of my pants, desperate for her. Then I pulled open the tie at the neck of her nightgown, which kept so much of her skin from me, pushing the shoulder of the fabric aside until I'd worked her breasts free.

"*Santa mierda!*" I swore as I drank her in.

"What does that mean?" she breathed out, her voice holding a note of insecurity. I tore my eyes away from her naked chest to fix on hers once more.

"It means you'll be the fuckin' death of me, *mi sol*. You're so god-damned beautiful."

She chuckled, until my mouth came down against her ample chest, kissing, licking, sucking until I'd made a mark on her warm brown skin.

"*Oh!*" she moaned, a hint of surprise leaking through the pleasure. Her soft breasts were perfectly round, large enough to fit beautifully in my hands and mouth. Like every part of this woman was *made for me.*

Her lithe body wasn't still, even in her lack of experience; she rolled and bucked against me instinctually, following every thread of pleasure, luxuriating in it, and I knew I'd never be able to stop. She was even more beautiful like this. Taking what she needed, giving in to it, clinging to me as her pleasure built.

"Tell me what you want, *mi sol*," I panted against her skin. She shook her head, eyes shutting as her hips ground against me once more. I smiled. The little brat. When I pulled away a few inches, she whimpered and grabbed for me, but I caught her hand in my own. I flattened her palm against the hard ridge of my cock and gripped her chin in my other hand so she couldn't turn those whiskey eyes away from me again.

"Then show me."

"Wh . . . what?" she squeaked, eyes widening slightly.

"Show me what you want, Savvy. I need to know you want this just as much as I do."

Steely resolve settled into the depths of her whiskey gaze, and she sat further up, answering my challenge with one of her own. *Mierda!* I clenched my jaw to keep myself from cursing aloud. *This* was the

Savannah Beauregard I'd watched obsessively the last few years. Fierce. Steady. Unwavering.

She never dropped her eyes from mine as she worked the button of my waistband open, the zipper swiftly following suit. She tugged and pulled on the damn fabric until my cock sprang free and her hand wrapped hard around me.

"That answer your question?" she asked, stroking me as I grunted confirmation into her mouth.

"I might need more clarification, maybe we should—"

"You talk too much," she said, arching her lips up to mine and dragging her teeth over them. *Was I dead? Was this heaven?* Gripping her wrist, I dragged it away from me and pinned it over her head, my whole body throbbing with feral *need* so strong it overwhelmed me.

The door slammed open, banging against the wall. Savvy stilled, tensing beneath me, the fire in her eyes quenched beneath sudden fear. Fear of discovery. My head fell, defeated, against the crook of her neck as I pulled the blanket up to cover us for her modesty's sake. I didn't give a shit if they saw me naked. Or making her scream my name. But Savvy cared.

"I didn't realize interruptions were *fucking contagious*," I grumbled hatefully, shimmying my pants up as Savvy righted her clothes, her cheeks blooming a fierce red. She averted her eyes from mine, but I saw a gleam in them before she did. One that intrigued me.

"About as viral as that *Ellis charm*, apparently." Bonnie's sharp voice pierced through the room, setting my teeth on edge. As soon as Savannah was covered, we both sat upright, turning to see Bonnie standing imperiously in the doorway.

"Did you actually *need* something?" Savannah asked, her tone just as irritated as my own. Bonnie held her hands up in a gesture of peace, offering Savvy a smile only friends could share. A little irreverent and teasing, but mostly happy.

"I didn't realize I'd be interrupting, but it *is* important," she said, walking farther into the room, Jesse tailing her with a weary expression.

He ran his hands over the stubble on his jaw, releasing the air in his lungs in a huff.

"Last night we found out a lot of shit. Like, life-or-death, end-of-the-world shit—"

"The world already ended," I said, pinching the bridge of my nose before locking eyes with Jesse briefly. He tilted his head slightly, as if to say *it's about time* in Savvy's direction. "Jess, my cigarettes are in the pocket of my jacket over there." I waved my hand at the vanity bench, and he dutifully went to rifle through it on my behalf.

"I *know* it already ended, but we figured out how."

Silence fell. I couldn't even hear breathing as all eyes turned to Bonnie.

"Alright, well . . . not *how*. But we found this map in my father's office and—"

Jesse handed me my smokes, and in a second I dragged sweet nicotine into my lungs. I wasn't prepared for whatever the fuck this new crusade was, but it didn't seem Bonnie cared.

"—he and Lucas are planning to move up the wedding. Long story short, I need both of your help stealing a ledger from him before we escape New Orleans for good. Oh, and we don't really have much time to do it."

With my cigarette dangling from my lips, I leaned over and started to put on my boots. Savannah's eyes were on me as I stood, taking my offered jacket and throwing it on haphazardly.

"Maybe we should give them a minute—" Jesse said.

"Which floorboards?" I asked Savvy, picking up the corner of her rug as she'd done before when she hid my weapons from me.

"Oh, no you don't." She pointed at me, brows low and stern on her forehead.

"I've done some thinking—"

"More like *plotting*," Jesse interjected.

"If we all help with certain things, we can get this done and get out of town quickly. Will, you're the closest to Lee. You can help us figure out where he's keeping the ledger and then—"

"No," Savannah protested, but nothing could stop the hurricane of Bonnie when she felt justice needed to be served. I knew that all too well. She was well and truly back. Ready to jump into action, impulsive and commanding.

"Aye aye, captain," I said, saluting Bonnie mockingly with my half-burned cigarette between my fingers. She scrunched her nose at my tone but didn't comment as I thunked the heel of my boot on the boards until I heard one that was hollow.

"With the wedding so close, I can keep Lee distracted. Jesse is going to help us coordinate assistance with Mickey's men and help with the escape plan. Savannah can—"

Prying the floorboard up, I pulled my gun from the depths of Savvy's floor. Still in its holster on my belt, which I wrapped around my hips and fastened. Savvy threw a pillow in frustration, hitting my side with a soft thunk before it fell to the floor. Her eyes were dark and murderous. I just shrugged at her. What did she want me to do? This was what I was good for. A soldier. An executioner. A player in Bonnie's cons.

It was what I'd always done.

"I know this sounds like *a lot*, but if I'm right, Lee is responsible for the Culling. And I think he sent Sixgun to Montana looking for something Jesse's parents hid from him. Something *dangerous*."

At the mention of my father and what he'd done in Montana, I shut down again. Numbing myself. Succumbing to the Beast inside me that needed to get the job done. My jaw clenched, and I started strapping my knives into place.

"Audrey, *stop*!" Savannah shouted, her chest heaving.

Guilt slammed into me. We'd been so caught up in each other and everything that happened last night, I'd forgotten to tell Savannah that Bonnie got her memories back. Bonnie stared at Savannah, neither of them turning away. The air in the room grew thick with all the things we *weren't* saying right now.

"Actually," I said, clearing my throat nervously. "I didn't get a chance to tell you last night but . . . meet *Bonnie*." I bit my bottom lip. "Her memories came back."

Savannah turned her head sharply, glaring at me hard enough that fear pulsed down my legs.

"While that is great news, we have more *important* things to talk about—"

"Savvy, *don't*—" I said, shaking my head at her. Jesse, who'd sat on the vanity bench looking bored, picked his head up at Savannah's serious tone. "It's *not important.*"

"*Not important?* I'm sorry, but I think the people who care about you deserve to know you had a gun in your mouth last night—" Her eyes widened at the harshness of her words, the realization of what she'd just revealed.

Suddenly, all their attention was on me, and I didn't like the scrutiny. Stubbing the butt of my cigarette out on the nightstand, I closed my eyes tight for a moment. No one spoke. Looking to me for answers, an explanation. Concern and pity weighed down their expressions, wriggling beneath my skin and making me feel sick. I didn't want that. Not from them.

"Goddamnit, Savvy," I said quietly, shifting my eyes to her.

"Will—" Jesse started, but I cut him off by chuckling.

"You should see your face, *pendejo,*" I said, slipping into my mask of frivolity with ease. "It's not a big deal. I was drunk and a little dramatic last night, but I'm sober now. Savvy just . . . "

But no matter how loose I made my shoulders, or how easy my smile was, the tension in the room didn't ease. I couldn't make myself lie. Not with Savvy's name in my mouth. The words just faded into nothing.

"Will," Bonnie said, her voice breaking on my name. I couldn't look at her.

"They deserve to know, so they can help."

"I don't need any fucking *help,*" I said, my words hard. Savvy flinched. Hurt flashed in those whiskey eyes I'd been drunk on a few minutes ago. I really was a piece of shit.

"We all need help sometimes," Jesse said, rising from his seat. He shared a loaded glance with Bonnie, who nodded in return. That was fucking annoying. Bonnie sat on the mattress next to Savvy and cleared her throat.

"Savannah, we both need some *tea*. How about you two hang out in my room while she gets dressed, and we'll see you in a little while?" she suggested carefully, sounding like socialite Audrey even though Bonnie's machinations drove the suggestion. That was pretty fucking annoying, too.

"Whatever you say, *Miss Audrey*," I said, my tone black. I stalked out of the room, picking up my shirt from the bathroom floor as I left, Jesse hot on my heels.

As soon as we were alone, it crept back in. More insidious than before. All the parts of me I thought I'd recovered were gone again. Sinking into the darkness within my mind. Shredding my self-worth to pieces. They all knew now. They knew that I was losing the battle for my soul. Knew I wanted to give up altogether.

Sinking onto the chaise, I buried my head in my hands and tried to forget the look on Savannah's face as she recoiled from me. I'd hurt her. Again. Because the truth was, I'd never been worthy of her. I'd only disappoint her.

Or worse, drag her down with me.

CHAPTER FOUR

JESSE

THE LAST THING I expected this morning was having to face the ugly truth that my best friend wasn't okay. I kept my gaze steady on Will as he settled on Bonnie's chaise, head in his hands. I'd been worried about him for weeks, ever since he killed Sebastian to save Bonnie. I *knew* he wasn't fine like he said, but I didn't push. I wanted to give him space. I wanted to give him a chance to figure it out for himself.

That's what I get for thinking Will would come around.

I leaned against the footboard of Bonnie's bed, staring at him. Thick, oppressive silence filled the air, even as movement sounded in the hallway just beyond the door.

Ever since that fateful day in Fort Hood, when Sixgun took Bonnie, I never felt like I was enough. I wasn't strong enough, fast enough, smart enough. My demons threatened to drown me on a daily basis, even after I arrived in New Orleans and entered the Lee household with the hope of getting the woman I loved back.

I only survived it because of Will.

When he finally lifted his head, our eyes met, and pain dulled his. He shifted uncomfortably, averting his gaze and reaching into his pocket for his cigarette case. As smoke curled in the air, his dark eyes darted toward the door, as if he were preparing to bolt.

"Talk to me," I finally said, breaking the silence.

"There's nothing to talk about, Jess," Will said, staring at his cigarette as he lifted it to his lips. "I'm fine."

"You're not."

"I am." Will ran a hand through his hair, once again avoiding my gaze. His hands shook. When he noticed my attention on them, he sat straighter and balled them into fists.

"You need to talk about this," I said. "I knew you weren't doing good, but fuck, Will, you tried to kill yourself."

He blew out a long, smoke-filled breath. "Like I said, I got a little drunk . . . There's nothing to worry about, *pendejo*. Now"—he rose from his seat—"can I go? I need to change out of this fucking suit."

"No."

"No?" Will stood straighter, towering over me by a few inches as he rose to his full height.

He was going to bolt, I could tell by the lines of tension in his muscles. I shoved away from the bed, positioning myself between him and the door.

"No, I'm not letting you walk out of here." I crossed my arms over my chest and widened my stance. He may have been taller than me, but I had a good fifty pounds of muscle on him. "I didn't push hard enough about Sebastian. I thought if you wanted to talk about it, you would come to me."

A muscle feathered across Will's jaw as he clenched his teeth.

"But you didn't," I said.

"What do you want me to say, Jess?" Will said blackly as he stubbed his cigarette out on Bonnie's desk. Loathing filled his eyes as he glared at me.

"I want you to open up to me. You've seen me at my worst. You helped me keep hope through all of this. I never would have made it without you," I said honestly. "Let me do the same for you."

In response, Will tipped his chin defiantly.

"Needing help doesn't make you weak."

"I don't want to talk about it, because talking about it won't fucking change anything. Okay?"

"How do you know that?"

"Because it doesn't change anything that I've done!" He took a broad step toward me, but I remained firm. "Or anything that's happened." I wasn't going to budge. Not until he talked to me. He blew out a hard breath, then paced across the room. "Whether it's Bonnie losing her fucking memory and me becoming an executioner to protect her. Or my father's constant presence even though he's hundreds of miles away. Or murdering people. Daily. Because they messed with Lee. Or owed him money.

"Killing someone I care about to protect Bonnie." Will flung a hand toward the closed bathroom door. "Or hurting Savannah because God fucking knows I will *never* be good enough for her. Or seeing you and Bonnie last night, reunited and happy together and *whole*. All of the things I'll *never* be. Talking about that shit doesn't change it."

His chest heaved as silence once more filled the room.

"You can," I said. "Have that, you know?"

"No, I can't."

"Yes, Will, you *can*."

"You don't get it. You can live without blood staining your hands. Because you do the *right* thing, no matter how hard it is. Things get better for you. I don't. I do *all the things* no one else will. Because they're necessary. And no one mentions how fucked up they are because . . . they have to be done. At the end of the day, you all excuse the horrible shit I've done because you're just grateful you didn't have to do it yourselves."

My hard stance wavered. "I may not have the same blood staining my hands, but I've done plenty that I'm not proud of," I said. "That doesn't mean I give up when the demons come to collect. I fight. Every single day. I lean on the people around me. I let them in."

Will lowered his head, a move I'd noticed when he wore his hat as it hid his eyes.

"Otherwise," I said, "the darkness wins."

"The things you aren't proud of don't haunt you the same way, Jess." I opened my mouth to argue, but he barreled forward. "You can't see their faces when you sleep. You don't get ambushed by grieving family members in the street. You don't hear *children* begging for their parents' lives. I've been hanging on for a *long time* before you got here. Seb wasn't the worst thing I've ever done. He was a fuckin' wake-up call."

A chill ran down my spine.

"I cared about him. He made me breakfast. We laughed together about stupid shit, like how picky he was about his food not touching. Or how long it took him to get ready in the mornings." The ghost of a smile curled along his mouth, then faded into a grimace. "Our relationship was fucking complicated. But, even when we weren't together, he talked to me like a person. *Treated* me like a person." He sat again, heavily, like he'd lost the strength to stand upright. "And I killed him. I know I *had* to. I know he lied. That he was a threat. But, Jess, it was *so easy.*

"Do you get it? I don't know where the line is anymore. I thought I was getting better, but I'm not. The truth is, the only thing I'm really good at is killing. Just like my father. And I'd rather be dead than become him."

The terse silence that settled between us rattled me. Will seemed so hopeless, so lost, and there was nothing I could do to help him. But I had to try.

"You don't want to be like your father," I said, stepping tentatively toward him. "What *do* you want, Will?"

"It doesn't matter what I want."

"Yes, it does," I said. "You can either lose yourself in this hopelessness, or you can admit what you really want and fucking fight for it."

Will clenched his fists together, his jaw tense as he glared at me. I lifted my brows in response. A moment passed. Then another. Eventually, the breath went out of him and the tension broke.

"I want to stop."

"Then, stop." It was easy for me to say that. Trepidation filled my friend's features, but I wanted him to believe that he *could.*

"If I do, Lee will kill me." He chuckled darkly, a note of resignation in his voice. "And if I'm going to die either way, I'd rather go out on my own terms instead of giving that motherfucker the satisfaction."

I nodded, running my thumb along my jaw in contemplation. "So you find ways around it. He wants someone dead, right? Help them get out of town."

"Jess, he expects to see bodies hanging from the bridge."

An odd smile crossed my face. "People die every day, Will. I doubt Lee will go out to the bridge to verify *who* is hanging. He trusts you, Bonnie is right about that." I gripped his shoulder, squeezing until he met my gaze. "You are more than Lee's monster, more than Sixgun's son. I believe that. Bonnie believes that. I bet Savannah does, too."

Some of the tension released from Will's shoulders. "Yeah, until I fuck that up."

I shook my head at him, a smile tugging at the corners of my mouth. "You really don't get it, do you?"

"Get what?"

"If Savannah didn't want you, she wouldn't be trying so hard," I said simply, opening my palms toward him. "She isn't the type to do anything she doesn't want to."

A half grin formed on his face, chasing the shadows away. "No, she doesn't."

"Just . . . remember that we care about you, that you aren't in this alone. Not anymore."

Will only nodded in response. I shuffled around the room for my boots. While I wanted to hide away and forget the things happening around us, I couldn't. Bonnie was right; we had things to do.

"How *did* that happen?" I asked as I tied my laces.

"What?" Will asked as he lifted a match to the cigarette hanging between his lips.

"You ending up in Savannah's bed."

Mirth filled his eyes as he inhaled deeply. A moment later, he blew out smoke, his grin lighting up his features. "I don't kiss and tell, Jess."

I rolled my eyes. "Since when?"

"Since I ended up in Savannah's bed," he said, narrowing his eyes at me. "She's a *fucking lady*."

I shrugged. "Well, good for you. I figured all you and Savannah needed was a good fuck."

Will's features lit up at my words, reminiscent of the morning after Bonnie and I spent the night in the truck just outside of Fort Hood.

"Come on," I said, rising from the chair. "We need to meet back up with Bonnie. We've got a lot to do. Starting with Mickey and The Kid." I slung an arm around his shoulders and guided him toward the door. "Do you have any idea how we can smuggle an army into the city without Lee noticing?"

While darkness lingered in my friend, I had hope that he would claw his way out of it. That we all would.

Chapter Five

SAVANNAH

"HE IS *ABSOLUTELY*"—I reached behind me to secure my dress's zipper—"infuriating!"

Bonnie chuckled from her spot on the edge of my mattress. I wheeled around to face her. While the bright blue of her eyes and her loose posture would have brought me great relief an hour ago, now it just annoyed me. The smile only slightly slipped from her mouth as I glared at her.

"Come on, Savannah, you have to admit, it's about time," Bonnie said.

I rolled my eyes and slipped on my shoes. "That's not *even* what we're talking about." I crossed to the vanity, snatching my hairbrush to fix my hair.

"Oh no?"

"No," I snapped.

After settling heavily at my vanity, I focused on fixing my hair and putting myself back together after the whirlwind of last night and this morning. It took far longer than I would have liked with my shaking hands, but I pinned my hair neatly back into place. I smoothed the flyaways down, creating the careful visage of control to which I so desperately needed to cling.

The walls I'd broken down built themselves back. I didn't want to be seen anymore.

I was a fool to think that this attraction between us was something real, something lasting. This was *William Ellis*. Notorious for breaking hearts.

35

As much as I'd enjoyed myself, it couldn't happen again.

"Care to elaborate?"

I rose primly from my seat. "No," I said, then headed for the door. We needed *tea* after all.

Bonnie scrambled from the bed and fell into step with me in the corridor.

"Look, Will didn't mean to snap at you. He just gets like that sometimes, when he feels cornered. And he's like *infamous* for trying to weasel his way out of tough conversations. I don't think he meant anything by it, if that helps."

I shook my head as Bonnie nudged me with her elbow. Though her stare burned against my cheek, I couldn't look at her. "It's not just that—"

The words faded to ash on my tongue. Yes, Will snapping like that hurt my feelings, but more than that, it reminded me of how different we were. How this thing that had blossomed between us wouldn't end well. Someone would get hurt.

That someone would be me.

"I care about him," I said finally, voice quiet as the maids sauntered by with fresh linen. They eyed me with the usual contempt, though their expressions softened when they looked at Audrey.

No. Bonnie.

Sensing my trepidation, she pulled me into the dining room and slid the pocket doors shut.

"What's wrong with that?" she asked, words soft. She was the only person who could get through to me in times like this. Even still, speaking my feelings brought them to life, gave someone power over me. Gave them the chance to destroy me.

"Everything," I said, brows pinched together. "I thought . . ." I heaved a sigh. "I thought that caring about him, showing him I cared about him, would help him. But clearly it doesn't matter."

"It matters. I know for a fact that, to Will, it matters."

I wanted to believe that. I wanted to believe that I was the exception. That Will cared about me, even though I knew his patterns. For God's sake, he was dating Sebastian and kissing me! My stomach roiled. There was just so much happening, and I didn't know how to process it. I didn't even know how to talk about it.

"If you say so." I turned to the door, intent on finishing the mission. *Tea.*

Instead, Bonnie gripped my forearm. I froze. "You can talk to me, you know that?"

"Of course, I know that, Audrey—" I stopped, eyes fluttering shut. *"Bonnie."*

That bothered me, too. Through the whirlwind of trying to get Will to listen, I'd learned that my best friend had gotten her memories back, and *that* brought an entirely new set of emotions.

Now that she knew everything, what did it mean for us?

My bottom lip wobbled as my anxiety swirled out of control. She wasn't *Audrey*, anymore. At least, not *just* Audrey. She was Bonnie, too, an entire person who had existed long before that fateful night three years ago when Will carried her death-like form into this very room.

"It's weird, right?" Bonnie said, her eyes unsteady on mine. "Suddenly remembering a whole life you didn't have before is pretty . . . confusing. I'm actually really nervous right now."

"Why in the world would you be nervous?"

She cracked a smile, albeit a small one. "Believe it or not, Bonnie was even worse socially than Audrey. And . . . I don't know . . . maybe you won't like me anymore?"

"You're kidding, right?" I asked, fighting against the smile threatening on my own lips. "I figured *you* wouldn't like *me.*"

"Are you insane? Now that I have my memories back, I think you're even more amazing than I did before. Remember, for a moment, that *Will Ellis* was my best friend growing up. I'd say I *definitely* upgraded."

"I know—" I started, but the pocket door slid open suddenly.

"Audrey, there you are." Lucas Rutherford may have appeared as he usually did—freshly pressed shirt buttoned nearly all of the way up, shined shoes, and perfectly styled hair—but something in the deep lines of his face unsettled me. "I know last night was a lot—"

"Lucas," Bonnie said, easily adopting a carefree smile as she brushed past me toward him. "Savannah and I were just heading to the kitchen."

Rutherford didn't spare a single glance in my direction. "We have a lot to get done," he said, his voice harsher than I remembered it ever being before.

"Right." Though her tone seemed very *Audrey*-like, from the tension in her back and shoulders, the last thing she wanted to do was engage with her fiancé. "I had a *really* late start. I need breakfast first. And coffee." She expertly guided him into the corridor. "How about I come find you after and we can get started on all of those *things*?"

It was so easy for her to mold into the part she had to play.

"Well, I don't think—"

"Perfect!" Bonnie pressed a quick kiss to his cheek, then grabbed my hand and dragged me away from him. Even though he protested, Lucas didn't follow as she led the way through the courtyard.

"This is such a mess," I murmured.

"Tell me about it." Bonnie shoved open the door to the kitchen, which already bustled with activity.

Etty had a large pot of gumbo cooking as she ordered her helpers about. She caught one sight of us and a brilliant smile crossed her features.

"Morning, baby." She touched my cheek with her fingertips as I brushed past her. "I thought for sure you two would sleep until noon."

Not likely.

I shuffled out of the way of a man carrying a large wooden crate who settled it on the opposite side of the kitchen island.

"We need tea, Etty," I said.

The woman's gaze went to Bonnie, who seemed unbothered as she settled on a stool and snatched a biscuit from the platter on the island. Etty retrieved the kettle and filled it with water. As she crossed to the stove and lit the burner, I cleared my throat.

"Enough for two, please."

Slowly, Etty turned toward me, narrowing her eyes. "Two?"

I nodded, unable to form words around my leaden tongue. Etty was protective of me; she always had been. She'd been a mother to me, given me all of the talks a mother normally would. The suspicion in her gaze made my stomach dip.

"It was that Ellis boy, wasn't it?" Her fingers wrapped around the rolling pin on the counter.

"Etty—" I started.

"Where is he?" She glanced through the kitchen window overlooking the courtyard.

"Please don't."

Etty moved toward the door, but I cut her off. The kitchen went still. The woman was a force, one that nobody got in the way of.

"Everyone out!" I ordered.

The other staff members eyed me with their usual scowls. When Etty didn't say anything, they shuffled out.

Bonnie sat at the island, picking apart the fluffy insides of her biscuit, pretending as if she *weren't* there. I reached for the rolling pin, tugging until Etty relinquished her grip.

"We talked about this," I said plainly.

"We didn't talk about *this*." Her gaze shot to the door, dark with murderous intent.

"Etty," I tried again, placing a tentative hand on her forearm. "We talked about there being a time this might happen. And what did you always tell me?"

Tension leached out of the woman. Her shoulders relaxed as she looked at me. "That it didn't matter, as long as it was your choice and you were careful."

I gave a terse smile, forcing myself to relax beneath her scrutiny. "This is me being careful," I said. "And it *was* my choice."

Etty let out an annoyed harrumph. Then, the normal sparkle returned to her eyes, and she turned away from me and stirred the giant pot on the stove. "You and Lucas sure aren't wasting any time, Miss Audrey."

Relief coursed through me. At least she wouldn't kill Will. Yet.

I settled beside Bonnie, who sat deathly still, biscuit still in hand. She set it down on a napkin and let out an uneasy chuckle as she wiped her fingers to rid them of the crumbs.

"*Right*, because he's my fiancé," she said.

Instead of responding, Etty hummed beneath her breath as she pulled two teacups from the cabinets. I shared a glance with Bonnie, lifting an eyebrow and shrugging. She tapped her fingers on the island.

A minute later, Etty plunked two teacups on the kitchen island at the very moment the door burst open and in walked the very men responsible for the need of tea.

"Bottom's up," Bonnie said, downing the contents of the glass in one go. I stared at her, wide-eyed.

"What is *wrong* with you?"

Bonnie coughed, then wiped her mouth clean with the back of her hand. "It gets worse the cooler it gets. You should hurry."

As I lifted my cup, my gaze caught on Will, hovering near the door. I rolled my eyes and sipped tentatively. Then I gagged. It was *awful*. Like rotten broccoli and skunk. I grimaced. "What is in this?"

"It's better if you don't know," Bonnie said, guiding my cup back to my lips. I opened my mouth to protest, but she forced the rest of the tea in my mouth.

The tea burned down my throat and made me tear up. I coughed, sputtering as I tried to force it the rest of the way down. "I hate you."

Bonnie leaned closer to me, whispering so no one else could hear. "Is there a way to get Etty *out* of the kitchen for a while?"

"No one gets me out of *my* kitchen, boss's daughter or not. Now, y'all wanna tell me what's going on, or do I need to pull it out of you? Because I have a rollin' pin I'd *like* to put through Ellis's skull."

"*Etty!*"

Instead of acknowledging me, Etty glared at Will. He shrank beneath her ire, eyes darting toward the exits.

"Please stop," I said, running a hand over my face. "It's not a big deal."

"I'll let you have a swing at him if you can help me get some people across the river and into the city without any guards being tipped off," Jesse said, slipping in front of Will.

Etty's features immediately softened as she took in *Montana*. Boyish smile, blond hair falling across his forehead. If I didn't know him, I'd think he really was charming.

"And why would I do that?"

Jesse's grin didn't falter. He moved around the island and settled beside Bonnie. "Things are heating up in the city. I think you know that. We've got two weeks to get Audrey and Savannah out of New Orleans."

Etty pursed her lips and placed a hand on her hip before fixing Bonnie with a stare.

"I'm not *married yet,* Etty. Don't look at me like that. You've seen Rutherford. He probably only fucks in the dark for five minutes and still thinks he's king of the world."

I snorted, unable to help myself. Jesse and Etty fell into a round of raucous laughter.

Through it all, though, Will remained stoic, near the door. He wouldn't look at me either.

"How many people are we talking about?" Etty asked as she wiped tears from her eyes.

"How many can you get?" Jesse asked as he placed a hand on Bonnie's shoulder.

A valet barged into the kitchen and headed for the pantry. I stared at my fingernails, picking at them unnecessarily.

"We'll circle back later," Etty whispered to Jesse before turning back to the gumbo pot.

"Lucas cornered me earlier wanting to rope me into wedding plans," Bonnie said, looking expectantly towards Will. "If you're with me, I bet he'll let me out of it. Do you think we could—"

"Well," he said, slapping his hand on the counter as he shoved toward the door. "I'm going to get changed. I'll see y'all later."

"Where are you going?" I asked, rising. He stilled, not quite looking at me.

I meant what I said last night. I wasn't convinced he wasn't a danger to himself, especially given the gun holstered at his hip.

"My apartment." As Will slipped out of the kitchen, I followed, unable to help myself. If I left him alone too long, I feared what he might do. He glanced over his shoulder as we neared the stables. "What are you doing?"

"Keeping an eye on you," I said, wringing my hands together. He lifted an eyebrow but said nothing as he continued into the alley beside the house. I fell into step with him.

The streets bustled with activity. The world continued on around us as if nothing had changed last night. But it had. *I* had changed. And I didn't know how to feel about it. I spared a quick glance in Will's direction, unable to read the tense set of his shoulders.

"You don't have to follow me around," he said as we shoved through a crowd at the edge of Lee Square.

"Yes, I do," I said pointedly, shuffling in front of him as we moved between two crowds.

When we turned onto Bourbon Street, the crowd parted. More than a couple of people stared at me with wide eyes, their voices going silent as we passed. I glanced over my shoulder as people whispered behind their hands to their companions.

Will guided me onto the sidewalk. People flinched away, clearing out in front of one particular establishment. His hand flattened on the small of my back as he opened the door. I took in a sharp breath at the sudden contact, remembering the feel of those hands on my bare skin last night, this morning. Heat rose in my cheeks.

Low light filtered from lanterns, casting harsh shadows across the room. A bar lined the wall ahead of us, with a handful of tables scattered across the room. Patrons drank and talked loudly. The moment the door closed behind us, however, silence fell.

First, the odd looks on the street, and now *this?*

I glanced back at Will, who kept his eyes low. He nodded to the barkeep before pressing his hand once more to my back and guiding me toward a staircase.

"It's true, then," someone whispered.

What was true? I turned back to the bar, but Will blocked me. Instead, he urged me up the dark staircase. The steps creaked beneath our feet. With furrowed brows, I reached the landing. Will brushed past, unlocked a door, and shoved it open. Inside was more of a single room than an apartment.

A large, unmade bed rested against one wall, filling most of the space. Small, unmatching tables were on either side, cigarette butts stubbed out on their surfaces. A sunken couch sat beneath the dirty window. Filtered light covered the space. Dust kicked up as I entered, as though it'd been some time since anyone was here. A single door sat into the wall on the other side of the bed. I spied a bookshelf hastily shoved into one corner, loaded with thick tomes.

Well, it certainly wasn't Lee's mansion.

CHAPTER SIX

BONNIE

BEFORE I COULD PROCESS the whirlwind of Will and Savannah's hasty exit, a maid said, "Miss Audrey, your father and Mr. Rutherford are waiting for you in his study."

And so it begins.

She waited to escort me, leaving me no opportunity to even say goodbye to Jesse with so many watchful eyes around us. To anyone paying attention, they would see *Montana* shoving part of a biscuit into his mouth, bored, and me smoothing invisible wrinkles from my skirt as I rose from the island. They didn't see the back of my hand slide against the side of his, a small, reassuring touch hidden from the outside world that spoke volumes between us. Reminding us of another time when a forbidden touch was the only comfort we had in the face of death.

"Presentable?" I asked with a bright smile. The maid offered a small nod in return as we left. Jesse's eyes, like a feather-light touch on my skin, followed me as far as they could.

It was strange how I longed for days slinking through the shadows, strapped with weapons and concentrated survival instinct as my main personality trait. But that wasn't who I was supposed to be right now. Right now, I was the pretty, broken girl who'd been trapped in this gilded cage. A blushing bride.

As I stood before the study door, I schooled my face into a weary mask of contrition, one that would appeal to my father's softer side and Lucas's savior complex.

Then I knocked.

"Come in."

The room smelled like charred wood, reminding me of campfires in the open desert and my rage last night. It simmered in my blood and soured my stomach. Shuffling in on clumsy feet, I gripped my skirt tight enough to bleach my knuckles white. The eyes of the two men landed on me like physical blows, assessing my rounded shoulders and downcast eyes.

"Here," Lucas said, pulling a chair out in front of my father's overly large desk. I sat demurely, ankles crossed and hands clasped in my lap as I finally lifted my eyes to Lee's. They were dark as pitch, gleaming in subtle malice. He had to do nothing to command a room. The threat of him was enough to force obedience in most people. It gave me a sick sort of satisfaction knowing that I'd burned his precious little map and ruined his makeshift throne room. He sighed, as if he no longer knew what to make of me.

"I'm sorry it took me so long," I started, adding a carefully constructed waver in my words. "I was still groggy from the medication this morning."

Lucas stood at my side, his hand resting on the back of my chair, his skin too close to the back of my neck. It made me uneasy to be so close to him, knowing what I did now.

"If you hadn't made a *spectacle* of yourself last night, it wouldn't have been necessary."

It hurt to swallow down my vicious words. Instead, I bit the inside of my cheek until I tasted metallic blood in my mouth. Lucas's hand came down on my shoulder then, running it across my back in the approximation of a soothing gesture. But I knew what it was. I had suffered unwanted touches like this for so long. This was a gesture of *ownership.*

"Well?" Lee asked, his black eyes looking wet with rage. "What do you have to say for yourself?"

Don't do it. Don't fucking do it, Bonnie.

I ducked my head, letting my hair fall forward to cover the expression in my eyes. I'd never been as good as Jesse at hiding my emotions.

"You nearly burned the whole fucking house down! In front of *every-one*!"

He slammed his fists against the top of the desk, rattling his lamp and decanter with the tinkling clatter of glass. I jumped at the sudden vehemence, my eyes trained on the ugly red rug at my feet.

"For fuck's sake! Say something!"

"Mr. Lee, maybe we should—"

"No! My daughter will explain it *herself*!"

Even Lucas's attempt at mediation wasn't enough to calm Lee's ire. *Good*, I thought hatefully. *Show them who you really are.*

"I didn't mean to drop the lamp," I said, forcing my words to sound pathetic. Small. Weak. Just like he wanted me. "It was an accident."

"An *accident*?"

I nodded, blinking rapidly to force a watery sheen into my eyes before lifting my gaze to his once more. The false display of emotion did what I intended: softened him toward me. The flames of his anger sputtered out.

"It's . . . *hard* for me. The people here in New Orleans, they don't like me. They say such awful things. *Especially* the mayor's daughter. Being the center of attention just invites their criticism. And Alice knows how to hurt me. I was looking for glowroot . . . to numb the pain. I know it was wrong."

My speech was convincing enough for him to take a seat and thread his fingers together. Silence, thick like fog on the river, billowed in the room as we waited for his judgment. I held my breath. Even though his opinion shouldn't matter, some twisted part of me still didn't want to disappoint him. There was *definitely* something wrong in my head.

We sat that way for a long time, and with each second that passed, Lucas's rhythmic touch grew bolder. It took every bit of my strength not to act on my violent impulses. And to think, a couple of days ago I'd fooled myself into agreeing to be his wife.

Fuck, what if I couldn't manage it all? What if, by attempting to take down my father, I ended up married to him? A shiver of dread coursed down my spine involuntarily.

"Well, considering your recent relapse, Lucas and I believe it's in your best interest to move the wedding date up."

Of course, that was a lie. I'd heard it all last night, or *overheard* it really. They'd already planned on muscling me into a shotgun wedding. My little foray into arson just gave them the perfect excuse to get me to agree without a fuss. Checkmate.

I nodded somberly, knowing I had no substantial argument. Powerless wasn't a feeling I tolerated well.

"Two weeks. Here. Then Lucas and I will settle up some business and you'll both travel to Manhattan Island together."

Lucas's hand squeezed my shoulder until I begrudgingly looked at him. Same warm brown eyes. Same stupid flop of hair over his forehead that once amused and infuriated me in equal measures. *Everything* between us was a lie. The vulnerability and compassion, the tenuous friendship and safe haven he'd become. I'd been deceived so many times without my memories. By every single man I trusted.

"Don't worry about it," he said, his dark eyes soft and kind like I remembered. "We'll take care of everything. It'll be perfect. Beautiful. As beautiful as you are. We'll make that bitch Alice Devereaux eat her hateful words."

I didn't want to, but I smiled. The thought of revenge always did give me warm, fuzzy feelings.

"Let's talk details," my father said, breaking the tender moment. Details? All the warm, fuzzy images of Alice Devereaux's insanely jealous face evaporated in an instant. They wanted me to plan my wedding *now*. Fuck me.

The next couple hours felt like a nightmare. One filled with talks of VIP guests to invite, floral arrangements in season, how much and how quickly they could import luxuries that I didn't even know still existed when I was Bonnie. No one asked for my opinion or input, content with a nod or tilt of my head when they glanced my way. I wouldn't have to worry about any of it, just like Lucas said. Because this event, the spectacle and opulence, none of it was about me. None of it was about celebrating love or family the way I imagined.

All the while, I felt like I was floating outside my body. Numb to the leather seat beneath my legs and Lucas's hand on my skin. Like I wasn't me anymore, this body wasn't mine, and nothing that happened to it really mattered.

Instead, I imagined I was with Jesse and The Kid. Heard their laughter and felt the warmth of the hot desert sun blistering my skin. I inhaled the animal scent of Eagle's coat, warm and musky. The desert horizon blazing with a riot of colors stretched before my eyes as I remembered what freedom felt like singing through my veins.

"Well, I think we're at a good starting point now. Though, the next couple of weeks will be incredibly busy as we sort through the finer details. I've kept you both long enough; I'm sure you're itching to spend some *quality* time together."

Being ripped from my daydream was akin to the torture I'd received at Jones's hands. The reminder of my powerlessness, abrupt and unkind. Lucas stood first, holding his hand out to help me up. As my palm slid into his, the friction of our skin made revulsion slosh through me.

But this was the con, and I was an artist at my craft.

I smiled and let him lead me out of the study, tucking my hand onto his arm as we headed downstairs in a comfortable silence.

"Let's take a walk. You've been cramped inside for too long."

I laughed a little in agreement. The sun was high in the sky when we arrived in the courtyard. My mind spun with fractured thoughts and too many questions. I needed to get a grip, find an anchor, and soon.

"You've been quiet."

Instead of answering him, I bit my bottom lip. All the things I wanted to say remained trapped inside of me. On the surface, I was the picture of compliance, but inside I was screaming.

I could run with Jesse and the others. It was an option. But, if I did, my father and Lucas and Jones would come for us. We'd never stop running. Never be safe. If anything happened to Savannah, or Will, or Jesse, or—

I couldn't even think it. Couldn't even say it within the safety of my own head. Because if The Kid was ever hurt again because of me, I wouldn't survive it. I'd put a gun in my mouth like Will and there would be no hesitation.

No. I would bury them all in order to free myself and the people I loved. And if they didn't let me go, I would die choking on my revenge. Never again would I allow myself to be their pretty, compliant little prisoner. Never *fucking* again.

"I know this is overwhelming. But once we're married, things will get better."

I turned to Lucas, his eyes tilted up to a bright blue sky and shadows playing over his face.

"How?" I asked, for no other reason than he expected me to. *Wanted* me to.

He looked at me, brushing a stray lock of hair behind my ear just as Jesse had done this morning. His fingers lingered, his palm cupping my jaw as he stared into my eyes.

"I'm going to take care of you."

Take care of me?

"We haven't talked about what your life will look like after the wedding yet. I'm assuming change isn't something you're comfortable with after your accident?"

I swallowed hard. Change wasn't something I was comfortable with, period. Lucas squeezed my hand and pressed his lips to my forehead.

"When we get to Manhattan, you'll be living in just as much comfort as you have been here. You'll be expected to come to social events with me, but there won't be any *Alice Devereauxs* there to contend with. Just show up, looking as beautiful and charming as you always do." His eyes dipped down to my dress for the day. The fabric was a floral pattern that was light and airy, with sleeves that came down to my elbows. He wrinkled his nose in displeasure as he took it in. "Speaking of, why are you wearing *that?*"

Fucking asshole. What was wrong with what I was wearing? It was one of the many breathable, comfortable dresses I owned.

"It's just so . . . old-fashioned, and it doesn't show off your better assets."

"I like it mostly because of the sleeves. You know I have a pretty horrible scar on my arm, right?"

"But your scar is such an interesting talking point, don't you think?"

I felt like I'd been slapped.

My Bonnie girl.

Jones's voice filled my mind the way it hadn't in years. I heard the echo of my begging and screaming, the memory of Sixgun's buck knife covered in dark crimson blood that he licked from the shining blade bright in my mind.

"A talking point?" I questioned, surprised that I sounded so calm.

"Well, yeah. Just like the masks. You don't remember getting the scar, and it's so distinctive. People *will* ask about it. You can tell them whatever witty, tragic story you want." He chuckled, turning us back toward the walk around the courtyard and patting my hand softly as we moved forward. My legs felt like stone pillars, numb and too heavy.

"The clothes, though, they have to go. You need to wear things that show off your figure, and your scar. No need to hide anymore, Audrey. Not with me."

He wanted to use my tragedy to gain favor among Manhattan society? What in the actual fuck?

"My clothes are fine."

"They really aren't. Besides, it's non-negotiable. Now that we're engaged, you are a reflection of me. So you'll smile and tell whatever story I want you to, wear whatever I want you to, and once I fuck a few kids into you, you can stay busy with them."

He kissed me then. My thoughts felt sluggish, and I didn't see it coming. But suddenly, his lips were on mine, too soft and unwanted. If this wasn't a con, I would make him bleed. I'd make him pray for a swift death if he ever touched me without my permission. It lasted too long. Before I knew it, we walked back inside. He'd rattled on about wedding details and complained about almost everything, like the entitled brat he was. I excused myself, telling him with a false smile about needing to update Savannah with wedding plans.

He tucked me close, his hands wrapping around my waist and wandering low on my spine. I hated this. I hated him. And it felt just like all the other cons. When I was a child. When I was powerless to stop it. The disconnect from myself grew as my memories assaulted me.

Large, hard hands roamed over my thighs, a knee between them to force them open. Hot lips trailed down my neck as the mark groaned on top of me.

Where were they? Where was Jones?

This was going too far. Tears stung in the back of my eyes, and I blinked them away furiously. Those hands were in my shirt, grabbing at me too roughly, bruising my skin.

Bang!

Blood and brains splattered hot on my front. The violence didn't bother me. It was so normal now, to be covered in viscera. Relief nearly knocked me to my feet as the weight of the middle-aged man fell away. One of his hands had been working into my jeans. Jones stared down at me, so I steeled my expression and blinked away the tears that I'd almost let show.

I'd be punished if I cried.

So, I reminded myself, it was only my body. And my body wasn't me. Straightening my shoulders, I knelt and started going through that mark's pockets, handing over anything I found.

"You did good, my Bonnie girl."

Jones's hand rested on the crown of my head, gentle and appraising. Then, with his approval ringing in the gunpowder-tinted air, I was one with my body again. I raised my eyes to his, and he was smiling. I smiled back, thinking maybe one day I'd do good enough to be a real part of the crew. That I could prove to him just how good I could be.

There were people in my room, maids, taking my dresses out of my wardrobe and pajamas from the small dresser. Piles of fabric lined the bed.

"What's going on?" I asked, walking into the middle of the fray.

"Mr. Rutherford has a new wardrobe coming. He and your father told us to clear out your old clothes," one of the maids answered. I looked over at her as she pulled my shorts from the dresser and stared down at them in confusion.

No. Not those.

I walked forward and grabbed them from her hands, clutching the worn denim in my arms. When did he have time to do this? I'd only just spoken to him about this a few minutes ago.

The realization hit me all at once.

They were already going to do this. I'd never had a choice in the matter. I was a doll for them both to dress up how they wanted. My hands shook as I stood there, in the middle of the chaos as my life as Audrey was stripped away from me. Blouses and sweaters, dresses and linen pants all taken out one pile at a time. The silly pajamas Savannah and I had picked out together last winter on a rare trip into the shops on the square disappeared. As if none of it ever happened. The dress from the damn tea party that Alice Devereaux stained was tossed unceremoniously on the floor. It was a lie, this life as Audrey Lee, but it'd been *mine.* At least for a while.

I clutched the shorts tight, and on wooden legs, I left the room and made my way to the parlor. On the back credenza were bottles and bottles of liquor, and even though I wanted nothing more than to disappear into the glowing blue euphoria of glowroot, this would probably be as close as I could get. So I grabbed a large bottle of something, anything, and shuffled into the library.

The afternoon sun spilled into the room like it was my own personal paradise. Words of long-dead philosophers and poets surrounded me like a warm blanket. Closing the door quietly, I sat on the loveseat where I'd once watched Jesse sketching me and popped the cap open.

I swallowed down burning courage, numbing myself to it all, the way I'd learned to cope before. This time was different. I wasn't alone. I wasn't being used. I was in control of this, even if it felt like I wasn't right now. I had to be.

But Bonnie was still there, screaming inside my head that I wasn't safe anywhere. And control was just an illusion.

CHAPTER SEVEN

WILL

Fuckin' hell. I NEVER wanted Savannah here in this place. Never wanted her to see the deterioration permeating my life. I wasn't one to set down roots or make anyplace my home. This apartment, like the tents I grew up in, was always supposed to be temporary. Though, as the years stretched on, it became clear this would be my reality for a while as I struggled to bring Bonnie's memories back. It was as depressing a thought then as it was now. Everything was broken, or dirty, or misplaced.

And there was Savannah, in the midst of it all, pristine and proper. She had no hair out of place, no wrinkle in her skirts, and her eyes were dim as she looked around the room. Fucking disgraceful.

Just like me.

I'd hoped for some solitude coming here. To have time to mull over the events of the last few days, weeks, and especially last night. But, lady luck had never taken a shine to me before. I couldn't expect anything different from her now. Instead, my friends looked at me like I was a nuclear bomb, ready to blow their world up into radioactive bits.

I pushed past Savvy, guiding her further into the room before I disappeared into the bathroom. It hurt to look at her. To know how deeply I'd hurt her. Even worse was the insistent urge to do it again. To fold her beneath me, strip away all those careful layers, and corrupt every part of her until she was *mine* and *mine alone.*

I turned on the shower and stripped quickly, shoving the fancy party clothes Jesse had bought me into the far corner before ducking my head

53

under the spray. I'd never felt right in the suit anyway. No part of me was gentle. Or soft. Not like the men who used those suits to hide behind a mask of civility. I scrubbed my skin hard, until the sting of my rough sponge woke me up and made me feel alive again.

"Honestly, I don't know what Lee pays you, but I'd think you could afford a maid," Savvy said conversationally from the room beyond. I snorted, turning off the water and slinging a towel around my waist as I shook the water from my long curls. She had *no idea* what I could afford. Money wasn't the issue.

Sounds of her skirt rustling and objects moving around the room piqued my curiosity. It was strange. As much as I loathed her being here, a part of me never wanted her to leave. A soft grin curled on my mouth as I hastily brushed my teeth and tongue. She was probably snooping. Hell, I would be.

"Who's Clara?" she asked, deadpan. No hint of jealousy or curiosity, which annoyed me deeply. It was almost like she wanted to forget I'd been inside her last night, and almost this morning too, if my friends weren't such assholes. Spitting and rinsing my mouth quickly, I moved to the doorframe and leaned out of it to see her reading an old letter from Clara. The early days. When she wasn't such a hateful bitch and came into town more, keeping me from being alone in the darkness of my own mind.

"A friend," I answered, though after the last words between us, I wasn't quite sure that was true anymore.

You are fundamentally broken, and there's nothing you can do to fix the fact that you're a failure.

Savvy's eyes felt like a branding iron on my skin, her gaze following the beads of water dripping from my shoulders as they rolled down the midline of my body. I smirked, because that blush of attraction she couldn't resist banished Clara's cruel words from my mind. Savvy burned it all away beneath the heat rising in her cheeks.

"Uh huh, and how often do you do that *thing with your tongue* with your friends?" she asked, quoting obnoxiously from the letter.

I chuckled, leaning my shoulder against the doorframe as she averted her gaze from my body and rounded the bed to the far side of the room.

"Clearly, I'm nicer to my friends than you are to yours," I replied unrepentantly.

She rolled her eyes, already irritated with me. *Finally*. Some semblance of normal again. The tightness in my chest abated at her ire.

"Clearly," she mumbled sarcastically.

"We're friends, aren't we, Savvy?" I asked, my grin turning into a wolfish smile as her eyes snapped to mine again, wide with panic and longing. Instead of turning towards me or bickering, she just sighed, wearily, like it was hard for her to be here with me. My stomach sank.

"Just get dressed," she said quietly.

When I headed into the bathroom, it felt like the walls were closing in on me. I knew what Jesse said earlier was likely true. Savannah wasn't some weak-willed woman who had sex with me out of pity. She'd never do anything she didn't *want* to. But the thoughts were louder than ever now. I'd taken advantage of her last night, there was no doubt in my mind about it. Now, she'd never see me the same. Never trust me again. The fact that she was even still talking to me was a miracle.

I shouldn't expect anything less.

Dressing quietly, I felt the layers of myself falling back into place. Old, familiar armor. Clothes I could move in, that reminded me of who I was and where I'd come from. *Before* the Beast in the graveyard, trying to drag me to hell.

Taking a steadying breath, I finally emerged, hair tied back in my leather strap as I looked for a hat. My favorite, the one I'd had for forever, was still in Jesse's room. The one I found on my dresser was newer, less worn, and pitch black. But it would do for now.

I heard Savvy shuffling around the corner but didn't see her right away. When I looked closer, I found her perched precariously on my dilapidated couch, trying to scrub the window with a dirty t-shirt. It was comical, to say the least, her trying to create order out of my chaos.

"What're you doin'?" I asked, careful to keep the amusement from my voice. She didn't seem in a lighthearted mood today. She startled, nearly toppling from her perch on the arm, and I moved forward a few steps. Just in case.

"Picking up."

As if it were an obvious answer.

"You don't have to do that," I told her. I was already ashamed of the state of my apartment. The last thing I wanted was her coming in here and trying to make it *right* somehow.

"I know." My annoyance shifted into anger. Irrational, desperate anger. They were all treating me like I would explode at any moment, and now I felt like I might just do it. I wasn't some project or experiment. I sure as hell didn't need the woman I was trying to figure things out with treating me like I needed a babysitter all the goddamn time. It was fucking humiliating!

"And you don't have to follow me around all the damn time. I'm *fine*," I snapped. Though, instead of backing off, she leveled me with those whiskey-colored eyes wide with renewed concern. *Fuck.*

"You're not fine, William," she said, her gaze falling to the dirty t-shirt in her hands. Goddamnit, I really was a fucking prick. "And it's okay to *not* be okay."

How could I tell her I'd *never* been okay?

She was so sweet, so goddamned sweet, and I wanted her to scream at me. To hit me. To tell me I was a fucking piece of shit for how I handled last night. I didn't want her to treat me softly, like she was now. I wanted her to lash out with all that fury hiding inside of her. So we could *finally* talk about it. But that wouldn't happen. She didn't see me as a man anymore. Just a broken little boy. Like Bonnie did.

"Look, I'll stop following you around if you promise me one thing."

I sucked in a shaky breath through my teeth. I didn't want her to stop following me around, I just wanted her to stop treating me like she could see right through me. It made me uncomfortable. Because the things inside me were dark and ugly and would drown her light that I loved so much.

"And that is?" I asked, crossing my arms over my chest and raising an eyebrow.

She climbed off the couch and stepped closer to me, close enough that I could smell the sweetness of her skin, perfumed with kitchen scents and warmth. It was like a potent hit from your favorite drug, sending my mind reeling into unholy places that made my obsession flare anew.

"If you ever feel lost, or hopeless, or anywhere *near* how you felt last night."

I wavered on my feet, leaning closer to her unconsciously.

"You'll come to me."

I'd come to her regardless. I always had. There was something addictive in how she tried to save me. Like maybe, there was still a possibility that I *could* be saved. Maybe that was what I found so irresistible about her. She wore hope like a ballgown, illuminating the world around her, and I wanted so badly to have another taste of it.

"You don't have to be alone," she said, gripping my chin and forcing my eyes to hers again. The friction of her skin on mine sent blades of pleasure between my ribs and twisted deep. I didn't want to be alone anymore. The air thinned in my lungs, and my chest heaved, my fingers twitching furiously as I kept them shackled by my sides. I could wrap my arms around her right now. Carry her to my bed. And between screaming orgasms, I could wrench promises from her gasping lips.

Fuck.

"Ever," she whispered firmly.

My cock pressed painfully against the seam of my jeans. I knew what she felt like now. How she sounded when she was lost in the throes of passion. There was no thought, just the desperate yearning to taste her mouth and drink in the sweetness of her words. Leaning forward, I felt the tremulous breath of her hesitation fall on my tongue. She twisted away, clearing her throat, instead running her fingers nervously over the spines of the books on my leaning bookshelf. Fashioned from cinder blocks and scrap wood, the shelves bowed beneath the weight of the books it held. My body went cold at her refusal. Numb.

Her eyes stayed trained on the books, her head tilting to read the titles of them as she peered curiously from shelf to shelf. Timidly, she pulled one of the larger ones out, testing the weight in her hands before cracking it open to find the vascular system detailed on the page and my messy scrawl of notes in the corner. She glanced up at me, startled.

"Good choice," I drawled sarcastically, crossing my arms over my chest. "It's probably not as exciting as the books *you* read, but it has more practical applications than some of the others."

She scowled at my teasing, and I bit the inside of my cheek to keep my smile contained. Then, her scowl faded beneath an expression I'd not often seen directed at me. Curiosity.

"Wait, you mean to say . . . you've read *all* of these?" she asked in astonishment. I shrugged. Hoping to irritate her into more easy conversation.

"Surprised the Beast can read?" I retorted.

"I know you can *read*," she said icily. "I just didn't think . . . Why medical books?"

"I wanted to be a doctor once."

The admission shocked us both. Not that it wasn't true—of course it was—only that it'd slipped out so easily. Too easily for a dream that would never come true. I tilted the brim of my hat lower on my eyes and reached for the book in her hand.

"Really?" she asked. I wasn't sure if she was asking because she didn't believe me or if that wellspring of eternal hope had her thinking I could be something different. Someone better.

"It was a long time ago."

I shoved the book back on the shelf roughly before gripping her elbow and leading her toward the door. She twisted away, forcing me to stop. I didn't want to do this. Hadn't she seen enough of me already? Enough of the bloody, gaping wounds that stitched me together?

"It doesn't have to be. You'd be good at it—great, actually, and—"

"Savvy—"

"I remember the way you treated my rope burns when they were hurt—"

"Just *stop.*"

"And you have some of the steadiest hands I've ever seen. You don't have to—"

"God*damnit*, Savvy, do you hear yourself?" I asked, leaning close enough that she took a step back, swallowing down whatever other arguments she'd been ready to barrage me with. Only, this time, I didn't let her pull away. I followed her, step for step, my boots thunking ominously against the hardwood planks, until her back pressed against the wall by the door. Slowly, I flattened my palms against either side of her head and leaned down until we were eye-to-eye.

"Didn't you hear anything I said to you when we were dancing?" I asked, remembering the feel of her in my arms and how I tried to break her heart just to make it stronger. How I'd *attempted* to tell her goodbye. Another fucking failure.

Stop trying to fix broken people. Stop trying to save your mother. All you can do is forgive her.

"I'm not a good man. But, for all my faults, I'm an honest one," I said, licking my lips as her breath stuttered against my mouth. "I won't stop killing." Her pupils were dark and wide, her pulse pounding rapidly at her throat. I leaned forward just enough to brush the tip of my nose along the thrum of it. She whimpered in the back of her throat, a pained sound, like it hurt her to feel this way about me.

Good.

It fucking hurt me, too.

"Don't make a hero out of me," I whispered into the shell of her ear, ruffling the tiny hairs that'd escaped from her tight updo. Why couldn't I stay away from her? She didn't scare easily, which had been a problem in the past. Now, I was addicted to that foolish bravery. How she never gave up on me. Even when I gave her every reason. Especially then.

I licked my lips, catching hers beneath them. The plump pink of them welcomed me like a soft embrace, parting like she needed the taste of me more than air in her lungs. Her fingers clenched the fabric of my shirt, and I groaned as I folded against her. She was so soft and warm. My palm cupped her jaw, my fingers twisting into her hair to anchor her against me.

The last shred of my self-control snapped, and I devoured her like I was possessed, hips rocking against hers as she clung tighter to me. My mouth traveled to the spot beneath her ear that'd driven her crazy before. Her palms flattened against my chest, pressing hard enough that I gave her an inch of space, even as I tried to pull her back into me.

"Stop," she whispered against my mouth, stilling me in an instant. I caught her eyes, full of regret and longing. "We can't—*I* can't do this."

I stumbled back a step, cold settling deep in my stomach where moments before had been roiling heat.

"Can't? Like you couldn't last night . . . or hell, this morning?" I asked, hurt and confused by the strangeness that'd descended on the two of us. It complicated everything.

"I won't do this again."

With the pad of my thumb, I wiped my bottom lip clean of the taste of her. Who the fuck was I kidding? It lingered. It *always* lingered.

"Right."

"Will, I just—"

"I'm not stupid, I get it. It was a pity fuck. Or you were fulfilling some fantasy. Maybe both. Now that you have, the, uh . . . novelty has worn off." My words were harsh. Probably too harsh. I wouldn't apologize for it, though. I wasn't sorry for what had happened. No matter how ugly it was.

"That's not fair," she said, a hint of that familiar anger flaring in her whiskey eyes. I chuckled coldly.

"Not fair? Life's not fuckin' fair, *princesa.* Like I said, not a good man but an honest one. I'm just callin' it like I see it."

She shoved me hard, words like needles poised and ready to pierce me. But she kept them locked inside, slinging the door to my apartment open instead and marching outside. Her sudden absence from the dismal room made this place sad and small in an instant.

"Fuck!" I swore, slamming my palm against the wall. I wasn't stupid enough to break my fucking hand like Jesse had, but goddamnit did I understand the impulse right now. The truth was, I wanted her to see every broken, bloody piece of me. Every dark urge and murderous corner. I just wished she were brave enough to see all of that and admit she wanted me anyway.

No. Fuck this.

Jesse was right, the sappy motherfucker. I couldn't let the darkness win anymore. I couldn't let it push her away again. I was moving before I knew it, slamming the apartment door behind me and locking it swiftly.

"Savvy! Wait!" I called, shoving the keys in my pocket as I marched toward her.

"For what? Another sanctimonious lecture about you being the big bad wolf? No thank you."

She was nearly at the end of the hall by the time I caught up to her. I wrapped my hand gently around her elbow until she stopped trying to escape. She whirled, all the fires of hell burning in her whiskey eyes. And I melted beneath the heat of them. She was so *fucking* beautiful when she was pissed off at me.

"Don't *touch me*," she hissed, wrenching her arm from my grip. I held my hands up like I was facing down the double barrel of a shotgun. Hell, that might've been safer at this point. My heart pounded in my throat, adrenaline racing through my veins and waking me up in a way that made me feel so alive.

"I wasn't done, *mi sol*," I told her, inching forward and crowding her space. "If last night was because you felt sorry for me, then *fine.*"

"That wasn't—"

"I don't like it, but I can't change it," I said abruptly. "I won't apologize for last night, or this morning, or right fuckin' now in my room." Her breath hitched audibly.

"I'm not asking you to—"

"I spent the last three goddamn years of my life using every bit of strength and self-control I had to stay away from you. Because I thought that's what you wanted. That you *hated* me."

"I never hated you. Been annoyed by you, sure. Wished you'd go the hell away, okay, but I have *never* hated you."

I nodded, tipping the brim of my hat up to look her directly in her eyes. She needed to know that, for once, this *wasn't* a joke to me.

"Yeah, well, it took me a while, but I figured that out. What I mean to say is, I'm not going to try to be the good guy anymore. I'm not going to stay away from you, I'm not going to hold myself back. The next time we have sex, Savannah Beauregard, will be because you want *me*. Not because you don't want me to blow my fuckin' brains out."

There. I said it. I didn't let the darkness win. Might have made an ass out of myself to a woman who just rejected me, but at least I'd taken Jesse's advice. Only time would tell if it would actually pan out.

"Now let's get out of here. Apparently we have to help our friends save the world or some shit. And I've not had *nearly* enough whiskey yet today to think about that."

Savvy didn't move or speak. Her mouth hung open slightly, and I didn't think she was breathing. Seeing her at a loss for words did nothing to help assuage my sexual obsession with her. In fact, her mouth had fantasies blooming in my mind that would scandalize her.

"Close your mouth, Savvy," I said in a husky rasp. "Unless you're already rethinking—"

"Oh my God!" she shouted indignantly, and a wicked smile curled over my mouth. She realized what she'd said the moment she saw my grin. "No! Nope. Stop it." I chuckled as she marched down the stairs.

"What? You know I love it when you call my name, *mi sol*!" I called after her, hearing her frustrated groan all the way from here.

A weight that'd been crushing my chest lifted at our familiar bickering and knowing that I wouldn't let go of what happened to us without a fight. Not this time. I may be the worst thing in the world for her, but as long as she wanted me, I wasn't going anywhere. Not anymore. She just didn't realize it yet. But she would soon.

I made my way down the stairs slowly, trying to wipe the stupid grin off my face the whole way. It might be more terrifying for people on the street to see me smiling like an idiot. After all, the dark legend of my misdeeds painted me as the kind of psychopath that rivaled my father. When I'd finally gotten a hold of myself, I pushed into the bar.

"It's not her, look at her," someone said up front. There were more people in the bar than I'd ever seen before. Most of them crowded around the entrance, where Savvy's uptight hairdo bobbed between them.

"Come on, girl, tell us what it's like to fuck a murderer," another man said, earning a round of lewd guffawing.

"How much, sweetheart? Rob only needs about three minutes!"

What the actual fuck?

"Leave me *alone*—" I heard Savvy's voice, high-pitched and fearful.

Suddenly, the warmth and levity I'd felt moments before evaporated. Instead, cold rage trickled down my spine. I took my gun from its holster, and the deafening bang of a shot rang out. A man dropped to the floor, a bloody hole blown straight through his palm.

Men cowered as the thunk of my boots approached slowly, bodies parting before me like a dark omen. Until I stood tall before the three men harassing her, right behind her left shoulder with the barrel of my pistol still smoking. They looked up at me in abject terror, and I drank it down. Cool confidence made my motions slow and deliberate.

My free hand wrapped around Savvy's waist as I guided her to my side. Without acknowledging the men in the room, my gaze raked over her in search of any sign of harm. When I found none, but the fear lingering in her gaze, I raised my hand to her cheek.

"Did they touch you?" I asked in a dark growl. She swallowed hard, eyes flicking toward the man sniveling on the ground. "Yes or no?"

She nodded gently.

I checked the rounds in my gun. Five shots left. One empty. Then I spun the cylinder of my revolver and clicked it back into place.

"I'm not a murderer," I said quietly, knowing with absolute certainty that everyone in the bar could hear me perfectly. "I'm a businessman.

"I just happen to be in the business of murder."

Two more shots rang out, and bodies dropped in the room, blood and viscera splattering against the walls in a gruesome display of violence. To Savvy's credit, she barely even flinched.

"Put your hand on the floor," I demanded the man still clutching his bloody hand.

His mouth gaped open and slammed shut several times, confusion and fear making the air sour in the room. Finally, with a whimper, he held his trembling, bloody hand flat to the dirty floor. I placed my boot over it, pressing down with all my weight. He cried out, and the people in the bar fell silent once more in quiet horror.

"Listen up," I said, catching their attention as my eyes scanned the room. As the pause stretched, I ground my boot harder against his hand, until his screams echoed off the walls. "Anyone lays so much as a finger on her again, you'll *pray* all I do is hang you over that bridge."

A final gunshot ended his sniveling, though now my clean jeans had new stains on them. Turning to Savannah, I was surprised that she seemed unfazed by the death. Without a word, I led her out of the bar with a hand on the small of her back. Everyone would know the consequences of harassing her. Word would spread quickly through the city, of that I was sure, and Savannah would be protected by the bloody legend I'd wielded as a weapon all this time.

I could have dropped my hand from the small of her back once we were on the street, but I didn't.

I wanted them all to see that she belonged to me.

CHAPTER EIGHT

JESSE

RIGHT FOOT. LEFT FOOT. One in front of the other. Ever since waking up this morning, I felt like I was in some strange alternate reality. Last night had been incredible . . . until it wasn't.

This morning, though I wanted nothing more than to lose myself in Bonnie, there were things to do. I had to figure out how to get the Fort Hood crew into the city, then re-convene with Mickey and The Kid.

I ran a hand through my damp hair as I entered the kitchen. There were still a couple of workers moving about, but most of the bustle from the morning was gone. My gaze met Etty's from across the space. She motioned with her head toward a door in the back. I moved through the room on silent feet, then opened the door and slipped inside the pantry.

What was Bonnie doing right now? Was her father berating her? Was Lucas trying to make a pass? My jaw clenched at the thought of him touching her.

There was no way I would last two weeks under this ruse. Not now that I had her back.

Etty entered, closing the door on silent hinges as she regarded me with suspicion. I was used to her normal jovial attitude toward me. I guess I couldn't blame her for not trusting me, given what I wanted to do.

"You do realize what you're askin' me to do could get us all killed." She placed her hands on her hips.

"I do."

"But you're still asking," she said, deadpan.

"I am."

We didn't have any other choice. We needed reinforcements within the city. Maybe we could get Lee's ledger and escape, but that wasn't guaranteed. We needed Mickey. And Bonnie needed The Kid. There'd been desperation in her eyes as she mentioned him this morning. She needed to see him, and this was the only way to make it happen.

Etty regarded me silently and tucked her hand into the pocket of her apron. With a heavy sigh, she said, "There's a ferry a few miles upriver." She pulled a silver coin from her pocket and handed it to me.

It looked like a plain silver bit except . . . there was something stamped on one side. If I didn't know to look for it, I'd have thought it was just worn down.

"Once they're across," she continued, "they can filter into the city in pairs or small groups. Depending on how big of a group you've got, the Riverwalk is a good place to hide them. It's not close, but Lee's men don't go in there. They patrol outside, but their focus remains on the bridge and anyone trying to get into the city from the river."

I offered her a smile. "Thanks, Etty."

As I tried to brush past her, she gripped my arm. "Don't make me regret this."

A shiver ran down my back at the seriousness in her expression. I'd seen Will flounder beneath the woman's glare, but I never expected it to be pointed at me. I nodded, throat bobbing as I ducked my head.

"And if you hurt my girls, *Jesse James*, it won't be pretty."

I opened my mouth to refute her, but she unlatched the pantry door and left me in the dark. How did she know my last name?

After a few seconds, I slipped from the darkened space. As I passed Etty, she handed me something bundled in a cloth. I didn't dare open it until I reached No Name's stall in the stables. Two large squares of cornbread.

Maybe she didn't totally hate me. Yet.

Ten minutes later, I was clear of the square and finishing off the cornbread before I truly felt like I could breathe. Away from the bustle of Lee Square, the streets were emptier. For probably the first time since coming to New Orleans, I missed the long days of travel. They'd been hard when Bonnie, The Kid, and I were just trying to escape Sixgun and find my uncle, and they'd haunted me every single time I left a town without Bonnie.

Now, I desperately craved the unknown of the wilderness. At least then, I never had to worry about breathing. No Name tugged against the reins as if he agreed with me. I patted his neck.

"Don't worry, boy. When we get across the river, I'll let you run." He snorted. No doubt the weeks locked up in the stables were getting to him as much as being stuck in the manor was getting to me.

Now that I had Bonnie back, all I wanted was to take her and run as fast as possible.

Mind whirring over the madness of the morning, I guided No Name up the cement ramp that led to the bridge. Its hulking mass of metal and concrete loomed ahead. My eyes strayed too far, to the center of the structure where bodies swung on the warm afternoon breeze. From my position in the saddle, I couldn't tell how long they'd been up. Were the corpses the same ones I'd witnessed Will hanging the night I returned to the city?

I felt even less certain of my friend since his hasty retreat from the manor. I couldn't be sure if Savannah accompanying him was a good thing. Will seemed so haunted this morning, by the things he'd done, the things he wanted.

I want to stop.

Shadows plagued Will. I'd known that since first arriving in New Orleans. He was different. Though he could still joke and enjoy himself, there was always that flicker of darkness lingering just beneath the surface. I didn't know how to save him. I didn't know if anyone *could*. But I'd be damned if we gave up trying.

"Halt!"

At the guard's order, I tugged the reins, slowing No Name. I'd been so lost in my thoughts I hadn't realized I'd reached the same checkpoint that Mickey and I had coming into the city. I sat straighter in the saddle, squaring my shoulders and slowing to a stop before three guards branded with the fleur-de-lis on their neck.

"What's your business?" one of them questioned while the other two scoped me out.

I lifted my eyebrows. I could understand questioning people entering the city, but leaving? Why would Lee care about that?

"Work," I said, keeping my voice bored. The less suspicion I caused, the better. The guard eyed me with suspicion, reminiscent of Etty back at the manor.

Instead of speaking, I tugged at the collar of my shirt, angling my neck to show the brand marring my skin. Recognition flitted through the man's eyes. He nodded and then stepped backward.

"Right. On your way."

Without further fanfare, the guards turned their attention back to the city. I dug my heels into No Name's sides and clicked my tongue, spurring him forward. The faster I got to Mickey, the better.

The crew from Fort Hood had made their camp in an old oil refinery a few miles downriver. After veering off of the decrepit concrete highway, the road opened up. Crumbling buildings lined either side of the road, but there were no other people. I crouched low in the saddle and clicked my tongue, digging my heels in hard.

That was all No Name needed.

My horse raced forward, the wind rushing through my hair and the sun warm on my skin. If the others were with me, it would be all too easy to keep going and never look back.

A metal fence that surrounded tall, rusted cylindrical structures came into sight a while later. The buildings may have been white once, though the elements and time had worn them down. I slowed my mount, narrowing my eyes as I tried to sort through the careful instructions Mickey had hidden in his letter on how to find him.

We passed through an opening in the chain link. I dismounted, then led No Name in the direction of a couple of armed men milling about near one of the structures. The metal looked like someone had taken a blow torch to it to create an opening. At the sight of me, the men straightened, hands tightening around their weapons.

"What do you want?" one of them asked.

There was something familiar in the slant of his mouth, the crook of his nose.

"Where's Mickey Kincaid?"

The guards shared a glance.

"I'm Jesse. His nephew?"

The men still hesitated. One of them glanced toward the opening, as if waiting for instructions.

"Don't let that asshole in here," a voice called from above.

A set of steel steps wound around the building, leading to a landing near the top, where a lanky teenager with blond hair and a scowl perched, glaring down at me. My heart sped up at the sight of him. It had been *months*. Even before New Orleans, the weeks that led up to my fight in Little Rock had kept us apart. My eyes heated as he shoved off of the railing and descended the steps.

"Hey, Kid," I said, though my voice broke on his name. I didn't realize just how much seeing him would bring back the three years of desperation, three years of constantly disappointing him.

"You finally decided to show your ugly mug." The deep grumble of his voice shocked me. In my head, he was still that little kid who'd charmed Bonnie in Vegas. He always would be, really.

"Figured it was time." I offered a tentative grin as he reached the bottom of the stairs. Though he continued to scowl at me, his lips quirked up at the edges. I threw my arms around him, tugging him tight against my chest. He was almost as tall as me now. I crushed him to me, exhaling a shaky breath. "I missed you, Kid."

After a moment, The Kid shrugged me off. "Alright, alright," he said, gauging me in that way The Kid did, making me feel self-conscious when no one else really could. "Where's Bonnie?"

"Still back in the city. That's why I'm here. It's time," I said.

"Time for what?"

I slung an arm across his shoulders. "Time to bring Bonnie home."

A brilliant smile reminiscent of our days racing through the desert lit up his face. The Kid shoved out from under my arm and headed into the building. I followed, immediately plunging into the darkness. I paused to give my eyes a moment to adjust.

The building reminded me of a farming silo, though much larger. Tents dotted the vast space, along with people hovering around campfires, like that first night we arrived in Fort Hood. People waiting, watching, milling about.

"Look who finally decided to show up," The Kid said. I snapped my attention to where he stood thirty feet away.

Mickey perched on an overturned five-gallon bucket. Gabriela sat on the ground between his knees. Her head turned toward me at The Kid's voice. A flurry of motion and voices filled the space as my uncle and his girlfriend moved as one to embrace me.

Aside from the joy I'd felt last night when Bonnie remembered me, I couldn't remember ever feeling so happy.

"Took ya long enough," Mickey said as he pulled back from me. He clasped my shoulders and gave me a once-over. "Good to see you're in one piece."

"That's debatable," The Kid remarked.

"I missed you, too," I said, unable to hide my smile.

This. This was what I'd been missing. Family. The pieces of myself I'd left scattered across the country were finally coming back together.

"So, Jess, what's the plan?" Mickey asked as he lowered onto his bucket.

"Bonnie got her memories back," I said. "There's . . . a lot we need to talk about, but I've found a way to get you into the city."

My uncle nodded, his eyes sharp. He listened with unwavering attention as I explained Bonnie's revelations from last night and how I intended on getting the crew across the river. For the first time in weeks, I felt normal. Laughing, sharing stories as we passed a flask. We were just missing Bonnie, Will, and Savannah.

At long last, when the world turned dark outside, Mickey and The Kid walked me out to No Name.

"We'll see you in a few days," Mickey said. Gabriela looped her arm through my uncle's.

"There's one more thing," I said, turning to face my uncle. I shoved my hands into my pockets. "I need you to talk to Will."

Mickey's curiosity turned to concern. His brows lowered, casting deep shadows across his face.

"He almost killed himself last night," I said, shaking my head. "I thought he was getting better, but after Sebastian . . . "

My uncle clapped me on the shoulder. "I'll take care of it," Mickey said with a curt nod.

"Here." The Kid tugged a small black box from his pocket. My heart plummeted at the sight of it. I took it from him and flipped open the lid. The dim light flickered off of the surface of the blue jewel centerpiece. I closed the box and motioned to my brother.

"I need you to hold onto it for a little longer."

"Why?"

"Bonnie can't exactly wear it when she's got that asshole's ring on." I ruffled his hair, and he scowled as he smoothed the locks down.

"Why don't I come with you?" he asked, tucking the box into his pocket. I frowned.

"I wish you could," I said honestly. Seeing The Kid would do wonders for Bonnie. "It's too risky. Lee's men have checkpoints set up on the bridge. I wouldn't be able to come up with a good excuse to get you through without questions." I gripped his shoulder. "I promise, as soon as I can, you'll get to see her."

Confliction filled his blue eyes. He clenched his jaw and gave a curt nod.

After another round of goodbyes, I mounted No Name and set out, keeping my eyes sharp as I made my return trip to the city. The guards on the bridge were different this time, but all I had to do was flash my brand and they let me through without hassle.

The city had come alive as the sun went down. People milled about the streets. Some were trying to get home as others prepared for long nights on Bourbon. I slowed No Name to a canter as I neared the manor.

I dismounted, taking care to guide him into his stall and get him cleaned up. Exhaustion weighed on me as I left the stables.

The house was in its normal state for this time of day: things shutting down, people going off to settle for the night. I passed by my room to change out of my dusty jeans. With some careful maneuvering, I made my way up to the front house, pausing at every corner to check for guards on duty.

I couldn't be sure what time it was when I finally pushed open the door to Bonnie's room. The smile on my lips at the very thought of seeing her slipped away as I shut the door behind me. The room wasn't really different from how I'd left it this morning, except . . .

It was empty.

My brows furrowed as I moved back into the hallway. Could she still be with her father, with Lucas? It was well after when I'd expect her to be back in her room. I headed down the hallway toward Savannah's door, but when I knocked, there was no answer.

Then I heard it. A small, drunken laugh.

I headed toward the sound, my eyes scouring the hallway for signs of a threat. The library door was open a few inches. I glanced over my shoulder again, then pushed open the door.

The first thing I saw was Bonnie's bare foot. She sat slumped against the couch, one knee tucked up as she brought a bottle of liquor to her lips. Her hair stuck out all over the place, as though at some point she'd pulled it back but it'd fallen out. Her dull blue eyes stared at a book in her hand.

It was like that old schoolhouse, when I found her alone in the library, only she didn't have a book in her hands. Because back then, she couldn't read.

"*Yeah*, because the girl *always* loses." She tossed the book across the room, where it thumped against a bookshelf and then fell, pages splayed open face-first on the floor.

My brows pinched together as I turned to Bonnie, the unasked question perched on my lips.

"Oh good, you're back." She brought the bottle to her lips. "Mrs. Rutherford has moved into my room."

"What?"

"Lucas. He's going to be a problem," she said, taking another small swig. "He's got it all planned out. How he'll dress me up, make my scar a *witty talking point*, and, oh yeah, 'fuck a few kids into me.' He makes my skin crawl."

Fury flared anew in my chest. I trusted Bonnie to know what she was doing, but, at the same time, I didn't like her putting herself in harm's way. I snapped the door shut and crossed the space to kneel at her side. Gently, I tugged the bottle from her hand and set it aside, clasping her fingers in mine. "Would my kicking his ass ruin your plans for the ledger?"

She snorted, tugging on my hand until I sat next to her. She folded against my chest, into the spot made for her. "Unfortunately, yes. But I'd love to see it."

"Do you want to talk about it?" I asked into her hair. I wanted to support her in whatever way I could, but I wouldn't push her. We both had a lot going on in our heads, and Bonnie would try to run if I pressed her. "You don't have to. But you can, if you want."

"This con just feels . . . I don't know, it's bringing up shit from when I was a kid."

I pressed my lips to the crown of her head. "What can I do to help you?"

She hummed a little in thought. The wheels of her mind never stopped turning, but sometimes, like tonight, it was like they were grinding together.

"Do you remember what you first thought of me in that bar in Vegas?" she asked, furrow appearing between her brows as she looked up at me.

"Oh yeah," I said, chuckling. "How badly I wanted to get my hands all over you again."

She shook her head, reaching across me to grab the neck of the bottle before taking a dainty sip. "That's a lie," she said quietly. "You thought that I was *dangerous*."

I opened my mouth to argue with her, but she pushed on, and I wasn't really sure what the point was. Why did it matter what I thought all those years ago?

"A murderer."

I tightened my arm around her, until I could feel the heat of her skin across my chest. I wanted to crush her against me and never let her go.

"You were right to be wary of me," she said, resting her head against my shoulder. "I *was* dangerous. And sometimes, during a con, or when shit hit the fan . . . "

She shuddered, her breath hitching as she tried to find the words that she was struggling so hard to say.

"I hear him."

My blood ran cold. I didn't have to ask who she meant. *Jones.* The last time I'd seen this caginess in her eyes was in Flagstaff. She'd scared me that night. I still remember how hard it'd been to see her press the barrel of her gun against her temple, ready to die instead of going back.

"It's been a long time since it's happened. After meeting you, I thought it was getting better. Then, of course, the memory loss." She waved her hand and rolled her eyes like it was irritating having to mention the last three years. "This con with Lucas . . . it came right back. His voice. Like he was just in the other room or right around the corner. Waiting for me to slip up and come back to him."

Her eyes were dark with fear, and unfocused, like she was looking at something far away. Her body trembled slightly. I wasn't going to let anything happen to her.

"I'll never let him get you back, Bon. I'll kill him before I ever let him touch you again," I vowed, crushing her in my embrace.

"Sometimes it frightens me how much of a hold he still has on me. It makes me wonder if I'm making the right choices, or if despite everything I'll end up just like him. A monster."

"Do you love me?" I asked.

She lifted her head then, glaring up at me in the familiar way she did when I annoyed her. "Of course I do, idiot."

"Monsters can't love," I whispered before leaning over and giving her a gentle kiss. "You're mine, and I intend to remind you every single day of that."

She cracked a smile, albeit a small one, but I could see her body relax beneath my words. "That was sappy, farm boy."

"Someone's gotta be," I remarked with a grin. "But . . . you are the love of my life. I hope you never doubt that." She settled her head against my shoulder. I tightened my arms around her. "I saw The Kid today."

"You did?" Immediately she straightened in my arms, eyes bright and curious. "How was he? Did he ask about me? When can I see him?"

"Soon," I confirmed. "He misses you. He wanted to come back with me tonight, but I didn't want the guards on the bridge to see him." I let out a long breath. "Mickey and the rest will be in the city within the next few days. As soon as they get here, I promise I'll bring you to The Kid."

"Will would have just killed the guards."

I scowled even as her eyes sparkled in amusement. My features softened at the joy in her expression. At least she didn't seem so haunted by her past now. "Lee would *let* Will do it. Me? Not so much."

"Such a goody two-shoes," she said, laughing. The banter reminded me of all our playful arguments in the desert. I'd missed it. "I know this plan about the ledger is a lot, that you'd rather just leave. But I need to make sure he can't come after us when we're gone."

I nodded. I knew that. I knew that she needed to feel safe when we left here. Bonnie had always needed to have her life in her own hands.

"Whatever you need, I'm here." And I would be. No matter what happened. "I hope you know that. We're in this together."

"Good. Because I plan on being stupidly happy with you. Living an apple pie kind of life, somewhere on a farm, with *lots* of kids."

A smile formed on my face, then slipped off of it quickly. Kids. *Emma.* My throat bobbed as I thought of that night, when she'd revealed to me that she'd lost a baby. *Our* baby. I hadn't been able to tell her the truth, and since then, I'd bottled it up and shoved it away.

"What's wrong?"

The concern in her eyes made my heart stutter. I looped my fingers with hers, squeezing tight.

"Emma," I whispered.

Bonnie's expression fractured. Devastation filled her eyes, and her bottom lip trembled as she seemed to realize all of the things I couldn't say. My voice caught in my throat, and tears stung my eyes. I lowered my gaze. Shame stuck hot in my chest.

"I wasn't there." The words burned, making my stomach roil.

"Hey, no," she said, twisting in my arms until she climbed onto my lap, straddling me and cupping my face in her hands. "No. You don't get to blame yourself for that. You *would* have been there. If you knew where I was, if you knew I was pregnant. Nothing would have stopped you. Not Mickey or Will, not Lee or all his guards. I *know* that. Emma knows that."

She kissed me, a thousand tiny brushes of her lips on my cheeks and wet eyes.

"This *wasn't* your fault," she said, pressing her forehead to mine.

A thousand arguments rose to the tip of my tongue. *If I had known . . . If Will had called for me . . . If I hadn't let Sixgun take her . . .* But they all died at the earnestness in her eyes. If Bonnie didn't blame me, how could I blame myself? We were in an impossible situation. I nodded.

"I'm still sorry. That I wasn't here. That you suffered the last three years, but, Bon, you have to know—" My throat bobbed again. Putting words to my feelings when I'd kept them locked down so tight hurt. But I needed to say them. She needed to hear them. "I fought for you. Every single day. And when I found out . . . I'm just sorry."

"I am too," she said, squeezing her eyes tight. "If I hadn't been so reckless in Fort Hood. Maybe if I wasn't so goddamned impulsive, we could have found another way. But I didn't even give us time to think about it—"

"He had *The Kid*. There wasn't time," I said, shaking my head.

"We could spend the rest of our lives trying to think of what we *could* have done differently. The truth is, if I'd stayed in Fort Hood, I'd have taken my glowroot tea and Emma never would have happened. If I hadn't been given glowroot, I would have died from my head injury. If you'd have come to New Orleans, guns blazing and me without my memories, Lee would have killed you. Or a million other things. Sometimes, things just happen. And they hurt. And we grow from them. So, farm boy, I want to have *lots* of kids with you one day. And when we do, you'll be there. For every time I throw up, and every long-winded complaint about aches and pains, and when I scream at you during labor. *That* is what we focus on. Not the pain of the past, but hope for the future."

My arms tightened around her. I brushed my lips across hers, wanting her to know that I loved everything about her. She quelled my haunted mind, made me feel like I wasn't a bunch of broken pieces, but, in fact, a whole man on my own. I didn't know if I'd ever truly be able to forgive myself for not being there.

But at least I would try.

"Do I want to know how bad it was today?" I asked after a long moment. I brushed her hair behind her ear, the pad of my thumb drawing slowly along her jaw.

"Nope," she said, smiling. "But it's a whole lot better now. You want to rip some of Mrs. Rutherford's clothes off of me? I think that could be *really* therapeutic right about now." Her smile widened lasciviously as she slung her arms around my shoulders.

"Hmm. Yes." I smirked, sliding my hands over her hips to pull her tighter against my chest.

This was the way it always had been with us. Easy. Seamless. Falling into one another was like breathing. I fell into the familiar feel of her in my arms. The little sounds she made as I slid the clothes from her body and took her there, in the library. The way we fit so perfectly together and moved as one. Until we were both spent, until we both knew without a doubt that this was what we wanted.

I fell asleep that night wrapped up in Bonnie, all of my worries a million miles away.

CHAPTER NINE

SAVANNAH

SLEEP HAD EVADED ME for nearly three days. After hours of tossing and turning, of not being able to force away the memory of Will's hands on my skin, I'd climbed into a scalding hot bath to rid myself of those thoughts.

Not that it helped.

Instead of the water washing away my conflicting feelings for the man, I thought about how much I'd liked him pinning my hands above my head in bed the morning after the graveyard. I remembered how reverently he treated my body, worshipped it, like I was some sort of goddess.

Jesus Christ, Savannah.

I yanked the plug from the drain and climbed out of the bathtub. Goosebumps pimpled along my skin as I wrapped myself in a soft white towel. Yet another image of Will filled my mind, of him in this very bathroom, showing me a tenderness I didn't realize he had.

I forced the thoughts away, turning my attention to the litany of lotions and oils that lined the vanity. I wrapped my hair in a second towel and went through my extended routine. Moisturizer, scents, the works.

My hair was still damp by the time I tugged on my nightgown. At least I felt clean. I shoved into my bedroom, eyelids feeling slightly heavier. Maybe now I'd get a good night's sleep—

"No wonder you've read this book so many times," a voice said. "It's absolutely *filthy*."

I bit back a screech and wheeled toward the window, where one William Ellis sat perched in my reading chair, my favorite book open in his hands. He grinned at me before turning his eyes back to the page before him.

"*What* in the hell are you doing here?" I snatched the book away, closed it, and set it on my nightstand.

"Something wrong, Savvy?" He lit a cigarette, his dark eyes glimmering in amusement.

I'm not going to stay away from you, I'm not going to hold myself back anymore.

"Of course!" I threw my hands up in exasperation. His declaration the other day loomed large in my mind. I'd kept to my room when I wasn't helping to maintain the image of the sham wedding as a way to avoid him. Because if Will didn't hold himself back, there was little hope for me.

When my annoyance only made him grin wider, I growled at him. He leaned back in the chair, perching an ankle over a knee.

I could *not* have him in here. In my space. Where just a few short days ago I'd woken up in his arms. I'd felt *needed* as his lips traced my skin, his hands—

Goddamnit.

"You need to go." I grabbed him by the wrist and tugged him to his feet. "Honestly, I can't—"

"You told me to come to you."

His words stopped me in my tracks. I faced him, throat bobbing at the tenderness in his gaze. He rubbed the back of his neck. I *had* told him to come to me. I bit my bottom lip and then dropped my grip from his wrist. I blew out a long breath, shaking my head back and forth slowly.

The tension went out of me. "I locked that door."

"You did." He took in a long drag from his cigarette.

"Then how did you get in here?" Jesus Christ, he was exasperating.

"I picked the lock."

I blinked, eyes widening. Just like that? He picked the lock? How many times had I been locked in here for one reason or another and never been able to escape? As a matter of fact, that must have been how Bonnie got into my room after Sebastian beat me.

"Could you show me?"

"What?" Will's jaw slackened, any hint of lingering amusement gone.

"How to pick a lock." I shuffled uncomfortably beneath his curiosity. I scratched my arm as a means to busy my hands, but it did little to distract me. When I finally met Will's gaze, a shock went through me. I didn't like it when he looked at me like that. Like he wanted to *see* me. "Sometimes, to punish me, Lee locks me in here. If I knew how to—"

"Why?"

"Why what?"

Darkness clouded his features, a hint of the Beast appearing. "Why would he lock you in here?"

I blew out a long breath and lowered myself on to the edge of my mattress. "Lee learned early on that I didn't like being isolated." I scratched at the invisible itch on my arm again. "A way to keep me compliant was to threaten to lock me up."

It was something my mother had done, locked me away after we were kicked out of the brothel and she didn't have anyone to keep an eye on me. *To keep you safe,* she'd said in the midst of her drug-addled ramblings.

"Never mind," I said, shaking my head. "It isn't important." I tucked my knees up, wrapping my arms around them as Will continued to stare at me. "Are you okay?"

Will's brows lifted. "Am *I* okay?"

"I told you to come to me if . . . " I shrugged.

"No, yeah, I'm okay."

Then why did you come here? I didn't ask the question, however. In truth, I liked having him in my space. I felt more comfortable with him around, safer. Even if I didn't trust *myself* around him.

"So you . . . broke into my room to . . . read my book?"

A grin crossed his face as he peeked at the scantily clad cowboy on the cover of the novel. "I was just curious what's gotten you to read it so many times." He stubbed his cigarette out on the side table. "That cover is far more worn than when I bought it."

"When you bought—"

Or the fucking romance novels. Sebastian had been standing right there, the night he beat me. *He has them delivered as if Lee bought them.*

I'd discovered weeks ago that Will followed me when I left the manor house. What I never quite put together was that it was because he *liked* me. Even if he'd convinced himself not to pursue me until now. Until we'd crossed a line that neither of us could go back over.

"It must be good." Will yanked me from my thoughts, quirking an eyebrow lasciviously. I crossed my arms over my chest. "I'm not big on romance novels, but I started it the other night, and I have to admit, I get it."

My eyebrows furrowed. The *other* night? "I'm sorry. Are you telling me that this isn't the *first* time you've broken into my room?"

"You've got quite the comfortable chair." He removed his hat and set it on my vanity bench. "Lock picking isn't hard, really." He extended a hand. "Let me show you."

I eyed his calloused palm, unable to breathe. My body wanted to lurch forward, to let him show me *whatever* he wanted, whether or not it had to do with picking a lock.

"I'm a gentleman." I heard his smile in his words. "I promise, nothing untoward."

My brows shot up in incredulity as I dared to look at him. "Uh huh."

"You wound me, Savvy." He flattened a palm against his chest as a grin lit up his features. "Seriously, get up. I'll show you."

I placed my palm in his hand, and he tugged me to my feet. I stumbled, falling into his muscled chest. He wrapped his arms around me, his breath making the stray hairs around my temples tickle my skin.

"Careful, now," he whispered, his voice an octave deeper. I cleared my throat and shoved back from him, smoothing my hair and shuffling my weight from one foot to the other.

Will grinned, unashamed in every way possible. My cheeks heated, but I shoved it all back, then motioned for him to proceed. He grabbed my hand, looping our fingers together as he tugged me toward the bathroom door. He pulled it open a few inches, then flicked the lock on.

"You'll need to get close to the lock," he said as he rifled in his pocket. He pulled out two slim pieces of metal: one flat and the other with a hook at the end. With his free hand, he guided me toward the lock, then put pressure on my shoulder. I lowered onto my knees, and Will followed suit, our arms brushing as he reached for the lock.

"This flat one goes in the bottom." He demonstrated slowly. I'd like to think I was a good student, but that was difficult to do with him so close to me. "With this one, you have to test the pins for tension." A few seconds passed, and then the lock on the door clicked. "See?"

I loosed a breath. "Sure?"

"Here." Will removed the tools and locked the door again. Then he shifted, moving behind me as he tucked the tools into my hands. His warmth enveloped mine. I settled back against him, the tension in my shoulders slackening at his familiar touch.

His calloused fingertips slid along the length of my arms, guiding the tools in my hands into the lock. He gripped my wrists, showing me the motions, even though all I could focus on was how it felt to be wrapped up in him. How I'd missed it, even if I wouldn't admit it to him.

"Pay attention," he breathed, tugging on my wrists. I blinked several times in an attempt to force my eyes to focus on the task at hand. Instead, he leaned forward, practically resting his chin on my shoulder. The only thing separating us was the thin nightgown. I really, *really* didn't want anything separating us.

When the lock clicked, I blinked in surprise. I didn't even realize I'd done it.

"Just like that." His breath brushed along the tender skin of my neck. He inhaled deeply, his lips millimeters from my skin. "You smell incredible."

My eyes fluttered shut at the husky tone of his voice. It would be so, so easy to turn my head and kiss him. To let myself fall into him. To lose myself in sensation. To give him every single part of me without reservation. His arms tightened around me, his hands dropping to wrap around my waist. I leaned into his embrace, back arching slightly as his fingertips brushed along the bare skin of my thighs just beneath the hem of my nightgown.

"Will," I whispered. His lips pressed against that spot just beneath my ear.

"Hmm."

I felt the deep reverberations all the way in my gut. He'd taken a stand the other day. He'd told me he wanted me. That he wasn't going to hold back anymore.

And damn it, that messed with my resolve.

Before the graveyard, it had been easy to let myself be close to him. Maybe it was because I didn't know where he stood. Maybe the not knowing made me braver. I bit my bottom lip, my mind and body warring with one another. If I gave in now, I knew I would experience pure bliss. He would do everything in his power to satisfy me. But giving in gave him the power to hurt me. I didn't want him to hurt me.

But I'd be a damned liar if I said I didn't want *him*.

I twisted in his arms, the force of the move knocking him onto his ass. I straddled his lap, wrapping my arms around his neck. With a shaky breath, I covered his mouth with mine. His fingers tangled in my hair, and he groaned against my lips. The familiar flavor of tobacco and liquor welcomed me home. I raked my fingernails along his scalp as his hands slid the hem of my nightgown over my hips. I shifted, grinding my pelvis against his.

"*Fuck*," he murmured against my lips.

That was the thing with Will. It was easy. *Too* easy.

"Savvy."

I tensed, flattening my palms against his chest. I shook my head, shoving backwards and off of his lap. I climbed to my feet, righting my nightgown and touching my fingertips to my lips.

I couldn't do this.

A small, square bottle sat on the table next to my reading chair. I crossed the room in quick strides, yanking it up. Then I stomped past Will and pulled the bathroom door all of the way open.

"Goodnight, Savvy." The grin in his words grated my nerves.

I moved quickly through the bathroom, slamming open the door to Bonnie's room. Inside, dim light showed Bonnie and Jesse curled up together beneath the sheets.

"Jesse, *out.*" His brow furrowed as he took in the sight of me.

"Why?"

"*Out!*"

When he looked at Bonnie, my best friend smirked at him. "Yeah, get out."

Jesse scoffed. He glanced back at me, and something in my expression must have scared him, because he climbed from the bed and headed into the bathroom. I slammed the door behind him.

"Girls' night?" Bonnie asked, a brilliant grin crossing her mouth. I leaned back against the bathroom door.

"William Ellis is going to be the death of me," I said thickly. I lifted the bottle to my lips, taking a tentative sip. It wasn't Will's usual whiskey, but it burned on the way down just the same. I shoved away from the door and crossed to the bed, where Bonnie had retrieved her own bottle from a side table.

After snatching a pillow from where Jesse had been, I settled against the footboard, bottle in hand. Bonnie slid across the mattress, settling beside me.

"The Ellis charm got you *bad*, huh?" she said with a grin.

"No," I said too quickly.

She sighed, taking a swig from her own bottle. "You wouldn't be the first. Will is . . . infuriatingly charming. It's kind of funny though. I don't think I've *ever* seen him try so hard with anyone else. What did he do this time?"

"Showed me how to pick a lock," I grumbled. My friend chuckled beside me. "*Not like that*! I swear, you two have such dirty minds."

"He learned most of his jokes from me," she said, giggling. "I guess it's just how we coped . . . for a while."

Right. Because the two of them grew up together. Because she was his friend before she was ever mine.

"I'm . . . conflicted," I admitted. Though I could see her staring at me from the corner of my eye, I couldn't look at her. "I care about him, and that scares me. Because I know him. I know his patterns. What happens when he finds the next shiny, bright new thing to chase after?" I took a long pull from the bottle, cringing at the burn on its way down. "I know how this ends, Bonnie, and I don't know if I can endure that."

My friend took a sip from her own bottle, her head falling back against the footboard. She loosed a long breath.

"That's probably my fault," she said finally. My brows pinched together, and I turned to face her. Instead of returning my gaze, however, her eyes glazed over. "We were each other's firsts, but it wasn't romantic . . . like at all. He was my first friend when Jones bought me off of the slavers that killed my mom." Her throat bobbed. "We relied on each other to get through the hard days. And there were a lot of *hard* days."

A part of me was shocked to learn that they'd been together, but I didn't feel envy or distaste toward my friend. I could only imagine the horrors they'd endured growing up.

"After a particularly hard day, I climbed into Will's bed. I begged him to be my first. So that Jones wouldn't own that part of me. I wanted it to be on my terms with someone I trusted." She met my gaze, then, a half-smile curled on her lips. "Will was kind, and . . . it wasn't good."

Bonnie let out a bitter laugh at the memory. "It was fumbling and messy and weird. I felt safe. But . . . I didn't love him."

At that, my own conflicting emotions rose in my throat. Not that *I* loved Will. No, I was determined to never let it get that far.

It was that I knew it would be *easy* to love him.

"For Will it was different. He thought it meant we were in love. Because, like me, he didn't know what love looked or felt like. He thought we were together. That he wouldn't be *alone* anymore." She bit her bottom lip in contemplation. "I tried to tell him it wouldn't happen again, I didn't care about him how he needed me to."

My bottom lip trembled at the parallels. I'd *just* told Will it wouldn't happen again. Had my rejection reminded him of that time all those years ago?

"Instead of trying to find the words to explain when he wouldn't give it up, I slept with someone else so he'd get the hint. We stopped talking." She took a long pull from the bottle, then fixed me with a stare. "Next thing I knew, he had a reputation as a heartbreaker, and *everything* was a joke to him. Things went back to normal, and we just . . . *didn't* talk about what happened. Ever."

It made sense. The lack of commitment, the lackadaisical nature with which he addressed everything. There was still so much I didn't know about either of them.

"What am I supposed to do?" I asked finally. I shook my head slowly. "I mean, he was kissing me while with Sebastian. I'd be stupid to think I was any different."

"You are," Bonnie said. I shook my head, but before I could argue, she pressed forward. "Savannah, when Will likes someone, he goes for it. Immediately. No hesitation, no holding back. Except for *you*. I've watched the two of you for *years*. I didn't know it then, but I do now. You *are* different to Will."

Her words echoed the very sentiment he'd laid before me at his apartment. That he wasn't going to hold himself back from me any longer. I ran a weary hand over my face.

"I don't know what to do. What would you do?" I picked at the label on the bottle, scratching it away from the glass. Bonnie leaned over and wrapped an arm around my shoulders.

"Probably not the best to ask what *I'd* do," she said.

I barked out a laugh and nodded. "Good point."

"I can tell you what Will would say," she said, taking another swallow before turning to face me fully. "*El dolor es fugaz.*" She put the bottle down and gripped my hand. "It's something his mom taught us when we were kids. *Pain is fleeting.* We used to say it like a mantra on any given day because, well, we were living in hell. But looking back on it now, I think it means not to let the possibility of pain stop you from taking risks. Because pain doesn't last, but regret does."

Regret. How many times in my life had I regretted not taking a chance? Will had mentioned his mother before, how I reminded him of her, and by the wistful expression in Bonnie's eyes, I wondered if she might think the same thing. I squeezed her hand back, nodding.

"Enough about me and Will," I said, forcing a smile onto my face. "I want to know about *you*. Bonnie. Now that we know what happened before you were here . . . I want to know you."

"That conversation may take a while," she said, half joking, half bitter.

I shrugged. "I've got all night. It's not like I'm going back to *my* room."

Bonnie's grin lit up her features. I'd seen Audrey smile many times before, but it had been different. There was always an edge there, the piece she was lacking. But now, seeing her whole and, while not completely happy, as close as she could be, my heart felt lighter.

As she started to tell me about long days in the desert, I settled further into the pillow with the warmth of the liquor coursing through my veins, pushing away all thoughts of the beautiful man who was more than likely still in my bedroom.

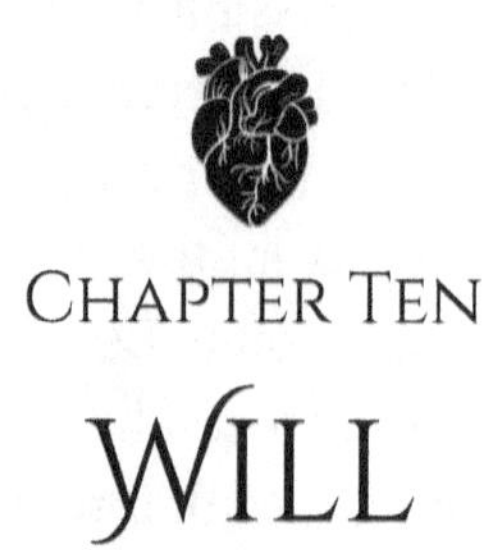

WILL

I COULDN'T WIPE THE stupid grin off my face. She'd *kissed* me. Savannah kissed *me.* I didn't want a cigarette for once. I didn't want anything to taint the taste of her in my mouth. So *fucking* sweet. Instead, I sat back in her chair and ran my thumb over my bottom lip in absolute shock. She hadn't just kissed me. She'd *wanted* me.

Whether she admitted it or not, I knew it was true.

The door creaked open, and my heart stuttered in my chest. Was she coming back? Maybe she didn't really want to leave. Unfortunately, it was just Jesse's hulking form, walking in half-dressed with a scowl. He pointed an accusing finger at me.

"Is this your fault?"

"Probably," I said with a shrug.

"I really *don't* understand you and Savannah. Is she pissed off at you or is this more weird flirting?" he asked with a frustrated sigh. "And why the hell do I *always* get the shit end of the arguments between you two?" He sat heavily on Savvy's mattress, leaning his elbows on his knees as he finally glanced at me.

"Wait, you look . . . good."

"Yes. You're nosy. And I *always* look good, *hermano*."

My shit-eating grin had his eyes rolling. "You know what I meant. Better than . . . recently."

"Well, I took your advice."

Jesse's eyes widened. "Fuck, really?"

I nodded, adjusting my hat on my head. "I told Savvy I wasn't going to stay away from her anymore. And I haven't. I've broken into her room the last few nights and—"

He pinched the bridge of his nose like a headache was coming on. "Wait, you *what?*"

I shrugged again. "She didn't seem to mind. I mean, she was asleep the last couple nights but—"

"I *swear to God*, Will, you're gonna give me a stroke."

I barked a laugh and leaned forward, clapping a hand on his shoulder. "Nah, you know you love the chaos."

"So, you told her you were *stalking her* and that's why she stormed into Bonnie's room and kicked me out?"

"No, she's used to me stalking her," I said matter-of-factly. "She stormed out of here after kissing me like the world was about to end again."

"What the fuck?" he said, holding his hands open in confusion. "I *really* don't get the two of you."

"Passion, Jess, *passion*. She's not done with me. Not yet. Not all the way. This is good news. It means I still have a shot."

"Yeah, in hell."

"I'll take those odds."

He ran a weary hand over his face and shook his head at my exuberance. "Well, I've been kicked out because of your hijinks. So, I guess we're bunking together tonight like old times."

"You missed the cuddling, didn't you?" I asked, holding my arms open wide. "C'mon, bring it in."

"Did you know that you're extra terrifying when you're happy?" Jesse asked, shoving my arm away. A small grin cracked on his face, though, one he couldn't hide.

"We don't have to tell Bonnie, but we *both* know you missed it." I stood and walked toward him, arms still open wide with an eyebrow raised in question.

"Shut up," he said, laughing in earnest now. I let my arms fall to my sides and expelled all the air in my lungs. It had been a while since I'd felt like this. In recent years, laughter had been hard won, genuine joy even rarer. Part of it was Savannah. A large part. But if I were being honest, my last few days had been spent exploring one of Jesse's other suggestions.

"There's a network of undesirables in the city," I said, watching his shoulders straighten at the serious change of topic. "I used to pay them for information on some of the targets Lee sent me after. They're desperate for money and supplies, and they're everywhere. In all the abandoned places, in the shadow of all Lee's seedy businesses."

"That's..." Jesse paused, his brows furrowing in thought. "Brilliant."

I shrugged, shoving my hands in my pockets to keep them from reaching for my cigarette case. "In the beginning, when I was new here, I had to get . . . *creative* to get the jobs done. I've been reaching out to them the last few days, but they don't stay in one place, so they're not easy to find."

"You think they'll help us?" he asked, running a hand through his hair.

"Hell no," I retorted with a snort. "But they're willing to help me smuggle any new targets out of the city through their networks and keep an eye out for any fresh corpses to replace them. For a price, of course."

Jesse's smile curled slowly as my words sank in, pride shining in his eyes. It made me incredibly uncomfortable. "You found a way to stop."

"Turns out not *all* your advice is shit."

"We need a drink to celebrate. This is a big deal, Will. You finally took back some control of your life. That's not easy under the best circumstances. I'm—"

"If you say you're *proud of me*, I'll be forced to kiss you. And I don't think Bonnie would appreciate that too much."

He blanched. His mouth dropped open in shock. I couldn't control the booming cackle that erupted from my chest. He was still too easy to tease.

"You don't—you know—see me *like that*, right?" he asked, still mostly mortified at the thought. "I mean, *we're friends*."

I looked him over slowly, watching him squirm beneath my appraising glance. Then I shrugged, waggling my eyebrows suggestively. "I'm not blind, Jesse. You're hot, but don't worry. I don't really go for guys with *violent tendencies.*" He barked out a laugh. One that seemed to surprise him, shaking his head at our running joke.

"It's crazy to remember how we met," he said, eyes glazed in memory.

"Speak for yourself. I still have the scar." I thunked my boot on the floorboards, listening for the hollow one. "Anyway," I said, circling back to the topic at hand. "When I was negotiating with the undesirables, they threw in some information they thought I'd appreciate."

"What're you doing?" he asked, watching me continue to thunk floorboards with the heel of my boot.

"You said we needed a drink. Savannah stole my whiskey, but I know where she keeps her contraband."

"Since when does Savannah have *contraband*?"

"She's a notorious prude whose best friend is an addict. This can't be a surprise to you." Just then, a hollow thud resounded through the space. Flipping up the ugly rug at the corner, I started prying up the board.

"I'm gonna tell her you called her a prude."

"Please do, she'll be determined to prove me wrong," I retorted with a wicked grin. "Stop distracting me, Jesus, Jess."

"Right, the undesirables," he said, half listening.

"They told me there have been whispers of Hanged Men outside the city. I'll meet with them soon for an update, but I think our timeline just got shorter." Jesse stilled, and I could practically feel the tension in his shoulders. I focused on the loose board beneath my fingertips and let the news sink in. The board came up after a little strategic jiggling, and I tossed it to the side. "Now let's see what Savannah Beauregard has been keeping in her secret little cubby for me."

"Is there any part of you that thinks violating her privacy is a bad idea?"

I looked up to see Jesse was leveling me with a *at your own risk* look that probably should have warned me away.

"No."

Jesse got off his high horse pretty quickly when he realized I wasn't having second thoughts and joined me on the floor. With great care,

I started pulling out items and arranging them delicately on the rug beside me. There was an old tin of tea that, when opened, was half-filled with different bits. Probably scrimped and saved over the years as she'd contemplated her escape from the manor. It was hardly any money. On the open road, it wouldn't get her even halfway to St. Louis. That wasn't what I saw looking at the coins, though. I saw her sheer determination to make a life for herself. I fished out all of the bits in my pocket and dumped them into the tin before closing it and putting it away.

Several really nice hairpins were stashed inside, none of them bent. Clearly, these were the expensive ones that Savannah didn't want Bonnie using for target practice. I smiled at the sight. A small leather pouch was next. When opened, the unmistakable musky herb scent of marijuana filled the air.

"What's that? It stinks," Jesse asked, peering inside at what could only be *really old weed*.

"That's gonna make you loosen up tonight, *hermano*."

I didn't think there was anything left inside, until the faint blue glow caught my eye. *Oh fuck.* The vial was wedged so far back that I had to reach in almost to my shoulder. My fingers brushed against something soft and worn. As tenderly as I could, I pulled out the vial of glowroot and a doll. It was made of mismatched scraps of fabric, the stitching loose around her face, drooping like she too had been touched by the Culling.

How long had this been hidden in here? So far back that she couldn't reach it without great effort. Was she that terrified that Lee would find it? Bringing the doll closer for inspection, my nostrils filled with heavy perfume. *Opium.* A favorite scent amongst women in a brothel. Almost like incense, earthy and warm.

I shouldn't be touching this. I didn't want the scent to dissipate. Memories of my mother flashed in my mind. Some of the few good times. I couldn't remember what she smelled like anymore, and I wouldn't wish that on anyone. It was like losing someone all over again, when you realized your memory couldn't retain the tiny details that made them important to you anymore.

Jesse leaned closer, reaching his hand out to take it from me.

"No. Not this."

Instead, I tucked it inside the cubby, careful not to snag the fabric on the exposed nails inside.

"No wonder Bonnie could never find the glowroot," I said, holding up the vial and deflecting the questions that lingered in my friend's eyes. I tossed it to Jesse, who caught it with a sneer.

"This is it?" he asked, glaring down at the vial like it was the devil himself. "This tiny little vial nearly stole my family from me."

I shrugged with one shoulder. "You sound pretty bitter for a man who used to be engaged to the biggest dealer in the city."

His eyebrows furrowed in confusion, blue eyes dark in pensive thought.

"Clara Higgins?" I said, reminding him of the blonde-haired hurricane that'd traveled from Montana with him years ago.

"God, you kept up with her? I figured she'd gone her own way after Fort Hood."

Scratching my eyebrow with my thumbnail and sucking a shaky breath between my teeth, I grimaced at him. "Well..."

"You're *still* sleeping with her?"

"Uh—"

"Jesus, Will!"

"Define *still?* I mean, I haven't seen her in months. She stayed in New Orleans for a while after we got here, and then she got into the glowroot trade. When she comes into town, we meet up for a little casual fun, then she's gone again."

"What on earth could possess you to keep fucking her after what happened in Fort Hood?" he asked, judgment ringing clear in his voice. I dropped my eyes to the vial in his hand, my stomach roiling with discomfort.

"She was the only person that knew me *before.*"

"She was working with slavers, Will."

"And I work for Lee. Monsters don't bother me, Jess."

"So how does Clara fit in with Savannah?"

"Like oil and water? I don't know what you're asking me. Haven't you ever had casual sex before?"

"Let's say Clara comes back to town. What does that mean for this . . . thing with you and Savannah?"

I picked up the pouch of weed and found some papers folded in an inside pocket. With deliberate carefulness I started rolling a joint like I did most of my cigarettes.

"Nothing. Things ended *badly* the last time Clara was here. I believe her exact words were that I was *fundamentally broken*. Pretty sure she's not going to look for me the next time she's in town. Besides, it was *casual*. Just fucking."

"Uh huh," he said, eyeing me with incredulity.

Jesse's lack of trust shook the giddy feeling from the center of my chest. He was my best friend, and his lack of faith chiseled away at the fragile foundation I'd been rebuilding my life on. Was this how Savannah saw me? How everyone did?

It wasn't abnormal for me to have multiple people warm my bed, but Savannah wasn't some casual encounter in a bar or a friend with benefits from years ago. She'd never had sex before our tryst in the graveyard. That *meant* something. Didn't it?

Doubt niggled its way into my mind, gnawing at all the convictions I'd been so staunchly holding on to. Pinching the joint between my index finger and thumb, I lit the end and inhaled the harsh smoke. Then I coughed horribly before passing it to Jesse. He opened his mouth to ask another question, but I shoved his arm and waved an impatient hand at him. It only took me a moment to pack Savannah's treasures back into her secret hiding spot.

The rest of the night consisted of Jesse and me passing the joint back and forth, philosophizing over nonsense and forgetting that I wasn't good enough for just a little while.

CHAPTER ELEVEN

BONNIE

LUCAS HAD CORNERED ME *again*. And my murderous impulses were nearly constant at this point. No matter how I tried to distract my father, Lucas was never far away, his hazel eyes turning cruel as he chastised me. Today, I'd nearly started breaking glasses in an attempt to piss off Lee for his attention when my *fiancé* gripped my arm and dragged me from the room with his fingers digging into my skin.

Audrey doesn't know four ways to break a man's hand. Don't blow your cover, I reminded myself as he slammed my back against the hallway wall, fury turning his unassuming looks grotesque in the dim light.

"What the *fuck* has gotten into you lately?" he said through clenched teeth. I tried to wrench my arm out of his hold, but his grip only tightened to the point of pain.

"You're hurting me," I said in response, but it fell on deaf ears.

"You're acting like a child! All you had to do was sit there and look pretty while we figured out the seating chart. I won't tolerate this *rebellious* behavior, Audrey."

"What happened to us being *friends?*" I asked, unable to stop the defiance that boiled in my blood as I tipped my chin up at him. "Wasn't that what you said? That we'd be friends until we learned to love each other. Then why, at every turn, are both of you ignoring me? It's *my wedding* too, or have you forgotten?"

His answering smile was chilling, hazel eyes cold as they turned dark with lust. They dropped to the clingy, revealing dress that'd been chosen

95

for me today. "Your father told me not to force you, but if you want to get closer, I can make that happen."

He dipped his head to kiss me, his body pressing hard into mine. I leaned on one of my oldest tricks: turning and offering my neck. It was less intimate. Lucas Rutherford, however, wasn't easily deterred. Since I'd been wearing the new, clingy clothes, his brown eyes often darkened with lust as he looked at me.

My body isn't me. This is just a con.

"You're so fucking sexy in that dress," he groaned into my ear, pressing me further against the wall. I was going to be sick. His lips on my skin made my stomach thrash, and I had to dig my nails into my palms to keep from breaking his nose.

His fingers gripped my hips tight, and I felt like I couldn't breathe.

I had to regain control of this situation. Fast.

Like an avenging angel, Jesse appeared. He was all the way at the other end of the hall, fingers clenched into tight, shaking fists. His blue eyes were dark and murderous. My lungs finally filled with air.

"Lucas," I said, running my hands onto his chest to push an inch of space between us. "If you don't get off of me, I'll scream." I let my voice waver, as if in fear. It wasn't hard to fake. I hated that Jesse saw this, worried what he would do because of it.

"So?" he questioned amusedly. "We're going to be married soon."

He would care when Jesse kicked his face in.

"Not yet," I whispered. "I'll tell my father."

He sighed. Eyebrows furrowing in exasperation. "Fine."

Then his weight disappeared as he retreated. "But soon you'll be in my bed, and I'll remember this." A clear threat. I nodded, swallowing down bile at the hard edge in his voice. His displeasure was clear. He would hurt me if he had the chance.

Jesse looked like he was two seconds away from ripping Lucas's head off with his bare hands. As soon as Lucas disappeared around the corner, I sank against the wall and squeezed my trembling hands into fists at my side. *Get your shit together.*

I didn't have time to cover up a murder.

With a steadying breath, I straightened my shoulders and marched toward Jesse who was glaring after Lucas. Gripping his arm, I tugged him away from the hall with little effort. Every muscle in his body was tense, his blue eyes sharp like shards of colored glass.

"I know."

"I fucking hate that guy."

"I know."

"Can I strangle him?"

"No."

"Are you sure?"

"Yes."

"Bon—"

I'd walked him out onto the courtyard, and we folded into the shadows of one of the pillars away from prying eyes.

"It's a *con*, farm boy. And I'm struggling hard enough as it is not to make him bleed." He stared back the way we came. Reaching up to cup his hardened jaw, I pulled his eyes back down to me. "You trust me, right?"

He expelled a shaky breath. One that showed me just how tightly he was wound. Honestly, if the roles were reversed, I'd feel the same. I couldn't blame him, I wouldn't. I'd tear someone apart for even thinking of threatening him.

"You know I do."

I nodded, letting my hand run down the side of his neck to settle on the place above his thundering heart.

"I can handle that prick. *I promise.*"

Promises were sacred. One of the few tenets I'd lived by after years on the run as a fugitive and an outlaw. My word was my bond. If I gave it, I never did so lightly. Jesse knew this. Knew *me* in his bones. Some of the tension released from his shoulders, but his concern remained.

"You'll tell me, if it's too much. Right?" I folded into his arms, and he clutched me tight, fingers burying in my hair. He cradled me as if he could protect me from Lucas. The more time that passed, the less certain I was of that. Still, I nodded against his shirt.

"Thank you," I breathed against him.

"For what?"

"Being *mine*."

He pulled away enough to stare down at me, then pressed his mouth to mine swiftly. His fingers at the base of my skull squeezed softly.

"Always."

As much as I'd love to fall into the safety and comfort of him, I knew I couldn't. Anyone could see us. If we got caught now, I didn't want to think about what could happen to him. Or to me.

"Why'd you come?" I asked, unable to stop myself from running my hands over his chest again. The familiar touch grounded me as much as it seemed to calm him. I felt the rumble of his groan beneath my palms. His eyes lit up at my question. Covering my hands with his own, he brought one wrist to his mouth for a kiss.

"I have a surprise for you," he said, with a small grin that set my skin on fire.

"Oh, you do, huh?" I asked, twining my fingers with his. He smirked and dragged me from the courtyard without another word. "Is this a surprise that requires *clothes*?" He barked a laugh, shaking his head as we dipped into the stables. Another few feet and we were in the alleyway on the far side of the house.

I made a satisfied humming sound, eyes lit in wicked delight. "An alleyway? How appropriate, farm boy." Just like where we first met. I'd been so terrified of how I felt then. I was afraid now, too. For different reasons.

Gripping his shirt tight, I pushed him against the dark stone wall just like I had all those years ago. When I was just a girl on the run, and he was a boy who didn't know how to trust. His eyebrows rose in shock at my aggression.

"*Don't pout*," I said, mirroring my harsh words from so long ago. His answering smile lit up the shadows. "Help me forget that slimy fucker had his hands on me." It wasn't a question, which he discovered when, rising on tiptoes, I slammed my mouth against his.

He didn't hesitate. With possessive enthusiasm, he gripped my waist and wrenched me close. My fingers buried in his hair, neither of us caring if we couldn't breathe. His hand tracked a familiar pattern across my body, curving over my ass and pulling me tight.

"Bonnie?" a deep but familiar voice said behind me.

Everything inside of me stilled. There was no more chaos, only quiet that spread through my veins like ice water. I pulled away from Jesse, blinking toward the opening of the alleyway that was bright with the afternoon sun. A tall, slim figure stood dark at the entrance.

"Who's that?" I asked in a whisper. Because a part of me already knew. A part that was terrified and buzzing with so many emotions I couldn't begin to name them all. Jesse only smiled at me. The figure approached, thudding on heavy, booted feet. My heart pounded in time with each step.

"Why is it every time I find you two in an alleyway, you're doing ungodly things to each other?" he asked, sarcasm dripping from each word like I'd spoken them myself. He remembered. He remembered *me.*

Tears burned in my eyes, and the air trapped in my lungs expelled in a rush.

"Kid?"

His name broke across my lips like shattered glass. A shaft of light illuminated his face, blue eyes lit in teary recognition. Seconds slipped, time slanting away from me, stretching into forever. I didn't feel the ground beneath my feet, didn't know I was running toward him, but the space between us disappeared in the blink of an eye. He had to lean down as I approached, throwing my arms around his suddenly broad shoulders. His hat fell forgotten to the ground as he lifted me off my feet, squeezing my ribs hard enough to hurt.

Hard enough to prove that *this was real.*

"Kid!" I half-gasped, half-sobbed into the familiar smell of his hair. Tears wobbled and rolled down my cheeks as, in no time at all, a part of me that had been gone too long was returned. He was *here*, so changed but still *mine*.

My smile trembled and stretched wide as he put me gently back on my feet, like he was afraid I would break. Like me, his eyes were wet and his smile so big it nearly broke his face in two. Just the way I remembered it. My shaking hands ran through his hair, a soft halo of russet gold, curling over his ears.

"Let me look at you," I said shakily. He was nearly as tall as Jesse, and I cupped his jaw.

He still gripped me tight, like he had when he finally learned the truth about his parents. When the well of his sorrow threatened to consume him, he'd clung to me like this. Sobbed against me like this. In the time since my memories returned, I'd tried not to think about him. Three years was such a long time for a child. I'd wondered what The Kid remembered of me, if the chasm of time that'd caused a rift between me and Jesse would be even wider with him. After all, he'd had to grow up so much since the last time I saw him. I pulled back to press my forehead to his, studying the light of curiosity that still lingered in his eyes. But it was buried now, beneath grief he'd carried for too long.

"You didn't lose me," I said in a rush.

"Someone told me once that I couldn't," he said, his voice deeper than I remembered. "After all, you aren't a sweater I flung off at bedtime." I laughed then, the swell of happiness expanding in my chest as I raked my trembling hands through his hair, over and over again. As if I could erase the three years lost between us if I just kept doing it. He may have grown up, but he was still The Kid. *My* Kid.

I stepped out of his embrace, smoothing my hands over the shoulders of his shirt and drinking in the sight of him. He'd lost the round youthfulness in his face, gaining some of the chiseled angles that reminded me of Jesse. Yet his arms and legs retained a colt-like gangliness that proved he wasn't completely grown up yet.

"Look at you," I said, gripping his hand in mine. He squeezed back, eyes full of affection and hope. Two of his fingers hadn't responded to the grip of his hand on mine. My eyes fell to the appendage, and I pulled it up, peeling back the sleeve of his shirt to see the pink scar on his arm.

I remembered the sound of his screams. The blood. Before the world went dark and I'd awoken as a different person.

This was my fault. I'd led dangerous men to a place where he was supposed to be safe. They'd hurt him because it would hurt me. It would force me to go anywhere, do anything, to keep him safe. He must've seen the dark thoughts cross my face, because he pulled his hand back.

"I'm better at throwing knives now," he said with a mischievous grin that made my heart soar.

"Guns?" I asked, and he breathed out a frustrated sigh. Answer enough. I dragged my palms over his cheeks, ridding them of the salt tracks left behind from his tears. "Well, it seems I still have a lot left to teach you then."

His smile was slick and malicious, the kind that promised trouble in spades. *Jesus, he learned a lot from me.* I should've probably been worried about that, but oddly my chest filled with pride instead. His eyes turned down to my hand, still clenched in his, to the left one where a large diamond glittered in the afternoon light.

"How much you think we can trade this ugly ass thing for?" he asked, scowling down at it.

"Enough to finally buy that assault rifle I've always wanted," I retorted, twisting my palm away. Shame like sour smoke filled my lungs and made it hard to speak. I didn't know how to explain this all to him, not in a way that would make sense to a surly teenage boy at any rate.

"I give you full permission to use her fiancé as target practice, Kid," Jesse said over my left shoulder. His hand drifted casually onto my hip, which I normally wouldn't notice except this touch felt more possessive than usual. My stomach roiled, and my chest grew vice-grip tight. It was like walking on a tightrope, and no matter how I tried to correct my balance, I was still falling.

"Hell yes!" The Kid hissed approvingly.

I glared at them both.

"No putting holes in the rich asshole until I have the ledger."

"You're supposed to be the *fun* one," The Kid grumbled blackly, retrieving his hat and slapping the dust from it before settling it back on his head.

"No, I'm the *smart* one."

"Not smart enough to keep from being trapped by that prick."

I didn't know what hurt worse. The Kid's bitingly truthful words or the fact that Jesse remained silent in agreement. They really had that little faith in me.

Long buried insecurities raised their ugly heads in the dark memories of my past, clawing with talons of doubt and scoring deep, until the illiterate slave of the past stared back at me like a bloody mirror.

"I'm not trapped by *Lucas*," I said, my words coming out hard.

"Then why are you still wearing his ring?" The Kid asked, his tone more argumentative than I remembered him capable of being in the past.

"That's not—it's—"

I *just* promised Jesse that I could handle Lucas on my own, yet here they both were . . . treating me like a victim. A damsel in need of saving. Anger heated my blood and pinkened my cheeks.

"Is that what you both really think? I wouldn't even be in this situation with Lucas to begin with if it weren't for Jesse. I can handle myself."

Jesse sighed wearily, squaring his shoulders, readying himself for a fight we both knew was coming. I forgot that we could be like this: as ready to rip each other apart as to hold the jagged pieces together. But the engagement to Lucas was directly related to all the lies he'd never acknowledged he told me, much less apologized for.

"You don't want to know what I think." His blue eyes were dark, sliding over to The Kid quickly as if in warning.

"Right. Because the great and powerful *Montana* can do no wrong. I forgot what a good liar you are. So impressive that you could even lie to yourself—"

"Oh, that's just *fucking great*, Bon—"

"You said you *understood*! That you knew how important getting the ledger is and—"

"And I don't have to like how you're doing it!" He threw his hands up, taking two steps back until his back was against the brick wall. As if he needed the stone to hold him upright.

"I'm just going to . . . " The Kid thrust a thumb over his shoulder before he disappeared into the stables awkwardly, leaving Jesse and me to fight without an audience.

"Great. That's just great," Jesse said, gesturing toward the empty space his brother disappeared into. "Exactly how I wanted this to go."

I crossed my arms across my chest and chewed on my bottom lip to stop myself from saying anything else. When did everything get so complicated? Silence blanketed us, leeching away some of the animosity from our words.

"I don't like it either," I said after a while. "Lucas. I told you he was going to be a problem, but—"

"You lost control," he cut me off. "It was terrifying. Usually, with cons, you're in charge. You run the game. Bon, you're *always* two moves ahead. But what I saw in there was . . . "

His words trailed into nothing. But I knew what he wanted to say. What he saw wasn't me running a con, but a pawn in one. A little girl, hiding under a bed. Thrown in a trunk. With a bad man she lured into an abandoned place.

But I wasn't that girl anymore. I hadn't been in a long time.

My eyes dropped to the cobblestones at my feet. I was out of my depth, water closing over my head, until the air was thin enough to rattle in my lungs. He'd lost faith in me. I'd lost trust in him too, after everything. How did we get here? How did we manage to find our way back?

"Every time I've tried to distract my dad, Lucas keeps getting in the way. He's starting to . . . it feels . . . I can handle it." My words were clumsy. The air wouldn't stick inside my lungs, and my heart squeezed so tight it was nearly unbearable. "I can. I can handle it." The Jesse I used to know would never make me doubt my capabilities like this. In a few steps he was in front of me again, lifting my chin until all I could see were the depths of his eyes. More familiar to me than anyone's. A place that always made me feel safe. He cupped my jaw, and we breathed together. I drank in his shaky exhalations. Sucking his breath deep inside of me, hardening my bones and my resolve.

"Who are you?"

Grounding questions. The same ones we'd asked each other a thousand times when things got too intense. But this time, all I could do was utter an incoherent sound from the back of my throat. My chest was on fire, my ribs caving in as I tried to sync my breaths through trembling lips.

"Someone who needs you to *support* me."

He nodded, his fingers flexing against my jaw. His nose brushed against mine, and his breath fell hot into my open lips. Why was it so hard for him to trust me? Didn't he know how badly I wanted the life that had been stolen from us? Couldn't he feel how hard I was fighting for that?

With steely resolve, I lifted my hand to cover his over my jaw and, with little effort, guided it down. My eyes stayed trained on his as I nestled his hand over my throat, fingers over my steady pulse at the sides of my neck. *I trust you*. His nostrils flared, eyes darkening as he realized my intent.

"You aren't playing fair, Bon," he grumbled in that deep pitch of his voice that reminded me of canyons in the desert. I smiled, the curl of my lips against my teeth slow and sensual.

"I never do."

Then I bit my bottom lip and raked it through my teeth, watching as his control snapped and he crushed me against him. His hand never left the collar around my throat, the pressure never increased against my pulse, but he liked having it there. Liked that I willingly put myself in his power, that I gave him this small measure of control when he'd been forced to watch at the sidelines earlier.

He kissed me then. Slow and firm. His lips took their time against mine, making me melt against him until I was a trembling mess of need. My nails dug into his sides as I whimpered greedily. Jesse pulled away and pressed his forehead into mine, breathing heavily.

"I hate him," he breathed against my skin. "I hate watching him touch you. It's torture."

"*Please*," I begged him. "*Wait.* Just a little longer. Once we're free of them, I'll never do another con."

He closed his eyes, his hand finally dropping from around my throat to land on my hip, caging me loosely in the strength of his arms. Then he nodded, and the chasm that'd been splitting me apart at the seams was slowly knitting back together. Maybe, just maybe, I'd been wrong. Maybe we could find our way back to each other.

Maybe we could finally be a family again.

CHAPTER TWELVE

WILL

I'D TRADED ONE ADDICTION for another. Savannah moaned in her sleep, the sounds soft and breathy in a way that made it hard for me to think about anything else. My obsession with her had grown *unhealthy*. I couldn't stop. Well, I *could*, but I didn't want to.

When I thought about her, I didn't think about hurting myself.

It was always there, of course, lying in wait for the moment I didn't have Savannah Beauregard as a crutch. It was a beautiful lie I whispered to myself in the middle of the night. One I wished for so desperately I'd actually started to believe my delusions.

One day, I'll deserve her.

These intrusive thoughts kept me company on my errands. I'd gotten an envelope from Lee. Just a name. A life meant to be snuffed out expeditiously. The closer we got to leaving, the more Lee seemed on edge lately. Paranoid. Drinking heavily. Suspicious of everyone around him. Everyone *except me.*

After all, I'd been his loyal dog for years. Why would he think anything would be different now?

Only, it was different. *I* was different.

And it was all *her fault.*

Even as I traveled into the worst parts of town, where emaciated children wearing rags begged for food or money or drugs, her taste lingered on my lips. Too fucking sweet for the slums. I hated it here. Near the swampy, stinking waters of the Pontchartrain where the humidity shimmered poisonously in the air. As I rode in, a gaunt woman with a bandaged hand appeared from the shadows of a burned building. I'd dealt with her before. Too many times. Her hair was a dull red that reminded me of dried blood, her lips always chapped, dark circles gouging canyons beneath her eyes. Sometimes I genuinely couldn't tell if she was young or old.

"Moira," I said by way of greeting. She didn't acknowledge me. Instead she just motioned for me to follow her inside. Normally, I'd keep my head on a swivel as I ducked under the fallen, soggy ceiling boards, and be on the alert for any others who may not know about my tentative deal struck with the undesirables. But no, Savannah *fucking* Beauregard haunted me. How she'd kissed me consumed my every waking thought. There had been an undercurrent of aggression as her mouth slammed against mine. Nothing like how I thought she'd want to be kissed, especially after the animalistic way I'd fucked her on top of Seb's grave.

I mean, that was pretty fucked up, and I had been certain every single day afterward that I'd done irrevocable damage to her. But that kiss made me start to believe differently. Fuck, my cock grew hard just thinking about the things I'd imagined doing to Savvy. Things that would start with a kiss like that and end with her screaming my name until she couldn't speak anymore. Until the very thought of me made her soak her little cotton panties.

Moira snapped with her good hand, dragging me out of my daze, and stared at me incredulously. *Shit*, it wasn't like me to lose my focus like this. Savannah really would be the death of me if I wasn't careful.

"I did some recon on the name I was given. He's a man in his early forties, stout build, approximately six feet two inches tall, with dark hair. Think you can find me a fresh corpse to match that description?" My words were clipped, one palm resting on the handle of my gun. She scoffed at me.

"Such little faith," she cooed in a gravelly, unused voice. She beckoned me on, through one dirty room into another to a large metal door with a hinged lock. Moira covered her face with her soiled shirt and pinched her nostrils closed.

I wouldn't like this.

She opened the metal door, and a flood of stench washed out that would curdle the stomachs of most grown men. Unfortunately, the smell of rotting corpses had long ago lost the ability to make me vomit. The corpses were piled high in some places and laid out in others, depending on how fresh and *intact* they were. I knew the undesirables, like vultures, often dragged away the dead. I assumed to steal anything left behind on their bodies, or to feed to Ponchartrain Patty, who lurked in waters nearby.

Once, however, I'd seen an undesirable crouching over a body and thought I saw teeth marks on the blue-tinged skin as I passed. A shiver of disgust fractured down my spine at the memory. We walked through the rows, my eyes roaming the unseeing eyes and bloated bellies of the stock I had to work with.

I have to find a way to stop.

The desperate thought made my fingers twitch at my sides. Jesse believed I could stop. He'd talked about it like it was so easy. If this didn't work, I didn't know what I'd do. Probably just finish the job and hope I was strong enough to live with the monster I'd become. Strong enough not to pull the trigger this time.

Moira stopped and pointed at the lifeless husk of a man in the corner, her eyes never leaving my face as I studied him. It would work. He was fresh enough to pass, and as long as I hung him high, he could be mistaken for my target. *It has to work.*

Hauling him onto my shoulders, I tried not to wince at how stiff and cold he was. Soon enough, I'd gotten him back outside, strapped onto the back of my horse, and ready for his trip to the bridge. I'd already warned the real target and given him instructions on how to find the undesirable network that would smuggle him out of the city.

After dropping a few coins into Moira's good hand, I turned to leave. "Wait," Moira said. When I turned, her normally blank expression was screwed up. It was hard to tell what emotion played across it. She was just so haggard from her life on the fringes that everything was distorted.

"There are Hanged Men in the city."

My heart slammed against my ribs at her rasped words, my mind spinning into a thousand different directions. *In the city.* I didn't know how they'd smuggled their way in, but if they were inside the city, then they were closing in on us. *My father* was closing in on us. Savannah's beautiful whiskey-colored eyes came to mind then, full of light and hope. Fear made my imagination see them as dim and lifeless as the corpses inside. Bile rose hot in my throat.

"Why would you tell me that?" I asked, suspicion hardening my jaw. Moira stepped closer, unraveling the rags that were always tied around her hand and arm. The skin beneath was grotesque. Several of her fingers fused together or were not quite formed all the way. Her hand was barely functional at best. I studied the joints and the articulation of them with each small movement. This was her disfigurement that made her an undesirable. I never thought she'd show *me* something this personal.

"You don't flinch," she said, studying me just as I'd been studying her hand. "You *never* flinch. We in the fringes are deformed on the outside, but I think you're one of us. *Undesirable.* You may have a pretty face, but your soul isn't pretty, is it?"

My eyes were wide, my tongue thick as her words crawled under my skin and lodged there. Slowly, because it hurt to be honest, I shook my head. My soul wasn't pretty. It was more disfigured and haggard than any of the people here. It was a gruesome, blackened thing torn to shreds.

"Good," she said, grabbing my arm with her disfigured hand and gripping me tightly. "It will take someone with ugliness to kill *him.*" My eyes were still locked on her disfigured arm, the one clutching me. It was hard to notice at first, because of all her ruined flesh. "He preys on us when he's bored." Her sleeve fell back, and shock numbed me as I traced the jagged lines of raised pink flesh with my eyes. I'd know those wounds anywhere. The scar on my face ached, as if it were new again.

The taste of Savannah's lips from earlier turned metallic on my ride to the bridge. Her soft, sleepy moans had shifted into the echoed words Moira had spoken earlier. The determination in her gaze as she looked at me like I was exactly the kind of monster she'd been hoping would one day come and free her from the torment of someone so much worse. Being a monster on those terms didn't seem all that bad, actually.

It wasn't until hours later when I got back to the house that my head finally quieted, the chaos of emotions and thoughts stilling as I rode into the stables and realized Savannah was safe. She would be in the kitchen with Etty, working on some sweet confection with all her goodness locked away tight behind Lee's armed guards. Something eased in my chest as I swung from my mount, looking for the groom to untack and brush my stallion, but even though I swore I had seen him as I rode in, he was nowhere to be found.

My stallion nudged the front of my shirt, lips fumbling along the fabric in search of sugar cubes. I shoved him off gently, untacked him swiftly, and pulled out a brush. I lost myself focusing on the long, rhythmic strokes of the brush against his pitch-black coat. He chuffed in annoyance, which made me smile. The stallion dropped his snout to my shoulder, teeth pinching me in retribution.

"Ow! You grumpy fucker!" I swore, jumping back from him with a scowl as he stomped impatiently. "Here!" I popped open my shirt pocket and shoved three sugar cubes toward him. "I hope you get so fat that you can't run anymore. Let's see you outrun predators then, asshole."

My swearing never bothered him before, and it certainly didn't now. He just happily lapped up the sugar cubes, tossing his head in a self-pleased manner when he was done. I rolled my eyes when he pushed forward, rubbing his nose against my cheek in appreciation.

"Uh huh, I know you're just sucking up for more treats," I chuckled, patting his neck and inhaling the warm animal scent of his coat.

"Should I leave the two of you alone for a while?" a gruff voice asked behind me.

I knew that voice.

A wide grin spread across my face as I found Mickey Kincaid in all his worn-leather and weary-eyed glory, leaning against a post across from the stall. The last time I'd seen Jesse's uncle had been months ago; it was one of the last times I'd felt I could actually defeat the demons inside me.

You do what you have to, son.

If he knew everything I'd done since, he probably wouldn't have that same faith in me. Still, he was here. Right now, with the still fresh threat of my father being near, that was more than enough.

"Jesse should've told me you were comin' into town, old man. I'd have saved a bottle of something good for you."

"I'm sober now, Will," he said, shaking his head.

"I know, but if you have to watch me drink . . . it should at least be the good stuff, right?"

I expected him to call me a name, or crack a smile, the way he usually would. Instead, he just stared straight at me silently, with eyes that could see right through me, in the best and worst of ways. Discomfort wriggled into my gut. Could he see the ugliness of my soul too? I exited the stall and moved closer.

"I guess you being here means that things are heating up. We're leaving the city soon, right? About damn time. I was starting to wonder if it was your age holding you up."

Still nothing. Just that all-knowing stare.

I couldn't hold it.

Adjusting my hat on my head, I cleared my throat and hung the brush up on a crooked nail. But my fingers twitched, and I wanted a cigarette. I reached into my pocket, thumb running over my case. Mickey refused to speak, and my wavering grin faded.

"He told you, right?"

He uncrossed his arms from over his chest, shifting his weight. I dragged a ragged breath through my nostrils and blew it out roughly. It did little to settle the disquiet in my mind. Of course, Jesse would've told Mickey about the graveyard. Which meant, despite my longing to keep him from knowing how fully I'd broken since his absence, he was already aware.

"So what? Is this an *intervention* or something?" I asked, glaring at him. "More words of wisdom to make me feel normal again?"

"Is that what you need?" he asked, stepping toward me. I flinched back, dragging the case from my pocket and flipping it open. With a cigarette clenched between my teeth, I could buy myself a moment to think. Lighting it swiftly, I let the smoke burn down in my lungs, the familiar pain of it steadying me.

"I don't need anything," I exhaled, letting the smoke pillow in the air. "It was a weak moment when I was wasted. That's all."

The lie rolled from my tongue so easily I could've fooled myself into believing it. If only the urge to die disappeared, maybe the lie would have fixed me. But the darkness was never really gone. Beaten back sometimes, by Savvy, or Jesse, but I couldn't escape myself. Being alone was when it came back for me, reaching for my soul in quiet moments.

"Yeah, I remember saying that, too," he said, nodding solemnly. "I remember a lot of us saying the same thing. Funny, I'm the only one still alive from my unit."

"Well, you're a tough old bastard. Lucky too, since you escaped the Culling."

"All but two died before the Culling, Will."

I flicked the end of my cigarette nervously.

"Some people called it an epidemic. Soldiers who couldn't let the horrors of war go when they returned home safely."

Screaming. Blood covering my hands. Carving. The bite of rope against my slick palms.

I shook my head, but the sounds and images flooding my mind wouldn't leave. I squeezed my eyes shut tight and pinched the bridge of my nose, breathing hard through my mouth to rid my nostrils of the phantom sting of metallic blood.

Mickey's hands came down on my shoulders. I hadn't even heard him come closer. He squeezed hard, the pain of his grip giving me something else to focus on. Something to keep me from drowning in the sea of dead men who haunted me.

"The first step to getting better is admitting you need help," he said, the gruff tone of his voice rasping in my ear.

"I'm not a soldier."

"The fuck you aren't," he swore, shaking me until I looked up at him. His eyes were watery. I'd never seen a grown man look like that before. Vulnerable. Clenching my jaw hard enough to grind my teeth, I shook my head. "You've been fighting in a war for survival since the goddamn day you were born, son."

Son.

I dropped the cigarette to the straw-covered floor, stomping on it with my boot as I gripped the back of Mickey's shirt and rested my head on his shoulder. My eyes burned, the stench of rot replaced with the smell of Mickey's soap.

"I need help," I whispered. He nodded, gripping my shoulders tight and pushing me back onto my feet. Steadying me. His eyes shone suspiciously with emotion, as if he were fighting back tears. It was as unnerving as it was oddly touching.

"First things first, no more fuckin' booze," he said, pointing a finger at me.

"What?" I scoffed. "You can't be serious."

"I am. Alcohol is a downer, so right now it's your enemy. Smoke as much as you want, but no more drugs and no more booze. At least until we get you out of danger."

"Mickey—"

"Don't make me babysit you. I'll drag you back to camp and not let you out of my sight if I have to—"

Panic shot through me like lightning. I wouldn't be able to see Savannah if he took me with him. But failing Mickey wasn't an option either. Resignation settled into my bones. If this was what I had to do, I could. At least, I hoped so.

"No booze."

"No more fuckin' jokes, either," Mickey said sternly. Frustration built in my chest. I couldn't do this. I couldn't. He was asking too much. I thrummed my hand on my thigh, *tap tap tapping* while I shook my head.

"That's just who I am, I can't just *change* who I am overnight—"

"I know, I know. Because being a sarcastic asshole is basically your whole personality. I get it. I'm talking about when you feel like you're going to hurt yourself. Don't joke about that. You don't owe anyone false joy. It's not making their lives harder if you're just having a bad fucking day, okay?"

I thought about Jesse and Savannah, even Bonnie. Had I been protecting them or just trying not to be a burden? Mickey didn't push me, or rush me; he let me sit with those words. What would happen if, instead of making stupid jokes, I just told people I wasn't feeling happy that day?

After what felt like years, I nodded, shocked at myself for agreeing.

"Lastly—"

"Fuck, Mickey, can we just *not*—"

"I want you to say three good things about yourself. Out loud. Every single day. *No motherfuckin' jokes.* If you want to get better, you've got to start remembering that you're worth the work it's gonna take."

"No."

"No?" he questioned, raising an eyebrow at me. As much as I didn't want to let him down, that was something I wouldn't do.

"No. I'm not doing that. It's stupid."

"Why?"

"Because it is!" I shouted, throwing my hands. "I'm glad you want to help, but I'm not going to spend half my day staring into a mirror and telling myself how pretty I look. I've got real shit to deal with."

I turned my back on Mickey then, my mind reeling. The discomfort that'd risen at the onset of this conversation took over. My whole body burned and screamed that I needed to punch something, someone, get in a fight, drink until I couldn't see straight, take someone to bed—fuck it, multiple people—anything, *anything* . . .

A whistle sounded, echoing from the other end of the stables. The Kid was perched near an empty stall, grinning at me in amusement. I almost didn't recognize him; it was the grin that gave him away.

"You might want to save the sappy shit for when you aren't being followed, Ellis."

"You little fucker—"

He flipped open the latch to the empty stall, and the door swung open, revealing a red-faced Savannah crouching behind it. Warm shock spread through my veins. My mind quieted immediately as I watched her awkwardly straighten from her hiding spot, clenching her fingers tight in front of her skirts.

"Well, I'll be damned," Mickey said, eyeing me too keenly.

Savvy couldn't hold my eyes. Instead, she tilted her chin defiantly and cleared her throat. Her gaze slid between The Kid and Mickey, all prim and condescending. I fucking loved when she looked like that. Battle ready at a moment's notice.

"Who the hell are you anyway?" she asked with all the commanding presence of Zachary Lee himself. Like she was the lady of this goddamned manor and to hell with anyone who said otherwise. Her confidence rang in my ears like a siren song.

The Kid flipped a knife from his back pocket casually, picking beneath his fingernails with it as his eyes slid over to me. "This one of the spies Jesse mentioned?"

"No," I chuckled. Savvy shifted uncomfortably on her feet, but I crooked a finger at her and motioned her closer. "Come out here, you little stalker."

Her nostrils flared at my taunt, and for a long moment, she didn't move, just to prove she didn't have to. Slowly, she made her way out of the stall to stand with us.

"I'm Jesse's uncle, Michael Kincaid, but all my friends call me Mickey."

Like the gentleman he might've been once, Mickey stepped forward and offered his hand for her to shake. She took it tentatively, eyes flicking to mine several times to make sure it was okay. That she trusted me with her safety made something warm and prideful swell inside me, and all my frustrated nerves were gone for good.

"So, you're Will's *friend*," she asked, eyes shifting to mine. Her tone implicated a disbelief that it took me a minute to comprehend.

"Not like *that*, Savvy, Jesus. Mickey's family. And that little *fucker* over there is The Kid. He's a pain in the ass, as I'm sure you've noticed already," I said, smiling wide when The Kid scowled in response.

She shrugged, not at all concerned with her mistaken assumption. "How am I supposed to know?"

"Will?" Mickey asked. I had to force my attention back onto him. "You want to introduce your..."

"Savvy," I said, eyes falling back to her like gravity.

"That's *not* my name, William."

The Kid snorted obnoxiously. "William."

"Call me that again, and I'll break your other hand, Kid."

"Savannah. Beauregard. I'm Bonnie's friend," she said before I could keep threatening the little brat. She widened her eyes at me in warning. It was fucking adorable.

"Nice to meet you, ma'am," Mickey said diplomatically. "No offense, but *why* were you in the stall there?"

Instead of answering, her mouth dropped open as if to respond and then snapped shut again. When Savannah blushed, it was like watching the sky after the sun sank past the horizon. Instead of an obnoxious, feverish red that pinkened her cheeks, her skin glowed. Like a light turned on inside of her that could never be put out. Her eyes darted toward me briefly, but I was so transfixed by the reaction I nearly missed it.

"She followed him," The Kid said, in a bored tone. "I watched her sneak over from the kitchens and hide when she saw Will."

Hope flared bright inside me, burning deep in my bones. The uncertainty faded from her eyes, her shoulders squaring defiantly.

"Well, someone has to look after you," she said, her words directed solely at me. Not ashamed in the least.

"Ah," Mickey said, looking between us like everything suddenly made sense.

"You *followed* me," I said, my fingers twitching as I fought the urge to sink them into her hair and kiss her breathless.

"Turnabout is fair play," she retorted sharply. I laughed, unsure how I got here. Where the world could make sense. Where I *might* be able to fight back those demons enough to not hate myself so much anymore.

Maybe my soul was full of ugliness. Maybe I was a monster. But I was a monster that *she* couldn't stay away from.

"You followed me."

"You've been following me for years, I don't see how this is relevant."

"I think you do," I retorted, wavering toward her. All I wanted was for the others to leave, for us to be alone so I could show her how ridiculously happy it made me that she'd sought me out. She'd wanted to see me. Even for a moment. She cared enough to make sure that I was alright. The pull of her was stronger than any drug. More inebriating than the strongest whiskey on a hard day. *Fuck.* I wanted to hear her scream for me. To feel the dagger-like clench of her nails on my back. I measured the hateful distance between us a thousand times, mapping each way I could span it.

"Kid, where are Bonnie and Jesse?" Mickey asked, clearing his throat.

"Mommy and Daddy are fighting right now. Best to leave them to it, in my experience."

"Well, I guess I'll have to leave a message with you then," Mickey said, wrenching my gaze from Savannah's face once more. "We heard rumors of Hanged Men, on the outskirts of the city."

I sighed, deeply irritated that I couldn't just forget what had happened earlier and sink into Savannah and her adorable blushing.

"They're not *outside* the city anymore," I said in a ragged breath. "I was informed this morning."

"We need to move up our plans," Mickey said stiffly. "It's time to get you kids out of here. We need to forget about the ledger."

"That's not true," I argued. Savannah watched me with careful eyes, as if she were seeing a whole new side of me. "It'll take time for them to smuggle in enough people to mount any real kind of attack. We have another two days, maybe three before we really need to start worrying. If we double down on the ledger, we may still be able to steal it before we're in too much danger."

"I'm not risking any of you—"

"What if I told you that we might have defenses within the city? Would you give us the two extra days?" I asked, my eyes sliding over to Savannah's once more. I said a silent prayer to a God that had abandoned me a long time ago that she wouldn't get pissed at me for what I would say next. She had no idea about the undesirables and my forays into the fringes. Mickey waited expectantly, and I groaned at being put in a position like this.

"There's an underground network of undesirables throughout the city and—"

"Will!" Savannah chastised, her hand coming up to grab my arm. I tugged her forward and wrapped my arm around her waist to secure her to my side.

"If we don't try for the ledger, Bonnie's right, leaving won't keep us safe from Lee. I've been the one in the corner of the room while he built his empire. It's larger than you can imagine. Endless resources. That ledger is like a roadmap on how to unravel it from beneath his fucking feet." My words were meant for both of them, but I held Savvy's gaze much longer than I needed to. If anyone deserved to be free of Zachary Lee, it was Savannah, and I intended to do whatever I could to make that happen. She gave a soft nod of understanding, and my fingers gripped her hip harder at her permission.

"I have a contact named Moira, and she's expressed an *interest* in having me do something for her people. A job." Savannah's elbow jabbed into my side as she twisted out of my arms, glaring at me. "I don't know the specifics of their operation, only that they work out of the fringes. They have a network in and out of the city, up and down the Mississippi River townships. They focus on attaining resources and relocating their people, but for the right price they'll be willing to help outsiders."

Mickey chewed the inside of his cheek, his jaw working as he thought long and hard before answering me.

"Alright," he said, clapping me on the shoulder. "You got your two days. Make them count. I'm headed back to the camp for now. I'll keep in touch by post. Good work today, son. Don't let me down."

He said it again. *Son.*

He'd never know what it meant to be called that by a man I respected. I nodded absentmindedly as he left.

Before I could stop myself, I followed swiftly after him.

"Where are you going?" Savannah asked, falling in behind me. I ignored her, jogging to catch up to Mickey before he disappeared.

"Wait!" I called, lifting my hand so that when he turned he would see me on the busy street. It was crowded today, and even though most people gave me a wide berth, it was still hard to navigate.

Mickey turned back, closing the distance between us.

"Where are you staying?" I asked, out of breath. I should stop smoking so much, but fuck it.

"On the outskirts of the city, we have a camp inside the Riverwalk."

I shook my head before he finished speaking. He couldn't be that far from me. Not right now. He'd given me an opportunity to get better, but if my dad was in town . . . all bets were off. Especially if facing him might be what I needed to get Moira on our side.

"No, you need to stay close. Just in case," I said, pushing back the brim of my hat. Savannah caught up moments later, puffing furious breaths behind my shoulder at being left behind. "Take my apartment. I'll stay here for a while."

"Are you sure?" Mickey asked, his eyes trailing to Savannah.

"I'm sure." The truth was, I didn't feel confident enough in making any real plans of my own. I'd always let Bonnie do that part before. Mickey, at the very least, had faith in my reasoning, but I wanted him close enough to intervene if I fucked up again. And if it came down to it, I knew I could trust him to keep Savannah safe if I couldn't. Digging in my pocket, I pulled out a key and dropped it into his palm.

"Thanks," he said, staring again with concern lining his eyes. It shouldn't have meant as much as it did, him helping me. Calling me *son*. Caring in the first place. I offered him a swift nod before he disappeared into the crowd.

The truth was, Mickey Kincaid had done more for me in a few conversations than anyone else ever had. I didn't know how to repay kindness like that. Without even glancing at her, I wrapped Savannah's waist in my arm and crushed her against my chest. Even amidst her protests.

Jesse didn't know how good he had it, having an uncle like Mickey.

Savannah twisted out of my grip petulantly, her face lighting up again with a flush of anger. With nervous hands, she smoothed down the wrinkles on her skirt. Nothing she was about to say to put me in my place would make me feel bad. Mickey was here. Savannah sought me out. In my books, I was winning today.

"You followed me, *again*," I said, enjoying her eye roll more than I should have. Instead of a vicious retort, she turned sharply on her heel to march back into the manor. "C'mon, Savvy! It was cute!" I shouted after her, chuckling.

Crack!

Pain blossomed across my jaw as my head snapped to the side. Blinking rapidly to clear my vision, all I could see were Clara Higgins's furious eyes and the waves of her agitated blonde hair. *The truth is you are fundamentally broken, and there's nothing you can do to fix the fact that you're a failure.* Familiar lips I'd kissed a thousand times had formed those words and jabbed them so far into my heart they'd never left.

"How *could* you?!" she screeched, her fists pounding against my chest.

My head hung, but I didn't do anything to stop her. After all, I deserved it. I knew it wasn't the ugly words spoken between us in my sweat-stained sheets that brought her here today. It was a sin far uglier than disrespect that had violent disgust curling on her lip.

"Leave him alone!"

Without looking up at Savannah's voice, I held a hand up to stay her. She was always trying to save me; it shouldn't have shocked me to hear her ready to rush to my defense once more.

"How *dare you*," Clara hissed through bared teeth. "Sebastian *loved* you. More than a piece of shit like you ever deserved."

"I know."

She scoffed at my answer, unhappy with the acknowledgement of my failings. No, Clara Higgins would never be content with anything less than torment. Her cruelty, once dispatched, was a stronger sting than bullets tearing through flesh. She wouldn't stop until I bled with the rending of her words.

She laughed, the sound cold and inhuman, teeth flashing like a crater beast in the dark. "You kill everything that loves you, Will Ellis. A scared little boy who destroys anyone trying to get close. One day you'll die alone and have no one to blame but yourself for it. Daddy's little killer, hands stained with innocent blood. Tell me, do you think you're any better than him?"

No. In fact, I was worse. Sixgun, my father, was lacking some part of his mind. Something integral to being fully human. He was little more than an animal, dragged along by his bloody urges. Ruled by them. Unable to distinguish his dark impulses from needs like hunger and exhaustion.

I understood every single thing I did with perfect clarity. And I killed anyway. Maybe that was what made my soul so ugly.

"I should have let him finish you off, rip that beautiful face away, and discard you in a ditch on our way to New Orleans."

"That is *enough*!" Savannah wedged between us, her body vibrating with rage. I'd forgotten she was here, sinking further and further into the misdeeds of my past. "I don't know who you are—"

Clara attempted to speak, but Savvy didn't let her.

"—and quite frankly I don't care. Sebastian got what he deserved, and you should remember who you're talking to. The next time I see you, if you aren't treating Will with *respect*, it'll be *your face* scarred."

People stopped and stared. The vicious snarl of Savvy's threat rang clear across the square. Whispers began behind their hands as they took notice of her. Fury made her beautiful in a way that shouldn't be possible. She was like a weapon, harmless if left alone but lethal the moment she was given purpose.

Clara smiled, her tongue darting from between her lips as if to taste it in the air.

"Oh, Will," she said, tucking a strand of pale hair behind her ear. "Your next victim is beautiful. And so eager to get hurt. Adorable."

"You shouldn't be here, Clara," I said, my voice too gruff. "Don't waste your time in the city on this."

"Don't you worry, cowboy," she said, leaning close and tapping the brim of my hat with the tip of one pale finger. "I have better things to do in this city than *you.*"

"Jesse's here," I croaked. It would be stupid to ignore the seriousness of her threat. Clara Higgins clawed her way up the ladder of the glowroot trade one horrible rung at a time. Anyone underestimating her would regret it. But at the sound of Jesse's name, all I could see in her face was the girl I'd met years ago in the desert. No, someone even more vulnerable than she'd been then. Maybe the innocence in her eyes had been true when Jesse knew her.

"How long?" she whispered.

"A while now."

"He came for her, didn't he?" she asked, her eyes glazed over as her mind worked through her next scheme. "Good. I hope it kills him to see her gone."

Savannah peered up at me over her shoulder, confused and angry. Even though she knew exactly what Clara was talking about, her animosity toward Bonnie was a new piece of information. Bonnie would have to explain that to Savannah herself.

"Daddy's home, Ellis," she said, turning sharply on her heel before disappearing into the crowd. I released all the oxygen in my lungs in relief.

"Who was that?" Savannah asked, her eyes like mine, fixed on the place Clara disappeared from.

"That," I said, adjusting my hat, "was the devil."

Chapter Thirteen

JESSE

IT WAS GETTING HARDER to control my temper.

Guilt settled deep in my gut as Bonnie and I made our way back into the manor. I wanted to let her handle this, let her do what she felt was right, because I did trust her. But goddamnit, it was hard when I had to watch Rutherford put his slimy hands on her and do *nothing*.

A steely calm settled over us; even the tense set of her shoulders said that she wasn't completely thrilled with me. Fuck, I needed to do better at showing my support. It was a challenge, because the need to run had seized me, the want to take what was mine and get as far away from this city as possible fought against every whisper of *wait* and *trust me*.

I'd waited. For three years, I'd waited, I'd fought, I'd risked my life and the lives of others as I searched for her. Now that I had her back, who could blame me for wanting to run?

"Let's go find The Kid," I remarked with a smile that didn't quite reach my eyes. I looped my fingers with hers, the smallest of gestures we could get away with once inside the house.

Watching Bonnie's reunion with my brother had brought me joy I didn't realize I'd been missing. I was used to being without my brother, but now that I had them both under the same roof, I didn't want to be separated from them again. My family was whole, more than whole, really, with Will, Savannah, Mickey, and the crew.

All we had to do was survive this fucking house.

The Kid perched lazily on top of one of the stable doors, grinning as he stared at something. As we rounded the corner, I caught sight of

Savannah and Will, to no one's surprise, arguing. The former reached up to touch Will's cheek, but between his height and squirming, she was unsuccessful.

"It's fine, Savvy. I've been hit harder by *men*. Besides, I sort of deserved it." His tone pitched down at the end, reminiscent of our prior conversations when he slipped into the dark recesses of his self-loathing.

"You didn't deserve it." Savannah crossed her arms over her chest, huffing in annoyance. Beneath her stern features, though, was clear concern. "She was completely out of line."

Something warmed in my chest at the sight of them. Even if darkness clouded his eyes, Will regarded Savannah with tenderness in a way I'd never seen from him before. A smirk formed on my lips.

"Did Will piss Etty off again?" I asked, meaning the words as a joke.

Heavy silence descended between us as Will's gaze found Bonnie. The softness he held for Savannah faded, replaced by cold apathy. My smile slipped away, my attention darting from person to person as I tried to understand what was going on between them.

Will turned his attention to Savannah. "You know what? It does hurt. *Bad*. Let's get out of here and find something cold to put on my face."

"O-oh," Savannah responded, the word clumsy. She glanced between us and Will, confusion and concern evident in the lines of her face.

Will turned, reaching for Savannah's hand as he started for the exit. "No."

One word. One single syllable. Bonnie's voice resolute in that stern way I was all too familiar with. There was no anger in it, only firm resolve.

Will stopped, his hand flopping to his side as he sucked in a deep, ragged breath. In an instant, it made sense. The harsh glares, the avoidance. I'd barely seen my friend except the night I got kicked out of Bonnie's room. Maybe that had more to do with Bonnie than I'd thought.

"No?" he asked, voice a furious snarl as he faced us, gaze dark on Bonnie at my side. He narrowed his eyes, jaw set hard. "I'm not your *fuckin' employee* anymore, Bonnie. You don't get to tell me what to do." He pointed an accusatory finger at her.

In response, Bonnie widened her stance, feet shoulder's width apart, bracing herself for a fight. I stole a glance at Savannah, finding a sort of panicked concern in her eyes.

"Alright," Bonnie said, holding her hands up, palms forward. "You're pissed at me. I'm invoking a rumble. Crew rules."

Will scoffed, a dark smile pitching up the edge of his mouth. He scratched his forehead with his thumbnail, pushing back his hat.

"You can't be serious. We haven't done that since we were children."

"What's a rumble?" I asked. Surely they weren't actually going to fight?

"Yeah," The Kid chimed in. "And what're crew rules?" A spark of interest lit up his eyes as he leaned forward from his perch.

"I'm dead serious," Bonnie said. "If you won't fuckin' talk to me, then we'll have to do this like when we were kids." She tied her hair back from her face with a strip of leather she'd worn on her wrist.

"Bon, what is this?" I asked, trying to meet her gaze.

"Nothin' you're gonna like, farm boy. You might wanna take The Kid and Savannah out of here until we sort things out."

"I'm not leaving," Savannah chimed in, crossing her arms over her chest as she glanced up at Will.

"Me either." The Kid practically buzzed as he hopped down from his spot on the stall door.

"You really wanna do this?" Will sucked his tongue against his teeth, nodding to himself as he tossed his hat onto the hay. "What're the stakes?"

"I told you. Crew rules, only no hitting in the face. It'd be hard to hide a black eye from my fiancé."

"*Hitting*—" My voice was cut off by Savannah's squeak of disapproval.

"Jesse'll shoot me again," Will said. "This is fucking stupid—"

"No, he won't." Bonnie didn't even spare me a glance. "This is between *me* and *you*. No interruptions." She shrugged. "Besides, he's a terrible shot. I doubt he'd hit you."

My jaw clenched. I didn't like this. Not one bit. They were two of the most important people to me, and I was supposed to let them hurt each other?

Will unclipped his gun belt and tossed it next to his hat, his knife following. He ran a hand through his hair, jaw shifting beneath the clench of his teeth. In response, Bonnie kicked off her shoes. I shook my head as they circled each other, bodies low and centered. Prepared. As though they'd done this hundreds of times before.

This was a terrible idea.

Will struck first, lunging toward Bonnie before she could maneuver out of his reach. He wrapped his arms around her waist, hefting her off of the ground easily and slamming her back against one of the posts. It rattled, and her grunt of pain made me clench my hands into fists at my sides. Much as I wanted to, I couldn't interfere.

Bonnie slammed her elbow into the soft part of his shoulder, in the crevice where his neck and back met. Will stumbled, shaken off balance by the blow. They collapsed together, but she rolled away the moment Will's knee hit the straw, and he released his grip just enough.

"Say it!" She swung a fist, landing the blow on his ribs. His breath whooshed out. "Fuckin' say it, Will!"

My eyes went to Savannah. Her hands were clenched together in front of her as if praying. Like me, I saw the confliction on whether to intervene or let this ridiculous fight play out.

Will kicked, his knee connecting with Bonnie's stomach. She gasped as her back hit the ground hard, gaping up at Will as he leaned down, their faces inches apart.

"I have *nothing* to say to you," he said between clenched teeth.

There was a flurry of movement between them, scratching and shoving and tussling, until Bonnie's small size gave her the advantage. She twisted, her arms wrapped around his neck.

"Say it! Out loud!" She gripped tighter, shifting behind him to restrict his airflow. Will's bronze skin darkened, eyes bulging as his neck bones cracked.

"Jesus, Bon! Let him breathe!" I took a broad step toward them. I didn't want to get between them, but I would if it devolved any further. Savannah seemed poised as I was, on her toes, ready to intervene.

After a long, terse moment, Bonnie's grip slackened. Will gulped in air. Then, using the leverage of their position, he twisted her arm and wrenched her wrist until she cried out. With one smooth move, my best friend flipped the woman I loved over his shoulder. She landed with a hard thump on the dirt and hay floor.

Bonnie glared up at him, the fires of hell in her blue eyes.

"Fine!" Will's lips curled back, teeth bared. "Fine."

"I was here, Will. I've killed my fair share," she said. Will scoffed through his bared teeth. "You went to that graveyard anyway."

"You *left me alone*!" His words filled the barn, filled the world. They sank inside of me, settling like heavy lead in my stomach. I frowned, brows knitting together. He *had* been alone. "You promised and you just . . ."

Both of them panted, eyes glued on the other, covered in straw and bruises.

"What?" Bonnie asked, voice barely above a whisper. Her eyes went glassy with tears, her cheeks flushing with heat.

"You left me."

She'd left me, too. I knew Will had been struggling, but I had no idea it was the very thing I'd experienced. I wanted to reach between them, offer them both my hand, because I knew. I fucking *knew* how it felt.

"I—" Bonnie blinked, falling silent.

"You promised me you wouldn't let me be alone. And you just *keep* leaving me. You left me in the camp. To be tattooed and used as a pawn in Jones's twisted fucking games. You left me with my *father*. Alone. Then I put my neck out for you. I left the crew, put a target on my back, and I came for you. Then you left me *again*."

For *me*. Fuck.

"I told you we should go north. I took a *fucking bullet* for you, but it wasn't enough." My guilt reared high at the memory of that ill-advised shot. "When my dad came for us, you offered me up to him. Because I'm worthless to you. Expendable."

His face fell then. His anger at Bonnie had been nothing more than a mask for his pain.

"I sold my soul for you. I held your bloody and broken skull together. And when my father . . . when he . . . when he *carved* my face—" His voice broke, lips trembling. "I thought it was justice. I'd done the same to you. It was . . . it was payback. But as hard as I fought all of those years for you to remember me, I never thought it would feel this bad when you *finally* did."

"Will—" Bonnie choked on our friend's name. Tears overflowed onto her cheeks, leaving salt tracks in their wake. With small, quiet movements, she inched closer, until her arms wrapped tightly around him. "You're not expendable."

Will took in a ragged breath.

"You're not worthless." They clutched one another tightly.

I glanced toward Savannah, unshed tears filling her eyes as she watched them. The Kid leaned against a post beside me. We shared a tentative glance.

Bonnie pulled back just enough to tug the sleeve of her dress up. Her own scar, *Jones*, was on clear display. "This scar—"

Will lifted his head to look at it, his eyes flickering back to Bonnie's.

"It came from a boy I trusted who risked his life for me." Her words were tender, kind. It reminded me of the first time we'd truly talked in the library, when she showed me a gentler side of herself. "The boy who wouldn't let me be a victim anymore."

All of those years ago, when I told Bonnie we should leave Will behind when his father was hot on our trail, I didn't understand the bond between them. I should have known then that I never truly would. They shared history, like me and The Kid. They'd fought and survived and endured horrors that I could never imagine.

"*El dolor es fugaz.*"

Bonnie and Will shared a breathy laugh, their eyes meeting. The tension slipped away, their features softening as they stared at one another. If it were anyone else, I'd be threatened, but I knew deep down, the love they shared was the bond of two people who had suffered, but had also *lived*.

"You have to know," Bonnie said, sniffling hard as she swiped at her nose. "I never really left you. All those times, I was being selfish and stupid. I broke my promise to you—" Her voice cracked, and she wiped her cheeks to rid them of her tears.

"I've been so lost since I remembered everything. I *miss* you. I miss *us*." She cradled his head in her hands, pressing her forehead to his. Her tears streamed anew, her body shaking with emotion. "I was so scared. Hearing about the graveyard. I can't imagine life without you in it."

"I'm sorry," Will whispered, his gaze dropping.

"*I'm sorry*," she said. "I'm sorry I didn't know what was happening. I'm sorry I left you alone. I'm sorry that I wasn't a good friend."

The tension broke. My own breathing became easier as they settled. Will nodded, blinking hard and turning his face away from Bonnie.

"But you have to know—" Bonnie motioned to me, to Savannah. "You aren't alone anymore."

It took me less than a heartbeat when her eyes locked with mine to cross the space and kneel beside them. She was right. None of us were alone anymore. I wrapped my arms around both of them, clutching tightly to those who had become my family. A moment later, Savannah moved in beside Will, tucking her head against his shoulder.

Bonnie lifted her head, glaring at my brother until, with a groan, he shoved off of the post and crossed to us, tossing his lanky arms around the group. My heart felt lighter, joyful almost, at having them all here, all together.

Our little, fucked-up family.

Savannah was the first to speak, lifting her head to fix Will with a look I couldn't read. "I could use a drink."

Will let out a breathy chuckle. "So could I," he remarked. "But. No booze."

"What?" I blurted.

"New rule."

I probably looked really stupid, mouth gaping, as I stared at him.

If that was what it took to heal, I'd do what I could to support him.

"Alright, enough of this," The Kid said. "Let's go kill some stuff."

"Kid," Bonnie said, slipping her arm around his shoulder. "I've got a wardrobe and some hair pins that have your name on them."

Even as we dispersed, Bonnie and The Kid going one way, Will and Savannah the other, I glanced at my friend. He met my gaze. Without a word, I gave him a curt nod, a promise, that we would get through this.

I followed Bonnie and The Kid to the staircase but stopped short at the bottom.

"Jesse?"

I glanced up at them with a half-smile, happy to see them together. They needed this, *time*. Without me. "I need to circle back with Mickey, check on preparations to leave."

Bonnie bit her lip, brows furrowing. I pressed a quick kiss to her lips.

"You and The Kid have fun," I said, giving her a brief smile. "I'll see you soon."

I shoved back from them and headed toward the front hallway. After our argument in the alley, maybe I needed some time, too. I trusted Bonnie, implicitly, but I couldn't erase the memory of Rutherford and his grimy hands all over her. This was a con, no different than the ones she'd done under Jones.

Did it make me better or worse than that monster by letting her continue this?

I headed for the front of the house, where I hoped to find Mickey. Maybe he could help ease my mind. If not, at least he could berate me, bring back some normalcy.

"Fucking cunt." Rutherford's voice filtered through the front hallway, stopping me in my tracks. "She really thinks she can get away with refusing me."

"C'mon, Luke, the wedding is days away. You'll have her where you want her soon enough," a lazy voice drawled from Rutherford's half-open door, one I recognized as Lucas's friend, the one who had set his sights on Savannah when they first arrived.

"It's the principle of the matter." There was a clink of glass and alcohol being poured. I balled my hands into fists at my sides.

Don't fucking do it.

"I haven't spent weeks trying to woo her just for her to clam up now. She's going to be my wife. It's high time she started thinking about her wifely duties," Lucas spat.

His friend said something I couldn't make out, but Rutherford let out a bitter laugh.

"I'll show her *exactly* who's in charge. Even if it means drugging her into compliance." The glass clunked onto a table, and footsteps thunked on the hardwood. My blood hummed in my veins as I slunk into a shadowy alcove.

"I'll be back before the wedding," Luke's friend said as they appeared together in the hallway. "Did Lee agree to sending his beast in the first shipment to Manhattan?"

My jaw clenched, fingernails digging into my palms. Schemes upon schemes with these people.

"Yes. Make sure your people are prepared," Lucas remarked. Footsteps receded in the hallway, and a moment later, the door shut.

I seethed. So not only were they using *Bonnie* as a pawn in their plans, they were going to bring Will into it too? And right when he'd finally started pulling away from the darkness inside himself.

Fuck no.

I marched purposefully, my boots echoing off of the hardwood floors. By the time I reached Rutherford's door, I'd steeled my expression. I banged on the door in quick succession, holding my breath for a long moment as he approached.

Bonnie's voice in my head told me to walk away, but I couldn't. Rutherford had taken things too far, and I was out for blood.

The second the door opened, I pounced. I planted one booted foot in the man's gut, eliciting a huff of air as I slammed the door.

Rutherford hit the floor on his ass, a haughty, choked sound coming from his mouth. Before he even had the chance to regain himself, I yanked him to his feet by his shirt. Recognition filled his eyes, widening them as I brought my fist against his left cheekbone. My knuckles ached at the contact, but the adrenaline that coursed through my veins was like a drug.

"Mont—"

I punched him square in the jaw, then released my hold on his shirt. He stumbled to the floor. The idiot didn't even have the sense to get away from me. He stared at me, horror and offense in his features as I loomed over him.

All I could see was the fear in Bonnie's eyes as Lucas had her pressed against the wall, his hands moving indecently over her curves, the darkness that loomed in my best friend's eyes as he spoke of the deal he'd made with Lee on the bridge. Who was next? Savannah? *The Kid?* When would it stop?

With me.

I pitched my leg back, then kicked him squarely in the ribs. Rutherford cried out, curling in on himself.

"I thought you were a gentleman," I said, squatting beside him, directly in his line of sight when he finally lifted his head.

The lines of his face showed his pain, but his eyes vowed retribution. He spit out pink-tinged saliva on Lee's ugly rug. "You're going to pay for this."

A smile crept across my features. I was fucking furious, but I radiated cool calm. "Maybe," I said, shrugging. He flinched as I lifted a hand to sweep my hair out of my eyes. It shouldn't have satisfied me as much as it did. "But not nearly as bad as you're gonna pay."

"What are you talking about?"

Because what he'd done to the woman I loved in the hallway meant nothing to him.

Because using Will in whatever fashion suited him meant *nothing*.

What I wouldn't give for a gun right now.

"You can wear your fancy suits, drink your expensive liquor, and walk through this house like you own the place," I said, leaning closer. I took hold of his shirt once more, yanking him toward me. "But if you lay another fucking finger on Audrey without her permission, you'll deal with more than an angry fighter."

Lucas's brows lifted, and he rolled his eyes. "Oh, really?"

"You have friends in high places, Lucas." I released my grip, shoving him hard to the floor. "But I have friends in low ones. And *he* likes to put his work on display."

The man's face drained of color, except for the bruise forming beneath his eye and the trickle of blood from the corner of his mouth.

I would never ask Will to do such a thing, but Lucas didn't know that.

"Don't forget, Luke. I'll be watching." I backed away slowly, enjoying the fear in his features far too much.

When I reached the door, I glanced back at Lucas, reveling in my handiwork. With one final, victorious smile, I twisted the doorknob and exited the room, flexing my fingers as I went.

CHAPTER FOURTEEN

SAVANNAH

I T WAS A RARE occurrence that Etty left her kitchen unmanned in the middle of the day. With Mr. Lee dining out tonight, the woman in charge had merely mentioned she had things to do, and there were sandwiches in the ice box if anyone was hungry.

"You do know that this wedding isn't actually going to happen, right?" William Ellis had kept me company in the kitchen for two hours now, his commentary non-stop as I mixed cake batter, poured it into pans, removed them from the ovens, and then got busy trying out different frostings and fillings.

"Of course," I said, gripping the edge of the kitchen island as I waited for my last batch to cool so I could assemble the cake squares necessary for tasting.

"So why are you doing all this?" He rested his elbows on the island, staring at me with that same intensity he'd been using for several days at this point, ever since I kissed him and ran away to Bonnie's rooms.

"Would you stop *looking at me?"* I'd demanded of him last night. He'd given up the pretext of waiting until I was asleep to sneak into my room.

No. Last night, he'd stared at me as he reclined in my reading chair, arms crossed over his chest and eyes full of amusement. Instead of listening to my demand, he merely grinned and lowered his hat enough to cover his eyes.

I'd been furious. Still was, if I were being honest.

"Because we have to make it look like there's going to be a wedding." I picked up a tray of freshly frosted cake squares. "It will help our cover if we appear as invested in it as they are. Now." I set the tray before him on the island. He eyed the colorful sweets warily. "Tell me what you think."

Will reached tentatively for the first square: a yellow cake with strawberries-and-cream filling. "You'd think with the shit he gave you about that king cake, he'd want to get the bakery to make Bonnie's wedding cake."

"He did." I snorted, a triumphant smile forming on my lips. "Two weeks was too little notice to create a five-tier wedding cake. They needed at least a month. Etty convinced Lee to let me do it." I shrugged.

Even if we did manage to get out of here before the wedding, my signature would be left all over the wedding preparations. It was my own brand of defiance.

"That one is like a strawberry shortcake," I said as Will chewed the square. "Bonnie loves strawberries, so I thought it would be a good choice." I thought I saw the light dim slightly in Will's eyes as he chewed thoughtfully. It flickered back to life a second later as he looked over the remaining squares. There was a decadent chocolate cake with a sugary, toasted coconut filling and topping. Another was a plain yellow cake with whipped chocolate frosting. My personal favorite was the almond cake with buttercream filling—classic wedding cake.

"What kind would you make for your own wedding?"

Will's question caught me so off guard that all I could do was blink at him. I knew him well enough by now to know that he never asked anything without a purpose, but . . . what the hell was the purpose?

Shifting uncomfortably beneath his curious gaze, I shrugged. "Probably something simple. Almond cake, like that one." I pointed to one of the squares. Will pinched it between his fingers and stared at it. "But I'd do something different with the filling. Buttercream with sugared, roasted pecans layered in."

Instead of responding, Will popped the cake into his mouth. The white buttercream smeared along his lips. I watched, brows lifted, as his tongue darted out to lick the sweet frosting away. He grinned at me. There was frosting on his chin. As he swallowed the cake, I moved around the island toward him, overly amused at the stark white frosting against his bronze skin.

A smirk crossed my lips as his eyes widened. I'd purposefully kept my distance from him. If I got too close, we both knew my chances of resisting his charm would diminish.

I just couldn't help myself.

Will tipped his head back slightly as I swiped the frosting from his chin with the pad of my thumb. Before I could wipe it on my apron, however, he captured my wrist. My heart pounded as he wrapped his lips around my thumb. His tongue flicked against my skin, cleaning it of the frosting. My lips parted on a sigh at the sensation, my stomach coiling tight as the memory of his mouth on my bare nipple flashed through my mind.

"Sweet," he said after tugging my finger from between his lips. His eyes crinkled as yet another dashing grin crossed his face. Though his grip on my wrist loosened, he didn't release me.

The real question was: did I want him to?

"Will—" I tried to turn my face away, but he reached up with his other hand. He brushed his thumb gently across my jawline. The intensity of his stare made my pulse thrum.

I hated when he looked at me like that. Like I was the only thing in the world that mattered. Like he couldn't ever get enough of me. Like I was precious. Like I was all that he'd ever wanted.

"What are you even doing in here?" I asked, staring into his eyes. "Don't you have anything better to do?"

Will's lips curled up at the edges. "Better than you?"

I rolled my eyes and opened my mouth to argue with him, but he captured my mouth with his own. It started as a gentle brush of his mouth against mine. He tipped my chin, his tongue parting my lips as he wrapped an arm around my waist and tugged me tight to his chest. A moment passed before he pulled back and stared at my mouth.

"Never," he finished.

Laughter bubbled inside of me. Will's eyes lit up at the sound, as if it were the most beautiful thing he'd ever heard. My heart thumped wildly in my chest at his beauty. He was gorgeous all the time, but joy made him absolutely radiant.

Would this be life with him if we ever escaped this godforsaken city? True happiness chasing away the shadows, making love all day until neither of us could keep our eyes open, experiencing a laughter I hadn't known since I was a child?

My heart ached, because that was a beautiful dream. One that I'd always wished for.

But could that dream come true with William Ellis?

"Tell me something good about yourself." I rested my hands on his shoulders. Will straightened, brows furrowing.

"What?"

"Your conversation with Jesse's uncle," I reminded him.

He groaned, lowering his head and averting his eyes, but I followed his gaze, forcing him to look at me. "How much of that conversation did you hear, little stalker?"

"Enough," I remarked with a grin.

"So, all of it."

I smirked, shrugging casually.

"Great," he deadpanned. "Then you also heard I'm *not* doing that stupid exercise."

"Tell me one good thing and I'll kiss you."

"Where?" A wicked smile curled on his lips.

"Where do you want?"

"*Mierda!*" he swore, gripping my hips and sending a thrill down my spine as his eyes lit up. "You'll be the death of me, *mi sol.*"

"Tell me one good thing." I fixed him with a hard stare, trying to be serious, even though a smile threatened on my own mouth.

The playfulness in his eyes dimmed, his smile falling. "I can't think of one."

"I can," I said without hesitation. "As much as you'll deny it, you are endlessly kind to those you care about." I rested my hands on his shoulders, smoothing down his shirt. "Now, your turn."

He paused for a brief second, then said, "I'm a really good kisser." He leaned down to show me how, but I turned my cheek instead, shoving at his shoulders to put distance between us.

"You know that's not what I meant." I cleared my throat and pushed away from him. I'd eavesdropped on his conversation yesterday. While I didn't know Mickey, he made valid points.

"*Savvy*," Will groaned.

I shrugged. "Then no more kisses."

Before I could put too much space between us, he gripped my wrist and tugged me back toward him. He surveyed my face, his gaze trailing like calloused fingertips along my skin. The next words he whispered against my skin, raw and wrenched from some painful place inside of him.

"I'm loyal."

I nodded, once again wrapping my arms around his neck. "And?"

"No," he said, his fingers sinking into the flesh of my hips. "You said *one.*" Then his mouth came down hard against mine.

Kissing Will felt like coming home, like the most natural thing in the world. Truly, it was. Falling into him had always been easy, but I'd never acknowledged just how it made me feel. Safe. Cared for. Happy.

Will gripped my hips, tugging me tight against his chest as he pulled his mouth from mine and kissed along my jawline. The friction of his stubbled cheek against my skin made me gasp. I'd never realized how much I missed being touched until he touched me. Until I gave in to the deep-rooted *need* that I kept so carefully locked away.

In one swift movement, he lifted me up, placing me expertly on the edge of the island countertop, as he had the last time we'd been alone in this very kitchen. I ran my hands through his hair, my fingernails raking against his scalp. He shivered against me. It was empowering to make a man like him tremble.

My arms wrapped tightly around his neck as his lips brushed along the column of my throat. His hands moved expertly on their own, dragging the long fabric of my skirt up. His calloused fingertips ran along my bare legs. Goosebumps prickled on my skin in the wake of his touch. The cool air in the kitchen licked against my thighs as my skirt settled up near my hips.

I didn't think about the fact that it was the middle of the afternoon, that we were in a public setting. Because, like always, with Will, the rest of the world drifted away, disappeared. All that mattered was now, was *him*, was how he set my skin alight, how he consumed me as though I were his savior, his salvation.

Goddamnit, did I want to be.

Will brushed his fingertips against the front of my silk panties. My hips jerked forward, encouraging him to continue. Instead, he stilled. I lifted my head, glaring at him. At the vulnerability in his eyes, however, my features softened.

"What do you want, Savvy?" he whispered before feathering a kiss across my mouth.

"Wh-what?" I blinked back the haze of arousal. It was like the morning after the graveyard, when he'd needed my reassurance.

"What do you want?" he repeated, an edge of desperation in his voice as he pleaded with his eyes. He'd needed to know that I wanted him. God, if he only knew that it wasn't *wanting* that kept me away from him.

"I want you to touch me," I whispered.

A heartbeat, then his fingertips brushed against me once more. My mouth parted.

"Like this?" he asked.

I nodded, pressing my forehead against his. "Like the graveyard."

Will brought his lips to mine, his fingers working a magic of their own as he shoved my panties to the side. The moment he touched that sensitive spot, I gasped into his mouth. Denying myself the pleasure of his hands had been absolute torture. Knowing he was *so* close each night, that all it would take was a single word and I could have him if I wanted.

I *always* wanted William.

He shifted, his hips pushing my thighs farther apart as he wrapped an arm around my waist. A second passed, and then he curled a finger inside of me. My breath stuttered at the sensation, at the memory of how he'd filled me in the graveyard. How he'd made me feel whole in a way no one ever had before.

"*Mierda*," he swore. He did that a lot.

"More," I whispered desperately, my hips curving toward him, back arching to give him better access. He kept his arm tight around my waist, lips trailing down my throat as my head fell back. He slid a second finger alongside the first, and I cried out. My nails dug into his shirt, gripping him hard as he set a steady pace. My stomach tightened, my senses narrowed to the way he moved inside of me, how he whispered sweet words into my ear, even though my heart pounded so hard I couldn't hear them.

"That's it, baby." He tugged my earlobe between his teeth, then ran his thumb along my sensitive bundle of nerves.

I shattered. I barely heard my own scream of pleasure as my vision wavered and the kitchen disappeared for a moment. A tingling sensation coursed through me as Will rode along with the peak of my pleasure, until I couldn't feel my limbs, couldn't sense my own breath.

"*God*," I whispered as my heart slowed. When I lifted my head, I spied the triumphant grin on Will's face. He so loved my use of the word. But I didn't have it in me to even roll my eyes. I pulled his face to mine, kissing him slowly, sweetly, until my arousal flared up once more, until I scratched desperately at his shirt to remove it.

"Wait." He pressed his forehead to mine, his jaw tight. I blinked rapidly to clear my vision, to focus on him. Because if Will was asking for pause, that was a big deal.

"What?" My chest heaved against his.

"You followed me yesterday."

The vulnerability in his eyes stalled any sarcastic commentary I might have spat at him.

"And you defended me to Clara." Will cradled my cheek, his thumb brushing along my bottom lip. "You *want* me."

The next time we have sex, Savannah Beauregard, will be because you want me. Not because you don't want me to blow my fuckin' brains out.

Words failed me at the hope shining in his dark eyes. My brows furrowed, and I let out a dark laugh.

"Wanting you has never been the problem, William."

"Then what is?"

My throat ran dry at his question. For the first time ever, it felt like Will was being truly earnest. This wasn't a joke to him, as so much else was. I blew out a long breath.

"I want *too* much," I said, lowering my gaze from his.

Will opened his mouth to respond, but he never got the chance.

"I'd say not to defile my kitchen, but it appears you already have."

I peered over my shoulder, finding Etty near the door to the courtyard. She crossed her arms over her chest as she glared between me and Will, who was already righting my skirts. My mouth hung open as I stared at the woman. Propriety said I should be ashamed.

The truth was, I wasn't.

If anything, I was annoyed. Will helped me down, and I turned to face Etty, the island between us. She glared at him just over my shoulder. That annoyed me even more. I'd thought I was clear when we spoke of him that first morning. She'd always been like this. Dismissive, angry when he came around me. Then, after a drink or two, she acted like they were the best friends in the world.

"Ellis, I think you should leave," she said, shoving off of the doorframe.

Will glanced at me, then started for the exit. I grabbed his hand to stop him.

"He's not going anywhere."

I felt his gaze on my skin in an instant. Etty's brows lifted, a sort of angry surprise crossing her features.

"Savannah, we need to talk."

"You're right. We do," I said. Will tangled his fingers with mine, gripping my hand so hard it hurt. He'd done his share of bowing before the force of Etty. "If you'd found me in here with anyone else, would you have ordered them out?"

Etty let out a long sigh, crossing to the opposite side of the island. Cool rage radiated from her shoulders as she flattened her palms on the granite surface.

"You don't understand," she said, her words coming out slow, as though she were having to pick through them carefully. "I know your gentle heart, Savannah. *He* doesn't deserve it."

I shook my head. "Why not?"

Will shuffled uncomfortably beside me, gripping my hand like a lifeline.

"Because—"

"Because it's *Will* or because he wants *me*?" I demanded, not wavering beneath her intense scrutiny.

"Because he's dangerous. If you knew half the things he's done, you would understand," Etty said, shaking even as she tried to maintain control. I'd never seen her like this. Usually, she was calm, collected. She was a force. "I'm not just talking about the stuff he's done as the *Beast*. He was a Hanged Man. He handed Bonnie over to *Jones*—"

Etty's eyes widened, and she shoved away from the island.

Will stiffened beside me, his free hand already finding the handle of his gun. The fear had gone out of him, replaced instead by the man who instilled fear in the city.

"Who are you." It wasn't a question.

"That's none of your concern," Etty said.

"No?" he asked. "Because you know a lot for someone who just works here." He tugged his gun from its holster.

An image filled my mind, of the night he'd brought Sebastian's corpse back to the manor. The implication in his voice was clear.

Etty was a spy.

"Who do you work for?"

"Don't use that tone with me," Etty snapped. "You think I'm afraid of you? You're just a *boy*."

"Etty," I cut in. When she finally brought her gaze to mine, I fixed her with a hard stare. One that said I wasn't leaving until she answered. Until she told me the truth.

Will wrapped an arm around my waist and tucked me tight against his side.

"I work for Zachary Lee." She tossed a hand flippantly. "I've been here for twenty years, child. I don't appreciate your implication."

"Then how do you know Audrey's real name?" Will asked, his grip tightening on me. "You've always managed to get letters in and out of the city without interception. You gave Jesse instructions on smuggling people in. You always know more than the rest of us. You were the one who tipped Savvy off to that riverboat years ago. So, I'm only going to ask you one more time. Who are you?"

A glaring contest took place for two heartbeats, three. On the fourth, the tension released from Etty's shoulders. She lowered her gaze to the island, staring intently at the untouched cake squares on their tray. After steeling herself, she glanced toward each of the exits. When she was sufficiently satisfied with the lack of wandering ears, she fixed Will with a hard stare.

"The resistance." She kept her voice low and even. "There's a network of us throughout the city, all along the major thoroughfares, the Mississippi."

"The resistance?" I asked, brows pinching together in confusion. I'd known her for half my life. It didn't make sense.

"I've never heard of any resistance," Will said.

"That's because no one knows where your loyalties lie." She stood taller, her anger flaring once more. "One second, you take the Hanged Man tattoo, and the next, you're a branded man. I tolerated you because I had to, to keep my position in this household, but I swear to all that is holy, William Ellis, I draw the line at Savannah."

"Because you think I would hurt her," Will said coldly. "Like my father does."

"Because you are no good for her," Etty said, the words harsh. "She may not be my blood, but Savannah is as good as mine, and I will *not* stand by and let you destroy her."

"Etty—" I started.

"She is young, and has been kept locked up in this household for far too long—"

"Did you ever think *you* were part of what's kept her here?" Will interjected.

"Stop!" My words were fruitless, because Etty's attention remained locked on him.

"And what? Are you gonna *save* her, Ellis? You can't even take care of yourself, much less *anyone* else," Etty spat. "I know you. I know why you came here with Bonnie. I know why you stayed. And I know that no matter what you *think*, you will *never* be good enough for Savannah."

"That is *enough*." I'd never heard Will's voice sound like that before. His words were calm, but infused with so much raw power that they shuddered through the space easily. Etty's eyes widened, her hackles raised as she stared at him with wide eyes.

In all the time he'd been here, he'd never spoken to her like that.

"For Savannah's sake I've allowed you too much freedom, which you've used at every turn to chastise her for her choices. The time for that is over."

Etty couldn't seem to grasp words, her mouth opening and closing as her cheeks darkened with anger.

"She is not a child, and her choices will be respected. Is that clear?"

Will stood tall, no hint of cowering in his frame, each movement filled with a confidence I'd rarely seen in him. Now, I wondered how much of Etty intimidating him had been for my benefit all these years, another way he had been keeping himself away from me.

Etty, it seemed, had finally found her wits as she settled him with a hard glare. "She's as good as my own child, and I won't stand for this."

I opened my mouth to argue, but Will gripped my hand. He narrowed his eyes on the woman, taking a step closer and pushing the brim of his hat back so she could see the serious intent in his eyes.

"You don't have a choice."

His words fell in the room like a decree. Unwavering. Unimpeachable.

"She won't be justifying her decisions to you anymore. Savannah doesn't owe you *anything*."

My brows shot up at the resolve in his voice.

"And neither do I."

Etty's mouth snapped shut, but she sucked in a large breath, her chest inflating as if to make herself seem larger in the face of him. It was as if Will had become a completely different person in the span of a few minutes. No. Not a different person. More of *himself*.

"I won't stand back and watch you hurt her—"

"I will never hurt her," he said before she could finish. "You wanted to know where my loyalties lie? I defied the Hanged Men, my father, Lee, and became worse than all of them to protect my friends. And I'll do worse than that for Savvy. I'll burn your whole resistance to the ground if I have to. Because I don't have limits when it comes to protecting what is *mine*."

A thrill raced down my spine.

Tension shimmered between them, and Will's harshness softened after a moment. Probably disarming Etty more than the way he'd snapped at her before.

"Don't make me an enemy, Etty. Not when we want the same thing: Savannah's happiness."

Etty blinked, rapidly, still flustered but also seeming oddly . . . touched. With one swift nod, she turned her back and furiously scrubbed the top of the counter, most likely to keep her hands from reaching for the rolling pin she was so fond of. Will's hand spread along the base of my spine, gently directing me to move towards the exit.

Before we could make it over the threshold, he turned back to her and said sternly, "Oh, and we'll be talking about *the resistance* again soon."

Chapter Fifteen

BONNIE

FOR THE FIRST TIME in recent memory, I was blissfully happy. The Kid's smile was infectious and hard-won. I never let him win while we threw hairpins, a fact he wouldn't let me live down. We talked late into the night, about familiar things, telling tall tales as the night grew long. Jesse joined us quickly, with bloody knuckles that raised the hairs at the back of my neck. When I questioned him about it, he assured me it was nothing. I wanted to push the issue, to drag the details out of him, but that would only ruin this time with The Kid like it had earlier in the day. So I tried to push it from my mind, determined to trust Jesse the way he trusted me.

The brothers sparred verbally as The Kid told me stories about life in Fort Hood. The friends he'd made as the base grew, with more families and children coming each successive year. How they roamed the base like a wild pack of dogs, pulling pranks on each other and getting into the innocent kind of mischief that made his eyes bright. The night grew long and then, like we had all those years ago, we curled up together in bed. Reminding me of the small, beat-up mattress in Quanah's house with my fingers running through The Kid's hair and Jesse holding onto me like his anchor to earth.

The Kid never left my side, even as Jesse snuck out the next morning to avoid detection. It was like he couldn't believe I was real, or if he lost sight of me I might disappear again. I'd nearly forgotten how it felt to be with him. Protective. Adoring. Instructive.

Like a mother.

"I don't see why you have to leave—"

We'd been arguing for ten minutes. There were wedding plans to attend. A con ongoing. And my part to play in it all. If it were up to me, I'd never leave him again.

"Because they can't know my memories are back. Not until I find a way into the study. Not until I get the ledger."

"Who the fuck cares about the stupid ledger! Let's just get on our horses and ride out. Into the desert, like before. We did just fine in the wilderness."

Clipping my earring into place, I gave him a placid look, raising my eyebrows in question.

"Alright, there were a *few* rough patches, but we did well enough."

"No, we didn't. We had no way to make money. Barely enough food and supplies to keep traveling. And let's not forget the many times we nearly died."

"It was fun though," he grumbled, the depth of his voice startling me again. There were moments I nearly forgot how much he'd grown in my absence. Then I'd see a glimpse of the surly teenager he was now and the reality of time snapped me back to the present.

"Besides, if we don't get the ledger, we'll have no leverage when we leave. I'll just be hunted again. On the run. When we go this time, I don't want *anyone* chasing after us."

He sighed, unable to refute my logic. After all, when it boiled down to it, we wanted the same thing. To be together. In a place of our own. Instead of launching yet another of seemingly endless arguments, he pulled his pack out from beneath my bed and rummaged through it.

"Hey, Bonnie," he asked, earning my attention again. "Could you read this to me?"

My heart hammered in my chest as he pulled out a familiar, worn book of poems. The same one I'd given Jesse in Fort Hood on our last night together. Back then, I couldn't read, so I'd only used it to press flowers between the pages. When The Kid asked me to read to him, I'd refused him, ashamed of my own ignorance.

Softly, I crossed the space and held my hand out for the book. It felt so fragile. Blinking away the emotion in my eyes, I ran my fingertips lovingly over the faded title. He'd brought this all the way here so I could have a second chance to do it right. Sitting next to him, I opened the pages, finding the name of one of my favorite poets. Emily Dickenson.

"'Although I could not stop for death,'" I read, my voice finding a familiar cadence when speaking poetry aloud. "'He kindly stopped for me, the carriage held just but ourselves, and immortality.'"

His eyes were glued to my face, a strange expression in his eyes. Not the eternal curiosity I was so accustomed to. Instead, his features were pinched with guilt.

"I thought about that day with the book a lot," he said, his face screwed up and brow furrowed. "I didn't understand why you couldn't read. Or that my questions were unkind. But, I know more about the world now. I have friends who were rescued from slave camps." I tried to keep my face impassive, but The Kid's voice wavered. He wasn't a child anymore, able to live in blissful ignorance while horrors happened around him. It was hard to acknowledge, but The Kid was becoming a man. "I'm so sorry, Bonnie, if I ever made you feel like you were . . . less."

I wrapped my arms around him and pulled him tight, filling my lungs with the clean scent of his soap, and pretended he was still that small, curious boy that I could keep safe. "You didn't."

He pulled back from me, his expression clearly argumentative, which seemed to be his new natural state of being. "I mean it," I reassured him. "I did that all by myself. You just poked at a sore spot that had been there for a long time. I would never hold that against you."

Something eased in his countenance, some sort of weight lifting from his shoulders.

"Will you read me some more?" he asked quietly, making my heart burst from happiness. I nodded, forgetting all about wedding plans. I read to him until my voice was raspy, all while he marveled at my proficiency and I regaled him about the subjects I'd studied and books I'd read. Telling him stories about each exciting addition to my library over the years. We got into a heated debate over the merits of J.R.R. Tolkien versus C.S. Lewis that dragged on and on. He opened his mouth, I'm sure to try another argument, when a pounding knock came at the door.

"Hide," I whispered, standing from my perch as he tucked himself inside the wardrobe and pulled the door mostly shut.

My door swung wide seconds later. Three guards filed into the room and spread out. One of them, with a cross tattooed on his hand, covered the entrance to the bathroom I shared with Savannah.

"What the hell do you think you're doing?" I asked, fear creeping up my spine. My instincts had kept me alive so far, and now, they screamed that something was wrong.

"Sorry, Miss Audrey, but your father sent us to fetch you." The guard in front of me wasn't familiar. His dark beard was immaculately groomed, and discomfort hid in his eyes.

"I was almost finished getting ready. He can wait another five minutes. It's just a seating chart; it'll still be waiting for me in a moment."

"I'm afraid I must insist, ma'am," he said, his Adam's apple bobbing with the heaviness of his swallow. "We've been told to use force if necessary."

What the fuck?!

My mind whirled. Could he have found out about my plans? Surely not. As of yet, I'd been completely unsuccessful. The only people who knew about my memories or plans for the ledger were in on it with me. I wasn't careless enough to let any hint escape.

But the guards, though cautious, moved forward and crowded me. The wardrobe creaked, and the guard with the cross tattoo snapped his eyes to it, suspicion making them cold.

My heart pounded in my throat. They couldn't find The Kid here. I couldn't trust anyone on my father's payroll. The guard didn't waver in studying the wardrobe.

"Did you guys hear that?" he asked, inching forward.

Fuck.

"Alright, I'll come with you, but I'm not happy about it and I plan to let my dad know," I said, crossing my arms and giving a very convincing pout.

"What's in your wardrobe?" the tattooed guard asked, gripping the handle of his gun a little too tightly.

I cocked an eyebrow at him, looking him up and down, and, with as much scathing derision as I could infuse into my voice, said simply, "Dresses. Why? Wanna try one on for size?"

The other two guards tried to hide their snickers behind coughs and turned faces but failed miserably. He scowled, wrapping his fingers tightly around my arm and yanking me after him. I didn't care, as long as we left the room with The Kid still hidden.

They marched me formally to my father's study. A place I'd been *trying* to break into for a week with little success. Either I was too busy with wedding plans and staving off Lucas's advances, or trying to put my real family back together again. The tattooed guard knocked on the door, and I rolled my eyes at him.

He scowled and, suddenly, I was in a better mood. It was a talent being able to piss people off so easily, and I was naturally gifted. I was ushered inside a bit forcefully and noticed my father's hair was disheveled.

That *never* happened.

Zachary Lee was never disheveled, never fazed or rumpled. No matter the situation, he was always four steps ahead. Disquiet settled in the recesses of my mind, the niggling itch to *run* pounding along my heartbeat in my ears. One of the guards in front of me shifted, and Lucas came into view. He held a dripping ice pack to one side of his face. Bruised and bloody, swollen and red.

"Oh fuck," I breathed, realizing instantly what this was about.

Jesse.

"My sentiments *exactly*," Lee hissed, his black eyes glassy with simmering rage. "Sit. Down." A violent edge lined the command, one that echoed through my memories as a young girl. He'd spoken to my mother like that often, anytime she raised her voice above a terrified whisper or wore the wrong thing. Anytime she took too long to answer a question or I was too unruly. Then came his fists. Usually in a wild, drunken fury.

I didn't balk, didn't question. Instead, on leaden feet, I shuffled forward, keeping my eyes trained carefully on him. Like hunting in the wilds, watching for any indication that he was about to pounce. Lucas tried to sneer at me but grimaced at the pain in his face. I sank into the leather armchair next to him, sitting gingerly on the edge of my seat. Ready to fight or flee at a moment's notice.

"Dad, I—"

"Not a word out of your mouth!" Lee bellowed. To my disgust, I flinched, my whole body recoiling from the familiar, explosive anger.

So we sat in a vicious silence that promised pain. I hated to admit it, but I was terrified. None of this had been part of my plan. Jesse's impulsive actions, Lee's strange attitude that made him unpredictable, or me sitting here completely vulnerable.

From the corner of my eye, I noticed Will shifting uncomfortably, his eyes hidden by the brim of his worn black cowboy hat. Will often lurked in the shadows behind my father: a weapon he used at his convenience. If he'd called in Will, then it was possible he knew *everything*.

Grunts and cursing filled the hallway before the door slammed opened and five guards shoved Jesse inside. He stumbled but regained his balance and stood tall, how he always did in the face of adversity. I jumped to my feet, bracing my weight on the arms of the chair beneath me when Lee's black eyes fixed on me again.

"Not a muscle, *baegopeuji anh-eun ai!*"

On quaking legs, I sat once more. A muscle in Jesse's jaw ticked at my rough treatment. I didn't know what the words meant. But they felt like a brand against my skin, burning away everything but the shame shackling me to my seat.

"In *my own goddamn house*, Audrey!"

I started at the fury of his words, nearly jumping an inch off my seat. He was absolutely *unhinged*. Lee straightened his spine, running hands over his hair and rumpled shirt. Lucas chuckled darkly at the sight of me, helpless against the tidal wave of my father's anger.

Lee fisted a crystal glass half-filled with amber liquid and drank heavily from it. That was when I noticed the sheen over his eyes, why his anger seemed so familiar. He was drunk. Like he'd been in nearly all my recovered childhood memories.

"Let's be clear," he said, swirling the dregs of the liquor at the bottom of his glass. "I don't care that you fuck the help."

Lucas's head rose, mouth dropping open in indignation. "I care—"

But my father didn't pay him any attention. Instead, he slammed his glass down, eyes burning into mine. "I know all about your little party during the storm and when you snuck out to his fight—"

"Daddy, *please*—"

"At least then you were smart enough not to be identified by anyone of importance. So even though it was dangerous and stupid, I over-looked that. You can't really think there's anything that happens in my house that I don't know about, do you?" he asked, his eyes swinging from me to Jesse, who had his fists clenched at his sides. I swallowed down fear. I ate it. Because if I didn't, if he scented it on me, he would rend through that weakness like a hot knife through butter.

"All I ask for, all I've *ever* asked for, is that you don't make your indecent behavior *public fucking knowledge*," he said, hissing the words through clenched teeth. He moved then, and it was like a sea parting. Everyone in the room shuffled to accommodate him in return. The guards shifted and jostled Jesse an appropriate distance away. "It's bad enough you nearly cost me my entire investment during the showcase match because of his broken hand, but look at Lucas. Look at his face—"

I didn't.

Lee's fingers clenched around my jaw tight, yanking my face to where Lucas sat, grinning through his bruised lips. "How am I supposed to explain this?"

"Don't touch her," Jesse growled. The guards crowded him as he stepped forward.

"*That*," he said, pointing an accusing finger inches from Jesse's nose. "That right there is *exactly* what I'm talking about. It'd be one thing if you were just fucking him, but you're not *just* fucking him, are you?"

I couldn't breathe. He *knew*. Or he'd guessed. I'd underestimated him and his powers of deduction. I was out of my depth, caught in a trap of my own design. It was like being waterboarded all over again, trapped in this little room, crowded by men who kept me pinned in place while the air whooshed from my lungs. Then I caught Will's eyes over my father's shoulder. Through my panic, he nodded slightly, and I knew what he meant without words.

El dolor es fugaz.

He already knew enough to punish us, but if he knew everything, I doubted my being his daughter would stop him from crushing the threat of me at all costs. That was just who he was. Ruthless and efficient. Whatever affection he harbored for me would disappear instantly if he knew that I was actively trying to tear his little empire apart. So I let my mask slip, just a little, raising my chin in defiance and setting my jaw. I'd admit to just enough to hopefully get us all out of this alive.

"I'm in love with him."

Pain blasted across my cheek as the back of his hand collided with my face. My ears rang with the force of it, my vision wobbling. Even still, Jesse lunged bodily for Lee, barreling through three poised men before he was subdued. They wrestled his arms behind his back, one kicking his knee out from behind until he was on the ground before us.

"Ellis," Lee barked, calling our friend over. He'd masked his face in stoicism, his eyes dead. "The gun." He snapped his fingers impatiently. Will unholstered his gun, but he didn't flick the safety off. "Get him under control."

Will pressed the barrel to the back of Jesse's head, and the whole world stilled. If Lee asked him to fire that gun, it wouldn't work. There would be an empty *click,* and then the guards would draw their weapons. We were locked in a stalemate, the room a powder keg ready to explode any second. I gripped the leather arms of my chair to still the trembling in my hands. Was this it? The moment all my plans fell apart and got us killed?

"You've dishonored me."

The words fell like stones into the pit of my stomach. I didn't want to care, but Audrey still lived inside of me. The girl who wanted nothing more than to earn the approval of her overbearing father. Even if he was a monster. Instead of wincing, I smiled coldly.

"How?" I asked, my finger coming up to press against the corner of my mouth. I raised it to see a tinge of pink blood. "Because I fell in love?"

"Love?" Lee laughed cruelly. "*Power* is the only thing that matters, and your marriage to Lucas will keep us strong.

"Look how much you've cost me," he said, staring down at Jesse on his knees. "It'll be a shame to kill him. I'm not fond of tanking my own investments." He stayed silent for a while, studying Jesse as he shifted beneath the hands holding him down.

When he opened his mouth next, my heart stuttered in my chest.

"I own you."

His words were directed at Jesse, but somehow they pierced straight into my dark heart. I felt those words in every moment that forged me into who I am now. Dragged into the back of a wagon. Sold for two bits and a dainty little gun. Thrown into trunks. Beaten, starved, scarred forever. I knew what it was to be owned, and here I was again looking at the man who would so callously strip the freedom from a person. Someone with thoughts and a wild imagination. Someone who could feel, could create art, could *love* so deeply. I watched Lee, the gears in his mind turning at a glacial pace. But I knew before he ever made the connection what he would do. Because he'd done it before. To *me*.

"*No you don't*," I snarled, my nails piercing the leather of the armchair. Jesse's eyes widened as they swung toward me. I knew antagonizing Lee would only dig our graves, that it would only make his cold rage burn hotter. But I couldn't stop. There was an ache where my inner child was supposed to be that wouldn't let me. Lee narrowed his eyes at me, pushed to his limit with my rebelliousness.

I didn't cower. Instead, I glared right back at him.

"You can't *own* a person."

Lee laughed coldly, abandoning Jesse as he turned on me like a feral cat. He stalked closer until he was leaning into my face, my chest heaving with the struggle it took to hold myself back. My muscles trembled with the effort to stay fucking *still.*

"Not only can I own them," he said calmly, gripping my chin. "But I can *sell* them, too."

I didn't think, or I would've tried to strangle down the murderous intent in my eyes. I spat at him. My saliva dripped over the bridge of his nose. One of his hands tangled in my hair, the other raised into a shaking fist, poised to break and bruise me for my insolence.

"Do it!" I shouted through clenched teeth. "Show them who you really are!" He stilled. His gaze darted to the guards, who'd gone very still at his outburst. Jesse hadn't stilled; he wriggled beneath the threat of Will's gun, his chest heaving with the effort to hold himself back.

Then Lee's eyes lowered to mine, shrewder than before. *Fuck.* I'd said too much. He was going to *sell* Jesse. He was going to put him in a cage and strip away his dignity. They would break him, the way they almost broke me. Instead of my farm boy who stood tall against every odd stacked against him, they would hollow him out until he forgot he was human. And the girl from under the bed, the girl from the back of the wagon, the girl in the trunk . . . Those girls won't let him go through that without one hell of a fight.

"What did you say?" he asked, shaking my head with his fist in my hair. "Who am I, *exactly?*"

"She was scared of you," I said, my lips trembling and my eyes heating. "Mom."

He dropped his hand from my hair like it'd burned him. Shock stole whatever cruel words he'd had poised on his tongue. He shook his head. Back and forth. Like he refused to acknowledge my words or what they meant.

"No. No, you were too young—"

"She had the most beautiful singing voice and would hum all day long. Make up silly songs for chores or to calm me down when I got upset. And the *moment* you came home, the entire house went silent."

He shook his head more now, refusing to meet my eyes.

"Silent like a grave. Silent like a prayer in the dark. That this time you'd be sober. That *this time* you'd wait until I was in bed to start slapping her around."

"You don't know what you're talking about," he mumbled.

"The night she left you, she *wept.* It soaked the collar of my coat. After *everything you'd done*, she still cried for you," I said, pushing to my feet slowly. Will adjusted his grip on the gun at Jesse's head. A clear warning. *Don't push too hard. Remember what's at stake.*

"You *loved* her. I know you did. *Please*, I'm marrying Lucas just like you want. Just—" I reached out to him with soft fingers, clutching his hand in mine. "Let him go," I whispered.

When my father lifted his black eyes to mine, whatever spark of hope lingered inside of me was strangled.

Nothing.

There was nothing in them but a cold, black rage that froze my blood in my veins. With strong hands, he gripped my arm and shoved me until I stumbled back into the chair.

"Your mother was nothing more than another man's whore, and if you didn't resemble me as much as you do, I wouldn't have even claimed you as mine." He snapped his fingers with a finality that stole the air from my lungs. "*Love* is a bad investment, sweetheart, and I don't make bad investments.

"Take him to the market. Tell Eddie I want him in the next auction."

Lucas grinned through his bruised lips, the cut at the corner reopening. Tears stung my eyes, impotent rage filling my body until it felt like I would burst. He couldn't do this to me. Not again. Not *fucking* again.

"No!" I cried into the room as hard hands wrestled Jesse off his knees, and Will stepped back, holstering his gun. "Please, just show him mercy! If you *ever* cared about me, you wouldn't do this."

"*I* didn't do this, Audrey," Lee said through gritted teeth. "You did. With all your sneaking around and lies. All you had to do was what you were told.

"How much do you remember?" he asked suddenly, his black eyes marking every expression on my face. I was too expressive, too open. I didn't have a poker face like Jesse. He would see *everything* the moment I tried to lie. So I slipped into Audrey's skin again, for the first time since my memories came back. I stepped into her sheltered, small life of ignorance and tamped down Bonnie. If only for a moment.

"Not much, mostly just Mom. With the wedding, I've been missing her so much . . . at first I thought I was daydreaming."

He ground his back teeth together, studying me and seeming to find my trembling and tears to be adequate signs of honesty. Lucas stood, pulling me up by my elbow, his fingers digging into the soft flesh of my arm.

"Get your fucking hands *off of her!*" Jesse roared, a vein in his neck bulging as he tried to free his arms and lurch towards Lucas, which only seemed to please the bastard more.

Lucas wrapped an arm around my waist and pulled me tight against him in a show of blatant ownership. "Why? She's going to be my *wife*. Have my children. Warm. My. Bed." I shoved Lucas's chest, but he held on with an iron grip, his eyes never leaving Jesse's. "Don't fool yourself, fighter. You were *never* going to have her."

"I'm going to kill you," Jesse vowed, his Adam's apple bobbing as if he had to swallow the weight of his words. "I'm going to kill you *slowly*."

"Get him out of here, boys."

In a split second, everything was wrenched away from me in a sea of bodies as we were shuffled out of the study and into the hall. The guards were too rough with Jesse, shoving him and grabbing him as they forced him down the stairs. One had a white-knuckled grip on the nape of his neck to keep him from looking back at me. With each step he took, another sliver of hope slipped from my fingers.

Not again.

My Bonnie girl. Jones's voice taunted me from the shadows of my mind, *tsking* at how quickly I'd lost control of the situation. *You can't trust anyone, remember? Only me. I'm the devil you know.*

Jesse's impulsiveness had thrown everything into chaos, and they were marching him out to be sold at market. Like smuggled goods. My stomach thrashed and heaved as I tried to regain my control. I couldn't be separated from him again. Not after last time. I wouldn't survive it. Of *that* I was absolutely certain.

Frozen in place, Lucas put his hand too low on my back, forcing hot bile to rise in my throat. I didn't remember making any conscious decision, but all of a sudden, I did exactly what my instincts had been screaming at me.

I *ran.*

My feet pounded against the stairs, my father barking orders as he marched after me furiously. But I had desert sand in my blood and the whip of rushing wind in my veins. My heart beat the rhythm of a Comanche war drum. They were nearly at the front door when I caught sight of them again. Jesse dug his heels in and tried to wrench their hands off him to no avail.

"Farm boy!" I shouted breathlessly.

He renewed his fight, twisting to lock the blaze of his blue eyes with mine in desperation.

"Stop her!" Lee shouted from behind me. A few of the guards on duty near the front door broke away, clawing at my arms to push me back. Jesse threw off two of the men who'd been holding him and lurched forward. I twisted out of the grasp of one guard to throw myself into his chest.

His arms, strong as steel bands, wrapped tight around me as helpless tears rolled down my cheeks. Here, in his arms, was the only place I had ever been truly free.

Jesse didn't waste any time; his mouth crashed against mine in a desperate slick of lips and tongues.

"Don't fight them," I mumbled against his lips. "Keep your head down, no eye contact, separate yourself from your body." I couldn't help the whispered instructions as the taste of his lips and my tears mingled together.

"Rule number seven," he breathed into my mouth.

"Rule number seven."

Just as suddenly, we were wrenched apart. I grabbed onto any part of him that I could. My nails scored deep against his forearms as I was bodily lifted away, until the only part of him still touching me were his fingertips. Until even that small touch failed against the forces tearing us apart.

An inch. A foot. Three feet. Then he was tossed onto the cobblestones of the square, watching as I kicked and screamed and fought for him. Because this time, *this time*, he had to know I fought for him. They dragged him up from his knees, one of the guards kicking him in the stomach before they allowed him to stand fully.

The door slammed shut, and the fight that'd propelled me forward shattered like glass against stone. My sobbing was quiet. I'd learned early not to be bothersome with my emotions. My father screamed at me for so long that my feet ached. I didn't hear any of it. Instead, I stood there with my head hung low. Which, eventually, seemed to be enough for him to finally relent. Guards ushered me forward on clumsy feet back to my room. When the door clicked shut, The Kid came from the bathroom, a million questions poised in his curious eyes.

One look at my face had them dimming. After I told him what happened, he tried to reassure me for a while, but I felt numb. After scrubbing my face and changing into my night clothes, I sat at my barred window and looked out at the square. To his credit, The Kid allowed me time to sit with everything. I watched from my window as hours passed. Then, he gripped my shoulder and squeezed hard enough for me to look at him.

All the youthfulness had drained from his expression, leaving in its wake a dark steeliness I didn't recognize. Something immovable in his eyes that hadn't been there before. Like once he made his mind up about something, nothing in the world could change it.

"We're gonna need a plan, Bonnie," he said, stepping back and allowing me to rise on my feet. Slowly, the blood returned to my fingers as they curled one by one into fists at my sides.

"Have you killed anyone, Kid?"

He shook his head, but his determination never wavered. A silent understanding passed between us. I'd taught him the honorable side of being an outlaw when he was young, but his real education would begin tonight. The only rule that mattered at the end of the day when it came to navigating the wilds of the world.

Kill or be killed.

"That might change."

CHAPTER SIXTEEN

JESSE

THE SLAVERS' PARADE RAN twice a day. At least that was what I heard from the workers shepherding a line of dirt-streaked people chained together.

The bloated banks of the Mississippi River greeted me, a reminder that no matter what happened, this was all bigger than me. It had been since long before I arrived in New Orleans.

The Slavers' Parade took place in an old rail yard, where a tributary from the Mississippi River broke off toward Lake Pontchartrain. Far enough from Lee Square, but not so far that Lee didn't still have his men on patrol.

First, they stripped me of my clothes and dumped a bucket of water over my head as I covered my cock with my hands. A pale-faced man with pockmarked skin and a pair of gold front teeth inspected me.

"He'll fetch a nice price," the man said, eyeing my flaccid cock, my shoulders, my arms. "He'll be the headliner for tonight's parade." He turned to a guard. "Keep him shackled. Don't want this one getting away."

After being given a pair of ragged jeans, my jailers had thrown me into a railcar, two of Lee's soldiers standing guard near the haphazardly welded bars that slammed shut behind me. It'd taken six of them to subdue me, to wrangle me away from the square after they'd ripped us apart.

Even hours later, the terror in Bonnie's blue eyes remained.

Keep your head down, no eye contact, separate yourself from your body.

A stab of fury went through me. Bonnie had been a slave for years. She knew more about slavers than I ever would.

I leaned against the steel backing of the car, one shackled wrist propped on my knee as I thought through the possibilities. If I fought the guards when they came for me, they'd shoot me. But would that be better or worse than the fate that waited if I was sold?

Of course, you fucking idiot. You have to live.

There were too many people depending on me. Bonnie. Mickey. The Kid. Will.

"Hey!" I barked at the guards. They shifted only slightly, one glancing my way from the corner of his eye. I shoved off of the metal floor of the car. "I gotta piss."

The only response from the guards was to adjust their grips on their rifles.

"Did you hear me?" I wrapped my fingers around the bar. "I gotta take a piss."

"Fuck off," one of them snapped.

So be it. I shifted my weight, my shackled hands going to the front of my jeans. A moment later, hot piss streamed over the man's head, steaming against the cool evening air.

He flinched away. "Fuck, fine!"

I couldn't help my satisfied grin as I fixed my jeans.

One of them called for the keys. They clinked together as a third person rifled through a heavy keychain, glancing my way every second as they tried to find the right one. His dirty fingernails and threadbare clothes made me wonder if he worked for the parade or was one of us. A slave. Except he wore a blue armband haphazardly stitched with a top hat.

The minutes ticked by until finally, the lock clicked open. The guards stepped back as he swung the metal bars open and scurried out of the way.

My chains jingled together as I climbed down. One of the guards gripped my arm, his fingers biting into the bare skin of my upper arm.

"No funny business, fighter," he growled. "To the latrine and back."

A cold gust of wind chilled my skin. It'd been warmer in the railcar. The guards flanked me as they led the way through rickety tents and buildings. People sat hunched together: men, women, children. I spied a large man with a giant manacle chained around his throat. A woman leaned heavily against his shoulder, her eyelids drooping and her hands shaking. At the entrance to a tent, there was a line of children waiting, but for what?

"Next!" a male voice called from the opening. It was the man who'd stripped me naked upon arrival. A young girl barely The Kid's age stumbled past him, tugging at the scraps of fabric that couldn't be called a shirt, as the first child in the queue disappeared inside.

I gritted my teeth against the sight. The guards shoved me away, through small groups of other slaves waiting to be sold. Some people's eyes widened as if in recognition, while others scowled. All wore shackles. There were more guards, some branded, but most not.

The stench of human waste reached me halfway through the camp. The "latrine" was little more than a deep ditch that fed into the river. I took my time with the front of my jeans, surveying the area around me. Across the camp, not far from the railcars, sat a rickety wooden stage. A ripped banner hung across the top. There was a large, open space before it where, I assumed, those looking to purchase would wait for the auction later tonight.

How the hell was I supposed to get out of here?

You aren't, Bonnie's voice reminded me. *Only in a pine box.*

I shook my head as I righted my pants and then turned back to the guards. I needed to find a way to give them the slip. That was the only chance I had. Could I cause a diversion? My gaze shot across the others waiting for the parade as they marched me back toward the railcars. Even if I could get these people to trust me, it would take time I didn't have.

One of the guards caught me eyeing his rifle. His knuckles went white as he adjusted his grip. "Don't even think about it."

I gave a smile that was more teeth than anything. "Don't worry, I'm a terrible shot," I remarked. "I'd rather kill you with my bare hands."

The guard's throat bobbed, which gave me a sick sense of satisfaction.

The sharp *crack* of a whip sounded as we neared the railcars. I stopped short, brows furrowing. Before us on a small platform surrounded by mud was a large post made from the base of a tree. A woman was chained to it, her bare back brandished to the camp as the man with the gold teeth threw his arm back. A small child whimpered, hiding between the woman and the post, snot and tears dribbling down their cheeks. The whip came down on the woman, who let out a muffled scream. Her nails dug into the wood of the post.

"Stop them," I said to my guards.

One of them snorted, then shoved me toward the railcars.

Crack.

"Did you fucking hear me?" I growled.

"If you don't shut up, I'll gag you," one of them said.

"Kinky. Didn't know you were into dudes." I spat at their feet, digging my own into the mud as they jostled me.

Crack.

No matter what these people thought the woman did, she didn't deserve this. Her child didn't deserve this. In my mind, it wasn't a stranger being tortured for sport . . . it was Bonnie. Her pale skin splitting beneath the definitive crack of the whip, dark crimson blood trickling from the wounds to mix with dirt and tears. A little girl cowered before her, no more than three or four, with tears falling from wide blue eyes. Her blonde hair was so dirty and disheveled it looked brassy with neglect.

I knew it wasn't Bonnie and Emma on that post, but my heart couldn't see the unknown woman's features anymore. When her child cried out, I heard Emma begging for mercy, incoherent with anguish. Each time the whip came down and the woman's body shuddered, her nails breaking from her grip on the wooden pole, I felt the pain of that lash in the center of my chest. I couldn't sit here and watch. Couldn't sit here and do nothing.

My hands clenched together in fists, and I whipped to the right, smashing my elbow into the guard's nose. He cried out and stumbled backward. I took my chance, crashing my chains against the top of his head. His knees gave out, and his gun slipped from his hands. I reached for it, fingers finding cool metal, and then turned to the other guard, who already had his rifle pointed at me.

"Put it down." A clear order. One that I had no intention of following. Without thought, I lifted my gun and fired twice. Another shot rang out as the guard crumpled to the mud.

I'd already garnered too much attention, but I couldn't stop myself. I advanced on the post, where the ringleader of this disgusting circus had turned his eyes on me. At least he wasn't beating the woman anymore. I lifted my gun again and fired, but the shot went wide and pinged off of a nearby boxcar.

"Get him," the man ordered.

I ducked beneath the arms of a man holding a machete and turned back to fire at him but missed again. *Fuck me.* Another guard wrapped his arms around my throat. I couldn't position the gun with my hands chained, so I bashed my head back into his face, reveling in the crunch of his nose and cry of pain.

Another shot rang out, striking the mud at my feet.

There was a crowd now. One that I wouldn't be able to escape.

I gripped the rifle tight, fingers going numb as I spun in a circle. A dozen or so armed men and women surrounded me.

"Don't kill him!" The ringleader shoved through the crowd, baring his teeth at me. "He's too valuable. Lee's giving me a fifty percent cut of this one." He fixed me with a hard stare. "Put the gun down, boy."

"Go fuck yourself." My gaze darted back and forth, shifting wildly as I sought a way out. I lifted the gun once more, pointing it at the man in charge. "Let them go."

The man turned back to the woman and child. The former sobbed against the post. Red welts had given way to lashes. Blood soaked the tattered edges of her clothing. The child buried their face in the woman's belly.

"Or what?"

"I shoot you where you stand," I said through gritted teeth.

An ominous smile lit up the man's features, his eyes practically glowing. Instead of responding, he brandished a pistol and pressed the barrel to the back of the woman's head. The child screeched, flailing and reaching for the gun. In the blink of an eye, the man fisted the back of the child's shirt and yanked her away from her mother.

"No! *Jo!*" The woman whimpered, fighting meekly against her chains.

"I said"—the man aimed the gun at me—"put the gun down, *boy*."

My jaw clenched. Everything in me wanted to grip the gun tighter, fire off a shot, and kill him.

"This isn't a ring," he said, regarding me with an almost amused expression. "There ain't no rules except one. Do what you're fuckin' told." His gold tooth glinted in the light.

I shifted my weight, my eyes darting between the man and the guards circling me.

The man cocked the pistol and fired a single round into the woman's head. As she went limp against her bindings, my vision wavered, the image of Bonnie in her place still haunting me. I gaped at him, watching with a horror-stricken heart as he pressed the gun to the back of the child's head and cocked it, lifting a single eyebrow in my direction.

The gun in my hands thunked into the mud at my feet.

A predatory smile crossed the man's face. He motioned to the guards, who took up both of my arms.

"I think it's time you learned your place."

While they dragged me forward, another person cut the bindings of the woman at the post and tossed her unceremoniously into the mud. Another guard yanked the child by her bindings away, even as she fought against them, screeching at her mother's dead body.

Splintered wood dug into the bare skin of my feet, mud marking each step I took across the platform to the post. Nails hung at different intervals above my head. I forced the tension from my body as someone yanked my chains and looped them over one of the nails to brandish my back.

A lesser man might've hung his head, accepted his fate. The people in this camp were already downtrodden, beaten into compliance. I felt their eyes on my bare skin as the ringleader called attention.

"Good day!" he cried out, that terrible smile spreading across his face once more. "I'd like your attention please!" He clapped his hands together. "Some might think what this fighter has done is good, even honorable." Deep bouts of laughter came from the guards. "I would like to present to you what happens when trying to be *honorable*."

Less than a heartbeat passed before the whip cracked against my skin. I bit my tongue to stifle my groan, and my vision flashed white. Before I could inhale, it cracked a second time, then a third. My muscles strained against their bindings, the metal cuffs around my wrists cutting off the circulation to my hands.

Again the whip cracked. Again. Again. My skin split beneath it, my body convulsing on its own with each lash.

Only when the world darkened did he stop.

I woke sometime after sunset, face down in the railcar. A small figure hovered nearby, scooting back in fear when I shifted uncomfortably.

The child.

"How—" I blinked rapidly, willing my vision to settle against the pain.

"Thank you," a voice said from beyond the bars. A boy hovered just outside of my prison, shifting their weight as if to keep watch. With a little hesitation, the child crossed to me with a canteen. They helped me to take giant gulps of water. It tasted like the spring of eternal life.

"You shouldn't have done that." There was a familiar certainty in the boy's eyes. It reminded me of The Kid, especially on our trip from Montana to Vegas. Except there was none of my brother's wide-eyed wonder. Only pain, only the haunted eyes of someone who'd see far too much at their age, forced to be wise beyond their years. More like me, even though I had to be at least ten years older, as if his youth had been sapped away.

"I had to."

"No one else would have," he said.

The little girl moved to my side, this time retrieving a small tin from her pocket. I hissed out a breath as she smeared some sort of ointment on my back.

"Why did they do it?" I rasped. "The beating? The killing?"

"The man with the gold teeth," the boy said. "He was trying to take Jo, and our mother wouldn't let him. Everyone knows he has an appetite for young children." His gaze flickered to the little girl as she backed a step away from me. "If they come back at all, they come back broken."

I opened my mouth to reply, but words failed me. I *knew* that things like that happened in the world. It didn't make it any easier to swallow seeing the real effects of it before me.

"Come on, Jo. The guards are returning," the boy said. The girl scrambled away from me, moving to the far end of the car, where she climbed up through a small hole in the ceiling.

Then I was alone.

CHAPTER SEVENTEEN

SAVANNAH

S TRAWBERRY SHORTCAKE. BONNIE WAS going to love it.

Except she's never going to eat it.

I'd made my decision on the wedding cake. One of the first things I learned about my best friend was how much she loved strawberries. Strawberry shortcake as her wedding cake was perfect. Even if my hard work would never truly be appreciated, at least the rest of the world would believe the wedding was still on.

That was my job, after all, to maintain the facade. Even if that grew more challenging by the day.

I'd given in to flights of fancy, imagining a life outside of this house and away from Lee, the guards, the others who hated me. A life where the shadows haunted Will a little less. A life that wasn't so hard all the time.

A commotion sounded, stealing my attention from the pen and paper on the kitchen island. My brows furrowed, and I slipped from my stool, glancing at Etty as she chopped vegetables. We'd barely spoken, working in tandem silently in the kitchen, ever since the blow-up with Will.

Could I trust her? I wanted to. Badly.

"What was that?" I headed for the door that led to the courtyard. Etty didn't reply.

Guards shuffled across the stone, rifles in hand, concern etched into their features as they headed for the front house. Had something happened?

I crossed the courtyard with brisk steps, shoulders tight. As I reached the propped-open double doors, however, an arm wrapped around my waist. I gasped at the sudden contact, my eyes widening as I took in the sight of Will. He tugged me into a darkened corner of the courtyard, lines deepening around his eyes. His long arms wrapped around me, and he buried his face in the crook of my neck, taking in several deep breaths.

"What's happened?" I asked, relaxing into the familiar warmth of his embrace.

Will was as tense as a bow string, so I threaded my fingers into the hair at the base of his neck and wrapped an arm around him. He took in a deep breath, then another.

"Lee sent Jesse to the Slavers' Parade," he murmured against my skin.

A breeze kicked up, the mixture of it and Will's words making my blood run cold. This wasn't the first time Lee had sent someone to the parade. I doubted it would be the last. I'd never been there, of course, but I'd heard stories over the years. Families separated, children whipped and abused, and Lee had a hand in it all.

"Bonnie," I whispered, my throat bobbing around my rising panic. I pulled back, cradling his face in my hands as I forced him to look at me. "Where's Bonnie?"

"The guards dragged her back to her room."

Without a thought, I took Will's hand in mine and pulled him toward the stairs, my heart pounding. We'd been riding a knife's edge for days as we enacted our plans, sneaking around the house, maintaining the status quo.

I halted the moment we rounded the corner to my and Bonnie's rooms. Guards. Heavily armed guards. I glanced at Will, then tugged him by his hand to my door, ignoring them as they catcalled and whistled at me.

Let them see Will going into my room. I wasn't ashamed.

After locking the door behind us, I dragged Will by the hand through the bathroom and into Bonnie's room. My friend stood over her desk, where Jesse's younger brother was quickly scribbling something on a piece of paper. They looked up at our arrival.

"What the hell did he do?" I asked.

Bonnie's eyes went dim, and her shoulders slumped. "He beat the shit out of Rutherford."

I sighed, shaking my head even as Will wrapped an arm around my waist, his hand gripping my hip tight.

"It's okay, we're going to get him back," The Kid piped up, his expression brilliant as he glanced toward me.

"Yeah, so I can kill him for ruining my con," Bonnie grumbled. A breath, and then she faced me, her softness shifting into rigid edges. Before me stood *Bonnie*, the woman who'd lived on the run for years, who schemed and conned and did whatever it took to get the job done. "What do you know about the Slavers' Parade?"

"They run auctions once in the morning and at night," Will said, moving toward the pair to glance at the paper on the desk. "Full of guards, but most of them aren't branded men. He really only sends them down there if he has an asset to protect."

"Like Jesse," Bonnie deadpanned, rubbing her hands over her face. "God, he is such a *fucking* idiot."

"No," Will said, pointing to the crude drawing on the page in front of The Kid. "It's farther east than that, right here"—while he pointed to something I couldn't see, I clasped my hands together uneasily—"where Patty enters the river."

"Patty?" The Kid asked.

Will let out a dark chuckle. "The crater beast that calls Lake Pontchartrain home. If they have unruly slaves or ones they can't sell, they'll toss them to Patty."

The Kid shuddered as I said, "Jesus Christ."

"That doesn't matter. We need to know more. Layouts, guard rotations. We can't go in blind," Bonnie said, shifting back and forth on her feet.

"We don't have time for that," I said. Everyone turned to stare at me. "*Jesse* doesn't have time for that. Besides, we have a larger problem."

They waited while I bit my bottom lip and twisted my fingers together. "You two"—I pointed between Bonnie and Will—"are far too recognizable. We can't just go into that camp guns blazing. Otherwise Lee will know we were there. Plus, we have to get past the guards parked in the hallway." I motioned to the door with my thumb over my shoulder.

Bonnie's gaze shifted, her mind working as she realized I spoke the truth. I wasn't a schemer; I relied on the rest of them for that. Will's eyes found mine as a slow, lascivious grin curled across his mouth. His features lit up, as if whatever brilliant idea he had would be more than effective; it would be fun. My stomach plummeted at the look in his eyes, one that said whatever he had in mind, it would include me.

"I know what we have to do."

A half hour later, I was alone in the bathroom, tugging on a pair of black jeans that were far too tight.

"Can you hurry up? The sun's going down," Bonnie said from her room.

I huffed, turning to my reflection. This was *never* going to work. I applied kohl to my eyes liberally, ignoring how my cleavage nearly spilled out of the ripped top we'd fashioned from one of *Mrs. Rutherford's fucking dresses*, as Bonnie called them. I tore the pins from my hair, the dark curls cascading over my shoulders and back. A shiver went down my spine. This was too risky.

After securing a black handkerchief around my neck and ensuring my brand was covered, I took a deep breath, steeling myself for what came next.

"*Santa Mierda*!" Will let out a low breath as I re-entered Bonnie's room, his brows lifting nearly to his hairline. An almost predatory grin crossed his features as he took me in, devouring me with his eyes. Rampant desire coursed through me as they darkened.

"Come on, you two," Bonnie said, tossing a jacket my way. I tugged it on over my shoulders and headed for the door. An arm shot out in front of me, and I glanced up at Will.

"You and The Kid go ahead. We don't want to cause unwanted attention, and the guards travel in pairs," he said.

Bonnie looked at him with skepticism in her eyes. Instead of speaking, however, she tugged the collar of her jacket higher. She placed one of Will's black cowboy hats on her head, tilting the brim so low that I definitely wouldn't be able to tell who she was. She had smeared black makeup around her eyes and across her nose to hide her identity. She gave a curt nod and then disappeared into the hall with The Kid. The moment the door latched, Will turned, invading my space like he always did. My back pressed against the wall, and I let out gasp at the sudden contact.

Then he kissed me and every single thought disappeared.

My arms wrapped around him on their own as he tilted my head back, deepening the kiss and stealing my breath.

Even through the layers of clothing between us, I felt every hard, lithe inch of him. He tugged one of my legs up around his waist, pressing his cock deliciously against me. I moaned into his mouth, and my fingers twisted in his hair.

Will pulled back, a mirthful glint in his eyes as he ran his thumb across my bottom lip. "Just don't want you to forget."

"Forget what?" I asked, my chest heaving as I sucked in a giant breath.

"Who you belong to."

My heart stuttered at the dead-serious expression in his eyes. He surveyed me for another moment, his gaze lingering on my legs, as if it were the first time he'd seen them.

"Come on, William." I shoved him back half a step, then reached for the door, my pounding heart drowning out anything else he could have said.

Will led the way through the corridors, peering around corners and keeping me close against his side.

"Where are the guards?" I asked in a hushed voice.

That grin I loved so much spread across his face. "I dumped them in one of the closets."

I'd known Will so long that his mischievous expression didn't surprise me, but it did make my heart beat faster. His joy was a refreshing contrast to the normally haunted eyes that watched me as I worked through the house.

Three horses were saddled and waiting in the alleyway. Will passed a couple of silver coins to the same stable hand I'd been paying to keep me updated on his comings and goings. In silence, Bonnie and The Kid mounted their horses. I eyed the black stallion stamping impatiently. I liked Will's horse, but riding had never been something I enjoyed.

"C'mon, Savvy," Will murmured into my hair as his fingers found my hips and he helped me into the saddle. I shifted uncomfortably; I couldn't remember the last time I'd worn pants. I'd ridden side-saddle when we'd returned to the manor after the graveyard, but now, I straddled the beast, my fingernails digging into the saddle horn.

Effortlessly, Will joined me, his legs pressing close on either side. He feathered a kiss along my jaw as he reached for the reins, grinning against my skin when I tensed.

Will led the way on his stallion, heading down the back part of the alley to avoid the guards at the front of the house. Three riders waited, hats low or hoods covering their features.

"What the fuck happened?" I recognized the man instantly. Jesse's uncle. Mickey.

"Jesse lost his mind and beat the shit out of Rutherford," Will stated simply. "I'm glad you got my message. I was hoping we'd have backup."

Mickey regarded Bonnie and The Kid and then nodded at me. "Let's do this then."

Will wrapped an arm around my waist and clicked his tongue, guiding his stallion through the back alleys of the city, places I'd never been. Every now and then, we'd pass a wandering soul who shifted their attention elsewhere. I thought I saw one with blue lips, but it was hard to tell in the fading light.

It was fully dark by the time the stallion slowed.

"You ready?" Will asked in a low voice.

I let out an unsteady breath. "Yes."

After dismounting, Will reached for me. The warmth of his embrace steadied me as I settled on my feet. He met my gaze, his eyes searching mine. Did I like this plan? Absolutely not, but we didn't have any other choice.

"Alright," Will said, capturing the attention of everyone in our group. "We'll have to split up. Mickey, you go with Bonnie and The Kid. I'll take Savvy." He surveyed the other two riders. "Stay with the horses."

A woman leaned down from her horse and kissed Mickey swiftly, offering a smile as she righted herself.

The chilly night air seeped through my clothes as we watched Mickey, The Kid, and Bonnie slip in through a large gate. Beyond the entrance, people milled about, carrying drinks or roasted meat on sticks as if it were some old-fashioned carnival. Vendor booths lined the pathway on one side. From what I could see, their wares ranged from iron manacles to gold teeth. A shiver ran down my spine.

Without a word, Will pressed a hand to the small of my back and guided me forward to follow the flow of the crowd. Voices kicked up, and music played from somewhere. My stomach turned at the people acting like this was some sort of festival and not an auction for human lives.

While most of the attendees walked forward without regard for our surroundings, I caught sight of tents beyond a fence. Small fires flickered. People huddled around them, shivering against the night.

These were the goods to be sold. Dozens of people: male, female, children, the elderly.

We'd come here with the purpose of getting Jesse back, but what about the rest of them?

The crowd slowed as we reached an area with a stage. A man stood in the center of it, his booming voice carrying over the noise.

"Ladies and gentlemen, up next we have a pair of sisters!" He wore a top hat, and his gold teeth glinted in the light. He extended an arm toward two women dressed in what could only be described as potato sacks, with barely enough fabric to warm them against the night's chill. Their faces were dirty and gaunt. Clearly they weren't being fed enough.

"For the meager price of fifty copper bits, you could own *twins*!"

My lip curled in disgust at the gleam in the man's eyes. I'd heard whisperings about the Slavers' Parade but never could have imagined this.

"Ten!" someone shouted over the chaos.

The man's brows furrowed. "Come now, my friend. These two are at least worth triple that apiece. I'm offering a bargain!"

"Twenty!" another shouted.

My stomach churned. I'd lived in relative safety all of these years, protected from the true darkness of this city by the brand on my neck. I reached up, scratching it through the fabric of my bandana.

"I'll take no less than thirty!" the man on the stage called back.

"Twenty or you can feed 'em to Patty," the purchaser said firmly.

My gaze shot to the edge of the crowd, where only a rickety chain link fence separated the market from the water where Will said Patty lurked.

"Will—" I said, shaking my head as I looked at him with wide eyes. "I can't do this."

"Yes, you can," he said without hesitation. He tucked my hair behind my ear, cradling my cheek as I implored him with my eyes. He only stared back at me, his faith unwavering.

My throat bobbed as I turned back to the stage. Apparently the women had been sold, as there were new slaves on the block.

"Where is Jesse?" I asked.

"They'll keep him separate, wait until the end. Probably locked in the railcars." He motioned to the far end of where the slaves were being kept. Armed guards milled about. Beyond, there were old train cars fitted with bars where doors should have been.

Familiar figures came into view. Our friends.

"Any sight of him?" Mickey asked from the other side of my friend.

With a shake of his head, Will said, "He'll probably be the last."

We stood that way, merely watching as the next person was dragged onto the stage.

"We have to help them," I whispered to Will.

His features tightened, even as his eyes softened on me. "We can't." He cleared his throat. "We're already risking too much by buying Jesse."

"But—"

"No. No heroes."

Something in me deflated at the finality of his tone.

Bonnie was as tense as a bow string as she stood beside me. I felt the same way, a spectator watching a sport I had no urge to participate in.

It felt like hours before the man with the hat quieted the crowd, his eyes gleaming.

"And for tonight's main event, ladies and gentlemen. Our final block is a man with the strength of a thousand and a smile to kill for. And—ladies—he most *definitely* won't leave you wanting." As he rattled off another ridiculous selling point, two guards dragged Jesse up the wooden stairs.

Red slashes lined his bare back. Bonnie flinched beside me.

"Fuck," Will said, his attention rapt as Jesse stumbled on the stage. "He's gonna need medical attention."

Jesse's uncle nodded. "We have basic supplies, depending on how bad it is—"

His words faded as I took Bonnie's hand, gripping hard. "He's alive," I reminded her. "That's the best we could hope for."

Before she could respond, the man called out, "Shall we begin?"

"Fifty silver!" one man shouted.

"Sixty!" another countered.

"Savvy—" Will said, nudging me forward as the bids flew.

"One-fifty!"

"How much do we have?" I asked, an edge to my voice as I peered over my shoulder at Will.

"Money doesn't matter," he said swiftly.

"Two hundred!" I shouted, but the numbers didn't stop there.

I shoved through the pulsing crowd, Will hot on my heels.

"Do I have two-fifty?" the auctioneer called, glee and greed in his eyes.

"Five gold!"

The crowd took a collective breath, their eyes finding me near the center.

"Five gold. Do I have six?" the man said, dismissing me immediately.

"Five gold, fifty silver," a man said from ten feet away, glaring at me.

"Six gold," I countered.

"Like you have six gold bits," my competitor said, his gaze sliding along my neck, down across my exposed cleavage. "*That* won't win you a slave, *girl*."

"Try me," I ground out between my teeth.

"Six gold, fifty silver," the man said as he turned back to the stage.

"Seven gold," I spat.

"You could get a dozen slaves for that price," the man said, his mouth working as if he were trying to figure out what I was getting at. "Seven gold, fifty silver."

"Twenty!" I glared at the man before turning back to the stage. "Twenty gold bits."

The auctioneer's mouth slackened. He cast his gaze across the crowd. "Do I have twenty-one?"

The hush that fell over the crowd chilled me to my bones.

"Twenty gold, fifty silver?" he prompted.

I glanced toward the man who'd been bidding against me. He glared in my direction but made no move to counter.

The ringleader's greedy gaze fell. "Sold to the woman in front for twenty gold bits."

I didn't miss the man's scowl at me as he departed from the stage.

Will flattened a warm palm against the base of my spine, his eyes shifting as he studied the crowd around us. As we started for the stage, the man who'd bid against me moved in front of us.

"You certainly don't have twenty gold. I'll take him off your hands for seven."

Will stiffened beside me, his hand going to the gun at his hip.

I forced a smile to cross my features. "Come," I said, staring directly at the man. "I'd like to see what I just purchased."

Without another word, I shoved through the crowd, my friends at my back, to save Jesse and get the hell out of this place.

CHAPTER EIGHTEEN

BONNIE

I COULDN'T BREATHE THROUGH the stupid mask, even though it was just a simple red bandana tied around my neck and pulled over my nose and mouth, keeping most of my face hidden. I couldn't hear anything but the buzzing in my ears and the *thud, thud, thud,* of my pulse as it raced through my veins and deafened me to my surroundings.

All I could see was blood.

Jesse's blood. Caked a dark rust color in lines across his back, a larger mirror of the scars on my ribs. His wounds were open to the grime and filth of the night air, and I knew that this place would seep beneath his skin. Dirty him from the inside. Just like the loss of my freedom had poisoned me all those years ago, twisted me into something dark and broken, giving me jagged edges that I used as weapons.

My nails broke against the immovable wood door to the wagon as I clawed for freedom, for a way out of this nightmare. "Momma!" I wailed, a keening cry that shredded my raw throat. I'd been calling for hours, days, eternity. Until her name was so garbled that it barely made sense anymore. The wagon didn't care; it kept rocking along, all my wet, desperate cries drifting along the path it made along the uneven ground. "Momma!"

Cold sweat beaded at my temples as we shoved through the crowd. Every muscle in my body tightened to the point of pain, and my eyes darted back and forth so fast it made me dizzy. Every single person was an enemy, no matter how disinterested or innocuous they seemed. Those who frequented the markets had no loyalty to anyone or any-

180

thing. No moral line they wouldn't cross. No principle they would adhere to.

I wanted them all to die horribly.

As Savannah led us through the crowd, my lungs ached beneath the weight of my loathing. Beneath the rage that had always been there, waiting for me to wake up, bathing me in the desperate longing for violence. The pommels of my knives dug into my palms, and I imagined them becoming one with my hands, a natural extension of myself.

We were led to a guarded railcar. The man in the tattered patchwork top hat grinned widely and bowed low, then ushered us forward with a flourish of his long arm. Moving ahead automatically, a guard brandished a dull, rusted machete to stop me.

"Ah ah ah," the ringleader said, waggling his finger. "You can look, but no touching or taking possession of him until payment is settled *in full*."

My eyes strained to make out Jesse's form in the shadows of the railcar, and when my eyes adjusted to the lack of light, I shook with the effort to stay my murderous impulses. He was slumped on the ground, leaning against the bars to keep somewhat upright. The deep, bloody gashes on his back were exposed to the night air. His eyes were closed, and though I could just make out the gentle rise and fall of his chest, my heart still seized brutally with the fear that he wouldn't make it to Mickey's camp.

Will counted coins with the ringleader as Savannah looked on with wide eyes, but I couldn't sit there while they haggled over bits. Naturally, I ducked under the guard's arm and made it three steps closer to the railcar before he caught up.

"Hey! You heard th' boss! Get away from there!"

I whipped my head around and locked my furious eyes with his, never uttering a word. The silence stretched between us, but I never broke eye contact, and whatever he saw in the depths of my vicious soul made his eyes widen in reluctant fear. He swayed on his feet, unconsciously putting distance between us, his breath trembling through dry, parted lips.

"You aren't capable of keeping me from him," I hissed quietly. I felt the truth of those bandana-muffled words in my bones. There was no one strong enough to separate me from Jesse. Nothing but death itself could accomplish the task. The guard's breath caught in his throat, and he took a half-step backward as I finally released him from my stare to study the lock before me. Too impatient to pick it, I pulled a borrowed pistol from the back waistband of my shorts and shot through the lock until the door swung open easily.

There was shouting behind me, but I didn't hear anything except the sound of Jesse's breathing in the darkness as I climbed inside. Replacing the gun and sheathing my knives, I lowered slowly to my knees and crawled between his long legs until our chests nearly touched, careful not to press anywhere that looked wounded. Cupping his jaw in one palm and pulling down my mask with the other hand, I covered his mouth with mine swiftly in a desperate press of lips that stirred him from his wounded sleep.

His hands always woke before he did. His fingers twisted into my loose hair until they were tangled at the nape of my neck, pulling me closer and opening my mouth beneath his. His body quaked, and I wasn't sure if it was from the pain or disbelief. He kissed me languidly, eyes cracking open as he finally pulled back to gaze up at me in half-dazed wonder. I loved when he looked at me that way. As if I were the only thing that sustained him. He hadn't done that in a long time.

"Mornin', sunshine," I breathed against his lips. Sweet relief fell over me like a warm blanket. The sight of his open eyes soothed my jagged feelings, allowing me to soften in ways that I could only for Jesse.

"What are you doing here?" he asked, shaking off the moment as he remembered where he was. "Bon, you have to get out of here—"

I silenced him with another kiss, resting my forehead against his when he quieted again. "Is that any way to treat your rescuer?" I asked with a sly little grin that had him scoffing arrogantly.

"I said, we'd pay for it!" Savannah yelled harshly beyond the bars. Jesse turned to see Will, Savannah, and The Kid as they haggled with the ring-leader and his guards. His eyes grew cold and dark, his face hardening into rigid stone. I always thought the sharp lines of his features looked as if someone chiseled him from marble, but it was moments like this when he stilled and his muscles tensed that he resembled a living statue. I envied how easily he was able to look like nothing could penetrate him. No weapons, no words, no chaotic feelings. His fingers clenched in my hair, and he tipped my chin up as his cold, loveless eyes fell back to mine.

"Give me a weapon," he demanded quietly.

"You can't even hold yourself upright—"

"That doesn't matter," he protested sharply. "That man needs to die."

I followed the line of his sight to the man in the tattered top hat. The wide smile on his face looked more ominous than it had before. Jesse, while ruthless and brutal in his own way, still shied away from killing. My noble farm boy always needed to assure himself that those who died at his hands *deserved* it or there was no other choice. That he followed some sort of moral code, even when inflicting violence. It was why he gravitated to the fighting rings. Even though there were those who played fast and loose with the rules, they still had them.

So why, exactly, was he advocating for murder?

As if he could read the questions and curiosity in the knit of my brow, he pressed his forehead against mine, our noses brushing together, and said through gritted teeth, "He killed a woman and stole her child."

I stopped breathing.

"He was beating her and I couldn't—" He clenched his jaw tightly for a moment, grimacing in pain. "I took her place—"

"Of *course* you did," I chastised him with a roll of my eyes. "I tell you to keep your head down, and the first thing you do is make a spectacle of yours—"

"Yell at me later," he said, shifting and then grunting in anguish as his wounds pulled tight. "He killed her anyway, Bon, the mother. Dragged her child away. All I care about right now is making that motherfucker *pay.*"

The rocking of the wagon stopped abruptly enough that I slammed into the side, bruising my shoulder. My eyes were swollen and my throat a gravelly mess from sobbing nonstop for hours, screaming for my mother, begging for help that never came. Men's muffled voices filtered through the wood slats, and the high-pitched, tinny sound of spurs clanging resounded in the air. It sounded like the windchimes Mom and I hung off the back porch in our little hideaway house. The hinge of the wagon door screeched, and I blinked against the blast of afternoon light. Hard, dirty hands with jagged nails clenched around my arms and dragged me forward before tossing me none too gently to the dirt.

"You want us to take her dress off?" one of them asked, and I clenched my fingers in my skirt, holding my arms stiffly to my sides in an act of defiance. Blinking rapidly, I tried to force my eyes to adjust to the light faster so I could assess my surroundings, but it was no use. I had no idea how long I'd been riding in that dark wagon.

"She's half-starved." The comment came from a man standing near a horse. His voice was deep and calculated. It reminded me of the dark princes in the fairy stories my mother told me before bed. In those stories, the dark princes were usually the ones locking away princesses in towers or turning them into swans. The glare of the sun stung my eyes, and I couldn't make out the man's features.

"Let me take a look at her." When he walked closer, I struggled against the hard hands holding me still, the musical clang of his spurs barely discernible through my heartbeat thrumming in my ears.

He knelt, the brim of his hat blocking out the glare of the sun and allowing me to see him for the first time. His eyes were dark and cruel, but curious, and for some reason, his stoicism made me brave.

"Tell me, girl, do you want to stay with these men?"

I shook my head furiously, my hair falling loose and into my eyes. He gently brushed the strands away and gripped my chin between his thumb and forefinger, studying me so intently that it was hard to breathe beneath the scrutiny.

"Say something," he demanded, but I couldn't. Not even if I wanted to. My ravaged throat wouldn't let me. The man scoffed and dropped my chin, standing once more. "She's a mute? What do you expect me to do with her?"

"That's not for us to judge, mister. If you don't want her, then I'm sure we'll find another buyer in Lubbock at the market."

"Just the gun then," the stranger said, fishing in his pocket for coins. That was when I realized he was going to leave. I was going to go back into the wagon, back into the dark, and this time I might not come out again. Something feral swept through me, and I sank my teeth meatily into the hand holding my upper arm. I bit down until a burst of metallic blood filled my mouth. The man howled and dropped my arm swiftly. As fast as my little feet could run, I sprinted towards the man's horse, thinking that I could ride away from these bad men who hurt my mother.

"Not so fast," the stranger said, gripping the back of my dress and hauling me into the air by it, thrashing in his grip. He stared at me, wild-eyed with blood dripping down my chin, and a slow smile curled on his lips. "I think I'll take her after all, what do you say? I'll take her off your hands if you throw her in for . . . two more silver bits?"

I nodded, pulling the bandana up over my nose and mouth once more. Resignation flooded my veins. I knew what it was to be stolen from the arms of a dead mother. Even though doing as Jesse wanted would ruin our easy escape, I couldn't deny him. And the truth was, I didn't want to.

"Alright," I said, rocking back on my heels and rising slowly to my feet. His brows furrowed in confusion when I didn't hand him a blade or a gun. "I'll be your weapon."

"No, Bon—"

But his protestations were cut short as Will and Mickey crowded inside the railcar and began the torturous process of hauling him to his feet. I helped get him onto shaky legs, his whispered pleas making Will's eyes widen in disbelief as he drank in the apathy falling over my features and dulling my eyes.

We shuffled out of the train car, my friends beckoning me toward the exit just a few measly steps away. Jesse's fingers gripped my elbow, imploring me to leave this place with him. It would be *so easy* to walk away. To take Jesse and his weak, broken body back to the camp to recuperate. To talk. To heal in all the ways we so desperately needed right now. It would be easy.

But it wouldn't be *right.*

My vision was red, murder calcifying my bones into steel as I stared unblinking at the man in the tattered top hat while he slunk into a dilapidated building across the field from us. He pulled out a key and opened the shed, where I caught a glimpse of a sobbing child holding her tattered shirt together where it had been ripped nearly in half. She cowered in front of a man in dirty jeans with pockmarked skin and gold teeth. His belt buckle dangled open.

"*Bonnie*," Will warned near my ear. "Don't do it. There's too fucking many of them."

"I don't care."

"What're you talking about?" Savannah asked, glancing between us rapidly.

"No," Will said firmly, like he was trying to heel a hound.

Too bad I was a bitch with teeth and a thirst for blood.

I backed away from Will toward the shed door that the man with gold teeth was trying to close. With a shrug of my shoulder, I spun on my heel and marched forward with purpose, tossing a "Sorry!" that I didn't mean back in his direction.

"Goddamnit, Bonnie," Will swore, shoving Jesse toward Mickey before the thunk of his boots trailed behind me seconds later.

"Kid!" I called, jerking my head to the right. He flanked me easily, naturally, as if we'd practiced this a thousand times.

"Get them out of here, Mickey," Will growled over his shoulder as he fell into step with me, twitchy fingers on the triggers of his dual guns holstered at his hips.

"Get ready, Kid, and don't hesitate." He nodded once, knives flipped into his palms as the guards noticed our approach and leveled weapons at us with shouted threats that fell on my deaf ears.

"Now!" I shouted, and the boys broke away from me as chaos ensued. My gun fired as naturally as breathing as I marched forward with all the conviction I'd learned from Jesse.

"We won't let it happen to anyone else."

It was an impossible promise he'd made when he realized I was an escaped slave. A promise filled with the conviction I felt now as hot, crimson blood splashed across my face and soaked my bandana. More guards came and I rushed them, a tiny woman they thought they could overwhelm easily. My knife sank deep into the throat of one man as it flew from my fingertips, meaty hands gripping me and an arm at my throat. I laughed as I tilted my gun up and pressed it beneath my captor's chin, the blast of the gunshot making a ringing start in my left ear. I laughed harder. A little hysterically.

"Bonnie!" Will roared. My eyes met his as the man fell heavily to the ground, the top of his head blown wide open and brain matter coating the mud at my feet. He took a steadying breath and nodded at me. An unmarked guard tried to surprise Will from behind, but with a quick maneuver I could barely track, he spun the man around with a sudden jerk of his arms. The man's neck cracked before he fell dead to the swampy filth at our feet, now slick with blood and viscera.

My grin widened beneath my bandana.

Swinging around, I watched as The Kid crouched over a body, pulling knives from the fresh corpse. A branded guard this time raised his rifle from the roof of a building nearby, putting The Kid in his sights.

I was running before I could blink. "Kid!"

His head whipped up, and he rolled onto his back, pulling the body half atop him as the shot blasted into dead flesh. I'd crossed to him quickly, holstering my gun and using the momentum to jump high enough to reach the dark underside of an awning below the shooter. Swinging roughly until I could wrap my legs around the support and crawl into the shadows of the building. I melted into the darkness, and it felt like coming home.

How had I forgotten the ease of this?

Shimmying up the support, I clenched my teeth as my arms screamed at the exertion. My fingers gripped the ledge tightly enough that I lifted myself onto my belly and crawled onto the roof. The shooter was ahead of me, panting panicked little breaths with his gaze glued to the sight on his rifle. I palmed my knife as I approached on soft, silent feet.

Human flesh takes some effort to slice into; you have to press harder than you think to part skin. My shaking arms screamed as I sliced along his throat. The effort it took to sever his windpipe made them shake harder. But the adrenaline that coursed through my veins as he tumbled from the rooftop was like a hit from a once-familiar drug. Murder might be better than glowroot. I stood from my vantage point, watching The Kid roll from beneath the corpse and stand confidently, blood coating his clothes as he offered me a mischievous smile that should have scared me.

Instead, pride filled my chest.

Will stood, panting heavily as bodies surrounded him, and for a moment, there was a lull in the chaos. Dirty faces watched from behind rickety structures. The remaining guards fled. But we weren't done yet.

"All slaves to the stage!" I shouted ruthlessly. The night grew deadly silent. Then, shuffling sounded and I saw movement. Weeping, scared, haunted faces dragged their feet through the mud to listen to my command. I slid off the edge of the awning, and with a short whistle, The Kid and Will fell into line behind me as I continued my march toward the shed where the man in the top hat had stolen the child away.

"Kid, you get the children to safety. Will, the ringleader is *mine.*"

"Understood." His gruff reply steeled my tumultuous feelings. Staring at the closed door and taking a breath, I shoved my foot against the doorframe, rattling it on its rusted hinges, but it held. A shout came from inside, but before they could do anything, I kicked the flimsy door off its hinges and the boys rushed in, Will making quick work of the man with the gold teeth until he gasped his dying breath on the floor. The Kid dragged the children out while I strutted inside, snarling behind my bandana as I approached the cowering man in the top hat.

"Who are you? What do you want?" he questioned in a high-pitched voice. I laughed coldly, the knife glinting in my hand.

"I came for a show," I said quietly, gripping the back of his shirt and shoving him out of the shed onto clumsy feet, his hat tumbling to the mud below. "You can't entertain me from over here. Now, *walk*, motherfucker, or I'll blow your goddamn kneecaps off."

He scrambled to his feet, the absence of the top hat revealing thin hair with bald patches. Will marched forward, twisting the man's arm behind his back, shoving him toward the growing crowd near the dilapidated stage. They stared, eyes sunken into malnourished faces, fear of the unknown making them shrink away and part from our path as if violence were contagious.

Will dragged him up the steps, throwing him toward the post covered in dull red, caked with layers of old blood. Jesse's blood. Blood of the mother he tried to save. Children's blood. This stage was a spectacle of stolen innocence and broken dreams. One that this piece of shit turned into entertainment for the morally bankrupt.

"Lash him to the post."

I turned, taking in the fearful stares of the slaves below, huddling together like sheep in a herd with no one to lead or protect them. I knew what happened in places like this. How they stripped away your humanity. Made you choke on pain until it was all you knew. Until you were hungry for it.

"Today," I said, loudly enough to garner all their attention, "is your independence day." They were rapt. Barely breathing. Barely able to hope. "Freedom isn't something that anyone can take from you. Even though this piece of shit tried. I know what it is to be beaten. Burned. Starved. Made to feel less than human. I took my freedom back with my fuckin' teeth! And then I made fuckers like *him*—"

I pointed an accusatory finger at the sniveling man, watching him squirm and struggle against his bonds.

"Pay in *blood*!"

I approached him, knife in hand glinting in the moonlight. Will stepped back, his head held high and meeting my eyes with pride.

"Who are you?" the man asked again, loudly this time. His lips trembled.

"Did you hurt those children?" I asked in response. He whimpered, shaking his head. Because the answer, he knew, would condemn him.

"Did you *hurt them?!*" I ripped his shirt open and dragged my blade along his chest. Not too deep, but enough to make the blood well and drip down his chest. He wailed desperately.

"Please, *please*," he begged. His agony was sweet in my ears.

"You wanna know who I am?" I asked, not caring if any of them heard me. My world had narrowed to the man. His face replaced so many in my mind. The men with the hard, dirty hands who dragged me from under my bed and threw me into the back of the wagon. The crew members who taught me how to run a con with my child's body. The men I lured, pawing at my underdeveloped form. The men who'd stolen The Kid and tried to force themselves on me. All of them turned into this man.

"I'm your *worst fuckin' nightmare.*"

I scrabbled with his belt and pulled his pants down, my knife plunging into his pelvis, where his sickness had stolen the innocence of those meant to be protected. He sobbed and wailed as I sawed at his flesh, slick with blood until his favorite appendage fell in a wet slap to the wooden slats beneath my boots.

His body jerked involuntarily as he continued to bleed and bleed and bleed.

I didn't turn to the crowd; I watched him as, with every heartbeat, he approached death, until he went limp and the light left his eyes. Then, and only then, did I take a shaky breath of relief.

My pulse finally slowed, the world around me snapping into focus from whatever rage-fueled trance I'd been in. Never again would I sit idly by while men like that got rich on the shattered bodies and minds of the weak. Never. Fucking. Again.

Then I heard it.

Clapping.

Slow at first. Then faster. Louder. Screams of *"Nightmare! Night-mare! Nightmare!"* pounded at my back. Turning slowly, I looked at the people below, their eyes filled with tears of hope or lust for revenge. But what I didn't see was the hollowness of before. Instead, they looked alive. *Alive.*

My hands shook. I'd done this for Jesse. For the child in that shed. For myself. I wasn't noble like Jesse; I never knew when I'd done the right thing. But this felt right. It felt *big*. Like the girl under the bed, the girl in the wagon, had finally taken her life back.

"They're coming with us," I told Will, unable to peel my eyes away from them all.

"All of them?" he asked, a note of incredulity in his voice. He followed as I made my way down the stage. The crowd screamed louder as we descended into them. They didn't part as easily now, and it was too loud to speak, so we shouldered through until I found The Kid at the back of the crowd, surrounded by children of varying ages, the girl I'd seen clutching his finger tight in her little fist and using her other to hold her shirt together. She couldn't have been much older than I was when I was taken. Six, maybe?

I reached for her, swinging her into my arms to press her tattered shirt against my chest and cover her. She squeezed my neck and sobbed into my shoulder, wetting my loose hair with her tears. My heart cleaved in two as I held her trembling little body.

"Every last one."

CHAPTER NINETEEN

WILL

"**T**HAT'S THE LAST OF them," I said, ushering in two women who clung to each other as they disappeared into the darkness of the Riverwalk. The crew from Fort Hood had been surprised when we first showed up with a long line of broken, half-starved former slaves, many of them now parentless children. They rallied quickly once Mickey and I started shouting orders, working together seamlessly to get the slaves inside and settled into groups, providing clean clothes, food, and the warmth of their fires to the weary souls.

There were a few places during our trek I'd worried about discovery, or that the bedraggled group wouldn't be able to stay on their feet. Their resilience through it all as the night darkened bolstered something in me. It was the right decision, even if it was risky. I'd burned a few favors from Moira and the undesirables to get them all through the city unnoticed.

My gaze fell to Savannah as she handed out blankets and organized a line for food. I was glad I'd done it. That Bonnie hadn't allowed me the easy choice of walking away. It was what Savvy wanted, and I shouldn't have doubted it could be done. She smiled at a woman who broke down and hugged her, clutching the blanket in her hands to her chest like something precious.

"Will," Bonnie's voice sounded from behind me, and I dragged my eyes away from Savannah as I took in the sight of my best friend. Still covered in blood. "Jesse is ready for you."

192

I nodded, following her farther into the makeshift camp. We passed Gabriela, who was washing a little girl's bedraggled hair and trying to comb through the mats. Mickey waved us behind a sheet fashioned as a curtain where Jesse lay face down on a rickety table, his hair falling in haphazard strands around his face. They'd made a sort of medic station, complete with a few medical tools, makeshift bandages, and a bucket of clean water and soap.

Before I could step farther, Jesse roared with laughter, and Mickey's eyes lit with a grin. Clearly, Mickey had helped Jesse imbibe enough alcohol to numb him to the medical attention he needed.

Bonnie sighed as I stepped forward, seeing the glaze of drink making Jesse's eyes bright. "You started the party without me, *hermano*? I'm wounded," I said, clutching my chest as he swung around to face me, the hint of laughter still forcing his breath to be uneven.

"Mickey has done some *dumb shit*, let him tell you—"

He tried to sit up and then winced and fell back onto his belly with a groan.

"Hey, hey," I chastised softly, "I've got plenty of time to get let in on the joke, man. Let's see about getting you fixed up first." I crossed to the bucket and rolled my sleeves up, then washed my hands vigorously. Infection was the enemy, and one glance at the mess of his back made it clear he'd need stitches if I had any chance of getting them to heal properly.

"How ugly is it?" he asked as I started inspecting the wounds. Bonnie slipped out a moment later.

"You want the truth?" I asked, forcing my voice into a playful, sarcastic tone.

"Hit me with it," he slurred in response.

"Unfortunately, I think the scars from these gashes are going to make you even more handsome." I sighed heavily. "As if I needed the competition. I'm supposed to be the pretty one, remember?"

"I didn't know we were in a competition." He blinked lazily.

"Never mind. Just shut up and let me fix you," I muttered, wishing I could smoke as I cleaned and debrided the wounds. I tried to be gentle, really I did. At the sound of Jesse's shouts, Bonnie reappeared with Savannah at her side. Which, of course, didn't help steady my hands. Not when I wanted them all over Savvy in those tight-ass jeans. Absolute fucking torture.

"Stop being a baby!" I shouted at Jesse, who tried to jerk away for the fourth time while calling me every swear word in his limited vocabulary. "I'm almost done."

And he wasn't going to like this next part. At all.

"Hey, Savvy," I said, catching her attention. "You know how to sew, right?"

Wide-eyed and confused, she said, "Yeah?"

"Good. I need your help with this part. Scrub up and get over here," I said with a salacious grin.

"What's happening?" Jesse asked with a note of slow panic in his tone.

Confusion gave way to realization. Savvy furrowed her eyebrows at me. "No. No way. Fabric and flesh are way different."

"Not *that* different, actually. Besides, I'll be doing the actual sewing, I just need an extra set of hands. Now, get over here."

She sighed and rolled her eyes but moved to the bucket, where she washed her hands and arms before stepping closer to me. I busied myself with laying out the tools I'd need within easy reach, then passed the tray over to her side.

"Thread the needle for me," I asked, close to her ear where I could smell the warmth of her skin. She'd been flushed most of the night, but her discomfort had given way to practicality a long time ago. She threaded the needle with deft fingers. Much faster than I could have done.

Bonnie crouched onto her knees, gripping Jesse's hand in hers and speaking softly to keep him distracted as we got things set up. I didn't have forceps to manipulate Jesse's skin where the stitches were needed, so I would have to pinch the flesh together. Picking up the needle holder, I took the hooked needle from Savannah and brought it down on Jesse's skin. He howled and jerked beneath me. She grimaced, turning away.

"Stay focused, Savvy," I told her, and she stared at me. "Watch how I do it. It's all in the wrist. Getting through one layer here, then the next, tie it off, then cut it." I put down the needle and held my hand out for the scissors, which she handed over quickly.

"You could have done this without my help," she mumbled beneath her breath as I started another stitch. I nodded.

"Yes, I could," I agreed. "But it's basic first aid, and a good skill to learn. You never know when you might need it. Especially once we leave the city."

"Could you get on with it?" Jesse asked, clearly irritated.

"Yeah, stop flirting over Jesse's bloody wounds, would ya?" Bonnie snapped.

"Ungrateful pricks," I mumbled, which made Savvy smile. I considered that a win. After another four stitches and some bandages, I cleaned Jesse's blood off just as Mickey stepped back into the room.

"Alright," he said, making eye contact with each of us. "When are we leaving?"

Jesse had managed to sit up, Bonnie helping him get his arms through a shirt, when he said, "Why don't we just go now?"

Bonnie went still.

"I mean, we're all here, outside of Lee's manor and influence. We could pack up and leave tonight. I can still ride."

I rolled my eyes. No, he definitely couldn't.

"We don't have the ledger," Bonnie said quietly.

"I know the ledger's important to you, Bon, but—"

"Important to *me*? It's important to *us*. All of us. I thought you agreed that we needed leverage so we aren't hunted down by Lee the moment we leave?"

"I do, but is it really worth you going back into that house?" His words were clipped.

My feet felt glued to the floor as Savannah and I watched the two of them square off. No easy escape unfortunately, since they were by the exit. *Great.* I wrapped my arm around Savvy's waist and tucked her into my side to ease the tension of the moment.

"I might have already *had* the damn ledger if you hadn't decided to beat Rutherford and get thrown into a slave camp. And yes, I think making sure that we have some kind of plan to keep us safe is worth me going back into that house."

Jesse grimaced and ran a weary hand across his face. "Fine."

Mickey shifted toward them, a calming force in the storm written across Bonnie's face. "How long do you need?"

"One day. Two tops. Any longer than that and I become Mrs. Rutherford. The rehearsal dinner is in two days. If we can't get to it by then, I'll call it and we can get the hell outta town."

"I—" Savannah started, but as everyone's attention shifted to her, she snapped her mouth closed. My arm tightened around her involuntarily, and with a soft nudge forward, she took a deep breath and tipped her chin up. *That's my girl.* "I can't leave without telling Etty goodbye. I may be ready to leave, but it's the only home I've known."

I felt like I couldn't breathe. Pride welled within me and expanded in my chest, making it feel hard to do much of anything except twist my lips into a bright grin that said everything I felt.

"It's settled," I said before anyone else could interject. "I'll take the girls back and we'll get in touch soon. Jess, rest your wounds as much as possible until it's time to leave or you *won't* be riding a damn horse." I leveled him with a serious glare that made him sigh. I waved Bonnie forward with an inpatient hand, reluctantly letting my arm loosen from around Savvy's waist.

"C'mon," I urged them. "It's getting late."

We shuffled through the camp, a few people stopping Bonnie or Jesse to offer weary thanks or shake a hand. The Kid noticed us moving toward the exit and peeled himself away from a group of kids before falling in line with us. Once we were outside and mounting horses, we filled The Kid in on the plan, and he wordlessly mounted his own horse. I swung up behind Savvy, happy to have her denim-clad ass nestled tight against me. She relaxed into my touch, letting herself lean against my chest. The smell of her warm skin filled my lungs with every inhale.

Savvy made a sound of discontent low in her throat, and I peered down to find her watching Bonnie and Jesse. When I looked up at them, I understood immediately. They stood in front of each other awkwardly, neither of them smiling, and even though Bonnie was finally reunited with her old steed, Eagle, she hadn't paid the gray, speckled mare any attention. She held her reins loosely in her hand as she struggled with what to say.

Savannah elbowed me and hissed at me to "stop staring," but there was little chance of that. It was like watching a horrific accident and being unable to tear your eyes away. Bonnie shuffled forward on unsteady feet, lifting on her toes to offer him a quick, closed-mouth kiss that he tried to prolong for a few extra seconds before she retreated. He didn't drop his hand from her jaw, however, and muttered something soft that I couldn't hear. Before I knew it, she swung her leg onto Eagle's back and clicked her tongue as she led us toward the city. I dug my heels into my stallion's sides only to glimpse a tight, stony expression on Jesse's face as he watched Bonnie disappear.

My thoughts raced as we made our way silently into the dark city streets. The rhythmic clomping of hooves on the cobblestones made my mind wander to days when I'd felt much like Jesse looked tonight: hopeless.

My face hurt. My heart hurt. Bonnie woke up today and asked me who I was. Because she didn't remember. For the millionth time I questioned if I was doing the right thing. But for tonight, I needed to be outside this city. I passed signs for Slidell on one of the ponies I stole from Lee's manor, until I was in thick, overgrown bush. It wasn't swampy here, but the grass was nearly as tall as I was and the cicadas sang a soft lullaby that soothed the ragged edges of my fractured mind.

I didn't know how long I'd stayed there, in the darkness, looking up at the stars in my saddle. Only that the cold temperature was harsher than in the desert, and the wet cold sliced through my layers of clothing.

A scream pierced the night, inhuman and bone-rattling. I should've been afraid. Should've run. Instead, whatever masochistic insanity had grown wild within me made me dismount and tie the pony off to investigate.

The inhuman shriek sounded again, high-pitched and keening, like the cry of a hawk but much, much larger. It was louder this time, which meant I was getting closer, tromping through the high grass in my boots to let any animals know I was approaching.

The moon was full and bright, the only light for miles, and it bleached the land of color until everything looked like shadows and bones. The crater beast had pinned down a herd of wild horses, snapping a curved beak to corral them between a thicket of thorns and a ravine so they couldn't escape. Leathery wings expanded wide, flapping once, twice in their direction. Cat-like paws the size of my head with long talons scored the soft earth beneath its feet.

Fuck.

What was I doing here? That thing could rip through me as easily as breathing.

Then I saw him, whinnying and stomping at the front of the herd, his coat a gleaming black like he was made of the darkness surrounding him. He reared on his hind legs, kicking toward the beast, knocking its snapping beak away from the others. Another shriek lit up the night, his paws flashing, and I watched as the stallion sacrificed himself, lunging forward, teeth bared and ears flattened so that the others could gallop away.

And they had. First one at a time, then all at once.

Until he was all alone.

In that moment, crouching in the brush, I knew I couldn't let him die.

I smiled, reaching across Savvy to pat his muscled neck. No one really understood why I hadn't named him yet. The truth was, he didn't belong to me. We were the same, he and I, both damned to be alone forever. I saved him once, a long time ago, and he'd saved me many times since. Bound together by darkness and blood.

I didn't own him. I *befriended* him.

Maybe, learning all his quirks and personality over time was why I noticed it: an almost imperceptible hitch in his confident steps beneath us. A slight flaring of his nostrils, a twitch of his left ear. My heart crawled up my throat, every muscle tightening as I clenched my arms protectively around Savannah. She was nearly asleep, if her deep, steady breaths were any indication.

It's just a fuckin' horse.

I was reading too much into this. Bonnie and Jesse were at odds, we were headed back to Lee's manor, and things just felt unsettled. Especially between Savannah and me. If tonight taught me anything, watching Bonnie and Jesse become near-strangers, I was done waiting. I didn't want any more distance between us. I didn't want another three years to pass until she finally admitted that she wanted me just as much as I wanted her.

His ears twitched again, and then he tossed his head, hooves prancing in place. *What do you hear, boy?* I wanted to ask. Wanted to explore whatever was making him nervous. But I didn't want to alarm the others.

"Will?"

I snapped my head up, locking eyes with Bonnie. She read the thin thread of panic in my eyes so easily it should have embarrassed me.

"What?"

". . . How close are we?"

She knew. She could read the growing fear in my body, could see my fraying control. Bonnie had always been too cunning by half. Like a fox. A fox from hell.

"Oh, *uh*..." I scratched my eyebrow with my thumbnail as I found a street sign that was familiar. "About a mile out," I said, watching as she barely tipped her head in The Kid's direction.

Brilliant.

I nudged Savannah until I was sure she was awake and slowed my stallion to a stop.

"I'm gonna let you three go on from here. The Kid knows the way."

Savannah opened her mouth to protest, but I offered her a strained grin that made her eyebrows furrow deep on her forehead.

"I need you to ride with Bonnie, *mi sol.*"

"But—"

"*Please*," I whispered against the shell of her ear, inhaling the sweet smell of her deep into my lungs. I needed her out of here. Needed her safe from whatever was stalking through the night. Savannah twisted in the saddle, staring into my eyes for a long moment before nodding quietly. I wanted to kiss her. Wanted to steal a moment of intimacy before the night swallowed me whole. Only there wasn't any time before she slid down to make her way onto Eagle's back behind Bonnie, who held my gaze for a long moment before turning in the direction of the manor.

"I'll be breaking into your bedroom soon," I called after Savvy with a forced, lighthearted grin. She scowled and flipped me off as I tugged the reins sharply to the left, offering a good-natured chuckle and a wave as I left them.

Moments later, my smile fell from my face, and I strained my ears trying to pick up any sound out of the ordinary. There was something wrong, some foulness polluting the air. I couldn't explain it. Perhaps it was because this city was mine, and once you've become the thing that haunts the shadows, you know when other monsters are near.

What I knew was that the farther I rode away from Savvy and the others, the more subtle signs I picked up that I wasn't alone. Shadows darted on the edge of my vision, sounds that were displaced, too soft or too subtle to usually be noticed over the echoing clop of my stallion's hooves against the cobblestone streets.

I rode on, even as the shadows converged around me, luring them as far from Savannah as I possibly could, seeking an opportunity, any really, to bottleneck them in somewhere. It was the only way I'd stand a chance being outnumbered.

There was a reason Bonnie came up with the plans.

Before I could put my half-assed idea into action, a rope whisked through the air, the lasso circling me expertly, holding my arms at my sides. With a hard yank, I was pulled bodily from the back of my mount. I landed hard on my back, the air whooshing from my lungs as I struggled to gasp it back in.

Those hints of shadows solidified in front of me, and the faces of ten men, most of whom I recognized, appeared above me. I struggled against the rope, managing to loosen it from around my arms enough to throw it off.

A sharp whinny pierced the night, furious stomping against the stone a testament to exactly how much they'd pissed off my horse.

"Boys," I greeted, wiping the back of my hand beneath my lip.

"You've really done it now, Ellis," said a man to my right. I was pretty sure his name was Rocky and that I'd fucked his wife a few times before I left the Hanged Men.

Plastering an easy smile on my lips, I opened my arms wide. "C'mon, I'm just taking a leisurely ride through the city. How's the little woman? Missing me, I bet." His fist cracked against my jaw heavily, and I tasted blood in my mouth. I grinned up at him through the pain, sure that my teeth were tinged red.

Spurs clanged against the ground, the ring setting my teeth on edge. *Well, fuck, looks like this just became a family reunion.*

My fingers twitched toward the handle of my gun. It didn't matter that I was outmanned, outgunned, I'd go down in a blaze of glory if it meant keeping that son of a bitch away from the people I cared about.

Savannah.

Her pretty face came to mind, smiling at me, brows furrowed in consternation, rolling her eyes at my latest antics.

You don't get to die on me, William Ellis.

Uncertainty shivered through my limbs as I realized I might not have a choice in the matter. I might not live long enough to keep my hasty promise to her.

The men parted, and my father stepped forward, not bothering to threaten or intimidate me. After all, he'd laid the foundation of fear my entire life. He knew he didn't have to do *anything* for me to understand the danger I was in right now.

Could I get to my gun in time? Was I a faster shot than him?

"Look'ee here, seems like we've caught us a little *beastie*," he said, chuckling cruelly. The others joined in, though there was no enthusiasm in it. No real mirth in the depths of Sixgun's black eyes either. I'd often wondered if he felt human emotion at all. Or, if by some stroke of bad fortune, he'd been born like a reptile inside. Hollowed out and cold-blooded.

"Dad," I greeted, widening my stance instinctively. Every nerve ending in my body alight. Ready to react, ready to help me survive this encounter. "Some things never change, I see. Still need a few sycophants to surround you at all times."

He snapped his fingers, and hands came down on me. My hat fell to the ground, and they stripped me of my gun. Someone slipped the lasso around me and tightened it with a yank. My father approached until he was inches from my face, sneering down at me.

"Look at him now, the *big bad Beast of the Bridge*! You think because you've made this little name for yourself that you've somehow earned the right to talk back to me, boy?"

No. No, I didn't actually. In fact, it was terrifying to face him with little more than a sarcastic quip on my tongue.

I was a child again, fingers gripping the arms of the wooden chair he made me sit in while he split my mother's skin beneath his blade, screaming inside the whole time. Desperate pleading locked inside my head because even then I *knew* it would do no good to ask for mercy. He didn't know what mercy was.

Instead of answering his question, I smirked at him. Falling back into old habits of false bravado to shield me from his wrath. I shifted my weight, testing how tightly they'd wrapped the rope around my arms. Loose enough for me to get a blade through pretty easily. My fingers twitched, and I rolled my wrist, loosening the hidden knife in my sleeve. Failsafes on failsafes. It was how I'd stayed alive this far.

My father wasn't quite as tall as I was, so he paced before me, dark eyes cold and calculating. His gaze tracked over my skin, my smirk, as if contemplating exactly how to tear me apart. The effect had my knees quaking beneath me, though I did my damnedest not to show it.

I had a feeling he knew how nervous I was anyway.

"What brings you to town?" I asked conversationally, as if this were a pleasant visit and not a fucking ambush. "I hear that you've brought some friends with you this time. Planning a party?"

My knife fell into my palm, and I kept it taut against my flesh with the pad of my thumb. I'd need a better distraction before I could use it.

"Afraid to have a real beast in the city?" he asked, startling me. "These people here seem to think you're someone to be afraid of. Dark legends making their way out of the city. If only they knew what a pathetic coward you really are. If only they could see you *now*."

His fixations were usually gruesome and bloody, and he'd always hated me. My entire life had always hung on how useful I could be as a bargaining chip. A tool he'd used against my mother to keep her compliant. By the time she ended her own life, Jones had taken a liking to me as a means to control Bonnie. And an annoyance to pit against my father.

A ruse that worked too well over the years, making me a thorn in his side that he wanted ground into dust beneath his spurred boots.

When my father left to burn Jesse's hometown to the ground, Jones used that opportunity to officially induct me into The Hanged Men. Freshly tattooed and given a gun and horse, my father had been *furious* when he returned. It'd shattered even the illusion of sanity, and that was when he slipped up. When I heard him talk about needing to go after Bonnie.

That was when I knew that no matter what happened between us, I had to get to Bonnie before him. Even if it meant betraying my new crew and putting a target the size of Texas on my back.

Now, it occurred to me that maybe his unnatural hatred of me *was* his only weakness. It was emotion, something he rarely, if ever, expressed. His fixation on my moniker and the bloody rumors that followed me around made me wonder if perhaps, like my humor, his hatred was masking some kind of vulnerability.

It hit me like a freight train.

Laughter bubbled between my lips, and his answering scowl confirmed my suspicions.

"You're afraid of me," I said, letting my smile curl viciously back from my teeth.

His cruel, dark eyes flashed, and he clamped his hand around my throat. Charging forward, he cracked the back of my head against a brick wall and squeezed harder. Like if he could steal my breath, crush my throat, it would make it less true.

My arms were still bound by the rope. I couldn't lift them high enough to break his hold. I coughed, spittle flying through the inches between us to spray his face with a mixture of blood and saliva. He only squeezed harder.

"Afraid?" he asked, slamming my head against the wall once more. "Of what? A whoreson like you? You only *exist* because I allow it. The moment you stop being useful, I'll leave your corpse to be picked clean by carrion birds. You'll be *forgotten*. Nothing."

My vision narrowed, and the pressure in my head and ears built to a fever pitch. With the last few breaths in my lungs, I choked out, "But... th-the Beast won't be."

He snarled, dropping me heavily and turning to his men. God, it was *laughable*. My reputation as a murderer, *that* was what ruffled his feathers. A reputation I despised.

I barked out a dark, bitter laugh. One that turned hysterical as I struggled to straighten my spine and stand tall in the face of him once more.

"No one will forget me, old man, because my legacy already out-weighs yours. That's what you're afraid of, isn't it?"

As our eyes met, I saw my death inside the black depths of his soulless irises. My bones felt like they'd turned brittle inside my body, ready to shatter. Because for the first time in my life, he looked truly afraid. The truth pierced through the inhuman armor he wore so well. Until all that was left was the cowardly, mortal bastard that lay within.

"Insignificance."

I thought of the women he'd hurt over the years. Carving gruesome scars into their flesh, knotted and raised, as a reminder that he'd been there. That he'd inflicted the pain. A way to preserve a part of him long after he'd gone. A walking sign that even after he was interred deep in the earth, the echoes of his misdeeds would never be forgotten. Or him, by association. Was that why he did it? Had I *finally* reached the frail humanity inside him?

I *knew* monsters. I fed them. I made them.

My father was no monster.

Just a man, afraid to be forgotten.

"Make it hurt, boys," he said with a whistle. I was grabbed roughly and thrown to the ground, my arms still bound. Fists and boots rained down, blackening my vision, and without the ability to fend off the strikes, they targeted my weakest parts. I twisted and jerked, trying to protect my abdomen and ribs, but it was no use. The bite of steel-toed boots had me grunting and crying out in pain. It throbbed and blasted through my skin, and I cataloged each one in my mind. It was all I could do, so I tried to think of each internal organ that could be vulnerable. The placement of them within my body. How to minimize the damage in those areas. Kidney. Liver. Spleen. Abdominal Aorta. Ribs. I had to make sure that the strikes weren't localized to one area, that the impact would be spread along the surface of my body to absorb the shock and hopefully keep me from bleeding to death internally.

I twisted and jerked as they laughed and spat on me, until my muscles trembled and my brain felt like it'd been shaken loose in my skull. I didn't know how much more of this I could take. Hadn't this been what I'd wanted not too long ago?

I caught a glimpse of the moon from my periphery, staring down at me in silent witness. I'd wanted to die in that graveyard, hadn't I?

But suddenly, Savannah was there, like she always was, a perfect image in my mind anchoring me to this world that hated me so much. I *didn't* want to die. I wanted to taste the sweetness of her skin and find new ways to irritate her. I wanted to know what it felt like to be worthy of her.

I had too much left to do to give up now.

El dolor es fugaz.

I endured it all, tears leaking down my face, teeth bared and clenched as whimpers of pain erupted between them. Even as the ferocity of the blows slowed with their exertion, I endured.

"Get him up," my father barked. The words barely registered in my mind. My grip on the knife was a white-hot brand of hope against my palm. My vision wobbled, head spinning as they hefted me unceremoniously onto unsteady legs. But as they shoved me into an upright position, I flicked the blade open with the pad of my thumb, and as they jostled me, I got the razor-thin edge against the rough jute binding my arms at my side.

One chance.

I only had one chance to get this right.

My father approached, a snarl on his mouth that looked devilishly mirthful at the state I was in. Triumphant in his victory over me. He didn't care that it took nine men beating me with my arms tied to gain it. As he got close enough for me to feel his fetid breath on my skin, I jerked my blade with every bit of strength I had left inside me, the rope falling away as I wrenched out of the grips holding me.

The blade arced between us, catching the scant light, and as I swung it I thought: *finally, it'll end.*

But my body was too weak and the swing went too wide. He caught my wrist in his meaty palm and slammed it against the bricks of the alley wall. Once. Twice. Three times. Until my grip weakened and the knife clattered to the ground. He pressed his forearm against my throat, anchoring me in place, and with a *shick*, he unsheathed his own knife. One I knew all too well. A large silver bowie knife that'd starred in my nightmares over the years.

"If you want a knife fight, *boy*, I'll give you one. After all, I don't like to leave my work *unfinished*," he growled between his teeth as I wriggled weakly.

No. No, not that.

Terror paralyzed me as he pressed the blade against my temple. Sweat rolled down my forehead as I raked in shaky breaths. He was going to do it. His intent bore down on me from the hateful darkness in his eyes. He was going to finish cutting my face off.

The knife was so sharp that at first, you don't realize it's cutting you. It felt like a pinch, a paper cut, then the deep throbbing of pain as flesh split and panic thrashed in the pit of your stomach. I remembered it like it was yesterday.

"No matter what you do to me, I'll always have something you don't," I said, through thin breaths. Barely above a whisper. He chuckled malevolently.

"Oh yeah? And what's that?" he asked, his voice filled with confidence that assured me if I didn't do *something*, I would die tonight.

"A damn fine horse," I stated, whistling shrilly and jerking my face away from the blade, forcing a long cut before the pounding crush of hooves and men's screams filled my ears. My stallion stampeded, slamming his hooves in the ground and threatening to trample the men between us. One tried to catch his reins and was sent flying as he rose on his hindquarters, kicking out and catching another in the jaw. He tossed his head, ears flattened, and shrieked into the night, charging toward us with a hellish intent in his eyes. My father ducked out of the way just in time, and I reached for the saddle, arms flailing as I caught the saddlehorn and held on for dear life as he raced us out of the alley.

"You're getting so many fuckin' sugar cubes," I said as he dragged me along, my legs barely holding me upright. After enough time, he paused and, with painstaking slowness, I threw myself onto his back. I tried to sit upright and grab the reins, but my head spun and I slumped over him.

"Take us home, boy," I said, tangling my fingers in the inky strands of his mane, letting my broken body rest as the darkness of the night caressed me like a lover, praying silently that we made it in time so I could keep my promise to Savannah.

CHAPTER TWENTY

SAVANNAH

THE CLOCK TOWER AT St. Louis Cathedral chimed two in the morning. I paced in front of my window, gaze steady on Lee Square below each time I passed the window. I'd cleaned up from our visit to the Slavers' Parade and dressed in one of my usual nightgowns, though I felt anything but normal.

Where was he?

Will should have been back hours ago. When he'd ordered us to return to the manor without him, I'd wanted to argue, but I knew better. He'd explain. Later.

Only, it was later and he hadn't shown up yet. I gritted my teeth, wheeled away from the window, and headed for the door.

Patrols were fewer now than when the house was locked down, but the eerie silence still unsettled my nerves. With wide eyes and a slow gait, I navigated the corridor to the back stairs.

I'd check the stables first. Then I'd . . . figure something out.

A shadow crossed my vision as I stepped into the courtyard. Moonlight slanted across a guard's face, highlighting his malicious smile. I froze as he tucked his rifle over his shoulder, the cross tattoo stark against his skin.

"Well, what have we here?" Jimmy asked.

"I don't have time for this," I said, giving him a wide berth as I tried to move around him.

"Right. Because you and the *Beast*," he said. Something in his tone rocked me. I stopped, turning to face him.

"What business is it of yours?"

Jimmy sauntered toward me, his eyes roving over my features, trailing along my neck and down my figure. I'd washed the dark makeup soon after returning to the house and changed back into my own clothes. His smile grew as he met my gaze once more. "Why hide it? We all know you two are fucking."

My jaw clenched at his words. "I'm not hiding anything."

"What's it like to fuck a monster?"

"That's enough," a booming female voice said.

Etty crossed the courtyard, anger in her eyes as she glared at him.

"Aw, c'mon, Etty." He shrugged nonchalantly. "I wasn't doing anything."

Etty's brows lifted. "Get back to work."

Jimmy looked me up and down once more, then stalked into the shadows.

"Why are you up so late?" she asked as she headed toward the kitchen. I followed close, not wanting to give Jimmy another chance to mess with me.

Once we shoved into the kitchen alone, I said, "I'm looking for Will."

Etty let out a heavy sigh. "Why?"

My throat bobbed as I wrung my hands together. "He's . . . " I bit my bottom lip. I didn't know if I could trust Etty. I squared my shoulders and loosed a long breath "He's late. I'm worried."

"You haven't asked me to make tea for you." She crossed her arms over her chest.

I rolled my eyes. "I tell you Will is missing and you're worried about *tea?*" I shook my head and turned toward the exit, intent on getting to the stables.

"Savannah, wait."

We hadn't spoken since our blowout in the kitchen, where she'd admitted she was part of some resistance, where she'd told Will that he'd never be good enough for me. I paused, glancing over my shoulder.

"I'm sorry," she said in a low voice. "I know that you care for him." I could see her struggle. She didn't want to approve of my choices, but she knew that her approval didn't matter. I forced my features to relax.

"I haven't asked you to make tea because there's been no need." That was all I'd say. "Now, have you seen Will?"

Etty shook her head. "Not since all of that business with Mr. Lee this morning."

"Something's wrong," I said. The concern etched on his face when he'd left us passed through my mind. "I have to find him." I turned from the kitchen, Etty hot on my heels.

"Take a guard with you," she said.

"Like I trust any of the guards." We moved briskly through the corridors, until the scent of hay and dirt filled the air. I stalked past the sleeping horses to the last stall which was . . . empty. My heart pounded painfully.

He should have been back by now.

The groom sat on a stool near the open doors, his hat covering his eyes. I stalked over and kicked the stool out from under him. He swore as he scrambled to his feet.

"Where's Will?"

The boy's eyes flickered to the empty stall. "He hasn't returned since earlier in the evening."

Dread filled my belly. "I need you to go out and find him."

The groom's brows lifted, and he shook his head. "Can't abandon my post, miss."

I gripped the front of his shirt, yanking him toward me. "I don't give a shit about your post—"

"Savannah—" Etty said.

"Look, miss—"

I glared at the young man and released my grip. He stumbled back, staring at me with wide-eyed shock.

I stalked into the nearest occupied stall and reached for the saddle tacked up on the wall. The horse chuffed at me and shied backward at my sudden movements.

Then I heard it: clacking on stone.

I sprinted into the alleyway. The moonlight cast an ominous glow across the cobblestones. Etty called after me, but I ignored her. A shadow moved through the darkness. The black-as-night stallion's hooves echoed in the silence, a figure hunched over in the saddle.

"*Will!*" I lurched forward. "Etty, help!"

The horse slowed as I approached. He pressed his muzzle against my palm as I reached for the reins. The movement elicited a groan from Will. I moved toward him, easing the horse to a halt.

"What happened?" I asked.

"Family reunion," he grunted.

Will tried to lift his head but instead hissed out a breath. This was *not* good. I touched his hand, my heart aching at the sight of blood on his skin.

"Come on, let's get you down."

Footsteps echoed in the alleyway as Etty approached. I murmured an apology as I reached for him and wrapped my arms around his waist. He bit back a cry, even though I felt his muscles constricting as if he were trying to help me.

"Ellis, what happened to you?" Etty asked by my side. She braced Will, taking on most of his weight until his feet hit the ground. His knees quaked, head still hanging.

"My father—" He cut himself off with a grunt. "The Hanged Men are in the city. They're getting closer."

Etty's face turned to stone, shutting down and turning steely, and her eyes glinted in moonlight.

"Etty, can you let them know at the Riverwalk camp? They need to be ready to move. We freed slaves tonight. They'll need help getting them away from the city. Your resistance can help with that, right?"

Etty's eyes widened and flashed between us. Something I had never seen before softened between Etty and Will then, through his pain-filled eyes lined with agony. She nodded slowly, the motion filled with something I never thought I'd see.

Begrudging respect.

Without another word, she marched off purposefully. I wrapped an arm gingerly around Will's waist, not missing the way he cringed at my touch. Ribs. Blood trailed from his lip. Bruises mottled his face and his scar—

My eyes fluttered shut, and I inhaled deeply. Now wasn't the time to lose my cool. Will needed me. But his father must have attempted to finish cutting his face off, because blood lined the side of his jaw, from the edge of his scar to his cheekbone.

"Savvy—" The pain in his voice made me nod.

"I've got you, okay?" I whispered. The groom stood at the door to the stables, watching with wide eyes. "Take care of his horse."

As we walked past, the boy said, "He'll bite me."

"I don't care if he kicks you. Take care of the goddamn horse."

Will let out a breath that sounded oddly like a chuckle. I never realized how heavy he was. We slunk through the hallways. Any sudden movement jostled him to the point of pain. He leaned heavily on the banister as I helped him up the stairs.

"Almost there," I said.

My back and shoulder muscles burned by the time I shoved open my door. I helped him settle on the edge of my mattress, but my work was only just beginning. He shook his head, straining as he tried to stand.

"Stop it." I placed gentle hands on his shoulders. "Sit down. I can't tend to you if I don't know where you hurt."

"Everywhere," he said, lines deepening around his eyes.

"Then lie down on the bed, William." Normally, I would have shoved him backward, but without knowing exactly where he was hurt, I didn't want to risk further injury. He met my gaze, something in his eyes showing that he wanted to fight me. I glared at him. "Let me take care of you."

His mouth opened, an argument poised on the tip of his tongue.

Instead, I pressed my lips to his. Even though he took in a sharp breath, some of the tension went out of his shoulders. He lifted a shaky hand, touching my cheek with blood-crusted fingertips. I cradled his hand gently and pulled back an inch.

"Let me take care of you," I reiterated, imploring him with my eyes. Something lit up in his, reminiscent of our bantering. "I'll kiss you as long as you do what I say."

Will's lips tilted into a small smirk that flashed into a grimace. "That is . . . a really effective way to shut me up." He let out a breathy chuckle. I couldn't help but smile in return and roll my eyes. He exhaled loudly, the tension between us breaking as he dropped his hand to his lap. "I don't . . . "

Vulnerability filled his eyes as he brought his gaze to mine. Through the bloodstains and the bruising, there he was. William. My . . . lover? Friend?

"I've never really done that before," he managed.

"What? Let someone take care of you?"

In response, he nodded solemnly. With the tip of my finger, I turned his head up toward mine.

"Me either," I said. I brushed my mouth across his again. "So let's learn how by taking care of each other." He ducked his head in response.

I searched his face, noting the split lip, the cut near his temple, and multiple bruises. When my gaze lowered, all I could see was his bloodstained shirt. I reached for the top button. Will flinched. I flashed my eyes up at him just long enough to provide reassurance. I would do my best to keep him from further pain.

Focusing on the task at hand, I made note of the blood staining his throat in finger-like shapes. I clenched my jaw at the thought of that man. His father. Sixgun. I never knew my father, but I couldn't imagine wanting to take a life you'd brought into the world. My fingers worked through his buttons.

As I bared Will's chest, my mouth opened in horror at the bruises mottling his skin and side. Someone with steel toe boots had gone to town on him. I tempered my features. The last thing he needed was for me to lose my cool. I slid my fingers beneath his collar, gaze flickering up to his. He cringed but lifted his arms enough for me to slip the fabric from his shoulders.

It was even worse without his clothes. I bit my bottom lip to stop its trembling.

"Bandages, ointment, alcohol," I murmured to myself as I surveyed his wounds.

"No alcohol."

I'd heard his promise to Mickey in the stable. Still, I asked, "Are you sure?"

Will nodded. I blew out a breath. Some part of me was relieved to see him sticking to his word, not that I doubted he would. I cleared my throat, my gaze scouring his bloody jeans, the boots on his feet. The idea of having him naked in my bed had passed through my mind more than a few times. I just never expected it to be because he'd been beaten bloody by a psychopath.

Well, I supposed we had to get this over with eventually.

I lowered myself toward the floor, a hand on one of his knees to steady myself as I started on the laces of his boot.

"Savvy, you don't—" There was pain in his voice, but I ignored him, working as quickly as my hands would go. I finished with the laces of the first and moved to the second, fingers fumbling and sloppy. "*Savannah.*"

I froze and looked up at him. I couldn't remember the last time he'd used my full name. Dark desire shrouded his expression and filled his eyes. My tongue darted out to wet my bottom lip. This was *not* the time. Though, judging by the bulge at the front of his jeans, I surmised no amount of pain could stop Will.

"Get up." His words were strained and laced with dark promise.

I bit my bottom lip, unable to hide my amusement. It was absolutely inappropriate. But triumph filled my chest as I returned to my work and tugged his other boot off. I didn't immediately rise. Instead, I settled on my knees and stared up at him through my eyelashes.

"If you don't get up right now, I'm going to fuck your sweet little mouth until you can't breathe."

A thrill ran down my spine. "You know, William, you shouldn't make threats that you can't deliver on."

His mouth tilted up, his eyes lighting as if accepting my challenge.

I knew about lust and the physicalities of it. I hadn't experienced it before him. I'd read thousands of stories, seen it growing up in a brothel. But I'd never truly understood just how empowered it made me feel affecting a man like this.

A man like *him*.

Someone strong and passionate and endlessly kind. Someone who saw the darkest of humanity. Someone who'd had plenty of partners in their life. Someone I could have never imagined would look at me like *that*.

Because I don't have limits when it comes to protecting what is mine.

Will would never intentionally hurt me, but I didn't know where he stood. Did he want just my body? Or did he want my heart? I desperately wanted to believe it was the latter. I wanted to wake up next to him in the mornings and fall asleep beside him at night. I wanted him to look at me like he had in the kitchen, like I was the *only* person in the world that mattered.

What kind of fool did that make me?

I forced myself to my feet and headed to the bathroom to gather supplies. My arousal faded through the routine of it, the plans in my head on how I'd address his wounds. Towels and water to clean them. Ointment to treat any open cuts. Bandages. God, I hoped he wouldn't need stitches. I didn't think I could copy the motions of his wrists from earlier at the camp.

By the time I returned, Will seemed more relaxed. His back straightened at the sight of me.

After setting the bowl of water on my nightstand, I deposited the rest of the supplies beside it and turned to him, once more surveying the damage.

"How did this happen?" I asked, placing my hands on my hips. I didn't even know where to start.

Will cringed as he lifted a hand to rub the back of his neck. "My dad was following us when we left the camp, so I led him across town." Dread settled low in my belly. Sixgun had been there. I dipped a towel in the bowl and took my time to wring the water from it. I turned to him, lifting the damp cloth to his cheek. "He got the better of me. Beat me to hell."

"You let him corner you to keep his attention off of us," I said, unsurprised at his self-sacrifice. He'd been doing it for years; why would he stop now?

Will told me not to make a hero out of him, but I wondered if he ever stopped to realize that he'd done that to himself.

"*You*," he said in a low voice. My brows furrowed as I met his gaze. "If he knew about you—"

My chest tightened at the revelation. I cleared my throat and lifted the cloth to the new cut, jagged but shallow, near his eye. He hissed in a sharp breath, tensing as I worked.

"It doesn't need stitches," I said gently, soaking the rag once more.

"Thank fuck for that."

My hands remained steady as I took his chin in my fingers and wiped away the rest of the blood from his face and throat. My tongue grew heavy at the bruises around his neck. I remembered how hard Sebastian had gripped my arm to leave marks like that. I didn't want to imagine how bad it would have been around my throat.

"Savvy," Will said gently.

I blinked. I was staring.

"Sorry," I murmured.

There wasn't much blood on his chest and arms. I didn't know if that was better or worse, because the color on his skin was bruising. I set the cloth aside and brushed my fingers along his ribs.

"Do you think they're broken?"

Will covered my hand with his, shaking his head. "Just bruised. I hope."

My gaze shot up to his. "That's not funny." He shrugged in response. I turned my attention to the blood crusting his hands. These, at least, were familiar. I'd cleaned them countless times over the years—one small act to help him.

"I've been through worse," he said quietly. "Besides, laughing it off is better than the alternative. I have *obsessive* tendencies."

"Fair point," I said before setting aside the cloth. I opened the jar of ointment, swirled my finger in it, and lifted it to the cut near his eye.

"Why were you in the alley?" he asked.

"I knew something was wrong." I spread the ointment, cringing at his pained breath. "You should have been back hours ago. I was saddling one of the horses when I heard your stallion."

"You were coming to find me."

I lowered my head, nodding. He grabbed my hand and gave it a squeeze.

"Someone has to look out for you," I whispered. "Especially when you won't look out for yourself."

Will tugged my chin so I'd look at him. With the gentlest of movements, he pulled my face to his and kissed me sweetly, slowly.

"Looking after me could get you killed," he whispered against my mouth.

"I'm not afraid, William."

He tipped back, his brown eyes intent on mine. The silver specks in his danced as he studied me.

"You aren't, are you?" he said, incredulous. "You vicious little thing." His brilliant smile sent my heart racing. "Fuck my ribs—" He wrapped an arm around my waist and lifted me. I straddled his lap, and before I could protest, he covered my mouth with his, stealing my breath, my heart, my senses.

My fingers tangled in his hair, heart racing as my back arched. Will moved with me, supporting my weight and keeping me flush against him. My blood hummed in my veins, need dropping into a deep throb between my thighs.

I'd never understand how something as simple as a kiss could knock me senseless.

I shifted my weight against him, and he fell backward onto the mattress with a loud groan beneath me. I stilled, then flattened my palms on either side of his head as I hovered above him.

Even through the pain lining his features, there was a glint in Will's dark eyes, something oddly familiar. Like how I'd seen Jesse look at

Bonnie. My heart squeezed at the sight. There'd never been an issue of passion between us. We certainly had more than enough of it. It was moments like this that terrified me, moments when I thought I saw something more in his eyes. Something like . . . love.

My chest tightened. *He doesn't love you. Not like you love him.*

"You . . . " I couldn't catch my breath. "You need a bandage. For your—your ribs." My gaze settled on his mouth, on the dried blood where his bottom lip had been split.

Heart pounding, hands shaking, I scurried from the room. I forced myself to ignore the delicious way our bodies fit together, instead focusing on dressing his wounds. A logical task, one that didn't involve kissing or sex. I'd done it a thousand times before, tended to Will's wounds.

But this time felt different.

I rifled through a low cabinet, squatting as I tossed out an empty box of bandages, a package of bath oils from Manhattan Island—Bonnie'd told me to throw them out, but I couldn't—and several older, threadbare towels that I'd discarded when Bonnie first arrived. I huffed when I couldn't find the longer bandages, ones that would wrap around Will's torso to steady his ribs.

Using my fingertips, I flipped open the top cabinet, leaning hard against the painted wood as I reached up farther, extending to my tiptoes, my fingers searching for the box of bandages that I knew had to be there.

Suddenly, an oppressive heat surrounded me, and the familiar scent of tobacco, of *home*, ensnared my senses. I gasped at Will's presence. I hadn't heard him enter the bathroom, I'd been so focused on the stupid bandages. He buried his fingers in my curls, gripping tight enough to send twinges of pain through my scalp.

"Will!" Every single instinct told me to pull away, to put space between us, but then he buried his nose in the crook of my neck and his tongue darted from between his lips, running along my pulse. He inhaled deeply, and my eyes fluttered shut, my head falling back against him as I fought for breath. His nails raked gently against my scalp.

This man would be the death of me, Jesus Christ.

"You—you're hurt," I stammered. He inhaled deeply, and my body trembled in response.

"Did you know that pain can heighten pleasure?" Will's rumbling voice reverberated through me and settled low in my belly. He wrapped his other arm around my waist, flattening my back against his chest. My breath shuddered, and I wriggled back against his stiff cock without even thinking.

"N-no," I whispered, the single word falling hotly from my lips.

"Don't worry, *mi sol*," he murmured against my throat. "I'll only hurt you if you ask me to." My toes curled at the promise in his voice. "Do you know what I realized?" I tried to shake my head in response but couldn't with his fist in my hair. His teeth grazed my earlobe, then tugged hard. "I've been treating you so *carefully* since I fucked you in the graveyard."

Our bodies still locked together, Will shuffled toward the bathroom counter, directly in front of the mirror. He wedged me between his lithe, muscled figure and the vanity.

"I felt so guilty for the way I took your virginity," he mumbled in my ear. "I was greedy. My self-control snapped. I was worried I'd hurt you or that I'd traumatized you. I hated myself so *fucking* much, I'd convinced myself that you only let me fuck you out of pity."

I met his gaze in the mirror, my eyes blazing up at him. "It wasn't." I exhaled sharply, my chest heaving as I raked in a ragged breath. "I . . . wanted you." My stomach flipped as Will's thumb grazed my belly. "You didn't hurt me."

You would never hurt me, I couldn't say.

"I know." A wicked gleam flickered in his brown eyes. "I read your book, Savvy." My cheeks heated beneath the implication in his words. "I realized, you were the one who lay down in that dirt and spread your legs for me." My pulse throbbed painfully between my thighs. "You didn't care if anyone saw us either. You screamed my name like you wanted the world to hear you."

Will's calloused fingers blazed a trail up my belly, over my silk night-gown, and twisted in the neckline. With a vicious yank, the fabric ripped down to my waist, freeing my breasts beneath his ravenous gaze. He tugged the sleeves down, pinning my arms at my sides.

"*Fuck*," he groaned. "You have the most gorgeous tits I've ever seen." He covered one with a hand, rolling my nipple between his thumb and forefinger. My eyes rolled back, and I bit my bottom lip to stifle the damn near purr that threatened to come up from my throat.

His lips grazed my jawline. "Look at yourself, Savannah," he whispered in my ear. I did as instructed, finding a very different woman staring back at me. My cheeks were flushed and rosy, eyes glazed with lust and longing. My body wasn't wholly mine anymore.

And I didn't care one bit.

"Look how fucking beautiful you are."

I blinked, my eyes shifting away from my reflection.

Will's jaw clenched. "You are a woman who likes it dirty and rough. Look how flushed you are from me manhandling you, *mi sol*. How your hips are wriggling against me. How dark your eyes are." He leaned closer and whispered into my ear, "And you liked me fucking you in public. You like the idea of being watched. Or being caught. The graveyard. The kitchen. The stables. You want someone to see. To *know*."

"Know what?" I asked breathlessly.

"That I'm yours just as much as you're mine."

A moan escaped my lips at the memory of the times we'd been together, how truly excited it made me at the thought of being caught. I wriggled against him, my words coming out as little more than pleas. I *burned*, and if he didn't touch me I would turn to ash before him.

His nails raked against the sensitive skin of my thighs as he slid the fabric of my ruined gown above my hips, then shoved down my underwear, his fingers expertly finding the one spot I needed them to be. A strangled cry came from deep within me as he circled my clit, and then he shoved two fingers inside of me.

He wasn't gentle. He wasn't sweet. He was exactly what I needed.

"Oh *God*."

My moans only spurred him on, his palm creating delicious friction against my clit as he pumped his fingers inside of me. Seeing my arousal coat his fingers in the mirror sent me even higher, my hips moving on their own against him.

"You know I love it when you call me God." The strain in his voice told me this was getting him off just as much as me. "Tell me no if you don't want to be fucked against this counter right now." I met his gaze in the mirror, my eyes blazing. I whimpered, grinding against his hand harder. *More.* I needed more.

Will bent me over the counter, my breasts flattening against the cold countertop. I gasped at the shock against my nipples. His hand remained firm in my hair, making me watch as he undid his zipper and freed his cock from the constraints of his jeans. My mouth watered at the sight.

I should have shied away, should have called him out for impropriety. Should have demanded I be treated like a lady.

But he wasn't a gentleman. And I wasn't a lady.

Will rubbed the head of his cock against me, and I nearly came undone. I wriggled against him, incoherent sounds coming from between my lips. He didn't tease me, didn't make me beg. With a single thrust, his cock stretched me as it had in the graveyard, hitting my insides in a newer, deeper way.

A strangled cry erupted from between my lips. He didn't give me time to adjust like before. No, he rolled his hips, withdrawing and slamming back into me.

"William!" My nails raked against my own skin as I wished desperately to reach back, to drive him deeper inside of me. "Oh God! I can't! I—"

Release hit me fast, my body spasming, my vision blurring around the edges. Will never slowed, never let up. Instead, he reached his free hand between my legs, fingers working against my clit once again as his hips set a brutal pace that made my eyes roll back in their sockets.

"Look at us, Savvy!" His fist tightened in my hair, forcing me to focus on our reflection. "Look at what I do to you."

It was the most erotic thing I'd ever experienced.

My gaze danced across Will, his lean muscles flexing. I loved him like this, not the man who made himself smaller around the others. The man who saw what he wanted and took it for himself. He recognized that I wasn't some simpering, weak girl, but a woman who could handle every bit of him and his darkness.

"This is what you need, isn't it?" he asked, our bodies coming together in an untamed, beautiful symphony.

Everything inside of me tightened, my body no longer my own but *his*.

I fell apart, the world narrowing to only this, only us, only how he made me feel. When Will released my hair and groaned, a deep satisfaction filled me.

A breath passed, and he separated our bodies, gently grabbing a towel and helping to clean up. I reached for the ripped straps of my nightgown, tugging the fabric up, blinking rapidly. I somehow managed to get my shaky legs beneath me, my eyes wide as I looked up at Will.

What now?

We couldn't go back to what we had been before, but how were we supposed to move forward? I worried my bottom lip between my teeth. He embraced me and pressed his lips to mine gently, in stark contrast to the harshness of moments ago.

While we shuffled back into my room together, I somehow managed to pull away from him as much as I just wanted to sink into him, into this. Whatever *this* was. My mind whirled with a mixture of hope and devastation, because this man knew me better than anyone I'd ever met. He knew me, he saw me, but it couldn't be what I wanted.

I discarded my ruined nightgown and changed into another, smoothing my rumpled hair down, grasping and failing at pulling myself back together. My throat was dry because I knew he was watching me, knew that if I met his gaze, I'd find things I wasn't ready to face.

"I-I think you should sleep somewhere else tonight," I said quietly, brushing past him and pulling the blankets down on my bed.

"Savvy—"

"It's late, and I'm tired. I'm going to go to bed, since I know you're going to be okay." I ran a hand through my hair, then busied myself with adjusting the pillows.

"Don't pull away from me." There was an edge to his voice, dragging me from my task. I blinked rapidly. "Can't we talk about it?" Will ran a hand through his hair, his own uncertainty breaking through the cracks in his usual confidence.

"Talk about what?" That he was right? That deep down, I enjoyed how hard he was with me, that I enjoyed the idea of getting caught, that I wanted to be fucked, but couldn't take it without being loved?

"You said *'I want too much.'* What did that mean?"

What *did* that mean? It meant that I wanted all of him. I wanted the good, the bad, the ugly. But more than that, I wanted him to want *me*. Not just my body. I wanted this man who claimed me to love me like I loved him.

I schooled my features into a carefully blank mask, blinking.

"Say something," he demanded.

"You're hurt, Will," I said, the words thick on my tongue. I took in the sight of him: the cut along his temple, the bruises on his ribs, the blood crusting his nails. "Now isn't the time for this."

I couldn't be the simpering girl that begged a man to love her.

"It'll never be the time, will it?" His fists relaxed at his sides, and a sad smile crossed his face, his eyes darkening with something I'd never seen before.

My bottom lip trembled as he gathered his things and shoved his hat back on his head.

"No, Will—"

He reached for me then, his fingertips touching my jaw and tilting my face toward his. "It's okay." Though the words were little more than a whisper, I felt the devastation in them. He pressed his lips to my forehead gently. A strangled sound came from my throat, and I lifted my hands to reach for him, for what? I didn't know. They dropped to my sides.

"It's okay," he repeated.

It was anything but okay.

Stop him. Don't let him go. Tell him.

Tell him what? That I was hopelessly in love with him?

The door clicked shut. My knees wavered, and I had to grip the mattress to stop myself from crashing to the floor.

I was in love with William Ellis, but he could never love me back.

CHAPTER TWENTY-ONE

BONNIE

THE BED FELT AS empty and hollow as I did. Nightmares of a different kind plagued me. Memories of my life *before*. Before Jesse, before The Kid, before Savannah . . . before I realized the depth of my loneliness. The sheer vastness of it stretched wider than the horizon across the desert. Fear grew inside me that I was slipping back into that dark place the more strained things became between Jesse and me.

He was right.

We should have left last night. I'd racked my brain over and over, but the timeline was incredibly short. Chances of getting the ledger were slim to none, and if I were being honest with myself, I'd already known that. I'd just been *so angry*.

Angry at Jesse's lack of trust in me that led to the situation last night. Angry at myself for not speaking up sooner about the issues we'd been having. Angry at the world for tearing us apart *yet again*.

I had today to salvage my plan to keep us all safe. *Only* today. A familiar wild recklessness settled deep into my bones. An instinct to warn me of approaching danger coming alive within me, setting my nerves on fire. Tomorrow was the rehearsal, and in two days, I'd be a married woman.

I had to play the part of the submissive bride for just one more day. Then, Jesse and I would find each other again. Once we escaped this place, *this prison*, back beneath the open sky we could untangle all this wrongness between us.

I'd been up since before dawn, fingers tracing the indent in Jesse's pillow where he last slept, trying not to hear his words from last night on repeat to no avail.

"I love you."

Nothing out of the ordinary. He'd said it often enough that it shouldn't have struck such a discordant note within me. It wasn't the words. It was the way he said them. A little unsure. A hint of question in his tone. As if he wasn't quite certain if he was allowed to proclaim his feelings anymore.

It hurt.

Shucking off my covers, I decided that if today was my last day here, then it was time to get to work. Choosing one of the most conservative dresses in my new Rutherford-chosen wardrobe, I gathered my hair and made my way into the bathroom to get ready. I passed The Kid, sprawled on the chaise and snoring lightly, all his gangly limbs at odd angles and his hair ruffled. Last night, I'd turned him into a murderer. I hadn't even thought twice about it. That probably should have bothered me, but I wasn't prepared to look too closely at those feelings this morning.

Passing through the threshold into the bathroom I shared with Savannah, I fussed over a few strands of my hair that wouldn't fall right. Perhaps I'd slept on them strangely, or I wasn't pulling them away from my face right. Either way, the whole situation was hopeless.

I was hopeless.

Dropping my hands from my hair, I sighed deeply, trying not to think of that waver in Jesse's voice last night. The door creaked open, and Savannah walked in with a bleary expression and a yawn stretching her mouth wide. She stood beside me, her sleep-glazed eyes studying me as if trying to solve a puzzle. Savannah didn't say anything, but the quizzical expression faded into one of determination as she picked up several items and arranged them on the bathroom counter.

Pomades and combs and leather hair ties all arranged in a neat, nearly obsessive, row. She pulled the deep forest green dress over and held it open to me. Without words we fell into the familiarity of our routine.

I shimmied into the dress that she fastened and then pulled the vanity chair in front of the mirror to sit on while she beat my unruly hair into submission.

Savannah would usually try to cut through my bad mood with some sort of quip or comment meant to make me laugh or distract me from my thoughts. Instead, there was only silence. The edges of Savannah's mouth were turned into a frown, and her eyes didn't seem as bright this morning. After how she and Will were last night, I didn't understand this cold, sharp demeanor.

There was nothing outwardly wrong, no external sign of struggle or hardship. It was only that the light that always lived inside of her had been snuffed out. I may not have recognized the subtle difference had I not seen it in the mirror several times over the last few weeks. Without words, I covered Savannah's hand with my own, stilling her furious brushing until she met my eyes in the mirror. A silent question passed between us, one that had her lips tighten almost imperceptibly, as if to keep them from trembling.

"Whatever Will and I had . . . it's over," she stated emotionlessly. I knew she wasn't, in fact, emotionless about it. But her stony expression made it clear that she wouldn't talk about her feelings, even if I tried to drag them out of her.

I didn't know what to say, my inept social skills leaving me strangled for any sort of comment or platitude to convey what I was feeling: helpless, empathetic, *sad*. Not just for Savannah and Will, but all of us. How had we gotten so twisted up? How did it turn out this way? We all cared about each other. Deeply. As friends, as family, as lovers. Instead of offering shallow apologies, I took a steadying breath and met her eyes in the mirror with a small smile. I was tired of talking about boys and relationships. Savannah and I had more important things to talk about anyway.

"I couldn't sleep last night," I told her, changing the subject. "Jesse was right, we probably should have left yesterday. I've been over it a thousand times, and the timeline is too tight. I might only have one chance today to try for the ledger, but we should make plans to leave after the rehearsal dinner tomorrow night."

Savannah nodded absentmindedly, as if her mind were far away, weighted with decisions. "I think I'm going to St. Louis when we leave."

Only Savannah didn't say it like a question, she said it like a fact. Suddenly, the air in the room thinned, and it was hard to breathe. Or maybe I'd just forgotten how. My eyes stung, and I blinked rapidly to clear the sudden blurriness in my vision. Savannah was going to leave. That loneliness inside of me stretched wider.

I nodded softly, not trusting myself to speak.

"It's just, I always said when I left New Orleans, I'd go back. Try to find my mom. If she's still alive, maybe I could help her beat it—the glowroot—like I helped you."

My hand rested over hers, and I stood, wrapping her in my arms so tight that I felt the catch in her breath through her ribs. How long had she been my anchor? Had I ever reciprocated? Did I ever say it aloud? I didn't think I ever had. Because I was shit at being a friend. Because I was shit at showing the people I loved how I loved them.

"Good," I breathed softly against her neck as I hugged her. "It's about damn time."

We broke away from each other, both of our eyes wet, staring at each other with a mixture of trepidation and hope. Before Savannah could say anything, I beat her to it.

"You've been putting me first for way too long already." My throat was thick, and I swallowed hard. "I don't think I noticed, as Audrey," I explained in a small voice. "But with my memories back, it's clear how much you've sacrificed on my behalf."

The words fell heavy between us, and Savannah shifted her weight uncomfortably from one leg to the other, as if she were desperate to assuage some confrontation she was afraid of. My smile only deepened.

"I was bought once," I said in a quiet voice that held her attention. "I know how that fucks with your head. Makes you feel all kinds of things about yourself, your *worth*, that makes you question everything. Every*one*."

I offered a shaky smile, tears wobbling in my vision once more. "There is no distance, or time, or circumstance that could ever make you less to me than what you are, Savannah." Her eyes, as round and deep as they were, seemed impossibly wider when they were filled with tears.

"You're my family," I reassured her, my sad smile stretching across my mouth as my own tears tumbled down my cheeks. "We'll write. And there will never be a day that you aren't in my thoughts, or in the corner of my mind. And no matter what it is you feel you have to go out in this world to do . . . you'll never be alone. Not for one *second*." I pulled back from her, taking in her flushed cheeks and the warmth of kindness that radiated through her skin and from her dark eyes. "If you need to be in St. Louis, then that's where you'll be. And I'll come to visit you, and your mother, sober and happy. Because there's *nothing* that you can't do."

She sobbed, her voice gasping in emotion that I couldn't decipher. I didn't know if it was sorrow or happiness or loss or all of them. She gripped me so tight that I couldn't breathe. And it felt righter than any sort of goodbye ever could.

"I love you, Bonnie," she breathed through her tears. Mine fell fresh at the use of *my* name. My *real* name. Maybe for the first time in my life, it didn't bring back memories of the girl under the bed. The girl that Jones found on the side of the road and bought to abuse. For the first time, it felt like me in a way that I could *own*. Not Jones. Not Lee. Not Jesse.

Me.

I was Bonnie. I was not Lee's daughter. I was not Jones's pawn. I was not the girl under the bed. Or Jesse's girl.

I was just *me*. A woman with something to offer. A woman who could save people. A woman who had control over her life.

I was a friend. Savannah's friend. Will's friend. The Kid's friend.

And *that* was so much more than enough.

"It's way too early for us to get all emotional," I grumbled in her ear. She laughed, because she of all people was used to my caustic personality. "We have work to do."

A moment later, we pulled away from each other, smiles and tears and the knowledge that *nothing* would ever tear us apart keeping us bound tight. Looking at my reflection in the mirror, Savannah had somehow wrestled my hair into a smooth braided style gathered at the base of my neck. Witchcraft, I tell you.

"Did you know that there was a period of six months when I was on my own that I didn't own a brush?" I said, running my fingers over the smooth style. Savannah gaped, and it made me giggle. "I'm serious. I couldn't waste what little I stole or bartered for something that *frivolous*. By the time I got a comb, it took me the better part of a whole day brushing out the mats."

"I'm packing you a brush," she said in a horrified whisper. "And conditioner."

I giggled at how silly it was, talking about such inconsequential things, and Savannah's eyes looked brighter than before. When we emerged from the bathroom, The Kid had woken, his golden hair standing at odd angles and reminding me of his younger self. His eyes were half-lidded as he shook off the last vestiges of sleep, but as he stifled a yawn, he waved to us in greeting. As if he hadn't killed anyone last night.

Maybe he would be alright. I hoped he would.

A knock came at the door, and everyone froze as I made way over, cracking it open just enough to see Will's black cowboy hat before pulling him inside and locking it behind us. "Alright—" I started, turning to see Savannah staring furiously into an empty corner while Will kept the brim of his hat low enough to cover his eyes.

"Today is our last day to find the ledger, but it's a long shot. Savannah and I will keep my father and Lucas busy with last-minute details and—"

"You have your final dress fitting today," Savannah interrupted brusquely. "They'll both want to be there."

". . . great idea," I said, trying not to let the tension in the room suffocate me. "Will, could you get a message to Jesse? We need to be ready to leave after the rehearsal dinner tomorrow night. Ledger or no ledger."

Will grunted in acknowledgement, keeping the brim of his hat so low I wondered if he was staring at his own feet. Shaking off the strangeness, I sat at my desk and pulled out a sheet of paper. I scrawled a quick message and then stilled . . . My pencil hovered over the blank space. How did I end the message? Where did we stand? My heart thundered painfully in my chest. Trying not to overthink it, I finished the letter and signed it, folding it quickly and handing it to Will. He grabbed it with his left hand and winced when he tucked it into his shirt pocket.

He *winced.*

"Will . . ." I dragged his name out long, accusingly. He sighed, a deep inhalation that caused a pained groan to wheeze out on his exhale. This time, when I reached for his hat, he didn't stop me from removing it.

Violence was etched across his face in splotches of dark purples, blues, and rust that painted his bronze skin and told a story of brutality that was as familiar to me as the dull, lifeless expression in his dark eyes. I knew immediately who had done this to him. My heart stopped in my chest as the memories crowded in my head, snippets of terror and blood-soaked horror, forcing my fingers to tremble. I clenched them along the brim of Will's hat, praying silently that no one would notice.

"It's *fine*, Bonnie," he said, his eyes unable to hold mine for long.

"But—"

"We're going to get out of the city before anything can happen. You said it yourself."

"It's *Sixgun*—"

"I won't let anything happen to you!" he shouted, yanking his hat back from me. He settled it on the crown of his head, straightening his spine and seeming to grow several inches in the process. "*Any* of you."

Before I could protest again, or remind him about the things we'd endured, the things we'd witnessed, he headed out the door with a scowl on his face. I could still feel the phantom touch of Sixgun's hands running along my skin. Bruising me. Violating me. Forcing Jesse to watch me become his willing victim.

I couldn't breathe.

I couldn't *breathe. I can't breathe! I can't—*

"Bonnie!" Someone shook me. My eyes focused on The Kid's concerned blue gaze, a furrow I'd never seen before carving a trench on his brow. "He can't hurt you. We won't let him hurt you again. *I won't,*" he said with a false confidence that made something in my chest crumble. I'd forgotten. Or I'd purposefully not remembered that he had been on the train with us. Hidden behind a wall of metal crates. A witness to Sixgun's cruelty as Will and I had been in our youth. I patted The Kid's hand on my arm, his grip tight enough that it was clear Sixgun's presence bothered him more than he was letting on.

As if realizing how hard he was clenching his hands into my flesh, he loosened them and let them drop awkwardly to his sides. Savannah stared at me with wide eyes, as if she were seeing me for the first time. As Audrey, I hadn't remembered my past, which had been somewhat of a blessing. I hadn't remembered the years of torture, abuse, neglect. I hadn't remembered being hunted down like prey across the country. Never feeling safe. Never slowing down. Never resting.

As Bonnie, I wasn't as fortunate. I remembered *everything* in pristine detail. Every lewd comment made about my too-young body growing up. How Sixgun's eyes trailed me throughout the camp, hungry and calculating. I remembered the abject joy in his eyes as his knife gouged into my skin, splitting me open over and over and over again. How he licked my blood from the blade, moaning as if it were the best thing he'd ever tasted. The curves on the letter 'O' were the worst. The muscles had been cut in an unnatural way, the nerves torn apart beneath his hands.

"Bonnie?" Savannah's voice was small, gentle. She approached me cautiously, as if afraid to spook me. Like a wild horse that had caught the scent of a predator and was about to bolt. "You're pale." She used her sweet voice to coax me onto the chaise. "Sit for a moment."

They both looked at me expectantly, but I wouldn't offer an explanation. I couldn't. The memories slithered through my mind like snakes, poisoning my mind and making me feel shame that didn't belong to me. It should belong to Sixgun. Only he didn't give a shit about what he'd done to me. The irreparable ways I'd been broken by him. Hot tears stung at my eyes that I refused to let fall.

"It's fine," I whispered. "I'm fine."

"I'm going to shoot whoever in that stupid camp taught you and Will that word," Savannah huffed, crossing her arms. "You are most definitely *not fine.* Neither of you!" She flung her hands in the air, her cheeks rosy and flushed with irritation. "Nor *should* you be. Sixgun is a monster. The fact that he's this close, in the city, terrifies me. I'm not afraid to admit it. I'm not going to pretend to be *fine.* I want to get as far away from him as fast as I possibly can."

Hearing her talk about her fear made the pressure in my chest ease. Admitting confidently that she wanted to run from the threat of Sixgun in the city was brave. I'd been conditioned for so long to think of fear as weakness. No, that wasn't entirely true. Anything felt too deeply had been considered a weakness. Fear, trust, love.

But it had all been a lie.

A lie told over and over again to a little girl who didn't know any better. A lie beaten and burned into my skin. A lie tortured into my mind. But it was still a lie.

"I'm worried that insisting on this extra time put us right in Sixgun's crosshairs," I admitted in a rush, the words blending together in my haste. "I'm scared to face him without Jesse."

"Well then, let's get the hell out of here before it comes to that," Savannah said matter-of-factly. "We have a dress to put you in to distract Lee and Rutherford."

"What about me?" The Kid asked. I looked at him, and his expression was unreadable. Like Jesse's at a card table. "What's my job? You assigned everyone else."

A sly smile curled over my mouth and banished the last remnants of fear lingering on the edges of my sanity.

"You get to break into my dad's office, Kid."

CHAPTER TWENTY-TWO

JESSE

WHISKEY MAY HAVE DULLED the pain in my back, but it did nothing to quiet the voices fighting in my mind.

Escape was right there. We had been so close to putting New Orleans behind us, but Bonnie insisted that we needed that damn ledger. While I understood her reasons, I disagreed that it was worth letting them go back to Lee Manor when we could have made a run for it.

"Wasn't that bottle full this morning?"

Judgment laced Mickey's words as he tugged the whiskey from my hand and set it aside. I sat up more fully, taking in the hard look in my uncle's blue eyes.

"Scouts spotted Ellis," he said, turning his attention from me. He glanced across the fire I'd been sitting at for hours into the dark recesses of the Riverwalk, as if expecting Will to appear like a shadow.

Instead, Gabriela approached. "He's moving slow. Something must have happened." She adjusted the strap of the gun slung over her shoulder.

I shoved to my feet, deep lines edging my face. We should have left last night. I knew it.

Together, we made our way down a staircase and across the vast mall. Will was climbing from his stallion by the time we arrived at the guarded entrance. He grimaced as he lifted the reins over his horse's head and guided him inside to the makeshift stable.

"You alright?" I asked when he finally approached, a hand splayed across his ribs.

With a grunt, Will retrieved something from his pocket and shoved it into my hand. "From Bonnie."

My heart plummeted like a lead weight in water. We hadn't parted on the best terms when they'd left last night. What if this was her throwing in the towel, deciding that whatever we once had wasn't worth the risk of further undermining her father? Could I live with that?

Did I have any choice?

"You look like you got beat to hell," Mickey said to Will.

In the dim light, I hadn't noticed the scab on his lip or the cut on his face.

"I'll be fine," Will said tensely, shoving past us and heading farther into the Riverwalk.

We followed in silent procession until Will found an empty fire to warm his hands over. Only then did I notice the full extent of his injuries. Bruises marred his face, and there was a red mark around his throat that looked suspiciously like rope burn.

"What happened, Will?" I asked, leveling him with my gaze.

Fingers twitching, he took his time retrieving his cigarette case and lighting one. "Sixgun."

Cold dread surged down my spine. "He's here?"

Will nodded, inhaling from his cigarette, the embers lighting up his dark eyes. "The Hanged Men have been circling for days. It was only a matter of time before he made a move."

I swore beneath my breath and opened the letter.

Jesse,

I tried but there just isn't enough time. Meet us after the rehearsal dinner. We'll be ready to leave then.

I exhaled loudly, relief, cold and soothing, coursing through my veins.

Together?

-Bonnie

Together? As if that were even a question. Maybe she felt as unsettled as I did. In a way, that gave me some relief. That if we were both unsure, we still had a chance to figure things out.

"Mickey, we need to mobilize. Bonnie's thrown in the towel on the ledger," I said, meeting my uncle's gaze.

"The rehearsal dinner starts at eight tomorrow night," Will added, cringing as he lowered onto an overturned crate and flicked his cigarette into the fire.

I stared at my friend as Mickey left to talk with a couple of his men. Will met my gaze, then averted his eyes.

"I don't wanna talk about it," he said gruffly.

"Fine." I stood and retrieved the bottle of whiskey that Mickey had taken from me. When I offered it to Will, he shook his head and stared harder into the fire. I'd seen Will after he'd been hurt. Hell, I'd shot him before, and he'd never looked so hollow. I sat beside him on a crumbling cinder block. "Did something else happen?"

Will cleared his throat and lit another cigarette, his gaze turning toward the floor. "I don't think Savannah's coming with us when we leave."

"Why wouldn't she?" I asked plainly. The two of them had been mighty cozy with one another.

"She's done with me."

Just last night, Will wouldn't let her out of his sight. Now he would let her stay behind?

"She's coming with us. Whether or not she wants to," I said firmly.

My friend's eyes flashed in anger as he looked at me. "Who the fuck do you think you are?"

"Excuse me?"

"You don't even see it, do you?" He swore beneath his breath. "You are the luckiest son of a bitch I've ever met. You fell in love. Twice. And she loves you back. Only you're ruining it all because of your goddamned pride."

My mouth snapped shut at his accusation.

"Whatever alpha male bullshit you're pulling, it's only driving a wedge between you two. Bonnie is struggling, yet all you can see is yourself." He removed his hat and ran a hand through his hair. "You can fuck up your own relationship however you see fit, but I will *not* let you force Savvy to do anything she doesn't want to."

"I didn't mean—"

"I know what you mean. You *mean*, you're scared to lose her again, but if you aren't careful you'll drive her away." He sighed, a long weary sound, and shifted on his seat before turning to face me fully.

"Imagine growing up with my father, Jess. I honestly didn't even know what love looked like, not until I saw the two of you together for the first time. You smiled so wide when she was at her absolute worst. That's when I knew that you weren't full of shit, you just loved her. Lately you seem to think you can just force Bonnie to do what you want. That's not *her*, Jesse. That's never been her and you know that. Wake up, man." He took a long drag from his cigarette. "I don't care what you do or how you fix it this time. You're a grown man. Figure it out or leave her alone for fuck's sake."

I swallowed around the lump in my throat. "Sounds like you're speaking from experience," I said, fixing him with a stare. "Savannah?"

"Nice deflection, shithead," Will said. "She's not ready, and I can't force her to be; that's all there is to say." He shuddered as he loosed a long breath. "And my ribs hurt."

"How the hell did that bastard get the drop on you, son?" Mickey asked, sitting in a rickety chair across the fire.

"I noticed someone tailing me when I left with Savvy, Bonnie, and The Kid last night, so I lured them away and landed myself in an ambush. Sixgun and a handful of Hanged Men. Lucky I made it out alive, since he seemed pretty determined not to let me," he said, voice oddly neutral.

"Could the two of you stop gettin' the shit kicked out of you?" Mickey asked, chuckling as he stared between us. Will grinned at me, the first hint of my friend returning.

"It took more than a dozen men to kick my ass. Jesse only had one guy who whipped him at the Slavers' Parade."

I rolled my eyes, unable to stop the corners of my mouth from quirking up. "Pot meet kettle."

"You know, you might both be havin' trouble with your ladies because you're too busy staring into each other's eyes," Mickey said.

My lips parted in shock at my uncle's insinuation.

"I keep telling him he's not my type, Mick, but he fell *hard* for the Ellis charm." Will winked at me, and I shook my head, sipping from the whiskey bottle.

"I hate you both."

My uncle chuckled.

"Who would've thought, out of the three of us, *Mickey* would be the one in a functioning relationship," Will said. A slow smile spread across my uncle's face. "Sober, by the way. Helping me get my shit together. It's like you're a whole new person."

Mickey shook his head, his smile never faltering. "If it wasn't for you kids coming to find me, that never would have happened." His voice was warm. Will was right. My uncle *was* completely different from the sad drunk we'd found in Fort Hood. "But having *family* again . . . being around The Kid, and the other children who started coming to the base, it reminded me that life is only as good as you make it. And nothing worth having comes easily."

If you'd asked me three years ago if I could depend on my uncle, I'd have said absolutely not. Now, he was probably the most stable person I knew.

"How are you and Gabriela doing, anyway?" Will scratched his eyebrow and avoided my gaze.

"Good," Mickey said, his smile turning into a full-on grin. "Better than good. Great, actually." There was something almost secretive in his answer, but neither of us pushed the issue. He reclined back in the chair, the wood creaking beneath him. "I took her for granted for a long time, boys. Too long. But I guess if there's a lesson to be had there, it's no matter how badly or how long you screw up . . . you can still make it right. If she's willing to forgive you." He rubbed a hand over his stubbled chin. "I honestly never thought I'd feel like this again."

"Again?" I asked. Mickey had never mentioned he'd been in love before. I'd just assumed he was a military man through and through, the job being his primary love in life.

My uncle nodded, the smile creeping off of his face and his eyes darkening.

"Mmm. I was in love once before. When she died, I didn't think I'd ever breathe again." His Adam's apple bobbed. "Much less care for someone the way I care about Gabi." His gaze went to her across the room, where she consulted over a pot of something with one of the others.

"How have we never heard about this before?" Will asked, leaning forward with a glimmer of curiosity in his eyes. "Was it the Culling?"

Mickey shook his head and ran his thumb over his lip, his gaze focused on the fire.

"Tell us," I pressed. Maybe he could give me some insight in how to fix things with Bonnie if we ever got out of New Orleans. *When*, I reminded myself.

"We knew each other for a long time," he said, clearly lost in the memory of another place and time. "She was my best friend's younger sister. Off limits. So I loved her in silence. She could light up any room, make friends with a brick wall. There was no one who met her that didn't love her."

His smile returned, but this time it was deeper, fuller, brighter than before. "Years passed that way. Looking back, I noticed all the little signs she'd been giving me that she felt the same. All the quiet pleas for me to get my head outta my ass. Back then I didn't."

Will and I were both glued to my uncle's words. This was the most we'd heard about Mickey's life before being a drunk at the base.

"She moved away, but it was easier to stay in touch from anywhere back then. I could hear her voice from the other side of the country with the push of a button. She could send me pictures and messages instantly. I could see her face with a flick of my fingertips. But she was kind of like a shooting star, with big dreams and ambitions, not to mention the stones to take the risks needed to make them come true. I'd always thought she'd make her name and come back home one day. That all I had to do . . . was wait."

Mickey's eyes dropped to his folded hands. Suddenly, he looked his age. The blond of his hair was fading slowly into an ash gray, though the bits of his beard stripped of color were dark as iron. The lines around his eyes had deepened, and even when he wasn't laughing or smiling, they remained.

"Did she come back?" Will asked quietly.

"Oh yeah," Mickey chuckled darkly. "With a ring on her finger and a rich fiancé in tow."

I sat up straighter, unable to ignore the similarities to my own situation.

"What did you do?"

Mickey leaned back, closing his eyes for a long while. "I confessed everything the moment we were alone, and *boy* was she pissed."

A startled chuckle sounded from Will. I grinned when our eyes met. We both knew how pissing off the woman you cared for felt.

"She screamed and punched me . . . a lot. Called me every name under the sun. Then she kissed me. And even though she was two weeks away from marrying another man, I took her and we left. We spent one whole week together, one *perfect* week. The kind you don't forget. Then, like it always does, life came between us. I hadn't told her I was deploying overseas for a year. But I'd already signed my contract and I had to go. She begged me not to, pleaded with me, and I didn't listen. It was the last time I saw her until . . . "

Nothing. Mickey shook his head and sat upright like he would end the story there.

Will stood, pacing as he ran a hand through his hair. "Until what? You can't leave it there. I think it's the most I've ever heard you speak, much less about your past. You took a risk, then fucked it up, and now is the part where you tell us you get her back, right? That it works out in the end."

I stared at him, dumbfounded. Usually, Will was closed off about his feelings, but this reminded me of when Savannah kissed him after he'd already committed to Sebastian.

"Because you *saw* her, in a way no one else did. And so what if you didn't admit it for a while . . . it's not the worst thing you could do. Sometimes it's kinder even, trying to spare someone from the fucked-up chaos in your head. The twisted shit that would lay waste to everything *good* about her. Maybe it's just unthinkable that she could want you despite all that. Maybe that was just too much to ask." He panted, boots thunking against the ground as he tugged at his hair.

"Until *what*, Mickey?" he asked, stopping in front of him with unfettered hope in his eyes. The silence stretched long between us. Mickey frowned.

"Until she died, Will," he finally said.

"Fuck that," Will said, shaking his head furiously at Mickey. "*Fuck that*. What was the point then? All that time was just *wasted*? You left and she died and that's it? What about the fiancé? What about him, what happened to him?"

Mickey stood slowly, reaching out to Will's shoulders to still him. "She married him."

I stood, brows furrowed. "What? How could she do that? She loved *you*."

"Yeah, and I let my pride get in the way of being with her when I had the chance," Mickey said pointedly. The air whooshed from my lungs, and I lowered back to my seat.

"If it wasn't the Culling, then how'd she die?" I asked after a long moment.

My uncle eyed the whiskey bottle in my hand as if tempted.

"You already know how she died, Jess," Mickey said, his eyes glassy as unshed tears formed.

It hit me like a runaway train. The photos of our parents. The stories Mickey had told me about my mom, about Jones, but also about Emma.

"Bonnie's mom?"

He nodded. "I hadn't talked about her in a long time before you all showed up in my house in Fort Hood. She haunted me. To the bottom of every bottle. Even though it was too painful to remember, it was impossible to forget. Then there she was—Bonnie. With Emma's eyes, and her fire, and in love with my idiot nephew."

I couldn't help the chuckle that came from deep in my chest and the smile that perched on my lips.

"What are you three doing over here?" Gabriela asked as she wrapped an arm around Mickey's shoulders.

My uncle fixed his blue eyes on her. Some of the glassiness disappeared as he smiled and wrapped his arm around her waist. "Just reminiscing," he remarked, then fixed me and Will with a stare. "Imparting wisdom on today's youth."

Gabriela laughed. "They might be a lost cause, Mick."

Watching the two of them together filled me with hope. I would fix things with Bonnie. We just had to survive the escape.

Mickey wrapped her in his arms, nothing but love shining in his eyes as he kissed her. "Nothing's ever a lost cause. Not even these two." He winked at us before ushering Gabriela away.

CHAPTER TWENTY-THREE

WILL

MY FACE THROBBED. THE healing cut burned and pulsed pain down my jaw with every ragged thump of my mangled heart. Mickey's words at the camp lingered in my ears as the cigarette smoke curled insouciantly around me in the humid air.

I'd been watching her for an hour now.

Maybe two.

Alright, it'd already been three and counting. . . the woman was relentless. She'd been frosting and decorating the behemoth of a cake that was nearly as tall as me with terrifying attention to detail. It was as if her mind were a thousand miles away. Lost somewhere in the wilderness of her subconscious between confections and engineering that had brought the five-tiered monstrosity to life. She hadn't stopped moving or concentrating in all the time I'd watched her.

It was exhausting to witness, and now that she was finally finished, I saw the weariness weighing heavily on her body. The way she rubbed her shoulders and stretched her neck, wiping sweat from her brow as she meticulously cleaned and put away all her kitchen tools. I shouldn't be watching her anymore. She'd made it clear that she didn't want this . . . want *me.*

I'd never thought of myself as masochistic before now, but *fuck* I couldn't help myself from staring at her. It was my favorite thing to do. I just didn't want to believe that she was done with me, even if she'd made herself crystal clear. At least this time I'd kept myself well-hidden. I'd gotten out of practice since the graveyard, and the last thing I needed was a pissed-off Savannah infuriating me and making me want to kiss her even more than I already did.

She poured herself a cup of tea and struggled with the knot at the back of her apron. I had to clench my fists to stop myself from doing something stupid. *Mierda*, I wanted to tie her wrists together with her apron strings and bend her over that counter and make her admit that she lied. That she *did* want me. I threw my cigarette butt to the cobblestones at my feet, viciously grinding the heel of my boot over the lit end as if I could crush this hollow feeling in my chest. The one that told me that I was *too late, not enough, too broken*.

As she turned off the lights in the kitchen, I tried to talk myself off the ledge. *Don't pin her to the wall and kiss her senseless. Don't beg her for another chance. Don't.* Do. *Anything.*

I'd taken my eyes off her for a split second, and the tinkling crash of a teacup made my head snap toward her.

Savannah was many things: neurotic, inflexible, easily angered, and more beautiful than words could describe. One thing she wasn't was clumsy. This late in the evening, the idea of hot tea before bed would've kept her grip on the cup white-knuckled in order not to spill a drop. I was moving before I even had a chance to think it through, my boots thunking purposefully in her direction across the courtyard.

"You shouldn't be out this late," a deep voice muttered. As I turned the corner, I saw one of the guards that Seb used to hang around with pressing Savannah against a stone column. His fingers dug into the soft skin above her elbow as she averted her eyes from him and tried to wriggle from his grasp.

My mouth dried up, my mind spinning into a thousand different directions. Was *he* why she didn't want to be with me? Were they *together*? My stomach thrashed and my blood ran cold. All I wanted was to murder this man or be him, depending on how they knew each other. What was his name again? James . . . John . . .

"Let me go, Jimmy," Savannah said, her voice firm. There was no playfulness, no warmth, no breathy quality to her voice. They couldn't be together. Right? Everything inside of me was numb and cold, as if I'd been killed by the thought of her with another man. How was I supposed to function knowing that she preferred this greasy, handsy, limp dick fucker to me? I couldn't tear my eyes away from them, my mind detailing every inch where their bodies touched and marking the exact positions of his hands on her skin.

"Not this time," he said, his eyes dropping down the front of her dress. Savannah's face screwed up, brow furrowing in an expression of fear and revulsion. Relief buckled my knees, nearly forcing me to stumble. Savannah didn't invite his advances. It was sick, how giddy it made me to know that she didn't want him. "Do you know how *hard* it's been, watching you saunter around in your little aprons and skirts, following around after the Beast all moon-eyed like no one else is even worth your time?"

I felt insane. Fuck, I *was* insane. My moods shifted so quickly from desperate sorrow to giddy relief, and now I plunged into a murderous rage that steeled my bones, readying my body for violence. Now that I knew Savannah wasn't moving on to someone new, I wondered what in the *actual fuck* this piece of shit thought he was doing touching her without her permission.

"Stop it!" she cried, her beautiful voice turning sour with terror.

"C'mon, it's more fun if you fight back—"

"J-just let me go and I won't tell anyone."

A shot cracked through the air, shattering the stillness of the night. Savvy fell to her knees with a startled cry that sounded like music. Jimmy clutched his bloody palm, a ragged meaty hole blasted through the muscle and sinew to show the scant light from across the courtyard shining through. He'd doubled over, wailing as his eyes bulged and saliva ran from his mouth.

"Jimmy, Jimmy, Jimmy . . . " I said lazily, the barrel of my gun still smoking as the shadows melted away from my figure.

"Will—" Savannah breathed from the ground, her whiskey eyes full of wide-eyed wonder that made me want to do things that most people would frown upon. Nothing major, just kill this fucker and his whole family so that his bloodline was completely wiped from existence.

"See, I was just trying to have a relaxing evening," I said, closing the space between me and Jimmy. He struggled with his good hand to grip the firearm in his holster. Guess he wasn't left-handed. "Burn a few smokes, watch my girl make a cake the size of the Mississippi River Bridge, and fall asleep in my horse's stall." He released his gun from the holster, and with little thought, I kneed him in the face. The crunch of his nose and gush of blood down his chin satisfied some dark urge that'd formed in my chest. His gun clattered to the ground, and I kicked it away.

"Now," I said, fisting his hair and shoving the barrel of my gun roughly past his teeth. "You might think that what's about to happen to you is due to this inconvenience—"

"Will—" Savvy tried to get my attention, but I never averted my eyes. Instead, I stared deep into the depths of Jimmy's dark, tear-filled gaze so that he could understand that he wouldn't survive the consequences of his actions tonight.

"I want to assure you, *Jimmy*, that the only reason for the pain and terror that you're about to suffer . . . is because you had the fuckin' gall to touch Savannah without her permission."

Savannah made a soft noise in the back of her throat, one that made my cock hard. *Ay dios mio!* I wanted her to make that noise again.

"Will—" Savannah tried to get my attention again, but I hadn't quite made my point yet.

"I'm talkin' to Jimmy here, sweetheart," I said, offering her my free hand without looking at her. Her palm slid against mine, soft skin against my cracked and calloused hands. Gripping her firmly, I helped her to her feet. She didn't let go of my hand when she stood; instead, she intertwined her fingers with mine, and I finally tore my eyes away from the sobbing man to look at her.

She was so *fucking* beautiful. Her eyes were the perfect color of bourbon, warm and sweet, and she definitely wasn't looking at me like she was done with this *thing* between us. She looked at me in that way that made my insides squirm uncomfortably. Like I was some kind of hero. Like I could save her. Like I was a *good* person.

That wouldn't last long. Not after I was finished with Jimmy, at any rate. Shouts from the patrolling guards sounded in the distance, but I didn't give a fuck. Jimmy would die tonight, and if anyone else interfered, well . . . I didn't have my bloody reputation for nothing. And there was no part of me that would let this piece of shit wannabe rapist keep breathing.

"Where did it come from?"

"Over here!"

"Who is that?"

The guards shouted orders, and mingled voices grew closer and closer, until at least a dozen crowded into the courtyard. I dragged my eyes away from Savannah's. With a swift kick, Jimmy fell onto the cobblestones at our feet, still clutching his bleeding hand and sobbing. Snot and drool covered his cheeks and gleamed in the scant moonlight.

"Is that Jimmy?"

"It's *the Beast*—"

"What do we do?"

Finally, one brave soul stepped forward. Another of the guards I remembered being close with Sebastian. Always laughing on rounds together, covering each other's shifts. I couldn't remember his name, but he looked familiar. Had he been part of this bullying too? Had he ever assaulted Savannah before?

Wild fury ignited within me, and the man's knees quivered as I stared him down. Swallowing heavily, he moved forward, his hand on his gun, holster unsnapped, ready to draw in a moment. I smiled grimly at the sight.

"You can't attack Mr. Lee's guards, even if you're also in his employ," he said, his words tight and high-pitched. He cleared his throat and tried to straighten his shoulders. "We'll have to take you to Mr. Lee and report what we found."

"*Take* me?" I questioned with a dark chuckle. "Which one of you is going to *take me* to Lee?" I looked around at each of them. Some averted their gazes, and others flinched outright. Jimmy tried to scramble onto his knees. "Ah ah ah, Jimmy," I taunted as I kicked between his shoulders, forcing his wet face back to the filth-covered cobblestones. The guard in front of me breathed heavily through his nose, nostrils flaring in either fear or anger at my mistreatment of his friend. A crooked grin curled on my face as something dark and ancient and bloody woke up inside of me.

Begging to be let loose and sink my teeth into flesh.

He wrapped his fingers around the grip of his gun, his thumb flicking off the safety as if I wouldn't notice. Savannah's fingers flexed in my hold. I'd never let go of her hand. It was a tentative squeeze, as if in warning. Like maybe some part of her was *worried for me.* The thought rumbled in my chest. The guard confronting me must have scented the change in the air, because he drew his gun.

Another shot rang into the night, cacophonous and echoing. Savannah screamed. Smoke swirled from the tip of my gun. The guard stood frozen before the electrical impulses from his brain gave out, the organ now splattered on the wall behind him as he fell to the ground. Savannah's fingers trembled in my grip, and I knew that if she stood here much longer, if she witnessed more of what I was capable of, that bravado I loved so much would shatter into fear.

I tugged on her hand until she was in front of me, with my body angled between her and the guards still standing shocked across the courtyard.

"Savannah." I spoke her name firmly enough to drag her gaze from the corpse on the ground. She stared up at me, her breaths short and ragged. I could taste her exhalations on my tongue, feel the hot waft of it on my lips. I wanted to kiss her so badly, but I didn't dare.

"I need you to do two things for me," I said, unable to stop my fingers from curling around her chin to keep her eyes on mine. She nodded quickly, the motions tiny because of my grip. "Look at the guards and tell me which of them harassed you with Seb and Jimmy."

"Will, I can't—" Her gaze shifted to where they stood. Two of them had crouched down to retrieve their fallen comrade while Jimmy wriggled beneath my boot.

"If you don't, *mi sol,* I'll kill them all."

She gasped, a small sound from the back of her throat that made her lips part. She trembled beneath my touch and searched my eyes for any hesitation, any sign that I might be bluffing. Her whiskey eyes, the color of umber liquor lovingly distilled and aged, crystalized into amber shards that were capable of tearing me to pieces.

"Those two," she said, pointing at the two men trying to drag the corpse away from the middle of the courtyard. I couldn't resist, I kissed the tip of her nose and tilted her chin up so that her eyes would fall back on mine.

"Good girl." A flush rose in her cheeks that I wanted so badly to explore, except now wasn't the time.

"Second," I said, earning her rapt attention. "I want you to go straight to your bedroom—"

"*William*—" She said my name breathlessly. Her eyes sparkled in the moonlight in a way that made my cock ache.

". . . and lock the door."

She gaped, stunned, and then her brows furrowed deep in that familiar indignation I adored.

"No," she said, pulling out of my grip and crossing her arms over her chest. Jimmy managed to wriggle out from beneath my boot, so I turned and kicked him swiftly in the soft part of his stomach until he curled around himself and struggled to suck in a breath.

"Savvy—"

"*No!*" she shouted, surprising me. It wasn't often I could get her to scream at me so vehemently with an audience.

"I'm not asking," I said, grinding my teeth together. "Go to your room, and I'll send Etty up with fresh tea."

"I said *no,* and I meant it."

Clenching my fists together so I didn't do something stupid, I tried to suck in a few steadying breaths. The woman was so damn *stubborn* sometimes! One of the other guards drew their weapon, and without thought, I covered Savannah's body with mine, and two more shots rang out in the silence of the night. The guards she'd indicated crumpled to the cobblestones.

"You want to see *this*?!" I shouted at her, waving my hand in their direction. "You want to see me slaughter and kill and torture?"

"No," she said, uncrossing her arms. "But I don't want you to be alone."

I sucked in a pained breath between my teeth. Could words physically hurt? Could they make you bleed? That was how it felt. Like I was bleeding. Like I was dying. She seemed to see the way her words hit their mark by how I flinched. I tipped the brim of my hat low over my eyes, obscuring her from my gaze. I couldn't look at her right now.

Savannah didn't want me to be alone, but she didn't really want to be here with me either. I was a charity case. A bird with a broken wing. Not a man she desired. Not someone she could rely on. I'd known that, hadn't I? Somehow, through the tender little moments and how she'd softened toward me, I'd fooled myself into thinking that she really could *see* me. Or maybe the problem was that she saw me too clearly, and the truth was that I was just a piece of shit.

Yeah, that was probably the case.

"So be it," I said roughly, grabbing her by her upper arm. I pulled her in front of me and dragged Jimmy along the cobblestones behind us as we approached the guards.

"Take a good *fuckin'* look at the woman here," I said loudly enough to earn their nervous attention. I pushed Savannah forward roughly, gripping her chin and tilting her face to the scant light. "You see her?" I asked one of them, and he nodded, Adam's apple bobbing. "You?" I asked another. "You?

"That one"—I pointed to the man with the hole where his face once was—"seemed to think that Zachary Lee would give a shit if I killed his guards. But if you all recall, I killed Sebastian and he had me running the interrogations on all the household staff... including all of you."

Savannah pulled out of my grip, her eyes ablaze with an inner fire that mesmerized me. Fuck, she was beautiful when she was angry at me.

"Stop with the sanctimonious little speeches," she mumbled grumpily through a scowling, kissable mouth.

"Those men," I said, glaring down at her for a moment, deciding to talk a while longer than I'd planned just to spite her. "Along with

Jimmy here"—I punctuated his name with a fistful of his bloody hair and dragged him onto quaking legs—"thought it'd be a good idea to put his hands on Savannah without her permission."

Savannah's anger quieted, her eyes softening as she realized I was threatening them *for her*. Making sure they knew not to fuck with her ever again. I wanted to tell her to stop looking at me like I was doing something noble. Threatening their lives wasn't noble, no matter the circumstances. All that did was make me want to kiss her, and let's be honest, when *didn't* I want to kiss her?

"And if any of you fuckers decide to do the same"—the night fell eerily silent, my voice reverberating throughout the courtyard even though I spoke softly—"you'll wish all I did was hang you." Jimmy sobbed again, trying to yank his hair from my grasp. "You'll beg for it."

"P-please, *please*, I'm s-sorry! I'm so sorry! *Have mercy!*" Jimmy cried and wailed until it made me sick to look at him, and I dropped him once more, letting him fall to his knees before Savannah. He clutched at her skirt with his good hand. Savannah looked down on him, and her eyes turned sharp as they had before. She glanced at me as if waiting for direction. My only response was to raise an eyebrow and wait for her decision.

I'd never forced her to make a decision before, and I certainly wouldn't start now. She wrenched her skirt free and stepped behind me, as if she were putting her safety solely in my hands, trusting my judgment. Questionable decision, since I had a tendency to eliminate threats before they could be leveraged against me, but I wouldn't doubt her resolve.

"Doesn't seem to be much mercy left for you, Jimmy," I mocked him, fighting the grin that curled at the corner of my mouth. I'd seen it in the mirror before when I grinned like this, how it pulled at the scarred flesh from my father's aborted attempts to cut my face off. How it turned me into something . . . *undesirable*.

Moira's words filled my head. *You may have a pretty face, but your soul isn't pretty, is it?*

The other guards thinned in numbers, as if several snuck away when my attention was elsewhere, unwilling to continue the conflict any longer.

"Anyone have a problem with me killin' him?" I asked, as if polling a large group of people. No one spoke. Most of them refused to even meet my gaze. "If there are no further objections, get back to your fuckin' posts!" One of the men eyed the bodies on the ground with a question in his eyes, but he didn't ask it aloud. Instead, he just turned and walked away.

I sighed deeply, running a rough hand over my weary face, bracing myself for the difficulty of the work to come. Not just physically, but in my mind. In the parts of myself that were still too fragile to shake too hard, lest they crack wide open again.

I set my jaw and got to work. An hour later, I'd finally dragged the corpses of the three guards into the stables. They were piled in a mess of awkwardly angled limbs next to a still sobbing Jimmy, though he was gagged now, which was a definite improvement overall. I'd trussed the bodies and tied them at the end of long ropes to drag behind my stallion on our way to the bridge. Jimmy would have to walk beside them as the broken asphalt roads tore them to shreds.

I knew how fucked up that was, making him witness the mutilation of his friends' corpses before killing him. I shouldn't enjoy it. I'd never enjoyed the torture before. And there was a part of me that wondered if I *did* enjoy it, if that meant I was more like my father than I wanted to admit. But remembering each part of him that had touched her beautiful skin, breathed her air, caused fear to dull her bright, brilliant eyes . . . It made me cruel in a way that *should* frighten me. But it didn't.

Savannah staged a silent protest that wasn't very silent. Huffing, scowling, tapping her foot impatiently, opening her mouth like she would say something scathing only to catch sight of me and snap her jaw shut. It took everything for me not to smile at her. She really was adorable all flustered like that.

I'd finally finished with all the preparations. I stood before Jimmy, looking down on him from below the brim of my hat, and he started thrashing again, screaming for help that wouldn't come. I'd shoved a dirty towel in his mouth and tied a rope between his teeth to muffle the noise he made. His terror made me giddy. I smiled as tears tracked down his face. Gripping the front of his disheveled uniform, I dragged him onto quaking legs and untied him from the stall door. I lashed the other end of the rope onto my saddle next to his friends' bodies. He yanked the rope, screaming pitifully into the makeshift gag.

When I glowered at him, the front of his pants gre dark and soggy as he pissed himself, and it ran down his boot to pool on the floor. Savannah's nose wrinkled in disgust, and I wrapped a lazy arm around her waist, guiding her away from him to stand between me and my stallion.

This was it. The moment of truth. She'd made some big declarations earlier, all of them tolling within me like warning bells. After all, she'd only ever seen me *after*. When my humanity had trickled back in on the ride from the bridge to drown me in my guilt. She'd never seen how good I was at taking them apart. How there was a part of me, a secret part, that reveled in it. The way I imagined my father always did. Would she be able to look at me the same after tonight?

"Savvy," I said, earning her attention. "There's still time to change your mind. You don't have to be there, you don't have to *see this*."

Her whiskey eyes turned sharp and amber in the torchlight of the stables. That fold between her eyes deepened with her resolve. "You're not doing this alone."

Fuck.

She didn't know how deeply those words affected me, how it reached somewhere wounded within me and dragged me closer to her, even though I knew that my actions tonight would only push her further away.

"So be it."

One way or another, Savannah and I would figure out if this *thing* between us was sustainable. Either I'd finally scare her away or learn that she was strong enough to withstand me. I didn't know what would happen afterwards, but there was no running from it anymore. No hiding behind witty one-liners or my hat. Wrapping my hands around her waist, I lifted her onto the saddle and swung up behind her. With a cluck of my tongue and soft kick, we moved forward, Jimmy screaming uselessly into the rag in his mouth the whole time as if begging for someone to intervene.

The night was clear, the moon lighting up the dark streets and washing it with an eerie silver-tipped hue that made the world look surreal. I felt Savvy's heart beating hard in her chest as her hands tightened on the saddle horn. She was nervous. Her breaths came in quick little gasps that made my fingers twitch against the reins. We didn't speak. Maybe because neither of us knew what to say, or maybe because until this was done, there wasn't anything left to say.

Windows shuttered much like the last time we'd made this ride together, back from the cemetery where we'd crossed a line that had changed us both irrevocably. I wasn't sure if she'd noticed it then, how the city turned away from me in the darkness, as if even the crooked alleyways couldn't bear to watch me work. She noticed now. Her eyes flitted from the guttered lights as we passed. She still said nothing, which made my heart pound against my ribs painfully.

All too soon, the bridge loomed before us, the enormity of the structure blocking out most of the light of the moon. At the base of the bridge, I dismounted from behind her and looked up at her shadowed face. It was hard to read her expression.

"You could stay here, if you wanted. No one would judge you for not wanting to see."

"Stop trying to convince me to stay," she said, her voice hard. "I've made my decision, William."

That was it then. I'd given her every opportunity to turn back. This was going to happen. I led the stallion onto the bridge, every clop of his hooves ominous in the quiet night. At the peak of the bridge we stopped again, the maimed bodies rotting above us jostled by the frigid wind. Jimmy was crying, his eyes bloodshot from his screaming and muffled sobs. He didn't sway me.

I reached for Savannah. She put her hands on my shoulders and let me pull her down gently onto her feet. Her trust in me shone brightly in her eyes as she allowed a murderer to cradle her until she stood upright. It should've made me sick. Instead, my heart thumped louder in my chest.

"I'll start with the dead ones," I explained, turning my back to the bodies of the guards. Their skin had peeled back in places, and one had his nose ground down to a stump. Was it really alright? Showing this kind of gore to a woman like Savannah?

With a grunt, I hauled the first man by his shoulders to the middle of the bridge. My ribs burned like acid in my veins, but it was only what I deserved. Sliding my knife from the leather sheath on my belt, I carved into his face. I kept my eyes on my task, never once looking up at her. I didn't think I could bear it. My hands were steady, his cold flesh parting like butter. Just like Savannah's confident hands could make beautiful pastries, mine could take lives. Once completed, I hauled the next body, then the next, finishing my work with an efficiency that would terrify most grown men. When I stood, hands and shirt bloody, I finally looked up at her. She unhitched the heavy loops of rope from the saddle, no hint of judgment on her face. I thought she might struggle beneath the weight of it; there had to be at least fifty pounds of the thick rope there. But I'd only underestimated her once again.

She was used to carrying sacks of flour and sugar in the kitchen. I should've known she'd be strong enough. Maybe it was the existential weight she would balk under. But, it seemed, she carried that easily as well. I wanted to smile but refused.

"Thanks," I said quietly as she handed over the ropes. Within a few minutes, I had them tied and ready to hang. But this was the easy part. We still had *Jimmy* to deal with. And my plans for that motherfucker would make most hardened criminals cry.

"Alright Jimmy," I said in a cheerful voice with a cold smile as I turned my attention to him. "You didn't think I forgot about you, did you?"

His hands were bloody from trying to untie the ropes, and he'd fallen to his knees. I assessed him, tilting my head as I ran through my plan in detail. How should I approach this? Savannah moved next to me, her arms crossed as she stared down at her attacker.

"Usually I'd ask you to pray to your Gods for the last time." I shrugged. "But I don't think they'd listen to a piece of shit like you anyhow."

Curling my fist into his shirt, I hauled him onto his quaking legs and dragged him to stand near his friends. "I'm going to untie your hands now, and if you do anything stupid, this will be *much* worse for you. Understand?" He was crying again, snot running from his nose to soak the rag in his mouth. I untied him with deliberate slowness, watching for the moment I knew would come. As soon as he had his good hand free, he swung at me, but with practiced ease, I grabbed his wrist and twisted until I heard a *crunch* of bones. He screamed into the rag in pain, but I just shook my head.

"What did I tell you?" I said with a beleaguered sigh. Why didn't they ever listen to me? It wasn't like I made a habit of lying.

"This changes things," I said looking down at his wrist in disappointment. "Your death wasn't going to be quick, but now . . . "

"Why did you untie him?"

Savannah's curiosity surprised me. I looked over at her taking in the scene with calm grace, like she was at one of her society events. *Ay dios mio!* She was beautiful. Even now. *Especially* now.

"Jimmy, unlike most of the people I bring up here, did something unforgivable. He's getting *special* treatment."

"Something unforgivable?" she asked, her sweet voice filled with innocent naivete.

"He touched what was mine."

Her eyes widened, and a beautiful flush of color warmed her cheeks. Why did she have to look so fucking beautiful right now?

I tied another length of rope around his injured wrist, knotting it tightly enough to elicit a whimper from him. Then I did the same on the other side and secured him to the middle of the bridge, his arms stretched painfully wide. Jimmy wouldn't get the honor of hanging. He tried to wrench one way then the other, but he was tied too tightly to move more than a few centimeters in either direction.

"Wait here."

From one of the saddlebags, I pulled out a small hatchet, flipping it lackadaisically as I approached Jimmy. He could hear me, feel me, but he couldn't see what I was doing. He trembled, a high-keening whine coming from the rags still stuffed in his mouth. I smiled. Widely. My years of studying anatomy filtered through my mind as I mapped where I would cut. Then I remembered, in vivid detail, everywhere that he'd touched Savannah earlier. Every inch of her skin that he defiled with his unwanted advances. A haze of red stole over my vision.

I swung.

The blade crunched through his ribs and along his spine. He screamed. "How many times did she tell you no?" I asked, swinging again as blood splattered onto my face. "How many times did you hurt her? Make her uncomfortable?" Another swing, another arc of blood, warm on my face. "Did you ever think of her at night? Did the fear on her face make you hard? Is that why you kept tormenting her?" I started on the other side, a wild smile of victory on my face as his bones crunched beneath my hatchet. "Savannah has always been too good for the pathetic likes of you." Another swing, another crunch. "She's too fucking perfect for someone like you to touch her with your filthy fucking hands." Blood dripped from my chin and rolled down my neck like red rivulets of water.

I dropped the sticky hatchet to the ground, my smile growing hysterical as I chuckled at the sight before me. "We're just getting started, *Jimmy*." With my bare hands I reached into the cleaving, open wounds and pulled sharp broken bones, opening his back with my arm muscles straining against the unnatural angle. He screamed and screamed and screamed and I laughed at the sound.

"Don't worry, Jimmy, you won't die for a *very* long time," I said as I reached into the widened wounds, feeling the expanding sacs of his lungs and yanking hard. Hard enough to tear muscle, hard enough that they finally came free. As I pulled them into the open air, something inside of me broke free. I placed them, still expanding and retracting on his shoulders. The sticky feel of his blood grew tacky on my skin.

I'd never liked it this much. I'd never *wanted* it this much. Death was a friend of mine, and I didn't shirk away from that. I embraced it.

I walked around him to face him, his head hung in exhaustion and pain, his lungs resting on his shoulders just like in the books I'd read.

"It's called a Blood Eagle, Jimmy. Your lungs are made to look like the wings of an eagle. You'll die of blood loss . . . but not for *several* hours." I tipped up his chin, so that he could look deep into my apathetic eyes, smearing his own blood on his face. "And for every second of agony you face, I want you to think of Savannah. I want you to regret ever meeting her. Ever touching her. Ever daring to make her think less of herself. I want you to beg for mercy within your own mind and know that the sweet release of death is only the beginning of the torment you'll face. Because if there is a God, he ignores what happens on this bridge. There's only the devil here. And he'll be the one to take his due."

I turned away from him, needing to finish this, needing to string up his friends as he watched. The final disrespect.

As I pulled the rope for the first body, my ribs screamed. The physical exertion of ripping Jimmy apart had taken its toll. I clenched my teeth and breathed heavily through my nose to stifle the pain, tugging hard with all my might as he rose foot after foot. Soft, clean hands covered mine, and I looked sharply to my left where Savannah stood, completely unperturbed by the gore on my skin. She was luminous in the swallowing dark. Like a star, refusing to let the ink of the night sky dampen her.

"Go wait by the horse. We're almost done, I don't want you to get blood on your—"

"Shut up, William, and pull."

Something soft and warm filled my veins at her words, at the sight of her, the feel of her next to me. I smiled. A real one this time. Together we hung the two men, and when we finished, she ran the back of her hand against her cheek, a smear of crimson left behind.

She stared up at me with those sunshine-through-whiskey eyes that I couldn't get enough of, dirty, disheveled, her hair falling out of its perfect chignon. She'd let go of her inhibitions and she'd never looked more beautiful. I had to say something, had to tell her how tonight had shifted my entire world. How much it meant that she didn't want me to be alone, and even in the face of such horror, she hadn't let me push her away. She'd carried the weight of it like she was born to. Like she was meant for me. She had to know, she just had to know that there was no part of me that didn't belong to her.

"You look so fucking beautiful with blood on your skin, *mi sol.*"

"What?" Her eyebrows scrunched in confusion. I smirked at my own stupidness.

"Right now, you look like you did the first night I met you. The way you took control of that house, commanded everyone to your will, like no one and nothing would stop you. You look like that."

"Oh," she said, her cheeks flushing again.

"Savvy," I said, moving closer, taking her bloodstained hands in mine. "The last time we spoke, you made it clear that you didn't want me. Want *this*. I told you it was okay, that I'd respect your decision, and I will. Even if I still did a *little* light stalking after that." She smiled and shook her head, her eyes turning glassy. "Is that still what you want? Because I can't keep doing the back and forth. I'm not good at this, so I just need you to tell me plainly. What do you want?"

"You."

Was I still breathing? I wrapped an arm around her waist, pulling her flush against my bloodstained body, no longer worried about sullying her. I tipped my hat up so that she could see my eyes clearly.

"You've had that all along. Don't you know that I'd do *anything* for you?"

"That's the thing, William, you don't have to *do* anything for me. I see you, I see your darkness, and I want *you*. Only you." She exhaled sharply. "You asked me what I meant when I said I wanted all of you." She flattened her palm against my chest, over my heart. "I want everything with you."

I sighed, part in relief and part in terror, because there were no more games to play. I had to be honest. "If you want me, you can have me. I'll never stray, I'll never long for anyone else. You've been the object of my obsession for so long, I think about you more than I think about myself.

I want to spend every night by your side, and every morning with the smell of your shampoo on the pillows. You make me want to be better, and you don't judge me when I'm not." I rested my hand over hers and stared into those eyes that held the multitudes of the universe within them. Eyes I could spend a lifetime drowning in. "But, Savvy, I *can't* love you."

Her breath caught in her throat.

"I'm not capable of love. And one day, when this isn't enough for you—"

"Will, I—"

"Because it *won't* be. I promise to let you go. Until then, say you'll be mine. Because I've always been yours. Whatever broken, fucked up parts of me there are left. They've *always* been yours."

Instead of her cursing me, slapping me, running away, she wound her arms around my neck and yanked me down until our lips met. My mind went blank. All I could do was hang on as she made me happier than I'd ever been. My hands and mouth had minds of their own, devouring everything she offered me. Memorizing the sweet taste of her, drinking in her gasps of pleasure, mapping the curves of her body as they melted into mine. I didn't realize until she made a soft sound of impact against my lips that I'd pressed her against one of the metal columns that held up the bridge.

"Say it," I growled against her mouth, tangling my fingers in her unkempt curls. "Say you're mine."

"I'm yours, William," she whispered, and the last thread of my sanity snapped. There would be nothing gentle or kind about how I would take her. Here. On this bridge. Overlooking the city that shunned me. With hardly any effort I ripped the top of her dress open, buttons clinking to the ground as I shoved fabric aside and freed her glorious breasts to the night air, brown nipples peaked in desire.

"Put your hands above your head," I ordered, my belt buckle clanging as I yanked it off. She licked her parted lips and crossed her wrists above her head in supplication. My cock throbbed in response. As I looped my belt around the crossbeam and tightened the leather around her wrists, she wriggled and arched her back, making her beautiful, full breasts sway in my vision. When she was restrained, I stepped back to admire her.

She was the perfect contradiction of beautiful and terrible. The shafts of moonlight highlighted the angles of her body, while the darkness of the night shadowed the planes of her skin. As if I were seeing her fully for the first time. Not just the epitome of feminine beauty, but the violent delight of it as evidenced by the smears of blood on her warm skin. If I was going to die, it would be by her hands alone. Until then, I'd live. I'd soak in every inch of her until she was all I knew.

I pulled my cigarette case out of my pocket and my lighter from another. She wriggled again, her thighs pressing together beneath her skirts, her plush lips parting on a question I could see written in her lust-filled liquescent eyes.

"William?" she breathed, beckoning me, questioning me, begging me for the rough hurried sex she'd become accustomed to. She didn't know yet what a masochist I truly was. How much I enjoyed denying my own pleasure so that I could soak in the agony of hers. I lit my cigarette, stepping close again as she tensed in anticipation, dragging a lungful of smoke to trap inside my hammering chest. Leaning into her warmth, I dragged the tip of my nose along her thudding pulse, exhaling the warm smoke against her skin. She bit her bottom lip and whimpered. With the lit tip of my cigarette clenched between my fingers, I cupped the heavy weight of her breast, so full and perfect it made me grind my teeth together in an effort to *slow down. Not yet.*

A throaty sound of fear and pleasure burst from her mouth as the heat from the cigarette dipped close to her skin and I rolled her nipple between my fingers. Like *she* was the intoxicating thing I wanted to inhale next. My teeth scraped against her ear, and she shuddered beneath my touch, forcing me to remove my hand until she stilled. I didn't want to burn her. Just heighten the pleasure building between us.

"Stay still, *mi sol*," I whispered against her neck.

"I-I can't," she moaned, wriggling her hips again. "I want you too badly."

I took another long drag of the cigarette and crouched low, sucking her other nipple deep into my mouth as I expelled the smoke from my nose. She arched her body so forcefully she nearly tugged her wrists from my belt. With a flick of my fingers, the lit stub sailed over the railing and disappeared into the darkness below. With both of my hands free, I traced the planes of her stomach as my tongue flicked against her. Then I mapped the shape of her waist and hips, her skirt slinging low as I explored her.

It would be so easy to shove inside of her. To fuck her so hard she couldn't sit for a week. I wanted that. I wanted it *bad.* I wanted to feel the warm, wet slide of her as she let me deep inside her body. My cock was so hard that it hurt. So hard that I would die if I didn't do something soon. But that agony was part of what I liked. With a *pop,* I released one breast only to slide the flat of my tongue over the other. I dropped to my knees before her, looking up at the long expanse of her exposed skin and knowing that this had to be a dream. It just had to. There was no way any woman could look this fucking beautiful, could stare down at me with passion-glazed eyes that burned so bright.

I reached beneath her skirt to her thighs, trailing upward with soft, tickling touches that made her throw her head back. I reached the soaked cotton panties beneath the fabric.

"*Mierda*, you're dripping for me. You've made quite the mess." She flushed, averting her eyes as if embarrassed. "I want to taste it." Her eyes snapped back to mine, wide and wonderful. "Spread your legs wider, baby."

"No, Will, I—"

But I didn't let her finish. Instead, I ducked beneath her skirts, forcing my shoulders between her legs. I could smell the warm musk of her, and I groaned as it surrounded me. Gripping her hips, I breathed against the soaked cotton so she could feel the heat of my mouth. Her legs were already trembling, thighs quaking against my ears as I licked her above the fabric.

"Oh God!" she screamed, and I smiled against her cotton-clad sex. I knew she could feel the twist of my mouth, knew it frustrated her that she'd let go enough to scream out something I could tease her for later. But I didn't let that stop me. I licked her again, savoring her taste, committing it to memory. Sucking at the top of her sex where I knew that little bundle of nerves would push her to the brink. She screamed again. This time it was incoherent, but it could've been some version of my name. I tortured her with the same glee I'd tortured Jimmy, drawing out her pleasure and nibbling on her inner thighs. She came so hard that I almost couldn't hang onto her as she bucked and writhed against my face. Only then did I emerge from beneath her skirt, my hand slipping into the soft cotton to impale her on two of my fingers, driven as deep as I could get them, something for her clenching inner walls to grab onto during the last waves of her pleasure.

"That was . . ."

"Just the beginning, Savvy," I said as I kissed her swollen mouth and fucked her with my fingers. Just the way I knew she liked. Slow and slick, keeping a rhythm that would have her seeing stars again in moments. She fought against her restraints now. Desperate to claw at me, yet powerless against the pleasure building inside her tight little body again. "Come for me. You're so beautiful when you come."

As if the praise was all she needed, she squeezed her eyes tight and sobbed through her orgasm. Her body jerked involuntarily, her cunt clamping down on my fingers as she rose onto the tips of her toes.

"Now you're ready," I said softly against her skin as I unbuttoned my pants. Lifting her legs to wrap around my waist, I pushed her panties aside and rocked forward, groaning as her body welcomed me. As I filled her, she sighed, like our joining was a relief. As if my cock being buried to the hilt inside her was as whole as she would ever feel. I wondered if she knew that was how it felt for me too. Complete. With her wrapped around me, it felt like coming home.

"*Fuck.*" I dragged the word out long as I shuddered with her in my arms. "You're so perfect." Tucking my shoulder beneath her chin, I thrust. Long, deep strokes. Reveling in the friction of every inch. She cried out, her voice ringing in the night air. It drove me wild. Knowing that the entire city would be able to hear how well I satisfied her. I thrust harder, until I knew it was too rough. Too wild. But I couldn't stop. I pulled back to see her face, lit in moonlight, open and vulnerable and tight with the sweet agony of sex.

"Say it again," I panted between us. "Say you're mine."

"I'm yours!" she screamed as I pounded into her desperately. "I'm yours, William! I'm yours!"

I couldn't stop. I couldn't slow. I couldn't think. She was close. I could tell by the way she rolled her hips against mine, but I didn't know if I could last. "Fuck, *fuck*." I tried to hold on. My fingertips dug into her soft flesh. She made me crazy. She made me weak. She made me feel *everything*. She tipped her chin up, defiant and beautiful, and through clenched teeth she said, "Come for me." Repeating my words back to her. And goddamnit I did. With a roar, I slammed into her as she tipped over the edge, the both of us making enough noise to wake the dead.

If there was a God, I saw her at that moment. Reality melted around me and all of my strength vanished. All I could do was hold onto her. My staccato breaths puffed against her skin as I untied her hands. Her fingers fell into my hair. Her mouth opened against mine, and all I could do was tremble in her arms as she shifted to separate us and stand on shaking legs. She held me and she didn't let go.

And I knew, at that moment, I'd never be able to let her go either.

SAVANNAH

RETURNING TO LEE MANOR was far less eventful. A haze of exhaustion weighed me down from the moment Will tucked me into the saddle with him. With the threat of wayward guards gone, I relaxed into him, into some semblance of safety. Everything had changed between us, grown stronger.

I loved him, and even if he couldn't love me back, I'd never be the same.

The easy route would be to ignore my feelings, shove them down until the end of time, but my heart disagreed. Even if it ended badly, being with Will felt right in a way that nothing else in my life had.

No one greeted us in the stables upon our return. Will put away his stallion and tugged me through the halls of the house and into my bedroom. We moved silently together to the bathroom, where we took turns cleaning the blood from our skin. As opposed to how the air seemed to charge when we were together, when I denied my feelings for him, peace filled the space between us.

The irony of Will cleaning my skin after I'd done the same for him so many times was not lost on me.

We fell into a routine, taking turns soaking towels in hot water and cleansing our skin of the night's atrocities. Not that Will was atrocious. No, any contempt I felt lay solely with the dead guards hanging above the river.

"Let me wash your hair." My voice was a shock against the silence.

Will's dark eyes flashed to mine, curious but not hard. His brows lifted in question. A small smile perched on my lips. We weren't good with letting other people take care of us, but this was something I wanted to do. He was so good at taking care of me in the tender moments when I needed it. The least I could do was this for him.

"Come on," I said, smirking as I tugged him toward the bathtub. I shoved him onto his knees and ran the hot water. Blood crusted his strands, making them look darker than they were. I took my time lathering the shampoo into his scalp, rinsing, and repeating until I was satisfied the remnants of the murder were gone.

Will rose, water coursing down his bare chest. With a gentle nudge, he sat on the edge of the tub, and I retrieved a fresh towel. I wrapped it around his head, digging in my fingers to dry his hair.

"For the record," I said kindly. "I would never ask you to kill for me." There was no shame in my voice, no judgment. I admired him for wanting to protect me, but I had to make it clear that I did not expect that of him.

"You don't have to." His voice was slightly muffled, so I let the towel fall from his head, using it instead to wipe the water droplets from his shoulders and chest. "I am not a good man, Savannah. If given the choice between doing the right thing or whatever it takes to keep the people I care about safe, there's no contest."

I nodded. I knew that. He gripped my wrist and tugged my hand, flattening my palm against his stubbled cheek.

"I am *selfish*. And I won't hesitate to do the bad things, the worst things, if it means you are never hurt again."

I swiped my thumb along his jaw, nodding. I'd accepted Will for who he was a long time ago, but admitting it to him had been almost freeing. I pressed my lips to his in a chaste kiss. His muscles shifted, but before I fell into his embrace, I pulled away, smiling at him.

"C'mon," I remarked, taking him by the hand. My muscles ached, and exhaustion weighed me down. I changed into a nightgown while Will settled on the edge of my bed. We needed sleep if we had any hope of getting out of the manor tomorrow night. Or was it tonight? I couldn't be sure of the time.

My bed welcomed us both into its soft depths. I curled against Will's side after he settled on his back. This felt right. It felt normal. I remained against his chest, eyes fluttering shut. I could have fallen asleep just like that.

"Savvy," he whispered, touching my cheek.

"Hmm?" My eyes opened, taking in his features as he lay beside me, landing on the scar that led from his cheek to his hairline. I brushed a gentle finger over it. Will stilled beneath me.

"I'm sorry he did that," I whispered. Instead of speaking, he gripped my wrist and pressed a tender kiss to my palm.

"I was too pretty before anyway," Will said, flashing a grin.

I tugged my hand loose and rolled my eyes at his sarcasm, my fingers sliding over his throat to the scar I'd noticed on his shoulder. "What's this from?"

Will let out a breathy chuckle. "Fuckin' Jesse." My brows shot up, the echo of a memory rising to the surface.

"He shot you," I said.

"He told you?"

"I think he meant it as a way to make me feel better at the engagement party." My fingertips trailed across the smooth planes of his abdomen, to the bruises that, though faded, remained from the beating his father had given him. Countless scars marred his arms, his stomach, but, to me, they were proof. Proof of his strength.

I ran my finger along a clean-cut scar on his forearm. His eyes marked the movement. "This one?"

Will cleared his throat, eyes shifting. "*El dolor es fugaz.*"

My chest tightened. "Your mother."

His eyes snapped to mine, pain and anguish flashing behind them. "How did you know?"

I leaned over and pressed a gentle kiss to the scar. "Bonnie."

He rolled his eyes but didn't seem shocked. "When I was a young boy, my mother sat me down and pulled out my father's knife. The one he always used on her." A low ball of dread formed in my stomach. His dark gaze was clouded, lost to the memory. "I was old enough to start asking questions and beg for mercy on her behalf. She worried I would try to rescue her and he'd kill me, so she decided to teach me about pain. She cut me here," he said, with a small smile curling on his mouth. He traced the straight line on his arm lovingly, the scar silvered with time against his bronze skin.

"I cried, and she took my face in her hands and kissed my tears away. She said *el dolor es fugaz, hijo.* 'The pain is fleeting, son,' and she was right." He took in a long breath and met my gaze, some of the fogged memory fading in his eyes. "After a while, the cut stopped hurting and she bandaged it. She told me never to forget, because it wouldn't be the last time I was hurt. And it wasn't. No matter how she tried to shield me, we both knew that a time would come when my father would start to cut me too."

A strange, peaceful curve crossed his mouth. "But this one, the first one, she stole that from him and used it to make me strong. Strong enough to survive him."

"You are, you know," I said. Will's brows lifted as he turned his attention fully to me. "Strong enough. Even when it feels like you aren't."

Will wrapped an arm around me, and I settled against the crook of his shoulder. "I don't know about that, *mi sol.*" He fixed me with a knowing stare.

"What do you mean?" I shifted to face him, resting my chin on his bare chest.

Tenderly, he looped one of my wayward curls around his finger and tugged gently. "You make me weak."

My skin heated beneath the intensity of his stare. Desire, mixed with longing, mixed with affection. Even though he claimed he didn't know how to love, the look on his face gave me hope.

"What about this one?" I asked, trailing my finger along a scattering of smaller scars around his wrist.

This time, Will's mouth twisted into that charming grin of his. "I fucked one of the Hanged Men's wives and got caught sneaking out the window. Jones let him tie me to a post with the ropes I'd bound that *pendejo's* eager wife with and give me twenty lashes."

My mouth dropped open. I blinked rapidly, not understanding what he was saying completely. "How can you be smiling at that?"

"It was worth it," Will said, snorting. A moment passed, his smile crumbling as he stared at his wrist. "It was a long time ago. I don't enjoy ropes anymore." I met his gaze but remained silent, not wanting to push. When he finally dragged his eyes up to mine, he hesitated and cleared his throat. Maybe he sensed the unasked question on my lips. Maybe he didn't realize it was something he wanted to share.

After a minute, he let out a gentle sigh and scratched his eyebrow with his thumb. "I know you read a lot, but . . . *Mierda*, I'm going to freak you out."

I couldn't help my amused smile as he covered his face and groaned sheepishly. I tangled my fingers with his, tugging his hands away from his face.

"As if my penchant for public sex isn't freaky enough?" I quirked my eyebrows suggestively. I *had* read quite a lot of romances over the years. I doubted anything he said would truly shock me. "Is William Ellis, *Don Juan* himself, embarrassed?"

Will peered at me through one eye, the hint of a smile curling his lips. "Alright. Alright." He tangled his fingers with mine once more, then bit his bottom lip. When our eyes met, the darkness of desire filled them, as if he were imagining the things he wanted to do. "I have specific tastes, sexually. I enjoy giving orgasms. Sometimes more than having my own."

So far, that wasn't shocking.

"With my hands, my mouth—" My stomach coiled at the memory of his mouth between my thighs. "Discovering every place on your body that gives you pleasure. Over and over again. I could spend hours, fuck, *days* even, bringing you over the edge."

I held myself very still, because, I found, I very much wanted *that*. With him.

"And *ropes* used to play a big part in that. Tying my partner up, having them surrender themselves to me intentionally, unable to move . . . "

I thought back to the morning after the graveyard, how Will had pinned me to the mattress, held my hands above my head, how just hours ago he'd belted me to the bridge. Thudding desire flared in my belly.

"It requires a lot of trust and patience and submission." His face fell, eyes shadowed as he averted them from my face. "I haven't done that in a long time though. Ropes have lost their appeal the last few years."

At his crestfallen expression, my heart slowed. I didn't like that look in his eyes, that shame. I never wanted him to feel ashamed about anything he enjoyed. Why would he— Suddenly, it hit me. What we'd done mere hours ago. Hanging men from the bridge over and over again.

Instead of offering him pity, I shifted on the mattress, straddling his lap as I took his head in my hands and forced him to look at me. "Use them on me."

Will blinked, brows crinkling. "What?"

"Ropes. I want you to enjoy this, too." I kept my voice gentle. His mouth popped open to argue with me, I assumed, but I said, "I trust you, William. Implicitly. You would never hurt me. No matter what others have made you do, you're still *you*." His features hardened, as if he were prepared to rebut me again. I cradled his cheek, brushing my thumb along his stubbled jaw. "I want *all* of you, William."

His eyes darkened slightly, even as he opened his mouth to argue with me. Then, as his gaze trailed down the curve of my neck, he closed his mouth and brushed his fingers along my thighs to rest on my hips. That devilish grin I loved so much crossed his features.

"You're going to regret saying that."

A shiver ran down my spine, and I twisted my fingers in his hair, raking my nails against his scalp.

"No, William," I said, my mouth hovering just above his. "I don't think I will."

Before I could kiss him, Will flattened a hand against the small of my back and flipped our positions. I let out a gasp as my heart somersaulted in my chest. Will settled his hips against the cradle of my thighs. Then he kissed me senseless.

We fell into one another, until my rational mind couldn't consider whether I'd made a mistake in choosing him. There was space for nothing.

Just him.

Just us.

Until our exhaustion took hold and I passed out against his chest, happier than I'd ever been.

A knock came at the door far too early. When I attempted to climb over Will and get out of the bed, however, he wrapped his arms around my waist and flipped me onto my back, barking at Bonnie at the bathroom door that we'd be ready in thirty minutes.

An hour and a half later, we entered Bonnie's room together, a flush in my cheeks and bliss on my heart. Morning light filtered into her room, casting a warm glow on everything, as if how I felt was reflected all around us.

Bonnie sat at her desk, a stack of papers with her scribbles on them. "Does everyone know what they're supposed to be doing?"

I tore my gaze away from Will, the smile slipping from my mouth. I'd gotten so lost in him last night that, admittedly, I'd need a refresher. The Kid shoved away from the barred window, his boots thunking heavily against the hardwood. He seemed a little . . . on edge. His clothes were disheveled, and he didn't meet my eye when I glanced his way.

"Savannah is on team exodus," Bonnie said. I snapped my attention to her. Right. We were leaving today. I had to get everything together. "And yes"—she eyed Will and me—"I will be breaking up you and Will today or literally nothing will get done." I grinned at Will sheepishly as she eyed us with suspicion. "Under the guise of regular house errands, I need you to get everything prepped to leave. Do you think you can handle that?"

With a nod, I stood straighter. Though I wanted nothing more than to get lost in my bliss, I was the rational one. The one with the lists. The one who made sure things got done.

"Will—" Her gaze settled squarely on him, though her eyes dulled a bit. "Secure our exit route. Liaison with Mickey and . . . the rest. Make sure they're ready to go."

I slid my hand into his, giving it a quick squeeze. I didn't like that he'd be out of my sight, but we'd have time for that later.

"Kid, team ledger. While I keep everyone busy and out of the office today, I need you to break in and find that fucking book. Find it, secure it, get it out of the house."

Without needing further instruction, The Kid gave her a quick salute with two fingers and headed for the door. Bonnie's shoulders slumped slightly as she turned back to the papers on her desk. Will wrapped an arm around my waist and tugged me hard against his chest. I smiled up at him, at the twinkle in his eyes.

This was really happening. We were leaving.

"Be careful," I said quietly, running my hands over his shoulders and smoothing down the front of his shirt. His father and the Hanged Men were still in the city. He had to leave with us. I *needed* him to leave with me. "Please."

"Don't fret, *mi sol.*" He leaned down and captured my lips in a hard kiss, then tucked one of my curls behind my ear. "We'll meet in the stables later while Bonnie's at the chapel?" I nodded. He gave me another swift kiss, then marched from the room with long, purposeful strides.

When we were alone, I turned to my best friend. "I'll see you tonight," I said cautiously. "Come hell or high water, we're leaving." The scariest emotion of all swelled in my chest. Hope. I'd been let down so many times before, but that was when I was on my own. Between the four of us, Jesse and his uncle's crew, we *were* going to make it.

I crossed to Bonnie and smoothed her hair down, then wrapped my arms around her shoulders and squeezed her tight. She gave me a half smile. I left her a moment later, already running through the things I'd have to pack. But first, while it was still early, I had to make a run to the kitchen and get some tea. The last thing any of us needed was a child right now.

The hope that blossomed in my chest only swelled more. For the first time in ten years, I was more confident than ever that I was leaving. With Will and Bonnie. Where we would go, it didn't matter to me, as long as we had each other. That hope faltered, though, as I made my way through the corridors.

My brows creased, and a frown rested on my mouth. I swallowed around the lump that formed in my throat. I'd be leaving Etty, the only real mother I'd ever known. My pace slowed as I entered the courtyard. People moved about, carrying floral arrangements or tables and chairs. Some of the maids hung lace streamers for the wedding.

"Don't bring those to the formal dining room until they leave for the rehearsal!" Etty's booming, authoritative voice snapped me back to my goal at hand. Tea for the road. The last time I'd seen her was when Will returned to the manor after being attacked by his father. I'd avoided her, working on the wedding cake only after she'd finished in the kitchen for the day.

Now, I had to face her.

I pushed through the kitchen door, the familiarity of it sending a thick wave of nostalgia through my belly. How many hours had I spent in this kitchen, learning from Etty, helping her, being treated as if I were her own? I didn't realize just how hard it would be to say goodbye.

When Etty caught sight of me, she stopped chopping vegetables and eyed me up and down. Her lips pursed, but not in an angry way. She seemed more resolved as she set her knife down on the cutting board.

"Everybody out." The others milling about lowered their gazes and left the room. Etty's shoulders lifted as she took a bracing breath, and then she turned to face me head on. "When are you leaving?"

I'd expected some commentary on Will, on how I'd been avoiding her, but not *this*. I glanced toward the exits, then moved closer to her.

"Tonight," I said.

Etty's bottom lip quivered. Her gaze lowered as she looked over my dress and nodded to herself. She placed her hands on my shoulders, continuing to nod to herself, before lifting her eyes to meet mine. She cupped my cheek gently.

"It's about time," she said, her brows knitting together slightly. Her eyes grew glassy as she looked at me. "My girl."

"It's not goodbye, Etty," I said quietly.

"We don't know what tomorrow'll bring. What do you need?"

This was the woman who'd mothered me, who'd taught me how to work in a kitchen, who'd helped me adjust to this life. Gone was her harsh persona that popped up when Will was around.

"Whatever provisions you can spare," I said. She turned from me then, purposeful as she bustled toward the cabinets. "And tea."

Etty stopped, her shoulders tensing. Dread coiled tightly around my heart. Instead of saying a word, she motioned me toward the pantry. Perhaps that last confrontation with Will had been enough to convince her that I could take care of myself. While she rifled through cabinets, I bee-lined to the pantry.

By the time we finished, Etty had packed an entire tote bag for me filled with provisions. It would work to get us out of the city. After that, we'd figure out our next steps. As I tucked the tea tin into the bag, Etty sighed and wrapped me in her arms. I clung to her, ignoring the bite of my grief as it welled in my throat.

"You could come with us," I muttered against her shoulder. She let out a breathy laugh and pulled back to look at me.

"Someone's gotta stay here in the aftermath. We need eyes on Lee."

Right. The Resistance.

"Don't put yourself in any unnecessary danger—" My voice cut off as one of the maids shoved through the door, carrying an armload of linens. She barely spared a glance at me before cutting to the other side of the kitchen that led to the laundry room.

"Promise me one thing, Savannah," Etty said, pulling my attention back to her. My brows lifted in question. "*Live*. Wherever you go. Whoever you're with, find happiness and never let it go."

My vision wobbled, tears stinging my eyes. This was it. This was goodbye. "We'll see each other again."

A sad smile crossed her face. "Be safe."

When she wrapped me in her warm embrace, I choked back a sob and gripped onto her, putting everything that I couldn't say into that one hug. That I was grateful for her. That I would have never made it here without her. That she had been one of the best things to happen to me.

We *would* meet again. I couldn't imagine any other outcome.

Etty cleared the back way for me, ensuring no one saw me with the tote. I brought it straight to the stables instead of lugging it back and forth to my room. It was safer this way. I loped into the stables, keeping my eyes peeled for the young stable hand. He was focused on brushing one of the other horses.

I slipped into the last stall on the left. Will's stallion was gone. I frowned. Even though I knew his orders would take him out of the house, my anxiety didn't like him being out there while the Hanged Men lingered. After covering the tote with hay in the corner of the stall, I made my way back out.

"He's gone, miss," the young man said.

"Thanks. Could you let me know when he's back?"

He only nodded. I didn't need him to tell me anything. Will would find me when he returned, but at least if the stable hand thought I was just looking for Will, no one would be the wiser when we escaped.

I returned to our rooms and went through our things, only packing the necessities as I saw fit. A couple of changes of clothes for Bonnie. A hair brush, as promised, but when I got to my own wardrobe, I paused. The dresses that made up who I was hung lifeless before me. My fashion had been my own sort of statement. Armor that I used to protect myself in this house of piranhas. But I didn't need them anymore. I shoved them aside and rifled through the boxes lining the bottom of the wardrobe, retrieving the pants and shirt I'd worn the night of the Slavers' Parade. They were far more practical, even if they set me outside of my comfort zone. I packed a couple of my frumpier dresses. Even if I wouldn't wear them, we could find use for the fabric in any case.

The clock tower at the cathedral chimed the hour loudly. It was getting late. I needed to finish up and head down to the stables.

I tossed the bag with our things over my shoulder and headed for the door, then stopped short. I was forgetting something. Something very important. I loosed a breath and turned slowly, eyeing the rug on the center of my floor.

There wasn't much that I cared about taking with me, if I were being honest. I didn't come to New Orleans with much of anything. My heart skipped a beat. But what I did come with was something I couldn't leave in this place.

I knelt against the hardwood, folding back the rug quickly. I pried up the loose floorboard to my hiding spot. It was the one secret I'd kept from Bonnie after all of this time. When she was heavy in withdrawal from glowroot, I'd hidden my supply there. *Just* in case. It was a failsafe, if I needed it. Thank God I never did.

First I found my coin tin, pulling it out of the hole and setting it aside. My fingers brushed against the nice hair pins, the ones I'd confiscated because I didn't want Bonnie to destroy them. Some of them were so old that the metal was tarnished, but the stones still shone brightly in their settings. There was a French ivory hairpin that I'd planned on using on Bonnie for the wedding when they'd first announced the engagement. Well, that would be out the window now. Still, I tucked them away in one of the small pockets of my bag.

Cool glass brushed against my fingertips. I sighed as I pulled out the vial of glowroot. The blue barely held any of its prior glow. It was so old at this point that I doubted it would have any real effect anyway. I flushed it down the toilet and crushed the vial, placing its remnants in an old washcloth and shoving it to the bottom of the garbage can.

There shouldn't have been much left in my hiding spot. I reached farther in, looking for the leather pouch I'd hidden two years ago. Instead, my fingers found something soft and delicate. My heart plummeted into my stomach. It was childish, really. I pulled the doll gently from its spot. The scent of my mother's perfume wafted up at me, stinging my eyes as tears filled them. I cradled the doll gently, bringing it to my nose and inhaling deeply.

My mother had made it for me during a period of sobriety. She would take on odd jobs after getting evicted from the brothel and thought it would keep me busy while she worked. My breath shuddered in my chest. It was the only thing I still had from St. Louis. When Mr. Lee noticed I carried it with me everywhere around the house, he'd ordered Etty to get rid of it. I'd hidden it here instead.

Much like Bonnie's clothes from the night she arrived, there were just some things that I couldn't throw away. I tucked it into the bottom of the bag gently, wrapping it in an old skirt. It didn't matter that it was impractical, a child's toy. I had to keep it.

After replacing the floorboard, I grabbed the tin of coins. My brows furrowed. It was noticeably heavier than the last time I'd retrieved it. I flipped open the lid, my heart pounding at the sight. There were gold bits in there. I hadn't put any gold bits in there, ever. In fact—I poured the coins onto my rug, counting the bits quietly as I realized there was more than triple the amount of money I'd saved.

The door to my room opened, and in walked Will, looking rather road weary. "Are you ready?"

I looked up at him from where I knelt on the floor, gratitude and love buzzing through my veins. "Did you do this?"

He glanced down at the piles of coins, then back at me and shrugged. "No."

I was on my feet and in front of him in the blink of an eye, a brilliant smile on my face. I pressed a quick kiss to his cheek.

"Liar." I grinned up at him. Before I could return to packing the coins, he wrapped an arm around my waist and pulled me flush against him. He tucked one of his hands into my hair and pulled me close, covering my mouth in a hard kiss. My body reacted to his lips, to his touch. Even as he feathered kisses along my jaw, I knew I couldn't get lost to him. Not now. I pulled gently from his embrace.

After packing the tin in our things, I turned back to him. "I'm ready."

Bonnie should be at the cathedral by now. Everyone's attention would be there, so we'd be able to slip out quietly once we retrieved her from dinner. Will tossed the pack over his shoulder and gripped my hand, tugging me toward the door. I paused at the exit, glancing back at the place that'd been my home for ten years.

"You okay?"

Yes. I was better than okay. I was leaving. These four walls would never again be my prison.

Instead of speaking, I just nodded and let him pull me from the room. We navigated silently through the halls, avoiding any patrols all the way to the stables. Will and I worked in tandem to prep his horse and load the provisions from Etty.

"Stupid fuckin' guards." A grumble came from the doorway that led into the house. I glanced over the door of the stall, finding The Kid kicking at a loose patch of straw.

"What happened?" I opened the stall door and headed toward him, leaving Will behind to outfit the horse.

"I made it into his office, but I couldn't find the ledger. A guard almost caught me, but I snuck out while his back was turned," The Kid explained. "I mean there was nothing in there, just those ugly books and that stupid burnt-up map."

Wait. The map. There was something about the map.

It hit me like a freight train. I blinked against the memory, the moments before Sebastian beat me to hell in my own room. When Lee asked I report on Bonnie going to Jesse's fight. He'd had the ledger right there on his desk, only I didn't realize it. He'd shown me where he kept it.

I marched toward Will and held out my hand. "Lock picks, please."

His eyes widened, but he reached into his pocket and handed me the two pieces of metal. "Where are you going?"

"I'll be right back, promise," I said before pressing a quick kiss to his mouth.

As I purposefully strode from the stable, I caught sight of a hammer, probably used in shoeing horses. I knew I could pick the door lock, but the safe lock was an entirely different challenge. One I doubted we had time for. I snatched the hammer from where it hung on the wall and slipped out of the stable.

Within minutes, I knelt before the door to Lee's office, fingers moving purposefully as I remembered the steps from when Will taught me to pick my own lock. I glanced around the corridor quickly for any sign of guards. A moment passed, and a familiar *click* sounded. I slid into the room silently, gripping the hammer after tucking away the picks.

The charred remains of the map stood out starkly against the rest of the well-put-together office. Why hadn't Lee replaced it yet?

I ran my fingers along the bottom of the frame until they caught on the corner. Then I swung the map out. My shoulders relaxed as the safe came into view.

"Well, here goes nothing," I remarked to myself as I lifted the hammer. I'd never prided myself on my physical strength, but we needed this. *Bonnie* needed this.

The resounding crash echoed in the silent room. I paused; I'd only cracked it. I shook my head and inhaled deeply, then lifted the hammer a second time and swung again. The sound of metal cracking was music to my ears as the lock fell apart. I dropped the hammer and reached up to the handle. It took some maneuvering, and when the door opened, I wanted to shout. I grabbed the ledger, scouring the pristine condition of the red leather cover.

Just a book. But it was so much more.

I didn't waste another second. I lifted the back of my shirt, tucked the ledger into my jeans, and tightened my belt to secure it. We were leaving with this damn book. I turned toward the door, but my blood ran cold at the sight of the man standing there.

"Well, well," said Sixgun, his gaze raking across my skin. "Savannah, isn't it?"

BONNIE

THE LIGHT FILTERING THROUGH the stained-glass windows dyed the pews of the St. Louis Cathedral crimson with late afternoon light. It reminded me of how blood filtered down the drain as you scrubbed it off your skin. Like it had the night I came back from the Slavers' Parade without Jesse.

"No, no, you stand *here*, Mr. Rutherford. Is there no one else in the procession before the bride walks in?" The coordinator at the cathedral was a red-faced, frazzled woman whose eyes never settled too long on anything, as if she were constantly in motion, endlessly solving problems, or just obsessed with perfection. She was younger than Etty, but her eyes showed the weight of her years and anxieties. By comparison, I was standing still enough to be mistaken for one of the decorative statues. Numb.

This whole farce, the rehearsal for a wedding that would never be, drowned me deep in memory. My chest was so tight that every ragged thump of my heart caused a hollow pain to reverberate through me. The chasm of agony inside me was shaped like Jesse in his absence. As I stood in this beautiful church, with frescos of cherubs and angels looking down at me with what could only be disdain, I'd never felt so small. Maybe for the many sins I'd committed in my life, or maybe because I stood with Lucas Rutherford and not the only man who ever made me feel like I had a future that was worth something.

Blinking harder than I meant to, I linked my arms with Lee's as instructed by the coordinator and tried to look as if I were paying attention. Lee looked at me sideways and shifted uncomfortably. I couldn't care less if he was uncomfortable; I didn't care about him at all. Not anymore. I banished the memories of the nights he spoon fed me while I recovered. I murdered the feeling every time he held me when my shattered heart at the loss of my child overwhelmed me. Or the forgiveness he gave me no matter how many times I relapsed in the throes of my addiction.

I *couldn't* care about him. I *couldn't*.

We were leaving tonight. I'd never see him again. I would never feel inadequate again. Never be a pawn in his twisted games again. There was no part of me, no matter how small, that I would allow to *miss* this flawed, violent, misogynistic man. New Orleans had become something between a home and a prison, and Zachary, while not really being a father to me, had given me a connection that was hard to leave. He could tell me more stories about my *halmeoni* and *harabeoji* and how they lived in Korea, and the journey they made here. But instead, I was leaving, and those threads of a culture and a past I might have belonged to once would be severed.

"What's that?" Jesse asked, his eyes glazed with drink and desire as he stared at my lips. "Korean?"

I pressed my lips together, but a small smile curled on them anyway as I remembered how his eyes had lit up with curiosity like The Kid's when I told him tall tales on the road. Would he understand the sense of melancholy I felt right now? Would he care? He'd made it abundantly clear that all he cared about was getting as far away from New Orleans as possible and not what it would cost those of us who'd been trapped here. Who'd built lives in the spaces between abuses and traumas and tragedies.

Step, step, pause.

We were on the move, walking slowly down the long aisle. Each step brought me closer and closer to Lucas, whose bruises were poorly covered with cosmetics and still clear in the waning light. Zachary tugged on my arm impatiently, silently warning me to keep up and stay present. I wanted to be anywhere but here.

"You could use my last name."

I could hear the words like Jesse was walking on my other side, whispering them into my ear. When my memories came back, there was a flood of ugliness in my past that I didn't want to look at too hard or be forced to re-contextualize. The memory of the morning Jesse and I (as Audrey) spent basking in our newly re-established love was a port in the storm. I'd revisited it so often I could tell the exact cadence of our nervous breaths before I finally had answered him.

"Did you just . . . ask me to marry you?"

Step, step, pause. My shoes hurt. Pretty, high-heeled, lace-covered things that resembled confections more than footwear, and they weren't designed for people who have all five of their toes. Zachary Lee was significantly shorter than me in these shoes, though it didn't deter him as he marched me down the aisle, his head raised as if this were the proudest moment of his life. What a joke.

"Very, very badly, it seems . . . I did *just ask you to marry me."*

My stomach churned as we reached the altar across from Lucas. The officiant directed Zachary to hand me off to him at the appropriate moment. Because *here*, with these men, I wasn't a person with autonomy. I was an object to be passed from one man to another. It was laughable, to say the least, how far I'd fallen. From quiet moments of adoration and awe written into my flesh as Jesse traced unconscious patterns, or his eyes drowned me in a depth of emotion that quite frankly terrified me sometimes, to *this*.

"Yes," I whispered against his open mouth, drinking in the taste of him. "I'll marry you."

The officiant looked between Lucas and me, and his bushy eyebrows pinched together in confusion. Perhaps he was puzzled by the lack of affection or nerves between us. He opened his mouth as if to ask but snapped it shut a moment later. Smart man. Zachary Lee wouldn't have responded well to being questioned by anyone, much less someone he paid. He would consider the interruption of services as a breach of the transactional nature of their relationship. Will had been dispatched on several similar occasions and come back looking hollower than he had the day before.

The officiant's voice was an inane buzzing in my ears, my eyes fixed on some point far in the distance as I played absentmindedly with the chain of my necklace, Jesse's father's ring hiding beneath the neckline of my dress. A shaft of red light caught my attention and reminded me how it felt to have hot red stone on my bare feet as Jesse and I stood, looking out at the violent beauty of the desert sunset on the horizon. Nothing but scorching miles ahead of us. Not knowing where we would go, or how changed we would be when we got there.

"You may kiss the bride," the officiant said. Lucas gripped my hands tighter, leaning in as if he'd done this a thousand times. A million. I turned my head, and his lips fell on my cheek. Cold. Stilted. He lingered too long. As if shocked that I'd deny him here, at the altar, as if he were *owed* something. The woman he bought with a shipping contract. When he pulled back, those warm brown eyes I remembered froze into livid pools of shit.

I smiled sweetly at him, showing the barest hint of my teeth. "Don't want to spoil the big moment before it arrives, do we?" The officiant was aflutter at that, taking it as a cue that the strange tension between us was just a part of the process. Nerves before the big day. The coordinator rushed in then, directing us like we were choreographing a dance.

Lucas leaned close, the stink of alcohol on his breath as he said, "We should talk after the dinner."

After dinner, I'd hopefully be on a horse riding like my life depended on it out of New Orleans toward the open desert and the possibility of figuring out this strange disconnect with Jesse. I nodded, even though I didn't mean it. There was no point in arguing. I didn't plan on talking to him ever again. Time dragged on and on and on as my heart galloped in my chest with the prospect of leaving this city and these awful people behind me. I wanted it. I wanted to ride towards my future more than I wanted anything else. Getting the ledger would keep us safe, but no matter what happened, the girl who'd arrived broken and bloody over three years ago would die tonight. I would strangle her into submission inside my body and my mind and force myself to move forward. I'd fucking *earned* a new start.

We did the walk twice more, making sure Lucas's rowdy and half-drunk friends knew where to stand and what order to walk down. The coordinator looked like she might have a stroke trying to stop them from making lewd jokes about the wedding night and wrangle them into some semblance of order. Every time Lee walked me down the aisle, though we didn't speak, I felt the tension in his hold on me, the waver in his breath. He probably never imagined that he'd get this moment, walking his only daughter down the aisle at her wedding. Not after I'd been gone for so long. Knowing that I was giving him false hope for such a significant moment made me viciously happy.

After all, I'd never been *his*. Not really. I'd always belonged to my mother, to Jesse and The Kid, to Will and Savannah. To the people who'd loved me.

We filed into the formal dining room an hour later, the sun nearly gone from the sky as twilight descended. Lit candles on every surface gave the room a romantic evening glow. Flowers in expensive arrangements perfumed the air. Plates covered with silver cloches were set in front of us, removed in sync with a flourish, showing dishes of food so beautiful it would be a shame to eat them at all. Etty had outdone herself. Wine was poured, glasses of clinking ice filled with amber liquid. The conversation was a buzz of excited murmurs. Lucas and my father were smiling, laughing, his friends showering him with attention. And there I sat, still and silent. Completely invisible.

After a while of pushing my food around my plate and answering questions with polite yet abrupt answers, I stood and excused myself from the table.

"Big day tomorrow. I'll need all the beauty sleep I can get."

Lee's eyes pinned me to the spot, full of some emotion I couldn't decipher. They were unusually soft and contemplative. It hurt to look at him, so I averted my gaze and turned to leave. The night had fallen in earnest, stars twinkling in a clear, beautiful sky. Like they were looking down at me and proud of me getting the hell out of here.

I made it all the way down the corridor that led to the stables where my friends were waiting to finally, *finally* take me away when someone called my name from behind me. I stilled, then turned to see Lucas marching determinedly my way. *Fuck.* I had hoped he was having too much fun with his friends and the flowing drinks that he forgot he wanted to talk. I sighed in exhaustion.

"Can we talk tomorrow?" I asked, my tone as weary as I felt dealing with him almost all day long. "It's late and I'm tired."

"No," he said directly, his hand resting on my arm as he led me back up the corridor and past the dining room, farther into the house. "Listen, before tomorrow, I think there's a lot we need to discuss. There's been bad blood between us with the . . . *Montana* incident, and it's not how I want to start our life together."

He opened a door and ushered me inside with a hand on the small of my back. Bile rose in my throat. If this conversation was the last hurdle on my way out, I'd withstand it. He closed and locked the door behind him, raising the hairs on the back of my neck. I crossed my arms. My dress tonight was sleeveless, which already made me feel exposed and vulnerable, but I didn't like being locked in this room with Lucas. Especially after he'd been drinking. He ran a hand through his perfectly styled hair, his palms flattening in front of him in a helpless gesture that I didn't expect.

"I meant what I said before," he said, swallowing hard. "I want us to be friends. I want us to get along. And yes, I got *jealous* about Montana. It's hard not to feel hurt and vindictive when your fiancé admits to not only fucking another guy but being in love with him. And to add insult to injury, the *same* guy who beat the shit out of me. So, now that he's out of the picture, I was wondering if we could start over?"

"Out of the picture?" I asked, my voice calm. "You and my father *sold him.*"

"Your *father* sold him. I just . . . didn't argue."

I sighed again, a headache forming behind my eyes. "Lucas, I haven't been fair to you. I can admit that," I said with genuine regret. I'd been a mess when Lucas showed up. And I hadn't been kind to him, toying with his emotions. But it didn't change the fact that he was a liar, a manipulator, someone who wanted to control and possess me. That wasn't love. At least not the kind of love I wanted. "But I need to be clear here: I will never love you. I may not ever *like* you after what you did. What you continue to do. You showed me *exactly* who you are and what you prioritize and *that*, not another man, is why I feel the way I do."

His face darkened with each of my words, his hands curling into fists at his sides. But I couldn't keep the con up anymore. I couldn't.

"That being said, you still won. I'm being forced to marry you, and I will. So take some consolation in your victory. Now, I'm tired, and I'd really like to return to my room. Okay?" He didn't speak, just stared through me with hurt and rage in his eyes. After a long moment, I turned back to the door, reaching for the lock, ready to be done with him for good.

Pain exploded at the back of my head. Glass shattered and rained on the floor, and my vision went white with panic. I froze, but Lucas dragged me backwards, toward his desk, shoving me face-first over it and pressing me down until I couldn't breathe. Was I okay? My head wasn't throbbing, but could I be sure? I focused on the injury, wondering if it would get as bad as the last time. If I could survive it this time. My breaths stuttered, and I could barely drag in air as I tried to push my panic down so I could assess the situation. Lucas shouted obscenities at me, but I couldn't hear him over my roaring pulse.

"You're going to be *my fucking wife!* Mine. I don't care if you fucking like me, you'll do as you're told and spread your legs for me. And I'm sick and fucking tired of you denying me what's *mine* by right!" He barely made sense, but I heard the ripping of fabric, and my green dress gave way beneath his hard hands, the seam ripping on one side. I took in a steadying breath as he struggled behind me, moving my forearms into position, fully prepared to defend myself how I'd been trained every single day by Will and Jones and a life spent surviving assholes just like him.

Except I never got the chance. Lucas's weight disappeared with a roar of protestation that shook me down to my bones. I paused for a moment to reorient myself in the room, standing on wobbly feet in the too-tall heels. My hand flew to the back of my head, where I explored my scalp only to sigh in relief that there was no gash, no blood, just a swollen bump that was a bit tender to the touch. My gaze flew to the other side of the room, where Jesse stood with Lucas Rutherford's throat in his clenched fist, having slammed him against the opposite wall. His biceps rippled with the force of his grip, making his tattoos shift. His jaw clenched so hard that it could cut glass. Blue eyes cold and deadly as he stared at the man choking to death.

The moment suspended, and I marveled at him, this bear of a man, standing tall and furious as he protected me. *God, I love him,* I thought as he slammed Lucas against the wall a second time before punching his jaw. The one that was already bruised. Lucas's eyes rolled back as he fell into a heap at Jesse's feet, unconscious. His chest was so broad, a fact that was even more evident as it heaved up and down.

"You came for me," I said quietly, unsure if he could hear me. Jesse whirled toward me, the rage in his expression fading to hurt. His eyes drifted over me, assessing, cautious, looking for injuries. They settled on my hand that rested in my hair. He wavered toward me as if he wanted to cross the distance between us but thought better of it.

"Of course I did," he replied carefully.

I dropped my hand from my hair, eyes growing hot, lips trembling. Of course he came for me. He watched my face crumple, and all at once we were moving, like a dance we'd practiced a thousand times before. He crouched, and I sprinted at him, flinging my arms around his neck, his iron embrace crushing me to his chest as he stood to his full height and hefted me off my feet. My face buried in the crook between his neck and shoulder, and one of his hands buried in my hair, fingers exploring just like mine did, making sure there was no injury.

I sucked in a ragged breath, inhaling the scent of his skin like a balm to my ravaged soul. "I wasn't sure," I choked out.

"I know," he breathed into my hair. "I know, Bon, I'm so sorry."

"I'm sorry too," I said, my voice breaking. "I'm so *fucking* sorry."

He shook his head, shaking off my apology. Then he put me gently back on my feet and ran his hands over my arms, his fingers tracing my scar gingerly, his eyes roaming over my form and catching on the ripped hem of my dress. His expression went from soft and concerned to murderous.

"I'm going to kill him," he declared with the type of intent that made something warm unfurl in my chest. He would do anything for me. *Had* done anything for me. I knew he'd kill for me, die for me, hold the bedraggled pieces of my soul together until they could heal on their own. And the certainty of him, of *us*, was all I needed to make the questions that'd swelled between us seem small and insignificant.

"Are we going to be okay?" I asked in a rush, ignoring his murderous intent. I didn't care if he killed Lucas or not. Lucas was unimportant, but I needed reassurance that Jesse and I would work through the last few weeks of this disconnect and find each other again.

His eyes softened, like the vulnerable note in my voice made him realize that even though I was strong and capable and independent, I was also just a girl. His girl. Who needed him.

He swallowed hard, his fingers threading through mine as he crouched to be closer to my height.

"Yes, Bon, we're going to be okay. We *are* okay. And we're about to get the fuck out of his city *together.*"

I nodded, tipping up on my toes and pressing a sweet kiss on his mouth.

"Together," I repeated. He nodded too, his half-lidded eyes on my mouth. Then he crossed the distance and captured my mouth in a searing kiss, crushing me against him like he'd needed the reassurance too.

Every stroke of his tongue and nibble of his teeth lifted a weight from my shoulders. There was something so affirming in the heat of his mouth on mine. Feeling his hands on my skin, cupping my jaw, brushing the hair from my face, melted the lead in the pit of my stomach. We parted reluctantly, but this wasn't the place or time to get caught up in each other. Looking into his eyes for a moment, I knew we were thinking the same thing. Soon, we'd have nothing but time.

Lucas groaned from the floor and stirred. As one, Jesse and I looked down at him.

"What do you want to do with him?" Jesse asked.

Crossing my arms, I contemplated it, trying not to show how happy it made me that Jesse was including me in this decision. "We're going to interrogate him."

With a nod and a few quick directions, Jesse hauled Lucas up and settled his slumped form into an armchair. I found a few ties in a drawer and secured his hands and feet to the arms and legs of it. Then I crossed to the corner of the room where a bourbon pitcher and glasses rested on a cocktail cart. Pouring a glass, I didn't hesitate to throw it in his face, which caused two things to happen simultaneously: Lucas woke with a start and then wailed as the alcohol burned his eyes. With another of the ties and a nod from me, Jesse fitted the material between Lucas's teeth and pulled tight enough to gag him. He blinked incessantly, trying to clear his vision, and mumbled into the material.

"Hey, Lucas," I said in greeting. "I know you're in a bit of pain right now, and incredibly confused since you thought you sold Jesse and that I was some sheltered debutante, but I'm gonna need you to focus for a few moments. Okay? No talking right now, just listening. I've killed like . . . definitely over a dozen people at this point, though I'm not crazy enough to actually keep count. And if you don't want to be one of them, you need to answer a few questions. Think you can do that?"

His wide eyes were bloodshot but clear as he stared at me, and then he nodded vigorously. With a flick of my eyes up to Jesse, he took the material from Lucas's mouth and stood next to me, towering in all his intimidating, muscled glory.

"H-how?" he stuttered, looking at Jesse's uncompromising form. I *tsked* loudly, gaining his attention again.

"You're not asking the questions, bud," I said sweetly with a vicious smile. "Remember?"

With a bracing breath, I ordered my thoughts. We didn't have much time. But there were things I still didn't understand. Details that might give me an advantage once we escaped.

"Let's start with this shipping contract. You and Lee came to an agreement to ship slaves to Manhattan, right?"

He swallowed hard but clenched his jaw tight, a clear refusal. I sighed wearily. "If you don't answer, we'll break a finger." His face paled as he looked between Jesse and me and saw the determination and unity between us.

"Y-yes, my father made Manhattan into a sanctuary city, and I needed . . . I needed to do something to increase profits in the textiles industry. So, I thought s-smuggling them into the city without him knowing could . . . you know?"

"How do the Hanged Men come into play?" Jesse asked, surprising me. *Hanged Men?* He gave me an apologetic glance.

Lucas paled impossibly further. "No." He shook his head and thrashed against his restraints. We'd hit a nerve. "No, no, I can't . . . " I snatched his hand, gripping his left ring finger hard. "Please! No, don't!"

"Either you talk, or I break you," I told him coldly. He clamped his mouth shut and sucked in deep breaths between his nose, his eyes wild and red from the bourbon. I pulled back on his finger slowly, stretching the joint so that he felt every moment. "Talk, Lucas!" I hissed at him, but he shook his head, tears wobbling on his lower lashes. With a quick yank and a loud *crack,* his finger went limp at an angle that was wrong. Jesse shoved the tie in his mouth again as he screamed around the fabric, spittle dripping from his lips to run down his chin.

After too long, he finally quieted into pitiful sobs, and Jesse let him go once more. "Ready for another finger, or are you going to talk?"

"Okay!" he cried, tears tracking down his cheeks and running the makeup meant to hide his bruises, causing purple and blue splotches to reappear on his skin. "It was Lee's idea," he wailed. "The Hanged Men have been interrupting his shipments and sinking his boats along his trade routes. He had me meet with their leader, a man named . . . "

His mouth opened and shut several times as he searched for the name, sniveling loudly.

"Jones?" Jesse asked, casting a worried glance at me. Because I'd stopped breathing. Stopped *everything* as my mind whirred with the implications.

"You met him," I said, more to myself as puzzle pieces clicked together in my mind, painting a macabre picture that sent fear-like shocks all the way down my spine.

"It was all Lee's idea!" he said, the panic in his voice a high-pitched whine that grated on my nerves. "He told me to act as a double agent under the guise of doing business. I told him I was entertaining Lee's offer but that I knew he had a corner on the slave market in the area and pretended that I would double-cross Lee."

I closed my eyes as horror washed over me. "No," I breathed out, trying to steady myself. Jesse's hand found the small of my back, warm and comforting, but I was already shaking. When I opened my eyes, Jesse studied the fear in them.

"We're setting up a trap for him. We're going to pretend to let him into the city and ambush him to take out the competition. The wedding was a part of it. I don't know why, but Lee was *sure* that news of Audrey and me getting married would ensure that he would take us up on the offer so we could spring the trap and—"

"You *invited* him here?" I said, my voice a garbled mess. Panic stole my breath.

"Bonnie?" Jesse questioned, and I turned to face him fully.

"We have to go *now*. Now, Jesse! NOW! Jones wouldn't fall for it. If he's already in the city then—"

But I didn't get to finish my sentence. The pop of gunfire, distant screams, and a loud *boom!* rattled the windows in their panes. It was too late.

"He's already here."

CHAPTER TWENTY-SIX

WILL

TEN MINUTES AND FORTY-FIVE seconds.

That wasn't too long for her to have been gone. I knew that, but I couldn't stop counting the seconds she was out of my sight. Cold dread solidified in my stomach like a lead weight the longer she was gone. Out of my arms. I secured the buckle on the last saddlebag and tried to breathe through the anxiety making me feel jittery.

"Will!" someone shouted in my ear. I looked at Mickey, his eyes dark with concern. "I've been calling your name." He'd gotten here moments after Savvy left with that determination in her eyes. And while it was so good to see him, a confirmation that we were almost out of this fucked city, he couldn't distract me from the mounting discomfort in my bones. "What's going on, son?"

With little thought, I took my hat off with one hand and ran the other through my hair to push the loose curls out of my eyes. "Sorry, it's just . . . Savannah's been gone for a while. I'm worried she might have gotten herself into some kind of trouble."

Mickey stared at me for a long time, studying me the way only he ever could. Those blue eyes peered into each corner of my mind. It used to unnerve me, but now, it felt natural. I didn't have anything to hide anymore. Not from *him.*

"Alright," he said, nodding softly in some sort of resignation. A soft smile played on his lips. "Go on." He waved his hand towards the door. "You're all but useless here now anyway." His blue eyes twinkled. "Go get your girl."

A grin curled on my lips. *My girl. Goddamn right she was.* After last night, and this morning, and honestly for the last nearly four years of my life, she had been. Mine. I wouldn't be able to concentrate on anything until I knew she was safe.

Then the gunfire started, popping and echoing in the air and making my heart plummet to the hay beneath my boots. The Kid rounded the corner with wild eyes.

"It's the Hanged Men, they're attacking! They've subdued the guards on the other side of the house and are overrunning the house."

"*Fuck*," Mickey swore as he pulled out his gun. Mine was already in my hand. "Jesse went after Bonnie, too. We can't leave without them."

Savannah.

"I'll get them," I swore, confidence thick in my voice. "I'll get *all* of them. Mickey, Kid, post up on the alley entrance and don't let any of those fuckers make it through. We need a clear exit. Lock and barricade the door behind me. I'll knock three times so you know it's me." As I spoke, I checked my weapons, tension coiling in my arms and breaths heaving in my chest. After a long, silent moment, I glanced at them. They hadn't moved yet. Instead, they stared at me, unmistakable pride shining in Mickey's eyes.

"C'mon," I said gruffly. "We don't have time for all that."

Then they were moving, and I marched forward, ready to take on a hundred men, a thousand, if it meant getting to Savannah. Employees and a few of the guests from the dinner sprinted through the courtyard looking for a way out. I went in the opposite direction, toward the cacophonous noise and screaming with my jaw set and gun loaded. It was so *loud*, people shouting, screaming, gunfire and the distinct *boom!* of some kind of explosive device. Pushing past several panicked people, I spied the Hanged Men rushing into the corridors like a flood.

"Savannah!" I shouted, scanning faces and trying desperately to tamp down the panic rising in my chest that I might not find her. That she could already be—

Bile rose in my throat as I stepped over the shuddering body of a man who clutched a gaping wound in his throat, bright red blood spilling too fast over and through his fingers. A grinning man with a tattoo on his neck dragged a woman by her hair down the corridor as she screamed. Without hesitation, I pulled the trigger of my gun, and he fell unmoving to the ground. A roar sounded from my right as another Hanged Man rushed me, knives flashing in the scant light.

"You shouldn't bring knives to a gunfight, *amigo*," I said as I raised my weapon and killed him swiftly. I paused to pluck one of the knives from his hands and tucked it into my belt. Shattered glass crunched under my boots as I pressed forward, screaming Savannah's name periodically while ruthlessly dispatching any Hanged Men unlucky enough to get in my way. I'd already changed my clip, trying to be more cognizant of my ammunition. They were a never-ending wave, it seemed, and I needed to conserve until I found Savannah.

After what felt like a year but was probably only another ten minutes, I heard it. *Her.* Through the clamorous din and the heavy gun smoke clouding my vision, I found her. Screaming. She was dragged into the courtyard by a man I would recognize anywhere. He was broad-shoul-dered and barrel-chested, a slight limp in his right leg from a bullet Bonnie put in his knee. His sun-leathered skin belied his many, many years baking beneath the desert sun where he'd committed crimes against humanity like it was a fucking competitive sport.

My breath stuttered, and I remembered the last time I'd seen him, the fear in his eyes that my bloody legacy would make him insignificant. She screamed again as he yanked her bodily farther into the courtyard, and something inside of me shifted.

Tonight, I would end his legacy for good.

Murder like cold shards of ice sliced down my veins, and I moved before I even knew it. The closer I got to the courtyard, the clearer his voice became over the crowd. "Where are you, *Beastie?*" He was calling to me, using Savannah, who had a split lip and tears on her cheeks, as bait to lure me into a trap. He shoved her toward two Hanged Men, who wrestled her arms behind her back no matter how hard she thrashed.

Red clouded my vision at the fear and anguish on her face, at the sight of their filthy fuckin' hands on what was mine! It was the only thought that pounded through me. *Mine. Mine. Mine. Mine. Mine. MINE!*

Two shots rang into the night, and their bodies dropped from around her as I stepped into the courtyard to face my father for the last time. Only one of us would leave this place alive.

"You wanted my attention, old man," I said, lips curled away from my gritted teeth. "You fuckin' got it."

He smiled, the dark hollowness in his eyes the same as it always was: reptilian and lacking any human emotion as he stared at me, calculating exactly how to kill me.

"Will!" Savannah half-gasped, half-cried. I wanted to turn to her, but I couldn't keep my eyes off my father. His knife was strapped to his belt within centimeters of his grasp, the other palm resting casually on the handle of his gun in its holster. At any moment, he could make his move.

"Savvy," I said as calmly as I could. The sound of her name broke our stalemate immediately, and my father lurched. I raised my gun, but he did too, and it wasn't me he aimed at. Savannah whimpered as she stared down the barrel of his gun. "NO!" I roared, but my father smiled at me again, canting his head to the side as if he didn't understand my rage and panic.

"She has such *beautiful* skin, don't you think?" He licked his lips. "Browner than your mother's, but I bet it cuts like butter. *So soft.*" I shook my head, batting away the memories trying to distract me. The way my mother's skin looked as she burned atop her funeral pyre, scars knotting every visible inch of her until she barely looked human anymore. The helpless desperation that had compounded over the years, growing wilder and wilder in my chest. Forcing me into a restless kind of recklessness just to take the edge off.

"You won't *fucking touch her*," I said coldly, confidently. With my other hand I gripped the stolen knife. His gun tipped down slightly, no longer leveled at Savannah's face. "Savvy, I need you to run, *mi sol.*"

"No." She shook her head, her voice trembling as hard as she was. "No, I can't leave you."

"Baby," I said softly, sparing a second to glance at her. "I need you to run." She made a choked sound in the back of her throat, like she was trying to stave off a hysterical sob. Then she moved slowly, inching away from my father.

"Guns down, *boy*," he said, flicking his eyes in Savannah's direction, his intentions clear. We were doing this. But if I wanted Savannah to leave this courtyard unscathed, I had to face him the way he wanted: with fists and knives. Savannah was far enough away that I lowered my gun and, with an open palm, set it slowly to the ground at the same time as he did. All I heard was my pulse pounding in my ears.

"To the stables, Savvy, three knocks," I said, only she didn't respond. Turning to make sure she was on her way, my heart plummeted once more. A Hanged Man covered her mouth and dragged her away. I started toward her, but I'd taken my eyes off my father for too long. He came down on me in an instant, Bowie knife swinging in an arc that I barely deflected by gripping his wrist and twisting. His other hand clenched in an iron fist and slammed into my jaw, knocking me off balance.

I didn't have time for this; I had to get to Savvy. Had to keep her from the Hanged Men. I knew what they'd do to her, had witnessed more horrors than I could remember. My mind had tried to protect me over the years, dulling or erasing the worst of my memories. A quick glance told me that she was still in the corridor nearby. She bit the hand of the guard who tried to drag her away, screaming my name. Calling for me. Calling for help. For protection that I'd promised her.

The flash of a knife illuminated in the dark as it whistled toward me. I leaned back just far enough that it sailed past my neck. A second slower and I'd have been bleeding out like the man from earlier.

Fucking focus!

Sixgun came at me again, but I was ready for him this time. I darted toward him and thrust upward with my own knife. It caught on his sleeve, a line of red blooming in its wake as he roared in impotent fury. His elbow crashed against my nose hard, making dark spots rise in my vision. I stumbled, and he used the opportunity to slam a fist into my gut. *Fuck,* I thought as I crashed to the ground. My eyes sought Savannah as I wheezed, sucking in to compensate for the breath that'd been knocked from my lungs.

Etty struggled across the courtyard with a Hanged Man who'd grabbed her, shouting things I couldn't hear. Over her shoulder, a man with a club loomed, but I had no breath in my lungs to warn her. The club came down on her head hard. Savannah clawed towards her body as she crumpled.

Steel-tipped boots clouded my vision as my father stood in front of me. "Pathetic," he drawled. "I should've bashed your brains against a rock when you were born like I told your mother I would. I tried to tell her that you had no purpose, no usefulness, but she was so . . . *sentimental*." He sighed, like it was exhausting to even think of.

He kicked me in the temple, making my vision blur and the world wobble unnaturally. The coppery tang of blood filled my mouth, and I spit it on the ground as pain throbbed and pulsed with every beat of my heart. Flexing my fingers, I realized I was still holding the knife. Gathering my energy, in a burst of speed, I rolled on my shoulder toward him and slammed the knife through his boot to wedge between the cobblestones, crunching through small bones, snapping tendons, separating muscle. He roared in pain, spittle flying from his mouth as, with both hands, he drove his Bowie knife down on me, weaponless below him.

My life flashed before my eyes as the glint of steel came toward me. A flurry of images and feelings.

My mother making *arepas* for my birthday. The sweetness of her smile.

Days with Bonnie, escaping for a few hours to catch lizards in the desert. Holding hands. Kissing with the taste of tears on my lips.

Jesse calling me his friend. Mickey calling me *son*.

Savannah. Savannah's eyes when she was mad, her eyes when she was lost in pleasure, or amused, infuriated, making plans. Savannah's constellation of freckles that I'd mapped so many nights staring at her sleeping face. Savannah's lips twitching as she ticked things off a mental checklist throughout her day. Savannah. Savannah bantering with me, rolling her beautiful eyes. Savannah.

Savannah.

Only Savannah.

CHAPTER TWENTY-SEVEN

JESSE

FOR SO LONG, PHILLIP Jones had loomed in my mind as a legend, a cautionary tale told around a campfire. I *knew* who he was, knew what he'd done, but it wasn't until the color drained from Bonnie's face as she met my gaze that I realized this legend, this boogeyman from her nightmares was here. Gunfire rattled the windows.

We were so fucked.

If Jones got his hands on Bonnie again, he'd kill her for what she'd done. Lucas had handed her right to him.

Panic rose like hot bile in my throat. After *everything*, Bonnie's nightmares were rearing their ugly heads. Because of Lee. Because of Lucas, a piece of shit that had the audacity to think he deserved even an ounce of Bonnie.

Will had come for us earlier in the day. The plan would be simple. We'd get in, get our friends, and then put this nightmare behind us.

Only now, the nightmare stood in the way.

"You stupid piece of shit," I growled at Lucas, still tied in his chair, his face not nearly bloody enough. Blind, red rage filled my vision as I rounded on the man, fists balled at my sides.

Then I caught sight of Bonnie's blue eyes, wide and fearful. I didn't have time to worry about Lucas fucking Rutherford. She needed me more than I needed revenge.

Lucas tensed, but I turned to Bonnie, crossing the space to cup her face in my hands. Her chest heaved as if she struggled to breathe, her eyes looking everywhere but at me, probably for an exit.

299

"Hey, look at me."

When her blue eyes found their mark, some of the panic receded. I brushed my thumb against her cheek.

"We're leaving. Now. I won't let anything happen to you."

Emotion sparkled in her eyes. I kissed her quickly, then took her by the hand and headed for the door.

"Wait! You can't leave me here!" Lucas twisted against his bindings as I gripped the door handle. I cut my eyes back at him and gave him a cruel smile.

"I pray that Jones makes your death a slow one," I growled.

Not waiting for his response, I twisted the knob and yanked the door open. Gunfire popped nearby, just out of sight. Screams rent the air. We had to get to the stables. If we did, we could use Jones's attack as cover and slip out unnoticed. There was too much chaos for anyone to be worried about us. I hoped.

We were nearly at the stables when two men filled the hallway that led to our exit. Knives flashed, the men spitting and cursing at one another as they struggled. A third appeared, the Hanged Man tattoo stark against his skin. His gaze moved from the fight in front of him to us. *Fuck.*

"This way," I whispered harshly, pulling Bonnie into the stairwell that led upstairs. We stumbled together. With a muttered curse, she kicked off the ridiculous high heels she was wearing, and we pushed forward. We would get out of this together. We'd been too at odds, leaving me with questions about our future.

There would only be a future for us if we got *out*. No matter what.

Heavy boots stomped up the stairs behind us, the Hanged Man calling out gleefully as he pursued his prey. Without a word, I yanked open a door to one of the various supply closets within the manor. I pulled Bonnie behind me and shut the door as silently as I could.

The Hanged Man marching past the door punctuated our heavy breaths. I squeezed Bonnie's hand to remind her I was there. A second passed. Two. Three. Ten. Only when the immediate silence settled did I dare to push open the door. Clear.

We emerged from the closet hand in hand. I was strung tight like a bow string as I took a tentative step toward the way we'd come. A clicking sounded, and before I could turn to see what it was, Bonnie threw herself at me, and we toppled to the floor. A bullet lodged in the wall where my head had been only a second ago.

I yanked the both of us up, and we darted down the hall and around a corner, Bonnie struggling to keep up with my long strides as another bullet passed.

"Where's Selene?" Bonnie asked in a rushed voice.

I swore beneath my breath. "In my saddlebag."

None of us expected we'd be in a gunfight, but we should have known better. A newfound determination filled Bonnie's eyes. We wouldn't get out of here being pursued like this.

"We have to rush him," she said. I nodded.

Like in those early days in the desert, when we'd established a system of hand gestures and learned to read each other's body language, we moved together. Bonnie perched right at the corner as the Hanged Man's steps approached.

"Come on, Bonnie," he called over the screams from beyond the house. "Jones is so relieved we finally found you." My hackles rose at the disgusting sweetness in the man's voice. I crouched, eyes on Bonnie. She nodded once. As soon as the Hanged Man came into view, I balanced my weight.

Like a crater beast, I attacked. I rushed him, slamming the bulk of my shoulder into his gut. His gun went off, the shot hitting somewhere near the ceiling as I tackled him to the ground. Bonnie kicked the gun from his hand. I'd almost forgotten how scrappy she could be as she retrieved his weapon and stood over the man. She leveled the gun with his face.

"I'm not going back," she said darkly.

The bullet landed squarely between his eyes.

Bonnie's entire body shook. I surveyed her from head to toe, ensuring there were no injuries. Slowly, as not to spook her, I tugged the smoking gun from her and tucked it in the back of my jeans. Then I took her hand

and pressed my lips to the back of it. She took in a bracing breath, then met my gaze.

Together we went down the hallway and past the library. It was a roundabout path, but hopefully we wouldn't find any more Hanged Men. I shoved through a door that led to the second level breezeway overseeing the courtyard.

A familiar female voice screamed, freezing me in my tracks. There was a scurry of activity below, but the unmistakable wail of Savannah as she clawed against a Hanged Man, fighting to get to—

Will. On his back, Sixgun looming over him. I heard the familiar, scratching growl of his voice as he said something to Will, but I couldn't make out the words.

"We have to help them," Bonnie said.

"We can't take them by ourselves," I said, noting the other Hanged Men looming near the edges of the courtyard, guns in hand. "We'll find Mickey and then go back for them."

Bonnie hesitated as I started down the breezeway but reluctantly followed me with a nod. This felt like the night we jumped off of that cliff, when we snuck through the town to raid the warehouse. Only, these weren't some normal townspeople. The Hanged Men weren't a crew you could fuck with. Everyone knew that. If you fucked with Jones or Sixgun, you were as good as dead.

Except for Bonnie. She'd somehow survived them both, and I refused to let her go back.

When we finally reached the door to the stables, it was locked firmly. I banged on it with my fist. "Mickey, open up!" My heart pounded as loudly as my fist against the wood. What if he wasn't there? What if the Hanged Men had blocked our exit?

We could double back through the kitchens. There was another exit there, but it was to the other side of the house.

The door slammed open, my uncle greeting us with concern mirroring mine in his eyes. Bonnie barreled past him into the stable. My brother lifted his head to look at me, clearly ready to fight.

"Ellis?" Mickey asked.

"Sixgun has him," I said, pressing a hand to the small of Bonnie's back as I placed myself between her and the door. Her gaze darted between me and the blocked exit. Hanged Men had swarmed the manor. All it took was one of them catching sight of Bonnie and everything that I'd fought for would be for nothing.

Coldness radiated from Bonnie's eyes as she figured me out. "We aren't splittin' up, Jesse."

My throat went dry. She would hate me for this, and I'd deserve it. "That's what Jones wants. You." She opened her mouth to argue, but I flashed my gaze to my uncle. He stepped toward Bonnie and placed a hand on her arm. "I'm fast, remember?" I flashed her a smile that didn't meet my eyes.

"No," she said, shrugging Mickey's arm off. "We do this *together.*"

"I can't lose you, Bonnie. Not again." I nodded to Mickey, who wrapped an arm around her waist.

"Don't you fucking dare, Jesse James!" she screamed, clawing at my uncle's arm as he dragged her toward the alleyway. She kicked back at him, her bare feet doing nothing against my uncle. I exhaled a bracing breath and pulled the gun from my waistband. "You promised—"

"I'm sorry." As soon as they reached the alleyway, I turned on my heel and retraced my steps toward the kitchen. Gunfire continued popping in the distance. I rounded the corner that led to the courtyard and stopped short, my path blocked by Hanged Men trading fire with Lee's branded soldiers on the level above.

Heart pounding, I doubled back, slipping in the blood of a dead man in the corridor and landing hard on my knee. I didn't have time for this. I needed to get to Will and Savannah and get them out. I wasn't losing anyone today.

Fear cloaked my heart as I remembered Bonnie's head being bashed in and The Kid's arm breaking with a sickening *crack.*

I shoved to my feet and sprinted around a corner that led to the front hallway but stopped short as two Hanged Men burst through the front doors of the manor. They lifted their weapons, but I already fired, the shot going wide. *Fuck.* I ducked as they pulled their triggers, the shots deafening my hearing. One pinged off the ground next to me. I turned back, but another Hanged Man blocked me as he rushed to see the cause of the commotion.

Years ago, in Flagstaff, we'd been cornered by the locals after a man accused Bonnie of robbing him. We'd been surrounded by unfamiliar faces and the barrels of too many guns to count. In that moment, Bonnie had been strung so tight that I could taste her desperation to run on the tip of my tongue.

I'd never felt that sort of fear before. Until now.

There was no stalemate, no warning shot fired into the air. Only chaos, only danger as the men approached. Deciding the single Hanged Man would be easier to eliminate than the others, I pulled the trigger on the gun.

An empty click.

"Don't kill him here," one of the men said from behind me. "Jones wants to give them a show."

The fuck? I threw the gun at him, but it glanced easily off of his shoulder. Something hard cracked against the back of my skull, and I stumbled, my side slamming into the wall as my vision wavered. I lifted a hand to the back of my head, my fingers coming away damp and sticky.

A boot slammed into my side, knocking me onto my knees. The world faded in and out. Vaguely, I registered rope wrapping around my torso. Hands hefted me up. Men barked at me to walk. A flash of wallpaper. Stinging pain in the back of my head. A stairway. Barking voices.

It wasn't until my feet hit the cobblestones in front of the manor that I forced my vision to settle. The men shoved me onto my knees at the end of a long line of people.

"Jesse?" a female voice whispered from my side. Savannah. *Oh god*. I looked up at her, but the devastation in her eyes made my heart shudder. "Bonnie?"

"She got out," I whispered harshly, brows knitting together. "Will?"

Some of the light went out of her eyes, and her expression crumbled. Tears brimmed over her eyelashes. A loud sob came from between her lips. Her shoulders quaked. I'd seen this woman buck up to the Beast countless times. My heart dropped into my stomach like a giant stone sinking to the bottom of a lake.

No. *Not Will.*

"Shut up!" a Hanged Man barked from behind us before delivering a swift kick to my ribs.

"Zachary!" a male voice called, followed by a solo gunshot. Savannah flinched beside me. A skinny man stood in front of the line of kneeling people, gun holstered at his hip. "All of your people are out here. Where are you?!"

There was a wild glint in his eyes.

"You gonna let your people die out here instead of facing me like a man?!"

I'd sworn to myself long ago that if I ever came face to face with him, I'd rip his fucking heart out for what he did to her.

Rage flared to life inside of me.

"Where's my Bonnie girl, Zachary?!"

CHAPTER TWENTY-EIGHT

WILL

MY ARMS TREMBLED WITH the effort it took to hold the Bowie knife two inches from my chest. I strained with every muscle in my body, my palms gripping my father's wrists as he leaned over me, using his body weight to bear down. I was losing space. Losing precious centimeters as I bared my teeth and, with a roar, forced every miniscule piece of strength in my body to regain distance.

"It's useless, boy!" he screamed into my face, his expression twisted into a cruel sneer. "I'll *finally* be rid of you today. Finally never have to hear your name or how people seem so *interested* in your insignificant little life." He shoved, and the tip of the knife dipped perilously, eating up the space towards my skin. It shook, back and forth, gleaming in the scant night.

"Get 'im, Sixgun!" someone shouted from my left side.

"Kill the traitor!"

"Beasts are meant to be *put down*!"

"You should fuckin' skin him!"

The shouts grew louder, clamoring, growing in excitement and viciousness. I didn't leave any friends behind with The Hanged Men, and this was exactly how they were. Bloodthirsty. More animal than I'd ever been.

"*Will*!" Savannah. Still calling for me. Her voice was far away now, causing a spike of panic, of desperation. Was it even real or just my mind tormenting me before I died?

Sixgun lowered his body over me, putting more pressure on my exhausted arms, close enough to speak near my ear.

"Once I've killed you, I'm gonna finish cutting off your face and then I'm gonna *nail it* to Zachary Lee's front door." He chuckled, the sound demonic. I thrashed beneath him, trying to push him off, to shift him, to make it out of this somehow still alive. I sucked in a ragged breath and closed my eyes, squeezing them so tight it hurt.

Strength alone wouldn't keep me alive. My mind whirred, trying to push past the cloud of panic tolling like warning bells in my ears. I knew the human body, better than anything else. My eyes snapped open. His knee. The one Bonnie weakened all that time ago. Calculating quickly the angle and distance of the knife to my chest, I gathered my strength for what came next.

I couldn't die here.

I couldn't die at all.

I had too much to live for. Too many people who needed me. Too many things I wanted to experience. With a wail of enraged anguish that split the night apart, I did a few things at once: I let go of his wrist with one hand, brought my clenched fist down on his injured knee with the strength I had left, and I pushed the knife with the other to guide it away from my body.

He cried out in pain, his weight shifting as his knee gave out.

For a moment, I believed I'd succeeded, that I'd actually done it. Until fire licked up the side of my chest. Pain exploded, and I prodded the wound carefully only to find my fingers covered in bright red blood. *Fuck.* That wasn't good.

Sixgun's chest heaved; the effort of our fight had taken a toll on him. He gripped the Bowie knife loosely in his hand, dragging the tip of it along the cobblestones as he rolled onto his good knee and rose to his feet. But everything in the world was pain and more pain. I pressed my hand against the long gash down my side. Fuck, it was deep, and the blood seeped between my fingers in a warm gush.

El dolor es fugaz.

My mother's tremulous voice echoed like the night she had given me the first cut. The first of a thousand. A million. She taught me to be strong enough to survive him. That's what I'd told Savannah. I meant it then. I thought I could. But here I was, my blood soaking the dirty cobblestones below me. I would die on my back in the goddamn dirt. My eyes drifted to the sky. A bright moon staring down at me. Light in the darkness. I thought it was a beacon once, a symbol of hope that I could escape the swallowing dark. And here I was, sinking into it.

El dolor es fugaz.

I heard the mantra again, more insistent this time as my father finally got his feet underneath him. He smirked, his spurs clanging as his boots stepped in the pool of my blood around me. Then he turned his back. I was so insignificant that he couldn't even be bothered to watch me die. Tears leaked from the corners of my eyes.

"*El dolor*," I whispered, struggling slowly onto my side. "*Es fugaz.*"

Hand clutching my throbbing wound, I said it again. Louder this time. "*El dolor es fugaz.*" Pressing my forehead onto the ground and bracing myself with the other arm, I screamed as I struggled to my feet, the wound gaping open wider with the movement. When the fresh wave of pain subsided, I felt lightheaded. *Don't pass out, you fucking asshole.*

My father chuckled darkly, his knife in hand. "What's that you're muttering?" he asked insincerely. On slow, clumsy feet, I stumbled upright. Clenching my teeth together, I made my decision. I was getting out of this house. Then, I would kill anyone standing between me and my girl. I took a steadying breath and blinked to focus on his face, sneering at me in the dim light.

With trembling hands, I dropped my arms by my sides, letting my wound bleed freely as I squared my shoulders and faced down the demon that'd haunted me my entire life. I was weak, bleeding. My knees could buckle at any moment. But I was going to end this. I *had* to end this.

"*El dolor es fugaz*, fucker!" I growled. His expression fell, no longer amused and victorious.

Pain is fleeting.

With that thought, I charged at him, eyes wild. His blade flashed as it arced toward me again, but this time, I thought back to my years as Zachary's beast. My arm came up and blocked his, twisting his wrist until his grip slackened and his knife clattered to the cobblestones. His fist slammed into my wounded side, and my knees tried to buckle, but I fought back. I lunged forward, and his bad knee gave out, making him go down. *Hard.*

I fell with him, unable to keep myself upright. His hands reached for my throat, but I was already in motion, using the momentum of our fall to drive his knife down. Until, with both arms and all my body weight, we grappled with it over his chest. My strength waned, but I shifted until my shoulder helped me drag the knife down.

It slipped between his ribs.

Easy.

Like it'd been easy to slip the knife between Seb's ribs. Easy to kill and kill and kill. He made a choked sound of surprise that I felt deep in my battered soul. But unlike Seb, this wasn't a killing blow. I ripped the knife out at the hilt, and he jerked beneath me. I brought it down again, this time puncturing a lung, if the release of air or line of blood dribbling down his chin was any indication. The frenzy started as I thought of all the people he'd hurt, all the pain he'd inflicted, the scars he'd carved into countless bodies. I stabbed him again.

Again. Again. Again. Again. Again. Again. Again.

I stopped to catch my breath and wipe the sweat from my upper lip.

Then again.

Again.

Again.

Again.

Until I'd lost count and he'd stopped breathing. I stabbed until my arms shook with the effort to keep going. I stabbed until my chest heaved and our shared blood splattered my face.

I stabbed him until I knew for sure he would never rise again.

Finally, I dragged my broken body upright, clutching my wounded side, and without a second glance left him in a bloody heap on the cobblestones. My gaze refocused, several pairs of eyes staring at me in abject fear.

"Alright, motherfuckers, who's next?"

I'd kill them all. Without mercy or remorse.

No one would keep me from her.

CHAPTER TWENTY-NINE

BONNIE

*H*E DID IT AGAIN.

I felt like I was coming out of a glowroot haze. As if the world was fractured around me, and I couldn't make sense of it. The sight of blood and death, the sounds of gunfire and screaming, the feel of Mickey's arms like shackles dragging me away. Shock and betrayal had stolen my senses when he first wrapped one arm around my neck and the other around my waist. I'd fought his hold, but only half-heartedly as something cracked in my chest when Jesse walked away. We'd made it through the alleyway, and I was still screaming for him. "You *promised!* You said *together*!" Gunfire lit the windows as we passed in blasts that reminded me of the flashes of lightning in a vicious desert storm, ready to tear my whole world apart.

Jesse was in there.

He broke his promise to me and he'd walked back in. At some point a hollow realization set in, and I stopped fighting Mickey as he shoved me toward the square and beyond an iron gate where The Kid waited with the horses. With concerned eyes, he rushed forward, scanning me for injuries. Only the worst ones were on the inside.

"Where is everyone?" he asked with a hint of anxiety as he looked between our grim expressions. I turned back to the house that I'd once thought was my home.

"We need to leave," Mickey said with somber finality. I laughed, a sorrow-filled, breathy little chuckle that showed how close I was to completely losing it.

"I'm not leaving *anyone* behind," I told him firmly. He gripped me by the shoulders, leveling pained eyes at mine.

"He would want me to get you both to safety, and that's what I intend to do," he said with authoritative conviction. Too bad I had a fucking problem respecting authority. I shook him off and marched toward No Name, rifling through the saddlebags until I found what I needed.

Selene.

"You can try, Mickey," I warned him. "But I don't leave people behind."

I glanced at The Kid, whose jaw was set, his brow furrowed. "Rule number seven," he said in a voice that was deeper than I remembered, filled with Jesse's conviction and my determination. I turned toward him, his hat tipped down and a knife in his hand. The hard glint in his eyes reminded me that he wasn't the same ten-year-old kid. He was an outlaw now. But he would always be *mine.*

Rule number seven. No one gets left behind.

"Kid," I said, sucking in a steadying breath. How did I tell him everything I wanted to say? That he was the best thing that ever happened to me. That if I had a choice, I'd never leave his side again. That I loved him more than I thought it was possible to love another person.

"I know," he said calmly, blinking away the glassiness in his eyes.

Without words, I took a moment to memorize every slope and plane of his face as it was now, with the hint of stubble on his jaw and the quirk of a grin on his mouth. I nodded, my eyes flicking to Mickey, who only shook his head in silent condemnation. With The Kid's too-long arms, he scooped me up, gripping tight for a moment, a breath. I tangled my fingers in the hair at the base of his neck before we parted.

"Go," he said, "bring them back to us."

I ducked beneath a crossbeam on the iron grate, slipping easily between the bars. I rounded the shadowed corner on feet that remembered what it was like to move with stealthy grace. A quick check of ammunition showed only two shots left, but I wouldn't let that stop me from bringing Jesse back. Bringing them *all* back. Crouching low, I crept across the street to the alleyway beside the house. A shadowed figure stumbled forward, and I raised Selene, finger on the trigger, until a shaft of light illuminated Will's bloody face.

"Will!" I breathed against him as he nearly collapsed on top of me. He was so tall that his weight dragged me down until I planted my feet and helped him balance once more. He clutched his side, and his bronze skin was sickly pale, his normally laughing eyes dulled in pain. My gaze dropped to his other hand, which gripped a bloody knife. Not just blood dripping from the hilt, drenched to the hilt, drying in rust-colored rivulets along a blade that was too familiar.

Sixgun's knife.

"You're hurt," I said, watching him swallow too hard and take too long to focus his eyes on me. There was so much blood. *Too much blood.*

"I'll survive," he managed to choke between his teeth. But I wasn't sure how much of the blood belonged to him. His eyes were determined in a way I'd never seen before, in a way that terrified me. I turned to him, forcing the arm with the bloody knife over my shoulders. He leaned on me the way we'd always leaned on each other.

"We always do."

He didn't speak, but as I supported his weight, I felt his relief in every muscle as he relaxed against me. I could get him to Mickey and come back. I could do it. I *had* to. Halfway back to where I left Mickey and The Kid, a voice rang out, stopping the both of us in our tracks.

"You gonna let your people die out here instead of facing me like a man?!"

Jones.

Memories I'd furiously beaten back since they'd returned to me raged to the surface, clawing deep inside of me. He was the nightmare in the dark. The man who'd stolen my freedom and my innocence. I'd run from him so long that I'd almost convinced myself that he was a fucked-up figment of my imagination, a boogeyman that couldn't touch me.

The foundation of who I was tilted, and my knees trembled.

I propped Will against the corner of a brick wall. Peering around it, I was unprepared for the scene in front of me. People were lined up in rows, sobbing on their knees with armed Hanged Men behind them, ready for mass executions. On the front steps of the manor, Jones paced back and forth, Jesse and Savannah kneeling two steps below him but above the others. As if they were in a position of honor, put on display for everyone to see.

I clenched my teeth and looked up at Will. His determined eyes only grew more purposeful at Jones's voice ringing in the night.

"They have Savannah," he said, shoving onto unsteady legs. He stumbled toward Jones's voice, but I rested my hand on his forearm to still him. His dark eyes dropped to mine.

"He has Jesse, too," I whispered. Will swore, wavering on his feet and smacking a hand out to catch himself on the brick.

"How?" he asked.

"He went back in for you," I told him. Will's eyes shuttered, and pain crossed his face.

"Of course he did," Will said, fury and anguish warring in his tone. "That fucking *pendejo*." His voice cracked, and it broke something in me. I knew that feeling too well. I was so angry with him, so angry and so scared of what might happen next.

"Where's my Bonnie girl, Zachary?!"

My name in his mouth felt like a death sentence. It choked the life from me, the claws of that darkness scoring deep inside over and over again, ripping my strength into shreds beneath a history of violence and abuse.

Jones looked exactly as I remembered: the severe line of his jaw, the long lanky stature that, up close, dwarfed me. It was his long, elegant fingers that I remembered the most, wrapped around my throat and promising me death for my disobedience. Those fingers twitched, a miniscule gesture that preceded a gunshot in the silence of the night.

A body thudded to the ground.

I scanned the people, recognizing too many of them. The woman who'd fallen had been there the night Emma died. With tears in her eyes, she'd bundled her little body in a pink crochet blanket and put her in my arms. She didn't deserve to die.

Beside a bleeding Jesse, Savannah sobbed. Will lurched forward, and I clawed his arm to still him. We needed to *wait*. To find a moment where we could get them away safely. If we barged in there now, we would die . . . or worse.

I tried to shake away the memories of the *worse* things that awaited us if we were dragged back with Jones. The torture. The beatings. The way he would break us into infinite pieces of nothing and bathe us in darkness and blood.

Darkness that Will had been steeped in for too long, that had almost claimed his life.

One of the Hanged Men, young but with a glint of cruelty in his dark eyes, approached Jones. He leaned close and said, "Losses in the courtyard."

"How many?" Jones asked.

"Thirteen, Sixgun included."

The shock on his face was unnerving. Something he didn't expect had happened, and if there was *anything* I knew about Jones, it was that he anticipated everything. Almost to a fault. He thought so far ahead that nothing *ever* surprised him.

"Well, that's unfortunate," Jones said, pausing for a moment to pull a cigar from inside his jacket pocket. It was only the stub of one, the smoke was thick and nauseating. He smoked them and then oftentimes put them out on my skin. Just for the hell of it. Just because he didn't like the expression in my eyes or because I was *there*.

He lit the stub with a match, his lips wrapping around it how I remembered, as if it were a ritual and not for any kind of pleasure. Just to order his mind by occupying his hands and those long fingers.

"Guards we didn't anticipate?" he asked the young man, who shook his head.

"It was *him*," the young man said as if afraid talking too loudly would summon the murderer. "Ellis. *The Beast*." I turned to Will, but his eyes were fixed on Savannah. One of his hands gripped so hard at his side that the fresh red blood stained his fingers. *Fuckin' hell.* I knew the expression on his face. He was thinking of doing something really fucking stupid. As exasperated and worried as I was, a thread of pride shivered through me.

He'd finally done it. He killed Sixgun. That inhuman piece of shit would never hurt anyone else ever again.

"I underestimated that boy," Jones said as if the taste of the admission was bitter on his lips, letting another lazy puff of smoke leave his mouth. He twitched his fingers again, and a gunshot rang on the wind. Another body dropped. A guardsman who told me jokes in the months after Emma died, trying to make me smile. He and his wife had six children, but for some reason, I couldn't remember his name. Something with an *S* or maybe a *T.*

"Is he still here? I'd like to offer him a job," Jones said, fingers twitching again. Another shot flared bright and loud in the darkness. I didn't see who it was this time. I'd closed my eyes. How long until Savannah or Jesse crumpled lifeless to the cobblestones, their heart's blood staining the square?

Will lurched, and it took my entire body to stop him. He fought against me so hard that I shoved my hand to his wounded side. With a choked cry, he fell against the wall. He opened furious, dark eyes at me.

"You can't stop me, Bonnie," he said through gritted teeth.

"If you go out there, he'll either kill you or he'll make you take your dad's place."

He reached a bloody, trembling hand out to me and cupped the back of my neck. His thumb brushed along my cheek lovingly. The way he'd always been with me. Gentle. Broken. They way we'd both always been.

"I can't let them hurt her," he whispered to me.

I leaned forward slowly, until our foreheads touched and my eyes fluttered shut. I felt the vibration of his words in my blood. Will had always felt too much to endure the hardship forced on us. I'd been strong for us both through our childhood. But it was him now, being strong for someone else. Someone he loved.

I nodded, sniffling back furious tears, with startling clarity.

Opening my eyes, I pulled away and took the safety off Selene.

With a steadying breath, I squared my shoulders, bracing myself to walk into the square outside the manor. Will's frantic, bloody hands grasped my arms and yanked me back.

"What are you doing?" he asked.

"Three more!" Jones shouted, and the shots rang out. Bodies dropped. The cobblestones reflected against the crimson stain of the massacre in the streetlights. Like macabre stars littering the night sky. A Hanged Man settled his gun at the back of Savannah's head, eliciting a whimper from her lips.

"Zachary!" Jones called out, his impatience clear in the tick of his jaw.

I feathered my hands over Will's face. No time left to argue.

"I'm going to get them back," I said, forcing the furious tears to recede. "Make sure they get to Mickey and The Kid."

"I don't understand—"

"Keep them safe for me," I said solemnly, offering a smile that was more of a grimace. I gripped him tight for a moment, in a broken approximation of a hug, then pulled away again.

"I can't let them hurt you either, not again. Not for me."

With those final words and a rough kiss to his cheek, I spun before he could catch up and marched. He shouted at me, his broken body lurching in a final attempt to stop me. He would never forgive me, but suddenly, it was so clear. With every single fiber of my being rebelling, I walked straight into the mouth of hell. It was time for me to face my demon, the way he'd battled his.

Jones raised his hand to motion for another round of deaths, ordering them as easily as swatting away a mosquito in the humid Louisiana heat. Savannah cried out as the hammers cocked back.

"Stop!" I called. Jesse's furious blue eyes found mine, and he struggled against his bindings.

Jones's gaze followed my echoing voice until his eyes landed on me. The darkness of his eyes lit in unfettered joy. The kind that held the edge of madness and promised retribution. Leveling Selene at his face, I stopped, feeling a breeze across my cheeks as the people in the square stilled.

"Ah," he said, a deep, pleasured sound rumbled from his chest. "*There's my girl.*"

My hands shook, Selene jerking so hard that I couldn't get a solid shot off if I tried.

"I'll come with you," I said, my chest heaving. My pulse pounded so hard that the echoing sound was deafening in the silence of the night. "If you let *them* go, I'll come with you."

Jesse was screaming, I could see his mouth open, the veins protruding from his neck, his whole body curled around whatever words he shouted. Only I couldn't hear them. Couldn't do anything but hold the gaze of the man before me. Unlike my mother, he had dark eyes. Mysterious and always slightly amused, even when he was being cruel. The first time I'd seen those eyes, I'd been dragged from the back of a wagon, my mouth bloody and my will to live thundering in my heart.

He looked at me the same way now that he had back then: like he could see every hurt and flaw and thread that stitched me together as a person. And that whatever he saw there intrigued him to no end.

"I'll let you have *one*," he said after a moment. "A homecoming gift. Your choice, make it quick."

My gaze dropped to Savannah, her tear-streaked face shocked and incredulous. I offered a small, conciliatory smile. One that said all the things I couldn't. *Thank you. I love you. Please forgive me.* She shook her head in disbelief, resignation falling over her features as painful as a knife twisting between my ribs.

I didn't look at Jesse. I couldn't.

"Savannah. Let Savannah go," I said, my voice firm.

Jones's gaze dropped to Savannah, the calculating glint returning to his dark eyes. After a moment of indecision, he jerked his head. A guard slashed her bonds, then jerked her to her feet and shoved her forward. Savannah didn't move for a long moment, instead holding my gaze and shaking her head softly. Will stalked from the shadows, and she found him over my shoulder. She ran to him until she grasped him so tightly that he grimaced. He whispered something in her ear and then ushered her away, both of them looking back with tears in their eyes before disappearing into the shadows.

"My Bonnie girl," Jones said, the words low and somewhere between too affectionate and deadly. "It's time."

My resolve quaked.

On numb feet I walked forward. One step. Two. Ten. Until I stood in front of him, Selene still leveled at his chest. There were two rounds left, and I could end this *right now.*

Only, I didn't.

Because Jesse still had a gun behind his head, and it didn't matter if I had my freedom. Not if I didn't have *him.*

When I was within arm's reach, he tugged Selene from my hand, leaving me naked before him. No weapon or bravado to hide me from him. No distance to separate me from his cruelty. No lost time to protect me from the memories of what he'd done. What he'd *do.*

Those long, elegant fingers reached forward, the ones that'd threatened to strangle me, and brushed a wayward strand of hair from my face. He tucked it lovingly behind one ear. For better or worse, he was the man who raised me, molded me into *this.* And whether he murdered me outright, tortured me for years, or made a gruesome example of me, the little girl inside of me remembered long days in the desert and a full belly for the first time in weeks. She remembered the scratchy wool blanket he'd draped over my shivering body. The brutal years of training that turned my frail body into one that was stronger, scrappier, feistier. There was the abuse, of course, that was ever-present, but after this place and Lee's deceit and lies, a part of me was relieved by the stark honesty of Jones. He'd never pretended to be anything other than what he was, torture and all.

Maybe he'd succeeded in making me believe this was the kind of love I could accept.

"I missed you," he admitted, a surprising gentleness warming his dark eyes. Horror filled my chest when I realized that I wanted to return the sentiment.

With furious tears wavering in my vision, he motioned for me to kneel before him. As my knees hit the slick cobblestone, sticky with blood and filth, I let my eyes drop with acceptance. I heard Jesse's voice protesting again, roaring into the night. I'd known this whole time that my execution was a probability. That if he got his hands on me after all this time, he might make an example out of me. What better way to send a message to my father than to leave my corpse rotting on *Lee Square* in front of his palatial home. I just never thought that Jesse might be witness to it. Regret curled into the pit of my stomach. I'd gotten the rest of them out, though. The Kid. Mickey. Savannah. *Will.* I'd gotten them out. I'd done something good, something they might remember me for.

Someone to my right wriggled and squirmed, a familiar swoop of hair making me pick my head up in interest. Lucas. Bound and gagged, piss darkening the front of his pants.

A shot rang out, and before I could even wonder about his circumstances, his body sprawled on the cobblestones, his arm at an odd angle. A mix of crimson blood and white brain matter stained the cobblestones now. Fatty and slick and horrible.

I couldn't catch my breath. I couldn't think.

I'd just been with him. Even though he was a piece of shit, I'd almost agreed to marry him. I was still wearing his ring, for fuck's sake. My hands shook, and I struggled to breathe as I stared at Lucas.

"He was a useful pawn for a while," Jones said, casual and dismissive. "Kill them all."

Gunfire popped in a sickening rhythm of violence. Bodies thudded to the stone. A cadence of death rocked the ground like thunder. My bottom lip trembled as I waited for my turn. For the crack of gunfire that would end me.

Instead, with a few shouted orders, he turned away, and I followed like I knew he expected. I didn't fight it anymore. There was no point.

Jones walked me to the wagons, not stopping when my feet grew clumsy. Instead he looped his arm through mine to keep me upright. He gestured sharply toward the back of a wagon with cruel efficiency before he handed me up, where I stood stoically and watched the door as it slammed shut.

"Just like old times," he said before clicking the lock and shouting at the driver.

The man dragged me from beneath the bed, wrenching my arm so hard it went numb. He threw me in the back of a wagon. I clawed at the wood until my nails broke and splinters embedded themselves beneath them, until my fingertips were bloody. I cried. I screamed. I begged for my mother to come. She never did. She'd stayed behind, lying in that pool of crimson blood.

I couldn't breathe, couldn't control my heart, which nearly beat out of my chest. It hurt. It hurt and hurt and hurt and it felt like I was dying. Like my chest was caving in and exploding outwards all at once.

"Bon." Vaguely, I registered Jesse's voice beside me, but I couldn't care about that while I was dying. Actively dying.

I slammed my shoulder against the door. Over and over and over again. Until it too had gone numb. When the horses moved, I pitched backwards, and the jaggedness of my broken pieces sliced deep. My fingers dug into my hair, pulling hard. *I can't cry. I* can't *cry.* They punished me when I cried.

"Bonnie!" Jesse called, moving toward me slowly, like he was afraid to spook me. Like I was a wild animal. A wild animal that'd been caged once again.

After a long while, breathing in a syncopated rhythm that stitched the ragged parts of me back together long enough to be coherent, Jesse sat next to me.

"Why would you *do* that?" he asked, quiet fury in his eyes. I slammed my head back into the bars and rubbed my aching chest. He didn't know what waited for us, but I did. I'd known this whole time what I was walking into. What I'd volunteered for.

"I made a promise," I said spitefully.

"Fuck the promise, I needed you *safe.*"

I leveled him with a glare that had him recoiling. He'd left me again. He'd broken my trust *again.* And while I'd do whatever was necessary to get him back to The Kid and Mickey, to get him out of this situation alive, I didn't know where that left us.

"I did what I needed to," I said after a long, tense silence. "You wanna be pissed off at me, go ahead. You're in good company." The wagon jostled and lurched, and suddenly, through the bars of the wagon, New Orleans shrank into the distance. This place had been a home, a prison, a safe spot to land, and now . . . was gone. Just like everything else. My friends. The life I'd built. And the support I hadn't realized I'd been leaning on so much all this time.

"What do we do now?" Jesse asked, though I wasn't sure if he really wanted an answer or was just posing the question to the night air. I answered him anyway.

"We do our goddamned best to stay alive."

CHAPTER THIRTY

SAVANNAH

THE UNSTEADY CADENCE OF my heart only made my panic *worse*. It pounded loudly, reverberating through me like a war drum, aching so hard I felt like I'd been punched. Will's body against mine was the only thing keeping me grounded.

I'd been used as bait by Sixgun.

I blinked hard against my watery eyes, forcing the bile back down my throat. I couldn't lose it now. Will's breath rattled ominously as we staggered together back down the alley to the stables.

I'd nearly been executed.

The ledger bit into my back, forcing my eyes to focus. What was even the point? I'd risked everything by getting that stupid book only to lose Bonnie and Jesse. To lose Will if I didn't tend to his wounds.

I lost Etty.

"Savvy—" His pained voice stopped me in my tracks just inside the stables. I paused long enough to settle him against the nearest wall, bracing him there so he didn't slide to the ground.

I could lose *Will*.

"It's okay," I said, feeling anything but. I surveyed his shredded shirt, stained with blood and other viscera. "Just hold on."

I darted into his stallion's stall, much to the horse's chagrin as he huffed impatiently, and rifled through the saddlebags, searching for the medical kit. Will would have packed it.

Red cobblestones filled my mind. There'd been blood *everywhere* and no way to stop more from being shed. With shaky hands, I finally

323

found the box with Will's supplies and returned to him. His head rested against the wooden wall, but that wasn't what worried me. He was struggling to keep his eyes open.

"Will," I whimpered, cradling his chin. "William, I need you to look at me."

A hot tear slid down my cheek as his brows lifted and he opened his eyes halfway. "Hm?"

"You've lost a lot of blood," I said, dipping my head to meet his gaze. "I need you to stay awake, okay? I need you to tell me where it's worst."

He lifted a bloody hand. Immediately, his shirt soaked through with thick blood. Oh God, how was I going to fix this? I pressed his hand down over the wound, nodding to myself.

"Keep as much pressure as you can," I said, trying to force the shakiness from my words. He mumbled something beneath his breath. I sprinted back into the stall and took out one of my old dresses, then ripped it into shreds. *Clean the wound, first.* I removed his hand, replacing it with my own and the clean-ish strips of fabric to staunch the bleeding.

Will groaned, jerking at how hard I pushed against the wound.

"Savvy," he whispered. The blood drained from my face. He was an odd shade of gray beneath the red that stained his skin.

"You hold on," I demanded.

"But Savvy—"

"Hold on, or so help me, I'll kill you myself." I bit back the sob threatening to escape from my lips. I leaned closer to him, cradling his neck with my hand. His ragged breaths mingled with my sharp ones. "You don't get to die on me, William Ellis. Not for a very, *very* long time."

This wasn't like the night we'd rescued Jesse from the Slavers' Parade, where there was a team of people who could step in at a moment's notice. Jesse's wounds had stopped bleeding then too. I needed clean hands. And clean tools. Stitching him up would do me no good if it just got infected later.

Footsteps pounded on the pavement toward us from the square. I tensed, snatched the knife from Will's hand, and put myself between him and the shadowy figures.

"Ellis?" Jesse's uncle. Something resembling relief made my shoulders relax. Moonlight slanted across Mickey's face as he and three others approached.

"It's okay," Will said to me. I lowered the knife to my side, turning my attention back to him. His normally vibrant bronze skin was concerningly pale.

It *wasn't* okay. He was hurt, badly, and I didn't think I had it in me to help him by myself.

Mickey's gaze narrowed as he took in Will's tattered, bloody clothing.

"I'm fine. Savvy can help," he huffed out, forcing himself away from the wall but staggering. Mickey darted toward him and tossed Will's arm over his shoulders. The woman with dark hair who'd been with us the night of the Slavers' Parade, Gabriela, cleared her throat.

"We have supplies back at camp. We can help."

I shook my head. "He won't make it back to camp." I exhaled a loud breath and fixed Mickey with a hard stare. "We have to do it here."

I barked orders at Mickey, Gabriela, The Kid, and someone I didn't know. While I retrieved the med kit, Gabriela and The Kid went in search of sterile supplies. Mickey and I supported Will's bulk between us.

"You're gonna be okay, son," Mickey said in a low voice, his words strained as we stumbled through the corridor.

The night Bonnie and Will had arrived in the manor, though ages ago, came back to me as we slammed open the door to the parlor. *Get him on the couch. Keep pressure on the wound. Cut off his shirt. Try not to freak out completely.* I needed to be the steady one, the one who could handle everything.

By the time Gabriela and the others returned with a bowl of steaming water, fresh linens, and two bottles of alcohol, I'd carefully laid out the tools we would need.

"Savannah," Mickey barked, yanking me out of my thoughts.

I turned my attention back to Will. His head rested against the arm of the couch. He was struggling to keep his eyes open. Hot panic licked up my spine.

I couldn't lose Will, too. *No.*

"Will," I whimpered, cradling his chin. "William."

"Hm?"

"Look at me," I said, dipping my head low to meet his gaze. "Please."

Will blinked hard, forcing his eyes open in an unnatural stare.

In a flash, I soaked my hands in alcohol and knelt on the floor beside the couch. My body quaked as I tried to thread the needle. I missed it once, twice, a third time. I'd only seen him do this once. What if I messed it up? What if I only made it worse? What if—

"That bastard doesn't get to take anything else from you," Mickey said, keeping his eyes locked on Will's. "He's taken too much already. You keep your fuckin' eyes open. You fought too hard. You keep 'em open. I'm not losing you, too. I'm not losin' you." Mickey kept pressure on the wound, talking in a low voice to Will. And he did. Will kept his eyes open, though each blink took a toll on him.

"Savannah," Mickey said firmly. I snapped my attention to him. His blue eyes offered to help silently.

"I've got it," I murmured, missing the eyehole a fourth time.

A gentle hand touched my shoulder. Gabriela. "Please, let him."

I shook my head. No. Will was mine. Mine to love and mine to heal. What was the point in showing me how to stitch wounds if I couldn't do this for him?

Hard hands covered mine, stilling my movement as I attempted a fifth time. Stark blue eyes stole my attention.

"Step back. I promise, I know what I'm doing."

Inherently, I knew it was true. With a sob, I relinquished the needle and thread and rose to my feet, staggering backward. Gabriela caught me, her arms cradling me like a child. But I wasn't a child. And I wouldn't leave Will alone in this.

Will hissed in a breath as Mickey removed the bandage from the wound. Blood oozed, gravity forcing it to trickle down and seep into the cushions. It was so much deeper than the lashes that we'd stitched together on Jesse's back.

I pulled away from Gabriela and moved to the arm of the couch, kneeling near Will's head. The damn ledger dug into my back, reminding me that this stupid book was the entire reason I'd left him in the first place. I tugged it out and tossed it unceremoniously to the floor. I'd been so afraid that the Hanged Men were going to find it when they dragged me away, when Sixgun captured me and used me as bait.

Will didn't speak when Mickey lifted the needle. He only elevated his arm above his head, grimacing as he did so. I laced my fingers with his, and he gripped me tight. Mickey grasped the gaping wound, eliciting a groan as he pinched the flesh together.

Pierce. Curve. Tie. Repeat. Whereas Jesse's had only been a few stitches, Mickey must have done at least ten before he leaned back. It wasn't pretty, and it would be a hell of an ugly scar, but it was done. At least the cut had been clean. Gabriela took the needle from Mickey and passed over bandages and medical tape.

"Mickey," Will said, his voice scratchy. "We're okay. Go help the people who actually need it."

Blue eyes cut toward me, a silent question in them. He hesitated, glancing between me, Gabriela, and Will. "Are you sure?"

"Savvy's got me," Will said.

Tonight had been too much. Too much bloodshed. Too much violence. Too much death. That Will still had confidence in me while I broke down so effortlessly made my heart thump erratically.

"Water?" he asked, his words tight.

I perched on the edge of the couch with a glass of water as the parlor door snicked shut. With the wound cleaned, stitched, and covered, the worst was over. I helped him sit up enough to take a few gulps of water, then gently helped him back down.

"You should get some rest," I said, reaching over to brush a loose strand of dark hair out of his eyes.

I stayed that way, watching his eyelids droop and his chest rise and fall in an easy rhythm. When I was certain that he was asleep, I leaned down and pressed my lips to his forehead.

My body ached as I sat back up. I needed rest, too, but my brain kept making its own lists. I needed to clean up all of this blood. I needed to find Mickey and Gabriela and talk to them about what happened next. I needed to come up with some semblance of a plan to get Bonnie and Jesse back. I needed to *help*.

But more than anything, I needed Will to get better.

Even as I rose from my perch, my body wouldn't move to do any of the things I needed to do.

So I slid to the floor in front of the couch and rested my head against the scratchy fabric, keeping my eyes on Will until darkness took me.

I stared at cobblestones as the cool, metallic barrel of a gun pressed against the back of my skull. I bit back my sob, knowing that any noise I made could elicit a snap decision from the Hanged Man. That I could be dead in a heartbeat.

Etty screamed. "Not my girl. You can't have my girl!"

A Hanged Man clubbed the back of her head. But he didn't stop when she crumpled to the ground. He smashed her head once, twice, three times. Until Etty's face was no longer recognizable.

Bonnie stood proud before me, her head held high as she demanded my release.

Will lay lifeless at her feet.

"Savvy." Will's soft voice permeated the square around me, like some God overseeing the horror, though he lay lifeless on the stone. "Wake up."

I blinked, finding Will's soft gaze on me from where he lay on the couch. I ran a hand over my face, through my hair. How long had I been asleep?

"You're awake."

"You were whimpering," Will said.

Some of the color had returned to his skin. He still wasn't his usual bronze, but it was significantly better than earlier. I lowered my gaze to my hands, wringing them together in my lap. He touched my cheek with a quaky hand, and I looked up at him, biting my bottom lip.

Blood still marred his skin. He had a ton of cuts and bruises on his face and chest. I should have cleaned him up before letting myself fall asleep.

I took one of his hands in both of mine and pressed my lips to his knuckles, fighting back the tears that watered my eyes. He was still here, still breathing. He *would* be okay. Then his brows knitted together, his concern evident in his eyes.

"I need . . . water," I said absently as I stood on shaky legs.

He caught my hand and gave it a gentle squeeze. I paused, my gaze falling back to his. "Don't leave."

How could I? I perched once more on the edge of the couch, turning my attention to his bandage. It was still firmly in place. Mickey had done a good job.

"Are you okay?"

A laugh bubbled up in my chest, but I forced it down. "I'm fine, I just didn't get a chance to clean you up earlier."

"That's not what I meant."

Concern laced his voice, making my heart squeeze hard in my chest. I was *not* okay, but I couldn't tell him that. Instead, I dipped a hand towel in the mostly clean water from earlier and started wiping away the blood crusting his skin.

"Savvy," he said more firmly.

"What?" I focused on my task. If I kept my hands busy, I didn't have to think about it.

"Savvy, stop." He gripped my wrists, stilling them firmly against his chest. He tossed the towel away, then looped his fingers with mine, brushing his calloused thumb along my knuckles. "You don't have to be okay."

"Of course, I do," I whispered harshly. "You killed your father. Jones took Bonnie and Jesse. Etty is probably dead, and I almost lost you. And if I let myself think about everything that happened tonight, I am going to shatter into a million pieces." I met his gaze, hardening my own.

It hurt. Everything hurt. And if I let myself feel it, it would destroy me.

There was too much to do, too many things that required my strength.

"You can't ignore it," he said, his words quieter than before. He tipped my chin to force me to look at him. "Because then it becomes inescapable and overwhelming. You're way too brave for that."

I wasn't brave. I was brash and foolish. I was useless in a fight. Useless as a medic. I'd only survived so far because of the people around me. Etty. Bonnie. *Will.*

"Do you know why I always make stupid fucking jokes?"

I lifted my eyebrows.

"Because if I don't . . . I'm gonna fall apart."

"I couldn't even thread the needle, Will!" I pulled out of his grip and stood, turning away from him. "You were *dying*, and you needed me. I can't make jokes about being totally useless!"

Will groaned, placing a hand to his wounded side as he sat up. "You *aren't* useless," he said, his voice firm and uncompromising, stilling my raging mind. "Do you know why I call you *mi sol*?" He took in a deep breath that seemed to pain him.

"You're the only reason I made it out of that courtyard alive at all, Savvy," he said, stark honesty coloring his words. "*Mi sol* means 'my sun.'" He shifted on the couch, reaching for me. I let him drag me to the couch beside him. His fingers traveled in a fidgety pattern along my skin, eventually sinking into my hair, grounding me, until our breaths were in sync and I relaxed.

"My day begins and ends with you," he said, pulling me in tighter, closer. "You're warmth, and life, and purpose."

My bottom lip quivered at his words. Because I knew exactly how he felt. My world didn't feel right without him.

He kissed me, then brushed his lips across my forehead, my nose. His soft kisses trailed over my shoulder and down to my hands.

"I wouldn't have been able to get off the ground in that courtyard if it weren't for you," he confessed. "I know what happens to the human body when adrenaline fades. Your hands shake. Your mind falters. Not being able to thread that goddamn needle doesn't mean *shit, mi sol,* other than you'd just survived a traumatic event."

He inhaled deeply, as if my scent could steel him against anything. "And I know your brain is making so many lists right now that you're doubting yourself. Questioning everything. But, *baby—*" His voice went tender and sweet on the word in a way that shook the foundation of my world.

"You had me. You *have* me. And together, we're going to get our friends back. Have faith in me." He said it like there was no other possibility. Like if I asked him to hang the moon, he'd make it his life's mission, until there was no doubt it would happen.

My heart had slowed, my hands steadied, and I wrapped my arms around his neck.

"Thank you," I whispered.

Will tucked his hand in my hair, cradling me gently against his good side. "It's you and me, *mi sol.* To whatever end."

CHAPTER THIRTY-ONE

WILL

PURPOSE, COLD AND HEAVY, settled over me in the hour after sunrise. Savvy had, of course, busied herself with fussing over me, insisting that she clean the blood on my skin and fetch me a fresh shirt. In the quiet moments alone, I replayed the night in my mind. Or at least, one specific part of it.

My father's face. His eyes as the blade sank into his chest. First, shock. Then, something even more sinister.

A hint of *pride.*

As if this was his plan all along: to make me no better than him, to strip away my humanity and truly become the legacy he so feared and hated. My stomach heaved, and hot bile crept up my throat.

Well, it was either that or the pain. Anytime I moved, fire lanced down my leg from my wound. It throbbed in time with my pulse, a reminder that I needed to be gentle with myself.

My destructive, fucked-up brain wanted to take Savannah to bed and drown the terror of the night in multiple orgasms. *Only, I don't do that anymore,* I forcefully reminded myself. *I will not avoid my problems with alcohol, drugs, or sex. I won't.* Instead, I braced myself against the arm of the couch and prepared for the worst pain of my life. In one swift motion, I stood. Pain barreled into my body from all sides, making my knees weaken and nearly buckle. I clenched my teeth so hard I swore they would crack. I wheezed, gripping my side as the room wobbled around me.

Fuck, I take it back. All the drugs. I need all the goddamned drugs.

332

But, of course, that was the moment Savannah came back, her eyes widening in horror at me. Quickly schooling my face into a mask of *not agonizing pain*, I offered her a strained grin that didn't fool her in the slightest. She white-knuckled a folded black shirt.

"What on *earth* are you doing?" she asked, brow furrowing adorably. It was a furrow reserved for me, the *'I'm-vexed-by-Will'* furrow. Not to be confused with the *'How-do-I-get-away-with-murdering-Will'* furrow, which was similar but significantly different because she gave that one to anyone in her general vicinity when I pissed her off. This furrow made me want to do very bad things to her. Things I was entirely too injured for and *not supposed to be thinking about.*

"I can't convalesce, Savvy, we don't have the luxury of time. Trust me, I'm as excited to be on my feet as you are."

That muted her irritation for the moment. She extended the shirt for me to gingerly thread my arms through. The fabric was soft, and though it was a little short and a little tight around the shoulders, it fit relatively well.

"I stole it from Luke's room," she admitted, her pretty mouth tipping down. *That's right,* I thought, *he's dead now.* At one point, Lucas Rutherford had been the only thing anyone wanted to talk about. Now he was just . . . gone. While I wouldn't miss him, it was still a difficult thing to wrap my mind around; the scale of death last night was staggering.

"Did you see Mickey?" I asked, buttoning the front of the shirt. Before she could answer, the man himself walked in with a pinched expression and weary eyes. Worry deepened the lines around his mouth and on his brow, setting all that cold purpose in my gut to roiling dangerously.

"Should you already be up?" he asked, assessing my condition. The memory of his bloody hands and soft assurances as he stitched me back together last night flooded my mind. I realized, somewhat dumbfounded, that he was worrying about *me.*

"No rest for the wicked," I retorted with a foolhardy grin. Mickey didn't smile. "What's it look like out there?" I hooked a thumb over my shoulder towards the windows.

"People gathering, trying to identify the bodies, but honestly, it's a mess," he said, running a weary hand through his gray-blond hair. Gabriela walked in, gaze darting between Mickey and me apprehensively.

"Have you told them?" she asked, tone careful. Mickey wouldn't meet my eyes. Savannah shifted closer to my good side, her arm brushing against mine.

"Told us what?" Savannah questioned.

"Look," Mickey started, talking with his hands open as if to soften a blow. "I know what you kids are thinking as our next step, but—"

"No." I cut him off abruptly. His nostrils flared.

"You have to think about this logically, okay, I mean . . . it's *Tent City* for fuck's sake, and we don't have the manpower we'd need to—"

"I said *no*, Mickey," I repeated more firmly. Savannah shifted uncomfortably on her feet, and I wrapped my arm loosely around her to steady her.

"You're not suggesting we *leave* Bonnie and Jesse there, are you?" she asked Mickey, glancing between him and Gabriela, their expressions a mixture of distress and guilt. "Oh my God." Savannah glanced up at me, her fingers covering her surprised mouth. "That's exactly what you're suggesting. But, you're his uncle. How could you?"

"It's not like I'm thrilled about it. I've been up all night trying to find a way . . . *any* way. But it comes down to numbers, and the simple fact is, we don't have enough. So, I can either march us to our deaths in a suicide mission, or we fall back, regroup in Fort Hood, and wait for reinforcements."

Silence fell like an anvil, a blanket of despair that smothered all the hope out of everyone in an instant. I let out a deep, rattling sigh.

"Fine," I said, earning everyone's attention. "I'll do it."

Still, no one spoke.

"Do what?" Mickey finally asked.

"You need numbers, and a strategy, right?"

Mickey nodded.

"Alright, I'll get the numbers and come up with the strategy."

"While I appreciate the thought, son, it's gonna take more than a pair of steel balls to get them out of Tent City," Mickey said, his eyes dark and hopeless. Savannah's gaze fell to the floor, and something inside my chest cracked open. While I was used to being underestimated and usually didn't give a shit, I couldn't stand the dejected look in her pretty eyes.

"Yeah, it'll take an army. Like the remaining guards Lee left behind who weren't killed, and what's left of Etty's rebellion in the city, your men, and I'm pretty sure if I put my mind to it, I could think of a few others who might be willing to join up along the way. And as far as strategy goes, I *lived* in Tent City, remember? Pretty sure I'm the best person, other than Bonnie, of course, to get them out."

Silence again. At this point, I was starting to get offended.

"Look," Savannah said, leveling those feisty eyes right at Mickey as she crossed her arms over her chest. "We can do it with you, or without you. We stand a better chance if we do this together, but the one thing Bonnie and Jesse don't have is *time.*"

Have I mentioned how hot Savannah was when she was bossy? It made tremors of pleasure course through my veins when she turned that sass on someone else. Especially when she was backing me up. Mickey shook his head, which was a bad sign. Then an incredulous smile tugged at his mouth, inciting a lopsided grin on my own. I shared a victorious glance with Savvy, who tried real hard to hide her triumph and failed spectacularly.

"Fuck it," Mickey said, smacking my shoulder. A hot spike of pain blasted through me, and I cursed below my breath. "If anyone's got what it takes to pull this crazy shit off, it's you." With that vote of confidence ringing in my ears, I squared my shoulders and stood to my full height.

"Alright, first thing, our plans stay close. I'm talking just us four and no one else. No telling if Jones had any other spies hanging around in Lee's house or Fort Hood," I said as I started walking. Mickey fell into line beside me. Savannah gripped my hand, and I linked fingers with her quickly. "Next, your guys should scour the house and grounds for supplies. Anything we don't have to waste time buying, packing, or hauling will help us get there faster. And like Savvy said, the one thing we don't have enough of is time. Mickey, you'll need to recruit some of Lee's guys to add to our ranks. After last night, there'll be plenty of them ready for revenge. Gabi, can you handle the supply run?"

Gabriela was a few steps behind us but grunted her acknowledgment.

I pinched the skin between my brows, rubbing at the ache starting to form there. "I wish we'd recovered that ledger. It'd make this part a whole lot easier in any case."

Savannah squirmed beside me, clearing her throat to get our attention. Her eyes were alight with smug satisfaction that could only mean one thing. Pride swelled in my chest, until it felt like it would crack wide open. Mickey and Gabriela looked between us, clearly confused.

"You didn't," I said, grinning mischievously.

"Well, none of you were getting the job done," she said with a nonchalant shrug. She released my hand, then headed back into the room we'd just exited, returning a moment later with a red leather ledger.

"Ho-ly shit," Mickey said, dragging the words out in awe.

"Anyone tell you lately that you're a beautiful, brilliant, menace of a woman?" I cupped her cheeks and kissed her firmly. Her answering smile was luminous in the dim corridor. Mickey took the ledger from her and started reading, laughing incredulously as he took in line upon line of Zachary Lee's contacts and business dealings.

"Just you," she said. Her eyes were dark and lusty, making my stomach clench with feelings so deep that they scared me. How'd I get lucky enough that this woman wanted me?

Mickey cleared his throat, trying to hide a grin as we separated. Gabriela snorted at us.

"Use that ledger to vet the Lee recruits," I told Mickey gruffly. Truthfully, I thought he would tell me to fuck off. Instead, he surprised me by nodding. Gripping Savannah's hand once more, I headed toward the front of the house, where the bodies lined the square, piles of discolored, mangled corpses that didn't look human anymore. Wide, unseeing eyes assaulted us from every angle, mouths agape, joints at the wrong angle, blood congealing on the cobblestones.

Savannah made a noise in the back of her throat. Disgust and despair warred in that sound, like she didn't know if she would cry or vomit. She buried her face in my chest to hide from the sight. The smell was even worse. Sickly sweet rot, and with the growing heat and humidity of the morning it would only get worse.

"Why don't you go check on my horse in the stables?" I suggested quietly, my lips close to her ear. "I'll take care of this." Her face tilted up, her eyes filled with unshed tears. My heart clenched tight.

"Will—" She cut herself off, blinking hard.

"What is it, baby?" I asked softly, because she looked so fragile that it made me ache deeper than the throb in my side. "Talk to me."

"I need you to . . . " She hesitated. "I need you to look for Etty." She gestured at the scene that had rattled her so badly, and all of a sudden, it made sense. Tears wobbled on her lash line.

"Did you see her . . . ?" I didn't finish my sentence, but the implication was clear. *Did you see her get killed?* She shook her head, the tears rolling down her cheeks.

"She wouldn't have left me in that courtyard if she hadn't been . . . " She couldn't say it either. "I just need to make sure. I need to take care of her if she's in there. I can't leave her *like this.*" I nodded, unable to swallow around the lump of gravel in my throat. Wrapping my arm tight around her waist, I tugged her closer, resting my chin on the top of her head as she buried her face in my chest for another few deep, steadying breaths.

"I know, *mi sol.* I've got it. I've got *her.*"

She nodded again, swiping beneath her eyes before heading toward the stalls, her back to the gruesome scene, shoulders straight and chin held high. I watched her for a while, amazed by her strength. When she disappeared around the corner, I turned back to the bodies. A few people gathered outside, some pillaging the dead, others in uniform dragging the bodies, their faces pale and stricken. Clearly members of the Lee household staff. The lucky ones who'd gotten away from the carnage last night.

They eyed me warily, unsure of my intentions, afraid of my reputation that'd only been reinforced last night. On one side, two lanky figures in oversized clothes with hoods drawn low rifled through pockets looking for anything valuable.

Immediately, I knew who they were. Undesirables. Probably here before dawn, scavenging what they could to survive another day, afraid that someone would see them slinking from the shadows.

"Hey!" I snapped, forcing jerky, startled movements and then ab-solute stillness from them. They wouldn't look at me, eyes instead fixed on the ground. On their task.

"You can have most of the spoils, but not weapons, medicine, or anything deemed sentimental by loved ones. And if you want the rest, you have to help with clean-up. Otherwise, get the fuck outta here."

They looked up at me, slowly. One of them had an eye covered in scar tissue, the corner of his mouth turned down in a gruesome approximation of a frown. A gasp sounded behind me, from one of the women hovering over the bodies of two women in housekeeper uniforms. I didn't flinch, just stared at him with expectation. After a long moment, his good eye glinted with curiosity and begrudging respect. The other figure, a woman, had no visible scarring on her face, though I stared her down just the same. They nodded slowly and stood beside me. I directed my next words at the woman who still had an echo of that shocked gasp on her mouth.

"You got a problem with extra help?"

She shook her head furiously, her cheeks burning in embarrassment.

"Good. Let's start by separating them. Lee's staff and guests and Hanged Men. I don't want any of those motherfuckers to be next to our dead. The Hanged Men we'll throw into the back of a cart. I'll grab one from the stable." I looked at the blushing woman again. "Bring as many sheets and linens and tablecloths out as possible. Our dead will get wrapped, and uh . . . " I pointed to a man in a dirty guard uniform with red-rimmed eyes, looking eager for direction, for anything to distract him from his grief. "You. Can you build a pyre in the middle of the square? A *large* one."

"Yeah, I can do that," he said, only a slight waver in his voice.

"You two," I directed the undesirables. "Strip them of everything useful. Weapons, medicine, and sentimental items in one stack. Everything else in the other for y'all to bring back with you. And if any of you see Etty, you find me immediately. Everyone got it?" I barked. They all set about their assigned tasks. They weren't looking at me in fear anymore. Instead, they were purposeful, looking slightly relieved if I were honest.

It was strange, being *listened* to. People respecting my decisions, like Mickey. Savannah's faith in me. Though it made the back of my neck prickle with discomfort, the responsibility I donned was for Savannah, for Bonnie, for Jesse. And for them, I'd do anything.

I pushed the thought of Bonnie and Jesse and what was happening to them right now away. I couldn't fall apart. Not now. Not when I had work to do. So instead, I marched to the stables where Savvy brushed my stallion and fed him sugar cubes, cooing to him in a sweet voice. I walked behind her, until I wrapped my arms around her and buried my nose in her curls, inhaling the scent of her warm skin.

"Did you find her?" Savvy asked. I shook my head. It would take hours to finish taking care of the bodies. Hours we didn't have.

"Not yet," I admitted. "I came for a cart to hitch to this guy. Wanna help?"

She nodded absentmindedly, and I could tell her mind was far away, trapped in the dark memories from last night. Fear and grief dimmed her normally bright eyes. I hated it. Giving her a swift kiss on the temple and some space, I made quick work of finding a cart and dragging it out. Savvy walked my stallion from his stall, and we hitched him to the cart. He wasn't too happy about it, which was evident as he stomped his hoof near my foot. But he was gentle with Savvy, not an asshole like normal, which was surprising.

I led him from the stables, through the alley and around to the front, Savvy warily following by my side. There were several more people in front of the building now. They looked up when we appeared. For the first time in a long time, none of them had fear in their eyes. It was jarring. Uncomfortable. A man walked up in dirty blue jeans with similar red-rimmed eyes to the guard I'd spoken to earlier.

"They said you would tell us what to do," he said simply, his hands in his pockets. I stopped short, my gaze traveling to the expectant expressions of those who'd gathered. They stared at me like they were waiting for instructions. This was . . . completely insane.

Savannah slipped her hand into mine and gave me a reassuring squeeze. Suddenly, it made sense. These people had been through something hard and horrible. Like all the nights I'd gone to that god-damned bridge. Or the times I watched as my father broke my mother, over and over and over again. In those moments when I felt the worst of it, I'd leaned on Bonnie's strength or Savannah's. No matter how contrived.

These people didn't care that I was *the Beast of the Bridge.* They just needed someone with answers. Someone with a plan. Someone to tell them what to do. How to feel. Even if it was all bullshit.

Setting my shoulders, I inhaled deeply and resigned myself to the task at hand: directing a shit-ton of traumatized-as-fuck adults with the emotional intelligence of toddlers. *Fuckin' brilliant.* This was not how I'd expected my day to go.

"Sure," I said, continuing my sojourn to the front of the house. "Hanged Men go in the cart. Don't touch the horse. He *will* fuckin' bite you. Sort the bodies, build the pyre, don't fuck with the undesirables or I'll kick your ass. Got it?"

The man nodded, jogging back to others and divvying out tasks.

"If anyone sees Etty . . . you notify me immediately. Do not touch her. Do not move her. Just run your little asses as fast as you can and let me know."

"Got it!" he called before someone else took my reins and started lining up the bodies that would be loaded into the cart. Someone dragged a *very* mutilated and familiar corpse through the front door.

What was left of my father.

"And you!" I called, pointing until they dropped the corpse unceremoniously to the ground. "Leave that fucker to rot. He doesn't get a burial or a burning. He gets to bloat and split open and soil this house for Lee to deal with whenever he shows his rat-fuckin' face."

No arguments. Or judgments. Or protests followed. Just blind obedience.

The discomfort only grew. "Well," I said a little incredulously as I was left with Savvy. "That's different."

"You're different," she corrected gently. I looked down at her with brows furrowed.

"What do you mean?"

"You're . . . good at this. Good at crisis management. They can see it. That you're not intimidated by this. That you know how to move past it." Her words rang with sincerity and honesty and a hint of pride. It made me want to kiss her and to hide, and I didn't know how to deal with those conflicting feelings, so naturally . . . I ignored them.

"Baby," I said, looking at the more than a dozen people working in front of the house. "Could you make something for these people to eat? I hate to ask you to go into the kitchen, but, honestly, it'd be a huge help. They'll get hungry quick and it'll be hard to keep them on task without fuel."

"Of course," she said softly, leaning in for a quick, performative kiss. "Honestly, I think I'd feel better in the kitchen right now."

I gave her a small, sad smile that she returned before she left me to my task. Mickey and Gabi checked in often, updating me on supplies and recruits. The undesirables were a huge help to Gabi, and more of them arrived with every passing hour. Each of them looked at me and the others with wariness until they realized that no one cared about their presence. They seemed reassured and a little baffled by that. Truthfully, they were invaluable. If they weren't helping Gabi with supply looting, they packed or arranged the wagons, horses, carts, and more that lined the far side of the square. Anytime I acknowledged or thanked them, their mouths dropped open in shock.

By the time the sun hovered high in the sky, almost all of the bodies had been processed. A man handed me a list of names as more than seventy people stared at me where I stood on the steps of Lee's Manor. Savvy had been passing out sandwiches and glasses of water to the workers with the help of two maids that I thought hated her. Mickey stood by my side, a hand resting on my shoulder in support. I didn't know if he realized how much I needed it.

Clearing my throat, the buzz of chatter stopped. Suddenly, it was hard to speak. How did Bonnie do this shit? Didn't she feel like she was on the edge of an angry mob when she addressed a crowd? I most certainly did.

"Most of you know me as *the Beast of the Bridge*," I started. The square went silent. *Fuck this is uncomfortable.* Savannah offered me a sweet, secret smile meant for just me, and that smile helped my lungs expand again.

"My name is Will Ellis, and for the last three years, I've been working for Zachary Lee." Mickey squeezed my shoulder in reassurance. "But what I want to say right now isn't about me. It's about *them*." I motioned to the massive pyre with countless wrapped bodies atop it. One of the workers stood sentry with a lit torch, ready to set the pyre alight.

"The people on that pyre were members of our community. Sure, there were rich socialites, but also good, honest, workin' folks. Like many of you. People just trying to make a few bits and provide for their families. People who didn't deserve the pain and terror that preceded their untimely deaths. They were husbands and wives, mothers and fathers, sisters and brothers, friends, and loved ones. I know what it's like to mourn the loss of someone you care for. I also know what it feels like to have blood stain your hands. The truth is, what happened last night . . . was inevitable. Zachary Lee and entitled pricks like him don't give a shit about anyone. They see us and think we're expendable. Like balancing a ledger. Wiping the accounts clean." Seb's face flashed in my mind, unbidden and painful. I cleared my throat, looking down at the list for inspiration. Mickey's firm hand squeezed my shoulder again.

"But we're *not* expendable." I lifted my chin and raised my gaze back to the crowd who listened with rapt attention. "The people on that pyre were loved. They were important. And they didn't deserve the senseless deaths they got. With that said, I'm gonna read a list of the dead, and afterwards, we'll light up the square to honor them."

The man with the torch lit the pyre.

"Edwin Montez."

The fire was slow to start, needing to be fed in several different places.

"Alissa Schneider."

The humidity was cloying in the summer heat.

"Shane Stephenson."

The list seemed endless, and my voice rasped with overuse.

"Kendrick Washington."

The fires caught, smoking horribly in the humidity, not fed by any kind of breeze.

"Demarcus Sutton. Gavin Landry."

"Hazel Wilkerson."

"Sean Choi."

And on and on and on it went. Until I'd spoken the names of all the dead and the crackle of flames rang out in the clear light of day. Everyone was silent, but no one left as the flames devoured the dead. The crowd looked like they expected me to say more. But I didn't have any more words to give them.

"Anyone who wants to avenge those we've laid to rest, we leave in an hour." It was a declaration, but also, a way out. A way to get them to stop looking to me and start moving. Whether it was moving on from the display or to leave, I didn't care. I needed to get out from under their scrutiny.

Mickey ushered me away, and I ducked my head immediately.

"Can you get your men to do some things for me?" I asked quickly. Mickey nodded. "I need someone to get my books from my apartment. I know it'll be a pain, but I have a feeling we'll need medical knowledge. Also, I need you or someone you trust implicitly to go to the bank. I don't know when I'll be back in New Orleans and need some things moved around."

Mickey stared at me and then pulled me to the side as others moved past us, silent until we were alone. He stared at me the way he did sometimes, like he could see right through me. Unnerving. Completely vulnerable. I hated it, but if I were being honest, I loved how I'd never been able to hide from him. How he never judged me or found me lacking.

"Will," he said, his voice soft like he was going to soften a blow. The way he'd sounded earlier when he wanted to leave Bonnie and Jesse in Tent City. I braced myself, completely unprepared for what he would say next. "Are you okay?"

Was I okay?

Did it matter? No—that was a stupid thought. I remembered Jesse's face looking the same after he'd learned about the graveyard. How he'd just wanted to know the same thing. If I was okay. If I would *be* okay. For the first time, the fear I'd been beating back seized my chest.

"No," I admitted, ducking my head. "I know what they're marching towards and the truth is . . . I'm terrified." My voice quaked, but Mickey didn't push for more details. He didn't rush me. "And I have *no idea* what I'm fuckin' doing."

Mickey laid his hands on my shoulders. I raised my eyes to meet his: clear blue and full of faith in me. It scared me. It scared me that I could make him believe in me and somehow fail him like I'd failed everyone else in my life. For maybe the first time, I desperately didn't want to.

"I've *never* been prouder of anyone, Will. And if there's anyone who can do this . . . "

I stopped breathing.

"It's you. You are so much more capable than you know."

My eyes burned, and I cleared my throat uncomfortably. I wasn't good at this. "I killed my dad last night," I said, unsure why I needed to say it out loud, or why I needed to say it to him.

"I know," he admitted, his voice heavy. "I know you did."

"I killed the last living family member I had left," I said, swallowing hard. "And I don't feel bad about it at all."

"No you didn't," he said, gripping me by the back of my neck and jerking me forward until I met his gaze. It was cold, hard, and insistent. "Your family is right here. *I'm* right here. And we're gonna get Bonnie and Jesse back."

Something in me snapped. Clean in two. I nodded furiously, blinking hard as he pulled me into a shoulder-slapping hug.

"I'm getting them back. I promise," I said through clenched teeth as I gripped his shirt. He nodded against my neck. After a moment, we broke apart, pretending the interaction never existed, which was fine by me, because quite frankly, I didn't know how to deal with it. With a gruff grunt of acknowledgment, he left, and I wondered if it'd really happened at all.

CHAPTER THIRTY-TWO

SAVANNAH

I DIDN'T THINK IT was possible to be prouder of Will. To stand in front of all of these people, to show these strangers even a sliver of vulnerability. To show that he was more than his dark legend took more than any of them would know.

But I did.

While Will went off to prepare for our departure, I made one last pass through the house. Even though I knew she wasn't there, as I peered into the courtyard, I found the bloody spot on the cobblestones where Etty'd been struck down. I prayed silently that her absence amongst the dead was a good thing. Maybe she'd gotten out.

In no time at all, we mounted the stallion, the cart of dead Hanged Men in tow, Mickey shouting for order as the procession started through the square. The cavalcade of horses, wagons, carts, and walking bodies was larger than anything I'd ever seen. We led them, Mickey and Gabi behind us to keep order.

The irony was not lost on me that this might be Will's final ride through the streets of New Orleans. Whereas before there'd been the slamming of shutters and doors, people lingered on their porches, on the sidewalks, staring at us with respect. Where once whispers of fear trailed Will, shouts of rebellion lit the air. I sat tall in front of him, one hand covering his.

Will had done this. He had brought himself into the light.

People left their homes, joining the march. The bridge loomed in the distance, but it didn't feel as heavy anymore. Even as it grew bigger the closer we got, the massive structure of steel and concrete was just that: a bridge.

By the time we made it to the base, hundreds followed us, the voices loud and chaotic. Will dismounted, and the chatter quieted to a busy hum. He gripped the reins and began the ascent, people moving single-file until we crowded the top of the bridge. The late afternoon sun washed the city in gold. Will removed his hat, allowing the sun to warm his face.

The hum of voices dissipated, and Mickey rode closer, his expectant eyes steady on Will as he pulled the horse level with me.

Before us stood two young, very scared guards in uniforms, staring with panic in their eyes and guns in hand. Will dropped the reins as one guard marked the gun on his hip, confusion in his eyes.

"Hey," Will said, his hands raised in a gesture of peace. He approached slowly. "Lee's gone." The color leeched from their skin. "Dunno if you heard, but a lot of people died."

They shifted their weight, shooting uncomfortable glances at one another.

"We're gonna make the people who killed them pay. And if you'd like to join us, you can." Will shrugged. "Either way, we're gettin' over this bridge, *hermano*. So . . . " He let the weight of his words settle, then added, "You can stay here and wait for Lee to get back, or tag along. Your choice."

"You're the *Beast*," one of them said, not lowering his gun.

"Yeah."

"Why should we trust you?" His voice wavered. Part of me felt a burst of satisfaction at their fear. Will shrugged again and offered him a disarming smile.

"Why not?" he asked. "I mean, I get it. I've killed like . . . a lot of people. It's a fair question. But, that was under Lee's orders. You really think all these people would be here with me if I were a threat?"

They considered his words for a moment, then lowered their guns and walked toward us, nodding softly as they fell in line with the others. Will walked forward unhindered, until we reached the tallest point of the bridge. He turned back to the crowd, still eerily quiet. He waved his hand at one of the men nearby.

"Start unloading the cart here." With a nod, he got to work.

Will sighed beneath the crowd's expectant attention, running a weary hand through his hair to push it away from his eyes. I offered him a gentle smirk as I slid from the saddle; I liked it when I could see his eyes. I bet other people did too.

"Here's what I'll say," he said, voice booming. "These motherfuckers"—he motioned to the bodies being unloaded—"came into *our city*. Hurt *our people*. They think they're unstoppable. But I'm *the Beast* of this fuckin' bridge and *no one* is untouchable."

A few people shouted encouragement at him. Will stood a little taller. "They call themselves the Hanged Men. So we're gonna hang 'em. From this bridge. For the entire city to see. I want 'em to know we're comin' for 'em. I want them to know that we won't stop until they're swingin' right beside them." The crowd surged forward at his declaration, many helping to drag the bodies into a neat line with fire in their eyes and purpose in their actions.

Will's eyes brightened, and my heart skipped a beat. He was so beautiful in his confidence.

Within minutes, people passed long coils of rope over the line of bodies. As the reluctant leader of this horde, he would be the first to raise a corpse. I grimaced as he yanked on the rope and pained lines crossed his face. *Damnit.*

As I rushed toward him, Will continued, hand over hand. Bodies rose around him, several others taking the initiative to hang the Hanged Men. I swore beneath my breath and ducked under one of the already swinging corpses. Then I found his ropes and pulled hard.

Our eyes locked. Neither of us spoke. But together, we lifted that first corpse. Others worked in tandem, too, until dozens of dead bodies swayed in the late summer breeze.

All of us beasts, determined to seek justice the only way this violent world allowed.

"Ellis," a voice called once Will tied off the rope. We turned to find an undesirable woman with a bandaged hand. I remained firm beside him, an arm wrapped around his waist. "My people have been bothering me all day."

"Sorry," Will said with a chuckle.

"They said you fed them, paid them, and protected them," she accused. My brows lifted at the tone of her voice.

Will nodded, because it was the truth. We'd made sure that each person who helped was taken care of. I wouldn't see it any other way.

"You killed him," she said again in that accusatory voice. Will tensed beside me. She meant his father. I gave him a gentle squeeze, acknowledging his pain even if he couldn't acknowledge it himself. "I knew you would."

That familiar pride blossomed in my chest.

"We're with you," the woman said, chin tilted high in defiance. "All of us. As long as you can guarantee our protection."

Will blinked, his eyes shifting in shock. The *undesirables* wanted to join us on our march against Tent City.

"How many?" he asked. Any help they provided would be invaluable. I could already see his mind whirring as he considered what this meant for us.

Mickey approached, stopping short when he spotted the woman.

"Three hundred," she said with confidence.

"Holy shit." Mickey's eyes widened.

"What he means," Will said, glaring at him, "is that you're welcome. We could use all the help we can get. And I'll make sure your people aren't harassed. They'll get fed and sheltered like the rest of us."

The woman smiled. "I knew it would be you," she said cryptically. "I want to make it clear—" Her tone deepened. "We don't follow this group. We follow *you*. You freed us from Sixgun. We won't take orders from anyone else." Her gaze shifted to Mickey, who nodded in acquiescence.

"Thank you," Will said as she turned away. "And—" She stopped. "If you or your people have time on our travels, come find me. I might be able to help with some of the mobility restrictions. Not everyone would be a good candidate, but if I can help . . . I'd like it if you'd let me."

The woman nodded again, smiling as her hand curled around her bandages. When she left, Mickey let out a loud breath.

"Not gonna lie," he said, still staring after the woman. "I'm a little stunned."

Will laughed good-naturedly. I stared up at him, and he smiled, his joy making my heart beat faster.

Will was so much more than the darkness. And just maybe, he would finally see it.

CHAPTER THIRTY-THREE

WILL

THE SUN SET HOURS later, and I was stiff from the long day in the saddle, Savannah sleepy in my arms. My side was murder, but I'd dealt with worse. Mickey and Gabriela had checked in several times on the ride to coordinate camp. Ideally, I'd have ridden through the night to get farther away from the city, but with this many people, we needed to get them fed, warm, and rested for the remainder of our journey.

Morale in the hours that passed had waned from the fever pitch of rebellion, into excited murmuring, and was now quiet with exhaustion. I tugged the reins, and we circled a large, flat area of ground, shouts of direction coming from across camp, Mickey's men with strict orders.

Savannah stirred, her deep breaths stuttering as she woke and tried to clear her bleary eyes. I kissed her temple softly, filling my lungs with her scent before whispering, "We're setting up camp. Are you too tired to help?"

She shook her head, pulling her shoulders back as the stallion stopped. I swung my leg over and then helped her down behind me. The Kid and his horse were only a few feet away. People gathered, some assigned to building fires, others to ration the food we'd brought.

Mickey found me in the hum of activity, Gabi, as always, not far behind, unrolling a map so we could plot the next day's path.

"We should stop here," I told him, marking a place called Acadiana, which looked like a large abandoned mall. Mickey's face screwed up, as if in pain, and Gabriela smiled widely.

"I don't think that's a good idea," he said with a groan. Gabi put a hand on his shoulder and looked at me with abject delight.

"We're stopping there," she commanded. My eyebrows rose as Mickey slid a look of betrayal her way. She patted her belly softly, and the fight fled him on a rough exhalation. I stared between them both for a few long seconds and tried to stifle the smile rising on my lips, without success.

"Then it's settled." I grinned wildly as Mickey knocked my hat off and departed.

The next hour was a different kind of quiet as people moved about their assigned tasks with purpose, bedrolls unrolled, fires lit, and two lines for dinner rations. Savannah and Gabriela managed one of the lines for food while I walked with Mickey, reviewing the progress and assessing our ragtag "crew."

"It's still unbelievable," Mickey said, surveying the patch of earth where many of the undesirables had settled. You could tell they were different because of how they were covered up, scraps of cloth wound around body parts, hoods drawn low, heads on a swivel looking out for danger.

"They'll be more valuable than you know," I told him. "I've been thinking on the ride and I've got plans for them . . ." I wouldn't say more in the open. Mickey had been true to his word, keeping most of the plans close. The unimportant things he delegated, but the intricacies of our plan remained between Gabi, Savvy, The Kid, and us. Though, The Kid never really spoke when we made plans. And several times I caught him glaring at me. I didn't know what I'd done to piss him off, but honestly, I didn't have time to deal with it.

"The inside of your head must be terrifying." Mickey chuckled and slapped his hand on my back good-naturedly.

"You have *no idea*, old man," I said with a grin. Shouting broke the lighthearted moment, followed by the thud of a fist against flesh, then louder shouting. Before Mickey could stop me, I ran toward the food line that Savvy was managing. After shoving people out of the way, I found two people, scrabbling on the ground. One had a torn guard's uniform. He was bulky, expression screwed up in anger as he slammed his fist into the pale, gaunt face of a young undesirable. The boy couldn't have been much older than The Kid.

"Give it back, you *fuckin' bottom feeder!*" the guard shouted.

"I-I don't have any extra rations! I swear!"

I strode calmly into the fray, using the heel of my boot to kick the guard off the kid. With a grunt, he toppled to the ground. In a surprising flash, he jumped up and turned on me with a sneer, fist raised as if to fight off the threat. When he saw me, however, his arm dropped. I cocked my head to the side before sliding my gaze over to the bloody-faced kid.

"What the fuck are you doing?" I asked, my voice quiet but firm, hands tucked into my pockets. The man pointed his meaty, bloodied finger at the kid, who was busy mopping up the blood streaming from his nose.

"He stole my rations," he accused, while the kid shook his head fervently. The back of my neck prickled with awareness. That was when I realized everyone was watching me now, watching what I would do.

"He says he didn't," I said, shrugging. "Did you see him do it?"

The guard's skin flushed, and, after a few attempts to say something, he snapped his mouth shut.

"Then why do you think he did it?" I asked, my tone careful. I'd expected something like this to happen eventually but had hoped that the camaraderie from the bridge and the pyre would last longer. The undesirables, like me, were the victims of rumor and legend and not seen kindly by others. And there were a *lot* of them.

"He was near my campsite earlier, before it went missing, and . . . and it's what *their kind* does. They *scavenge*."

I nodded, as if contemplating his point for a moment. Gaze sliding over to the kid, I crouched to him. "What's your name?"

"Billy," he answered around his hand on his nose. He didn't drop his gaze from me; instead he stared straight on, waiting to see what I would do. A flicker of defiance in his eyes reminded me of Bonnie when she was younger, before her spark of defiance blossomed into a blaze of world-ending anger.

I liked this kid.

"Show me your bag," I demanded. That flicker of defiance sparked in his eyes with offense. "I didn't stutter. Show me your bag." Reluctantly, he handed over his pack, and I glanced inside. No rations, not even his own. The guard's face crumpled as I held the pack open to him.

"Satisfied?" I asked, and he nodded. "Good." I handed the bag back to Billy and then slammed my fist against the guard's nose hard enough that it cracked and he shrieked in pain.

"You broke my fuckin' nose!"

Shaking my hand out, I nodded again. "Yeah." I sighed. "I can't punish you for being a prejudiced *pendejo*, but I don't tolerate anyone hitting kids. I *really* fucking hate that." The camp went silent. So I raised my head and stared back at the expectant faces watching the scene.

"You got a problem with somebody, you come to me. But the minute you decide violence is the answer in *my* camp, you'll be met with violence. And if you need something, you ask. If you're caught stealing you'll answer to me. Any questions?" No one spoke, so I turned back to the two bleeding people in front of me and sighed again.

"Alright, now you two follow me so I can patch you both up."

The guard nodded and followed after me, but Billy was more suspicious, taking a long time to follow. After cleaning and bandaging the guard's broken nose, I waved Billy forward and examined his bruises and scrapes. It was only when I finished dressing his wounds that Billy found the courage to speak.

"Some of us in the fringes talk about you like you're some sort of hero, but I don't see it," he said snidely. I chuckled.

"Me neither," I admitted. After another moment, I leveled him with a challenging stare. The little shit. "So where'd you hide the rations?"

His gaze dropped, and I shook my head at him.

"I-it's . . . I mean . . ." I raised an eyebrow at his stuttering until he said, "I gave it to old woman Alice. She's mean as a rattlesnake and wouldn't be left behind, but she's sick and that guy's built like a bull! It's not fair that—"

I raised a hand to stop his vehement protests. "Alright, alright, I get it. No worries. I'm not going to rat you out."

"You aren't?" he asked, his voice small. That was the first time I noticed how young he was, looking up at me with hopeful eyes. I shook my head. "Why not?"

"Because I know what it's like to be hungry, and to see people you care about go hungry," I told him honestly. "But you aren't gettin' off the hook just like that." Looking around, my eyes caught on The Kid walking toward Savvy.

"Kid!" I called, waving him over. With another scowl, he begrudgingly crossed the distance toward us, glancing between Billy and me. "This is Billy, and while we're on the road, you're giving him his assignments, got it?"

"Me?" he asked, shocked. I nodded.

"Yeah, why not?"

"Well, why do I have to?" he questioned with a scoff. Billy scowled again, but this time at The Kid. Honestly, I was over teen angst for the foreseeable future.

"Don't want to get mixed up with an undesirable, pretty boy?" Billy shot at The Kid, who rolled his eyes.

"No, just don't feel like *babysitting*."

I stood as they bickered and left them there, thanking every God I could think of that I didn't have children. I found Savvy wrapping up at the food line, my body relaxing at the thought of curling up together for the night. She snickered at me as I wrapped her in my arms and tucked her in tight to my body.

"What?" I whispered.

"You're good with people," she said, chuckling again.

"Is that surprising?" I asked, slightly offended. Instead of answering me, she shushed me and kissed me goodnight.

CHAPTER THIRTY-FOUR

SAVANNAH

"I DID *NOT* INTENTIONALLY throw you from your horse." I walked between Will and The Kid as the former led his stallion across a giant concrete lot. Faded yellow lines indicated that at one point, it'd been a parking lot.

"So how'd I end up on my ass?" Will asked, his voice lined with amusement.

I narrowed my eyes at him playfully. He knew *exactly* how he ended up on his ass. Someone got a little too playful after handing me the reins. I wasn't the best at driving the horse, but Will knew that, yet he'd taken advantage of his free hands by putting them on *me*. I may have yanked the reins too hard, and the horse might have bucked.

"Maybe your horse just likes me better," I said with a snort.

The Kid chuckled on my other side. He'd laughed so hard that tears filled his eyes when Will's ass hit the ground. I liked it when he smiled. He looked like Jesse. A sharp pang went through my chest at the thought. We still had a mission to accomplish.

I said a silent prayer for their safety. They needed it.

After days of endless traveling, I felt disconnected from Will. While we spent our nights wrapped up together, when we weren't riding, he was huddled off with Mickey, discussing our plans and strategizing about getting into Tent City.

Last night was the first time we'd spent together outside of riding or our tent. We'd wandered away from camp so Will could teach me how to shoot. I'd never had a reason to learn, but after being manhandled by

356

Hanged Men, completely unable to defend myself, I needed to learn. I wouldn't be caught so helpless again, by anyone. He'd set up a bottle on top of an old fence post, which wasn't the problem. The problem was when he put the gun in my hands, he wrapped himself around me to show me how to plant my feet, using his hands harder than necessary to set my hips and help me spread my weight.

That bottle still sat atop that fence post, because we didn't get any further than clicking off the safety before I got lost in him in the overgrown grass.

It had always been like that with Will, but I missed his constant presence, his watchful gaze. While I admired him for stepping into himself, I missed *him*. William. My William.

We approached a set of glass double doors, armed guards posted on either side. Will shouted orders to tie off the horses and for most of the crew to wait outside. The guards eyed us curiously over the shotguns in their hands. They were armed to the teeth with knives strapped across their chests and pistols tucked into holsters at their sides. Mickey met Will's gaze and gave him a nod before speaking quietly with the guards, and they granted us access.

The place brimmed with activity. People milled about in a long, wide hallway, excitedly chattering to one another. In New Orleans, people hadn't been the friendliest to me, most likely because of the brand on my neck. I tugged my collar higher and tossed my ponytail over my shoulder. I fell in line with Will, watching as two women embraced in front of a large plate glass window, then laughing as they separated and promising to talk later. Some of the people walking about carried weapons, but there was a relaxed set to their shoulders. I couldn't remember much about my early years in St. Louis, but it was never like this.

We passed what appeared to be old storefronts. Instead of being run down, each felt friendly, cozy even. I spied phrases like *Welcome* and *Home Sweet Home* painted on the large glass windows, thick curtains the only thing separating them from the main corridor. The farther we walked, signs indicating different wares lined the way: one for a jeweler, another for weapons, even a barber shop.

"This used to be a mall," Gabriela said, falling into step beside me. "Like the old Riverwalk."

The din of echoing voices rose as we reached a wide-open space. Skylights filled the ceiling, highlighting the cloudless blue sky above. Below, a largely constructed bar was surrounded by people sitting at cafe tables, chatting as if there wasn't a war going on outside their doors. For the middle of the afternoon, there seemed to be quite the party going on as a three-piece band played a fast tune. Others danced to the music, their smiles contagious.

This was the kind of place I wished New Orleans had been.

"Didn't I warn you that the next time you brought an army to my city, I'd shoot you?" An obsidian-skinned woman with long braided hair approached, guards flanking her on either side. At least, I thought they were guards. They didn't carry guns like the ones outside, but their eyes marked every movement we made. When they settled on Will, that familiar fear flashed bright.

Just how far-reaching was the legend of the Beast?

Mickey's tan skin blanched beneath the woman's scrutiny. She wore a simple outfit of jeans and a t-shirt, but there was something about her presence that radiated power. Her eyes went to Gabriela, and a smile crossed her face.

"Yeah, well, you kicked my army's ass, didn't you?" Mickey rubbed the back of his neck sheepishly. Then the woman pulled him into a warm hug. When they parted, Mickey said, "Sorry to do this to you, but do you have space for my crew for a night?"

"For you?" she questioned. "No." She turned her attention to Gabriela. "For my goddaughter, absolutely."

The women shared a laugh as Gabriela moved to embrace her. "It's good to see you, Elena," she said, then turned back to us. She introduced us to Elena one at a time. The woman's eyes turned curious when it was Will's turn, but she said nothing.

"There's plenty of space in the old Dillard's on the southeast side."

Mickey thanked her, then turned to one of the others and gave instructions to bring the horses around to the appropriate entrance. Elena guided our small group through the busy place, sharing small talk about their recent travels. I tuned them out quickly, instead focusing on the world around us.

The sight of a clothing store made me excited. I was sick of the too-tight jeans and shirt I'd been wearing for days. Already, I had a list of half a dozen stores I wanted to stop at when I had the chance.

The group slowed as another woman approached Elena, her eyes sparkling. Elena introduced her as her wife, Marie. She embraced Gabriela, the pair of them sharing a warm smile.

"We appreciate the hospitality," Mickey said as we slowed near a wide-mouth entrance to a vacant part of the mall. "We've got to get to Tent City, so—"

Elena turned her sharp gaze toward him. Marie stiffened at her side, eyes widening, shoulders slumping as she closed in on herself. Though she never spoke, I recognized the emotions running through her. Fear. Mortification. Elena wrapped an arm around her shoulder and guided her away, whispering quietly in her ear.

Tent City must have lived up to its reputation.

Our group took in the expansive space. It must have been a giant warehouse pre-Culling. There were walls dotted throughout that split up the space, but for the most part, it was wide open. The rest of the crew entered through the outside doors.

"Why the hell are you getting mixed up with Jones?" Elena asked in a hushed voice as she returned.

"He took my nephew and the woman he loves," Mickey replied, using his thumbnail to scratch his eyebrow.

Elena huffed. "Since when did you become a big softy?"

Mickey's gaze settled on Gabriela. "Since they reminded me of what's worth fighting for." A loud smack sounded in the space. Mickey rubbed the back of his head. "What was that for?"

"For taking ten years, asshole," she replied, much to Gabriela's chagrin. She motioned to a table set off to one side. "Let's talk logistics.

I'm not sure how up-to-date your information is on Tent City. My last scouts returned from there a couple of weeks ago."

Will eyed me with a silent question. I motioned for him to go ahead. He was a leader here, and I couldn't fault him for that. His gaze traveled along my cheek and rested on my lips, his eyes darkening in that familiar way though we were in public. My fingers curled into the fabric at the front of his shirt. We could dip into a bathroom—

"Ellis!"

The moment broke. Will's eyes closed, and he let out a gentle sigh. Mickey leaned over the table with the maps, pointing to something for Elena as he glanced our way.

"You should go," I said, smoothing down the creases of his shirt where I'd wrinkled them.

"I know." He pressed his forehead to mine, inhaling deeply. There was work to be done. I almost missed New Orleans, when people weren't looking at him to take charge. While things were crazy, we didn't have a choice. We had to get Bonnie and Jesse back. There would be time to take things slow after. At least, I hoped.

Will lingered, covering my mouth with his. I tangled my fingers in his hair, holding him there for a long moment.

"Will!"

We broke apart. The longer I stayed here, the longer Will would take to get back to his duties. I couldn't stand in the way of that.

"I'm going shopping," I said suddenly. If I weren't here to be a distraction, maybe he could focus better on the task at hand. I understood why he felt the way he did. After all, we'd only just made things official.

"Ask someone to go with you. This place is safer than most, but you never know."

"I'll take The Kid." I flashed a smile, then lowered my arms from his neck and started to brush past him. Will put a hand on my arm, and I let out an impatient huff. If I didn't extricate myself from him right now, he'd never get back to Mickey.

"You need money," he said quietly. He reached to the pouch tied to his belt. I expected him to pass a few coins over, but, instead, he handed the entire thing to me. With furrowed brows, I opened it, finding a *lot* of golden bits. He'd filled my tin with coins back in New Orleans too. This was too much. I opened my mouth to protest, but he cut me off. "Get whatever you want."

A brilliant smile crossed my face. I rested a hand on his forearm and leaned up to press a quick kiss to his cheek. Before I could turn away, his long arms enveloped me, and he covered my mouth with his, stealing my breath away. I softened against him, wrapping my arms around his torso. A breath, and then he pulled away.

"What was that for?" I asked, staring at him with wide eyes.

"Don't want you to start missin' me," he said with that grin that made my insides heat up.

"That's impossible," I whispered, then kissed him swiftly and headed toward The Kid. He was off in a corner near Mickey's stuff, unpacking his saddlebag and grumbling something to himself as he eyed the undesirable kid he'd been partnered with from across the way.

"Kid." He turned at the sound of my voice. "Wanna go spend Will's money with me?"

Light filled his blue eyes as he abandoned his work and donned his hat. I tried to ignore the familiar guilt that stabbed my chest. He looked so much like Jesse. It was okay. We'd get them back. We walked together, passing Will and Mickey talking to Elena over maps they'd spread out on a table.

The farther we walked, the more The Kid relaxed. I squinted at him, noticing how his eyes moved around the corridor, marking every single face before he moved on. It reminded me so much of Bonnie. He glanced over his shoulder as if searching for something.

"Fuckin' Billy," he murmured. I tilted my head toward him and narrowed my eyes.

"Why do you hate Will so much?" I asked.

He shoved his hands into his pockets. "Not *Will*," he said. "Billy. That kid Will's makin' me babysit."

Huh. That *kid* was at least a year older than *The* Kid. A vague sense of familiarity flashed between us. When *I* had been griping about Will all the time, it was really just denial that I liked him. The Kid had been awfully close with the stable hand back in New Orleans.

"I mean, *Billy* is way more handsome than that stable boy," I said nonchalantly as we entered a clothing store.

The Kid sputtered. "I—*no* . . . I mean, at least I'm not married to *the Beast*."

My mouth gaped. I was *what*? My mouth opened and closed as I tried to make sense of his words. He stared back, blue eyes confused as I struggled to find my voice. Married. To Will? Where did he get an idea like that?

"I'm not—*Kid*—what?"

"That's what they call you," he said, his voice gentle.

"Who? What do they call me?"

"The *bride*."

"The *what*?"

"On one of his midnight rides, people saw a woman in a white dress with the Beast," he explained, as though it were obvious. My heart pounded loudly in my chest. The night of Bonnie's engagement party. The night Will nearly took his own life. The night that changed me irrevocably. "They say he reaps souls, and in return, the devil gave him a bride."

That next day, when we'd gone to his apartment, people had stared in the bar. The man Will shot for touching me. He'd called me a whore, but the others . . . they'd been whispering madly.

I burst into laughter, unable to help myself. I flattened a palm against my belly as I erupted into a coughing fit from laughing so hard. I swiped an errant tear from the corner of my eye.

"That's ridiculous."

"Is it?"

"Yes," I said, shaking my head. "Will is just a man. He's not a beast. He's not some reaper of souls. He's a man."

"So you *aren't* married to him?" he asked, the corners of his mouth threatening to smile.

"No," I said, chuckling. At The Kid's grin, I smacked him in the shoulder and walked away to explore the store. My mind whirled, going over every time I'd gone somewhere with Will since that night. How people whispered behind their hands and stared. How they almost pitied me after realizing who Will was.

Did he know? He had to know. Because he knew people talked about *him.* Why didn't he tell me?

I found a couple of pairs of jeans, some sleep pants, and a few shirts. As I set my purchases on the counter at the register, I spied a mannequin in the window wearing a long, flowy skirt and matching top the color of red wine. The top banded around the chest only, leaving an expanse of exposed skin between it and the skirt's waistband. The sleeves, which could barely be called sleeves at all, looked like cuffs that slipped over the arms.

It was beautiful. And frivolous. I wouldn't have a chance to wear something like that on the road. But . . .

"I'll take that, too," I said to the woman behind the counter. The dress may not be appropriate for the road, but we were in a city of sorts. Maybe there was something special I could do for Will tonight, something to help us reconnect in the midst of this madness.

After sorting out the proper underclothing and shoes for my new outfit and paying for my things, The Kid and I made our way out of the store. I'd gotten what I needed, but the purse still felt obscenely heavy.

We wandered, stopping at a small kiosk where the vendor served giant scoops of ice cream. The Kid shared stories of Montana and the early days of his and Jesse's travels with Bonnie. He mentioned her outlaw rules, reiterating number seven. *No one gets left behind.* He was sweet. The longer we walked, the easier he smiled. I told him about my time in New Orleans, the good, bad, and ugly.

Lavender wafted from one of the shops nearby. I paused, peering inside. A man stood behind a chair, chattering animatedly and using a pair of scissors to cut another man's hair. I ran my fingers through my own tangled hair, catching sight of two more women cutting working beyond.

"Do you need a haircut?" I asked, reaching for his hat. He slid out of my reach and pressed it harder on his head. "What? Are you growing it out like Will?"

"No, I just don't want to cut it."

"Well, I'm getting one." I shoved my bags into his hands and entered the shop. Hair held memories, I firmly believed that. It was time to make some new ones.

An hour and a half later, the stylist whipped the chair around so I could look at her work. Before, the long, black curls fell to my mid-back. Now, they barely brushed my shoulders, the product in it defining them quite prettily. I leaned toward my reflection, my smile bright.

This was who I wanted to be.

The stylist swatted my hand as I reached up to touch the curls, chiding me about ruining her hard work. I left an extra gold bit as a tip. She handed me a couple of bottles of product, making me promise to keep it styled, before I met The Kid outside.

"What do you think?" I asked, shaking my head so the curls bounced. It felt so freeing.

"I think it's not gonna last past the first ten minutes riding tomorrow," he said. I rolled my eyes, then hooked my arm in his, guiding him back toward the vendor from earlier.

As The Kid waited for ice cream, a shop with a rack of guns in the window caught my eye. Without a word, I crossed to it. Inside, guns lined the walls in various shapes, sizes, and colors. A rack in the center of the store displayed knives. From penknives to giant machetes, the place had everything.

"Can I help you, miss?" When I turned, a balding older man with kind green eyes greeted me.

"Yes, I'd like to buy a gift for my . . . " I trailed off. While I knew the appropriate word was boyfriend, it didn't feel significant enough to explain what Will was to me. I let out a breath. "What do you get a man who wants for nothing?"

The man stepped back behind the counter. As he rifled in one of the cabinets, I spotted an open leather pouch on display in a glass case. Inside, a variety of silver medical instruments rested against black velvet. I thought back to the day at Will's apartment when he said he'd wanted to be a doctor, and how Gabriela mentioned that he'd wanted to join the medical team at their base.

What if, instead of purchasing a gift fit for a beast, I bought one for William?

The man seemed disappointed as I asked for the kit, but when I put two gold bits down on the counter, he didn't argue. The Kid wandered in as I tucked the medical kit into my clothing bag.

"What else do you want to spend money on?"

A grin lit up his features as we walked from the shop.

CHAPTER THIRTY-FIVE

WILL

I'D BEEN STARING AT the map for so long, the lines and boundaries blurred together. There was too much that needed to be done in so little time. Every minute, it was something else, a dispute between two drunk or prejudiced assholes that got ugly, so I needed to stitch them up. Roadblocks that cost us hours and days of travel time that we could've avoided if we'd been better prepared. The constant resource management for a group this large and varied was *insane*. And for some reason, it all fell to me.

"Did you hear what I said, son?" Mickey's voice finally registered, and I looked up, startled to find several pairs of eyes on me. Expectant and hesitant and some downright antagonistic. I pinched the bridge of my nose and blinked to clear my mind.

"Sorry, Mickey," I said, trying to ignore the woman rolling her eyes at me. "Repeat that."

A scoff sounded from across the table, and my eyes narrowed on the woman who'd scrutinized me so hard when we arrived. Mickey'd called her Elena, and other than clearly being the leader at this outpost, she proclaimed herself as Gabriela's godmother. Yet, since the moment she caught sight of me, she'd worn a dark expression and a scowl.

"I was explaining the issue we're going to have around this area." Mickey pointed to the map. A headache crept up, digging into my temple like a railroad spike. "The problem is the lack of vegetation. We'll be fully visible when we break the tree line and this big area here"—he

366

indicated a large stretch of barren flat land between the trees and the walls of Tent City—"is called the—"

"Badlands," I finished for him. "I'm familiar."

"I bet you are," Elena said loudly enough that the few people in the room shifted uncomfortably at the tension.

Finally, I looked up, straight into her no-nonsense dark eyes, and said, "Are you trying to fuck me or fuck me over? Because whatever it is, get to the point already, lady." Her jaw fell open in shock, and there were several gasps.

"Excuse me?!" she shouted, outraged. Mickey groaned and smacked me in the back of the head.

"What?" I asked, hands raised with my palms up. "Either you're going for an enemies-to-lovers thing here, which won't happen by the way, or you've got some sort of issue with me. Probably the latter, if I had to guess, but if that's the case, I'm gonna need you to air it out or suck it up, 'cause we don't have time for this."

Mickey buried his face in his hands. Elena looked like she was chewing on nails. Instead, after releasing the clench of her jaw, she said tightly, "You're the Beast of the Bridge."

I gasped mockingly, looking around as if for confirmation, and pointed a finger at my own face and mouthed "*Me?*" Her scowl darkened, and the murder in her eyes galvanized into something steely. "No shit."

"I don't want a murderer in my city, and especially not here while we make plans."

I nodded thoughtfully and leaned closer to her, the feral expression in her eyes amusing me. If I wasn't careful and got too close, she might actually try to bite me.

"This," I said, indicating the map and the people in the room, "is my plan." Leaning back, Mickey emerged from his hands to peer at me. "And while all of you have been doin' a great job of giving me a killer headache, I've figured out our next steps. That is, if I can continue . . ." I looked pointedly at Elena, and after several tense seconds, she relented with her arms crossed over her chest.

"The badlands are a problem, for sure, but so is Jones. Ya'll keep forgettin' about him, but I haven't. See . . . he's gonna expect everything you've suggested and will have countermeasures in place. If we go around, there'll be scouts with higher artillery in seemingly less guarded areas. The thing he won't expect is to go at him directly, right across the badlands, head-on—"

"Because it's suicide!" Elena threw her hands out in frustration. I held a finger up to still the rest of her exclamation.

"No, it's suicide for *us*," I told them, a grin curling on my mouth. "See, it would be nice if we had a really large group of people who are overlooked and adept at sneaking through the fringes. *Maybe* they could find the weak points in the wall for us . . . " I trailed off and then smiled widely at Elena. "Oh wait, *I do*."

I could practically hear her teeth grinding. Mickey's eyebrows were furrowed as he considered my words.

"Where are you going to camp the rest of the forces then?" Elena challenged.

"Right in front, just outside of their range. We're gonna roast fuckin' marshmallows and sing 'Kumbaya.'"

"But they'll see you!"

"Yes," I agreed. "They're on a twenty-foot wall with parapets, they'll have a *great* view. And Jones will expect it to be a trick so that he'll divert his artillery and forces away from the front, and instead, he'll put them on all the spots you and these people suggested for a way around the badlands . . . making it *easier* for us when we make our move."

Silence.

I was really tired of people underestimating me.

"You can't seriously consider this!" Elena turned to the others, imploring them to see sense. Mickey cleared his throat, and when I glanced at him, pride shone in his eyes.

"Actually," he started. "It's kind of genius. Jones won't expect something so direct. The element of surprise is something we've *never* had. Not with him. It could be the edge we need to win. So . . . " He took a deep breath and shot Elena an apologetic look. "I'm with the kid on this one."

"You have a sizable force of people with you," she said as if it hurt her to admit it. "But, with the wall and protections Tent City has in place, do you think it'll be enough?"

I smirked at her again, leaning a hip against the table. "That's why I sent our fastest riders from New Orleans to Fort Hood and Flagstaff before we left the city. Backup. Even if our first push only manages to weaken them, we'll be flush with reinforcements by the time we need them."

Fuming, she nodded for us to continue.

After more discussion, the finer details of the plan came together, and it took much longer than I'd like, but we finished for the day. I was ready to see Savannah, to take her to a dark room and bury all my exhaustion in her body. To remind her of the man she gave a chance.

"Good work," Mickey said, his arm wrapped affectionately around Gabi's waist. Elena glared at me from a corner where a woman muttered in her ear. Her eyes were glued on me. I winked and chuckled at her murderous expression.

"Don't feel bad," I called as she left. "Everyone falls for the Ellis charm eventually." She bared her teeth at me, and I guffawed. Mickey groaned loudly beside me.

"You're trying to get me killed, aren't you?" he asked. Gabi slapped his arm playfully.

"She's not so bad," Gabi said, staring at Mickey with a soft adoration in her eyes. Mickey leaned down and gave her a lingering kiss.

"Nah," he said, wrinkling his nose. "Not bad at all."

For a long moment, they stared deeply into each other's eyes until I cleared my throat to remind them I was still standing there. When they dragged their eyes away from each other and back to me, I stared at them expectantly.

They said nothing, so I finally said, "How far along *are* you?"

They wore the same shocked expression as they closed in on me. Gabi gripped my arm, and Mickey shuffled close so that our words were quiet.

"You can't say anything," he explained.

Gabi looked up at me with apprehension. "Four months, but at my age I'm still high risk."

I nodded and offered Mickey a genuine smile. "Congrats, *dad*."

His answering smile made him look so much like Jesse, it almost hurt. His blue eyes lit up with possibility and hope. My heart squeezed tight at the sight. It felt good, calling him *dad*, in a way that had nothing to do with their child on the way and everything to do with Mickey and me.

But, I would never say that aloud. I couldn't.

"Thanks," he replied. "We didn't think it could happen for us, but . . . I'm so happy." He blinked rapidly and cleared his throat.

"Gabi." I turned to her. "If you need *anything*, I know a lot about obstetrics. I studied it at length when Bonnie was pregnant. So, if you have any questions or get worried about something, you come to me. Okay?"

She nodded, happy tears shining in her eyes. She hugged me tight for a long time. For some reason, I didn't pull away. I just couldn't. When she finally released me, Mickey gave me a nod of approval that I felt all the way down in my boots. They waved their goodbyes before they left, wrapped up in each other. And I watched them leave, wishing I'd had parents like them and thinking about how lucky this kid would be.

When I was finally alone, I only had one thing on my mind, one *person*. I'd had too little real time with Savvy recently. I craved her presence in a way that was wildly unhealthy, and I didn't care one bit. I needed to be reminded of that goodness inside of her. I needed to feel her warmth and know she was still in this with me, even through all of this insanity.

It took me asking several people if they'd seen her until I made it to the bar, where Savannah sat with The Kid. He talked animatedly, seemingly complaining about something that had a small amused smile playing across her full mouth. Leaning against an open doorframe, I watched her for a while. Old habits died hard, I guess. I loved seeing her like this, free to enjoy herself. It was so simple and normal, and Savvy hadn't been allowed this for so long.

Her hair was different. Shorter. The curls that clung to my fingers so tightly were loose and defined, framing her pretty face like they'd always been that way, instead of tied up. It suited her. After I'd had my fill of watching and couldn't stand not touching her for a second longer, I shoved off the doorframe and crossed the bar, patrons parting for me as I moved through the room. Well, I supposed Elena wasn't the only one who'd heard about my beastly reputation. She'd done a pretty thorough job warning her people about me.

Before I was halfway across the room, Savannah sat up straighter and turned toward me, like she felt me approaching. Her eyes lit up as she locked them on me, filled with that inner light I was so drawn to.

Sunlight through whiskey. Warmth coursed through my veins as she smiled. It was strange, but I didn't feel fully alive until she looked at me like that. Like she was the center of the entire universe, and without her, I didn't know my place in it anymore.

The Kid said something, but I ignored him. Instead, without sparing him a glance, I said, "Where's Billy?"

With a soft swear, he shoved off the barstool and glared at me before stalking off. Savannah shook her head, and I leaned against the bar so that I was the only thing in her direct line of sight. I swirled my finger until one of her curls clung to me. I smiled softly down at her.

"What?"

"Why do you like torturing him like that?" she asked, leaning into my palm. I shrugged.

"I can't deal with the teen angst. Better they fight each other than me," I said with a weary sigh. "I honestly don't know how Bonnie and Jesse deal with it."

Her smile faltered at the mention of our friends. It was a reminder of what we were doing here. Why they weren't with us now. Hating that I'd been the one to dim her good mood, I changed the subject.

"You cut your hair," I observed, my eyes mapping the new haircut. The stacked layers of curls fell prettily above her shoulders and framed her face. Her face flushed as she looked up at me through her eyelashes.

"Do you like it?" she asked, her voice shy. There was *nothing* shy about this woman, but that she felt safe showing me this side of her made my cock stiffen in my jeans. It thickened even more quickly when her tongue darted from her mouth to wet her lips.

Oh the things I want her mouth to do.

"*Mi sol*," I breathed, drinking in the taste of her breath. "You look . . ." I trailed off, my eyes roaming over her soft curves. A strangled, growling sound escaped from the back of my throat. The bass in the sound vibrated in the air between us. "You look like you feel beautiful, and that is *so fuckin' hot.*"

Her answering smile was wicked, and suddenly, the seam of my jeans was painful. *Fuck.* Even in the immediate aftermath of what had happened at Lee Manor, regardless of injury, I'd been insatiable for her. I'd taken her at least once a day every day since, not caring if we were in public and someone could see us. Yet still, I couldn't get enough of her. As if sensing my thoughts, she averted her eyes, playing coy.

"Maybe you should get a haircut then," she teased me. After a moment's thought, I pulled her off the stool and, with a firm hand on the small of her back, led her away from the bar.

"Where are we going?"

"The hairdresser," I answered matter-of-factly. She looked at me curiously. "Lead the way."

Linking our fingers together, she led me to the barber shop where a hairdresser was finishing up with someone in her chair. She looked up and smiled when her eyes landed on Savannah. When the patron handed her a few bronze bits and left, she turned to us and said, "Back again, gorgeous?"

Before Savannah could answer, I plopped into the chair. The two women looked at me expectantly. I pulled the hat from my head and tugged the leather strap out of my hair, letting it fall to my shoulders.

"Don't look at me," I said, motioning to Savannah. "Do whatever she wants."

Savannah gaped, looking from me to the hairdresser and back before saying, "I want to see his eyes."

With a shared smile between us, she settled into the chair beside me, and the hairdresser got to work with her scissors, letting long locks fall to the floor. As she worked, it was strange, but I felt lighter. My soul was lighter. Before long, she turned me toward the mirror, where my hair was shorter than it'd been in years. My dark curls still fell nearly into my eyes, but the style left my every expression open to the world.

After a cursory glance, I faced Savannah, twisting the brim of my hat in my hands. "What do you think?" I asked.

She walked closer, brushing a stray lock from my forehead before giving me a smile that melted me into water. "Beautiful."

We left together, paying and thanking the woman. Savannah led me back to the bar, me trailing happily in her wake. She walked so straight now, with her shoulders back and her chin held high. I'd given her this, I realized. This confidence. The safety to be wholly herself without worrying about anyone else's opinion. Because she knew I was here, right behind her, ready to defend her at any moment. I thought back to Mickey and Gabi earlier. Was this how they felt?

"I want you to wait for me here," she said, glancing over her shoulder. I raised an eyebrow in question. "I have a surprise for you, but it'll take a couple of hours."

With our linked fingers, I tugged her to my chest hard, wrapping my arms around her and covering her mouth desperately with mine. I plunged my tongue into her mouth and swallowed the surprised sound that bubbled up from her throat. My lips moved to her neck, licking and kissing her pounding pulse.

"Don't keep me waiting, *mi vida,*" I said against her throat. With hazy eyes, she nodded, shooing me toward the bar, where I promptly found a seat and ordered a glass of water.

I only got to the second long gulp before The Kid and Billy found me. I groaned as they approached, The Kid's arms crossed over his chest and a glare in his eyes that I knew I couldn't escape.

"No," I said, holding up a palm to stave them off. The Kid didn't leave. In fact, he glared at me even harder. "I'm not in the mood for this shit tonight, Kid."

"Oh well," he shot back, not caring in the slightest. "He's slowin' me down."

I sighed deeply, rubbing a weary hand over my face before finally turning to them. They glared at one another.

"What do you mean?" I asked begrudgingly.

"Nothin'—"

"Billy's foot is messed up and it hurts him to be on it," The Kid said, interrupting Billy.

"Yeah, well, his arm's messed up!" Billy retorted sharply. "It's his own fault he's being held back. Not mine."

Fucking teenagers.

I pinched the bridge of my nose to stave off yet another headache. "Just *shut up*, the both of you, and come here."

With many protests and grumbles, they cooperated. Billy approached first, baring his teeth at The Kid as I noticed his limp. He raised his pant leg, displaying a significantly disfigured left foot. The ankle was at the wrong angle, the bones seeming to have grown in wrong. Twisted.

"Take off your shoe," I demanded. He grumbled as he removed it. The muscles of his lower leg were distended, and his foot curled unnaturally. Just looking at it, I didn't know how he stood upright. The pain of every step must be excruciating. If I had time, I'd break the bones and set them to heal in the right way, then over weeks or months help him re-train the muscles to work properly. But, on the road, I didn't have that kind of time.

"You're gonna need a lot of help with this," I told him, reaching out and rolling his ankle to test his range of movement. "I can't do what I need to on the road." I looked over to find him masking the disappointment in his eyes that I might have had a solution, or a quick fix. "But I can make you a brace. It'll help with the pain and support the muscles and bones there. It's a short-term solution, but might give you some relief."

"You could do that?" he asked, his voice soft in amazement and tentative hope. I nodded.

"I *told* you Will could fix anything, didn't I?" The Kid said, rolling his eyes so hard it was any wonder that they didn't fall from his head.

"Oh yeah? Then you shouldn't have a problem showing him your arm," Billy shot back, filled with a familiar caustic vitriol that reminded me of Bonnie when we were kids.

The Kid hid the arm in question behind his back and looked like he might take a chunk of flesh with his teeth if I approached. So I stayed still, staring at him until he shoved his arm in my direction while averting his gaze as if it were the absolute last thing in the world he wanted to do. His arm didn't appear injured at first glance, but a knotted, pink scar on his wrist caught my attention.

"What's the problem?" I asked him. He grunted and flexed his fingers. Only three of them responded. *Oh.* I pressed my fingers along the top of his hand to articulate the bones. "Try again." He flexed, and I nodded, thinking for a while. "This is definitely a problem."

"I told you he can't help me. It's impossible."

I gripped the front of The Kid's shirt and tugged him toward me until he looked at me and not Billy.

"Did I tell you I couldn't help you?" I asked. He shook his head, looking younger than he had since I'd seen him in Fort Hood. Afraid to hope. "You need to do the work." He didn't speak, his eyes wide like I remembered back then. "I can give you some exercises that will help mobility. But it'll only work if you follow my instructions."

For once, both teens went quiet as I released The Kid's shirt.

"Thanks, Will," The Kid said quietly.

The back of my neck prickled with awareness, and my eyes were drawn to the bar entrance. Through the bodies and smoke, the figure of a woman emerged wrapped in crimson fabric. The curves of her body were as familiar to me as the back of my hand. As I drank her in, noting her long skirt and the exposed skin of her belly and shoulders, my breath caught in my throat. The air shifted wrong, and a sound of shock and awe erupted from my chest.

"Get the fuck out of here," I growled at the kids without looking at them. Savannah sauntered toward me, a sensual sway to her hips that made me want to cry.

Jesus, I need her naked. Now.

As she approached, I stood in front of her, hands fidgeting and itching to touch her instead of reaching for a cigarette. Like she was my drug. Oh, who the hell was I kidding . . . she'd always been my drug. She smiled as I struggled for words.

"Like what you see?" she asked with that wicked little grin from earlier, the one that had me feeling like a lusty teenager. I nodded dumbly.

"You look . . . " I couldn't say any of the things that were running through my mind right now. "*Fuck.*"

One of her eyebrows arched suggestively. "That's kind of the point, William."

"You're going to be the death of me." I meant every single word. It felt like my heart would pound out of my chest. Like it would explode just looking at her. My cock throbbed painfully.

"Come on," she said, rolling her eyes as she led me from the crowded bar. All of the male patrons turned their heads in her direction. I noted faces in case I needed to kill them later.

She led me on and on and on. Not that I cared; I'd follow her anywhere. The swish of her red skirts made me dizzy. I went down one corridor and then a narrower one. Until she pushed open a set of double doors to a large, industrial kitchen, all stainless steel and open space.

Curious, I followed her to a table set with two places and lit candles in the center. The flickering lights contrasted with the industrial ones overhead but still lent intimacy to the scene. I didn't know what to do, or think, or feel. This seemed . . . *romantic.* Something I wasn't familiar or comfortable with.

"Savvy," I said, stilling her as she fussed with the table settings. "What *is this?*"

She looked at me and smiled so sweetly that it made something inside of me clench. Was I going to fuck this up? Had I already fucked this up?

"Do you remember when we talked about taking care of each other?" she asked. I nodded, remembering the conversation vividly. She'd tended to my injuries and begged me to let her take care of me. It had been terrifying then, but *now*, it was worse, like I couldn't shoulder the weight of her expectations.

"Well," she said, sitting primly on one of the chairs and smoothing her skirt down. "You've been taking care of everyone lately, and the best way I know how to take care of people is to feed them." She gestured to the other chair. On stiff, terrified legs, I crossed to the table and sat gingerly. "So, I'm feeding you."

Raking in a deep breath, I forced the tension from my muscles at her words. She seemed happy enough that I sat across from her, the plates covered with fancy silver cloches.

"So this is . . ." I trailed off, letting her explain, but she shook her head and smiled wryly.

"Just dinner."

A relieved sigh built in my chest. I reached for the covered plate, but before I could pull the cloche off, she asked another destabilizing question.

"How long have we been married exactly?"

I choked on the air in my throat, coughing unattractively as she folded her hands in front of her, the epitome of grace and class. And here I was, an absolute heathen acting like I had any business sharing a table with her, much less her bed.

"Uh . . ." I had no answer to that. I was well aware of the rumors that had sprung up since that fateful day in the graveyard. But I didn't have a good explanation for not telling her about it, or about letting them fester unchecked. Instead of giving me the tongue lashing I was expecting, she laughed.

Not just a performative laugh. A full laugh, straight from her belly, one that brought tears to her eyes. What was happening? I was so uncomfortable. Was she mad at me about the rumors?

"You're not mad?" I asked, but she waved me off and wiped the corners of her eyes before leveling me with her dark stare.

"Of course I'm not mad," she said, shaking her head like it was ridiculous. "You should've seen your face." As her laughter faded, she looked up at me with wide, glimmering eyes. It reminded me of how Gabi had looked at Mickey earlier. Something inside of me turned soft at the sight. "Why didn't you tell me about it?"

I shrugged, but she wouldn't let me off the hook that easily. Instead, she stared me down until I sighed.

"I don't know. I thought you'd get mad that I didn't . . . deny it."

"Why didn't you?" she asked, curious. I bit my bottom lip hard.

"I thought, if people knew you were *mine*, they'd be too scared to mess with you," I told her quietly. "And maybe . . . I didn't want anyone else to take you away from me."

Savannah's smile was luminous, brighter than the candles on the table. The small admission didn't make everything fall apart. Instead I felt relieved to admit it. She removed the cloches and set them aside.

The smell hit me first. Fried bread, spice, something ripped straight out of childhood memories that I hadn't dared to remember in years. Staring down at the plate, my mother's scarred face flashed in my mind so clearly that heat welled in my eyes.

"You made *arepas*?" I asked, my voice thick with emotion.

"You should have told me you didn't like sweets, I wouldn't have—"

I didn't know what she said next. All I saw was the cornmeal flatbread topped with avocado and chilis and some kind of salsa or pico de gallo, and I wasn't there anymore. I was seven years old, my mother pushing the rest of her plate onto mine and demanding I eat more. To grow up well. I blinked rapidly. I didn't bother with utensils; instead I picked up the flatbread and took a large bite, wiping my mouth on my sleeve as my eyes burned at the familiar taste.

It wasn't exactly the same as hers. The *arepas* my mother made were simple. With whatever ingredients were available. This was more decadent, spicy and filled with cheese. A noise I couldn't name crawled up my throat.

It was grief and love and bittersweet memories.

I remained silent as I put the food down and wiped my hands on a napkin. Then I dragged my burning eyes to Savannah's, alight with hope. "My mother used to make these for me." She sat so still that I didn't think she was breathing. "She'd give me half of hers too." I chuckled, but the sound was sad. "I didn't think I'd ever have them again."

"William." She breathed my name, reaching over the table to tangle her fingers with mine. I gripped them tight.

"How?" I asked, incredulous. "How are you even real?"

Swallowing hard, it felt like I was on the precipice of something I wasn't ready for. I pulled her hand to my mouth and kissed her palm, pressing it against my jaw. I just needed to have her touching me. Her skin on mine.

"I'm the luckiest son of a bitch on the planet, *mi amor.*"

"I'm lucky, too," she said. "I'm so proud of you. I know these last couple of weeks haven't been easy, but *you're* the reason we're here. You brought everyone together, kept us from falling apart, and gave us a purpose. And you're *mine.*"

"Fuck the food," I said, wrenching her from her seat and into my arms. I wasted no time hauling her from her feet and crashing my mouth onto hers. I needed her. I needed her *now.*

I was a man possessed. There was no forethought, no foreplay, nothing but the animalistic *need* to be inside of her. She clawed at my shoulders, the little gasps of pleasure she gave ringing in my ears as I crashed us both half atop one of the stainless-steel tables. The folds of her skirt were in my way, keeping me from touching her, and I gripped the fabric tight in my hands and ripped until my fingertips found the hot flesh of her thighs.

"I liked this dress!" Savvy exclaimed breathily as my teeth grazed her collarbone.

"I'll buy you another one," I told her, my tongue tracing the curve of her breast. "I'll buy you a hundred."

"William!" she cried out as I found the place I so desperately wanted to be, feeling her slickness coating my fingers. *Fuck*. She was so wet. So ready for me. "Wait!"

It took every ounce of my strength to still my body and step back. Her face was flushed, lips swollen, eyes dark with desire. I felt like begging. Like whining. Bringing my fingers to my mouth, I sucked the taste of her off of them, a means to stay my wild impulses. I groaned around them as the taste of her flooded my mouth. She gaped at me, and I fixed my attention on her open mouth with the filthiest images coming to mind. *Fuck*. I wouldn't last like this. I wasn't going to make it. I'd die if she didn't do something soon. Tell me *I* could do something soon.

Instead of speaking, she spilled from the table. She kept her eyes on me as she slowly lowered herself onto her knees before me. Like I was a *beast* and she needed to be careful not to antagonize me. Her hands went to my belt, our eyes still locked. As my belt buckle clanked, I realized I was *finally* going to have her hot mouth around me. No matter how hard I tried, I couldn't stop the involuntary flex of my hips toward her. She ran her palm along the bulge in my jeans, making my eyes roll into the back of my head.

"*Mierda!*" I swore. "You'll be the death of me."

Savannah flashed a wicked grin up at me, then unbuttoned my jeans. She made quick work of the zipper, and just as she wrapped her fingers around my cock to free it, the door banged open.

"No!" I shouted, more frustrated than I'd ever been before. My arms shook as I found The Kid and Billy, because *of-fucking-course* it was those two, marching purposefully into the room, completely unfazed by my compromising position. Savannah murmured blackly and shuffled to her feet, adjusting her skirt as I fastened my pants.

"Will!" The Kid called. A hint of panic in his tone banked my anger. "The riders are back."

I shook my head. It was too soon for any reinforcements to get here from Flagstaff or Fort Hood. That didn't make any sense. "From where?"

"It's Fort Hood," The Kid said, wide-eyed as he stopped in front of us. "It's gone. The Hanged Men burned it to the ground."

CHAPTER THIRTY-SIX

JESSE

IT HAD BEEN THREE days since Bonnie spoke to me, even longer than that since she'd spoken in full sentences.

The jostling wagon was a steady hum in the background, like a bee-hive readying for an attack.

My eyes never strayed far from Bonnie. Even when exhaustion weighed down my eyelids, I forced them open. The Hanged Men never left us alone; at least one of them remained prowling beyond the metal bars.

Jones hadn't stayed with us. He'd left us as soon as he escorted Bonnie out of New Orleans, as though something were more important. Her stories of the man hadn't been exaggerated. There was an eerie calm about him. He didn't rule with a loud voice and iron fist like Zachary Lee. All he had to do was give one look to his men and they shuddered beneath his scrutiny. I'd never seen anything like it before. He'd ignored me altogether.

On the morning of the seventh day, the wagon ran over a particularly rough patch of road. Wood creaked and metal groaned as it jolted me into full consciousness. My eyes found Bonnie, who sat a little taller against the bars across from me, her eyes focused behind me, ahead of the wagon. I bit back a groan at my stiff joints as I turned to follow her line of sight.

A crudely made wall loomed twenty feet in the air. Patchwork metal sheets made up the structure, some shiny as the day they were manufactured, while others were stained with rust. Figures stood atop it, their guns in hand.

The wagon jerked to a stop. One particularly ugly Hanged Man with a crooked nose and pockmarked skin lingered outside of the bars, leering at Bonnie. He'd been our jailer for most of the trip, casually slinging barbs at her as the long days dragged on.

After a round of shouts between the guards on the wall and the ones surrounding us, metal shrieked and groaned. An opening appeared in the wall.

"Bon," I said quietly.

"Not now," she whispered harshly, her attention fully on the way forward.

My already scratchy throat went dry at the tension in her small form. She sat straight, her eyes wide and alert as the wagon rolled through deep depressions in the road.

Even when she talked those first couple of days, her words were brash and brief. The fury that lit her eyes the night we were taken from Lee Square had dulled in the days since, but the tense set of her shoulders told me she was still pissed.

Honestly, I was too.

I needed her safe. I needed her to be with people I trusted. I could handle anything thrown my way, except when she was in the hands of her abusers. And she'd thrown herself back into the lion's den with me.

Why couldn't she understand that losing her was my biggest fear? That the three years we'd spent apart had irrevocably changed me, had kept me hypervigilant when it came to those I loved? That it didn't matter what happened to me, as long as *they* were safe?

Instead, Jones had us both.

I'd forced down any thoughts of our friends back in New Orleans, but those fears rose as the wagon went between the metal gates.

Tent City had always seemed like a bad dream. *You don't want to go within a hundred miles of that place*, Mickey had said once as we rode through Texas on the fighting circuit. *Trust me, Jess, that place is nothing but a living hell.*

My uncle never wanted to talk about Jones. As if speaking his name would will the man into existence. Any time I asked questions, he redirected the conversation.

Tents stretched in either direction in the morning light. The sun shone brightly as it burned away the morning dew clinging to the tarps and other makeshift fabrics held up by metal posts or wooden stakes. Light reflected from muddy rain puddles.

A bell tolled from deep within the camp. What had been a mostly quiet scene shifted quickly as we rolled forward. People exited the tents, their scrutinous gazes settling on the us. Within minutes, lines of men marched through the muck behind our wagon, all brandishing the Hanged Men tattoos on their necks.

The farther we went, the louder the bell tolled. My hackles rose as I took in Bonnie. Her jaw was set, but her blue eyes shifted dangerously around us, assessing every jostle of the wagon, every voice that pitched a little higher behind us. Her already pale skin went ghostly. I knew what she looked like when she was scared. I'd known since the first day I'd met her.

I'd never seen her terrified.

Fuck. This was all my fault.

The wagon lurched to a stop, the metal bars biting into my back. My muscles tensed, the still-healing wounds on my back from the Slavers' Parade screaming at me. The Hanged Men dismounted from their horses, most of them moving away to tie them off. Our ugly jailer approached and unlocked the metal padlock with a sickening *click*. His eyes grew brighter as he slammed the metal door open and settled his gaze on Bonnie.

"Welcome home," he said with a menacing grin. His teeth were yellow, and he was missing more than a couple.

He gripped her upper arm and yanked her from the wagon. I grunted in protest, but Bonnie's eyes found mine. As she settled on her feet, she gave me a single shake of her head before the Hanged Man dragged her away. Another approached and pulled me out by my bindings, sniffing at me. His lip curled in disgust.

The days of travel stained my clothes, my skin. We'd barely been given water, a crust of bread here and there, and we certainly hadn't been able to bathe. I clenched my jaw against the man's judgment.

"Move," he said, shoving me forward.

I sought Bonnie the moment I turned around. Before I could find her, though, my gaze caught on a huge structure surrounded by three feet of barbed wire. No, not structure. As the wind blew in over the dusty desert, the fabric fluttered and snapped around its framework. It was a massive tent. Faded stripes decorated the sides in pink and white.

One of the men shoved the barrel of a rifle into my back, urging me forward.

A line of women walked together, shackles around their wrists and chains connecting them. Their haggard appearance shocked me, reminding me of the junkyard on the fringes we'd escaped into. Gaunt faces framed by dirty, matted hair. Through the tears in their ripped clothing, I saw little more than skin and bone. One of them dared to look at me. Fear and disgust and a little defiance flashed back at me before she ducked her head and continued on with the group. They weren't the only people wearing shackles and averting their eyes.

Disgust roiled through me as I felt the barrel of the gun at my back again. I'd known that Jones dealt in slaves, but seeing it at a scale larger than the Slavers' Parade in New Orleans was something else altogether.

Morning sunlight blared down on the surface of the tent. My steps slowed as the man ahead of Bonnie spoke quietly to another wearing a black jumpsuit of some kind. A bulletproof vest covered his torso, and he peered at Bonnie through the plastic visor of a black helmet. He nodded to the other man, and the guards parted to allow us entry.

All I could see of Bonnie was the back of her head. She faced forward as we passed through the tent flaps being held open by railroad ties piercing into the thick canvas. Noise filled the air. People crossed the space quickly, some screaming excitedly as they looked at Bonnie, at me. Stale sweat and booze filled my nostrils as my eyes focused in the dim light. Lanterns hung haphazardly throughout the gigantic space that gave Lee Manor's front house a run for its money in size.

Even though it was early, there were more people than I could count. To my right, I spied a makeshift casino, with playing tables and spinning wheels. People shouted over one another, tossing their bets at the dealer. A loud bell rang into the hazy air, and the people around a single table erupted into cheers and chaos.

The guard shoved the tip of his gun into my back once more. "Move," he growled. I scowled at him, then marched after Bonnie and the others past a hazy curtained-off area. A dim glow cast through the opening, as well the burning scent of incense. A person staggered out, their eyes landing on me for a long moment. Their blue lips moved soundlessly before they stalked away. People danced and music played.

In the far corner, a fight was taking place in a raised ring. A large man landed a punch to the smaller. The crowd booed as he went down. Two women with ribbons around their throats beckoned onlookers from the match into haphazardly painted red tarps.

A tall man with a red ribbon tied around his throat sauntered toward us. My guard paused, his eyes trailing the finger the whore ran down the front of his shirt.

"Not now," the man said, eyeing me and dipping his head in Bonnie's direction. "Maybe later?" The whore turned to me, strutting over as he scrutinized me.

"Make me wait too long, and I'll take a bite out of this one." He winked before disappearing amongst the sea of people. With a scowl the guard shoved my shoulder and steered me to the left, where giant black tarps separated part of the tent from the rest of the space.

Six guards were posted against an entrance. They didn't carry large rifles like those out front, but they were armed to the teeth, holsters at their waists and knives strapped to their chests. These men reminded me more of Sixgun, dressed in jeans and plain shirts. One of them wore a leather vest with patches all over it. The man plucked a toothpick from his mouth and eyed me curiously before settling his gaze on Bonnie. The edges of his mouth curled upward, and his eyes lit up.

"Well, well, look who's finally come home," he said, grinning. I clenched my hands into fists at my sides. At the motion, the man flicked his gaze to me. "This big bad Montana?" He circled me, surveying my stained, tattered clothing, then snorted to himself and retook his post. "Good luck."

Our escorts separated and shoved me behind Bonnie through the black tarps. I blinked, letting my eyes adjust to the scant light of the room. It spanned the length of the tent, with several more tarps curtaining off other areas.

Ahead of us, highlighted by lanterns dotting the space, a tall figure stood with his back to us, facing a giant mahogany table littered with papers. The man reached over to pick up the glass he'd been using to pin down a map layered on top of the disorganized desk. Brown liquid swirled in the glass as he lifted it to his lips.

Two of his men remained behind us as Bonnie and I stood side by side. I glanced at her through my periphery, but she didn't look back. Her expression was careful, cool, no hint of her fear from earlier.

Jones set his glass back down, then retrieved a cigar and brought it to his lips. The cloying scent of its smoke filled the small space. A flash of Bonnie's scars from where he'd burned her went through my mind.

I'd promised that I would end this man if I ever met him.

Slowly, Phillip Jones turned toward us. His dark eyes practically glowed as he focused on Bonnie. He leaned back against the front edge of the desk and brought his cigar to his mouth. His eyes were cold and calculating as he inhaled, the orange glow making his features even harsher. A small, almost cruel smile crossed Jones's lips as he slowly stamped out the stump of his cigar.

"I've never been prouder of you, my girl," he said to Bonnie, the words sincere and chilling.

Jones stared at her with pride, but it was a different kind of pride. Cold. Calculating.

"Funny, I hoped I'd never see you again," she said, her voice gravelly with disuse.

Jones chuckled softly, seemingly amused with her response, which sent a cold bolt of lightning down my back. He acted like he'd won a great victory. Like he was basking in the delight of it.

"Still haven't figured it out, I see," he said, rising from his half-leaned position on the desk to his full height. His eyes shifted to the guards behind us. Wordlessly they stood straighter, waiting for his commands. "Bring some chairs and secure the boy to one."

I opened my mouth to protest, but it was no use. I was weak from our travels. The guards yanked me bodily backwards into a cold metal chair. They tied my bindings so tightly that in moments, my fingers tingled from the lack of circulation.

With a small jerk of his chin, Jones dismissed them. Bonnie sat in the chair beside me, her back ramrod straight, tension snapping every part of her into place. I'd seen many different sides to Bonnie, but her cold acquiescence made my stomach flip. One of her hands found the chain of her necklace. It was the first sign of emotion as she anxiously rolled it between her fingers.

"I figured out plenty," she said once the guards departed. "*Uncle.*"

The word made a true smile cross his face, wide and terrible. Victory shined even brighter in his eyes. I couldn't help but compare that evil smile to my own uncle. How had Mickey been friends with this man?

"Good," he drawled, the word dragged long from his mouth. "You're so smart. I knew when Sixgun reported that you'd found Mickey you'd start to piece it together."

"If you knew where I was, why didn't you come for me sooner?" she asked, her voice cracking like it pained her to address him like this. I knew that Bonnie's trauma ran deep, but seeing her fight against Jones's conditioning made me see red.

Somehow, I kept my fury locked down tight. My gaze tracked between them. How could we get out of this? Maybe we could appeal to one of the guards, but that could take weeks. We wouldn't survive this place. *Bonnie* wouldn't survive it.

"I knew where you were every single day since you walked out of this tent, little girl, and if you'd been ready before now, I would've called you home a thousand times. Thought about it. But I didn't spend all these long years molding you into the perfect weapon to fuck it all up because of sentimentality." His smile dropped slightly, the edges of his mouth dipping as that cold pride faded from his eyes.

"You know what happened to my baby sister, because you were there to witness it. What you don't know is that she'd written to me. Begged me to come get the two of you, to protect you both from Zachary motherfuckin' Lee and his plans to sell his six-year-old daughter into slavery so that he had enough money for his first steamboat."

Bonnie shook her head, her nostrils flaring as she inhaled. Her knuckles turned white from how hard she gripped the chair beneath her.

"Mickey James, the piece of shit—"

"He's a better man than you," I interrupted, my voice gruff.

"The piece of *shit*," Jones repeated, louder this time. His eyes never wavered from Bonnie. "Said he loved her. That he would 'move heaven and earth' to keep her safe." He used mocking air quotes as he spoke, staring directly at Bonnie, who swallowed hard. "But he was the reason we didn't get there until the next morning. That we walked into that house to see what had been done to her." His jaw clenched, a rare display of emotion I assumed, and a sneer of disgust slashed across his face.

"He couldn't be bothered to leave her body," he explained. My brows furrowed. "Not even to save you."

"That's bullshit," I growled. "Mickey would never—"

"Speak again and it'll be the last words you say, boy. This is between me and my girl." His voice was sharp but not loud. Bonnie flinched, and I turned toward her, snapping my mouth shut. She still didn't look at me.

My temper could get us killed. This wasn't New Orleans, wasn't Fort Hood. I had to tread carefully.

"At first, it was impossible to look at you," he explained, stepping toward her. "You just look so much like *him*. I thought about leaving you there. But I saw something inside you when you were dragged outta that wagon. When you drew that slaver's blood with your teeth. I knew that inside, behind that fucker's face, you were like *me*. And that if I were patient, I could make you into the one thing that could finally end this. End him."

He knelt in front of Bonnie. A quiet gasp escaped from her mouth, as though Jones had never knelt before anyone. He raised his hand slowly, gently. She trembled as he lifted his hand to tuck a strand of dirty hair behind her ear and cup her cheek.

Bonnie relaxed into his touch. Like she'd relaxed into mine in the quiet moments. I took in a sharp breath, biting my tongue to keep quiet.

A whimper came from her throat, and I felt that deep down inside. Not because I was disgusted by her reaction, but because I could relate. How many times had I wished for one more moment with my parents?

"You needed to be forged," Jones said, yanking me from my thoughts. "In pain and suffering and blood to make you strong. To make you deadly. To make you cunning. And I did that. I made you all those things. And I knew that you'd need a villain. I was alright lettin' it be me." He stared into her eyes, but his expression remained the same. "When you needed an ally, I gave Sixgun's boy to you. When you grew defiant and independent, I let you think you were on your own. I let you leave.

"But, make no mistake, I was never far from you. Every slaver's wagon you freed, every camp you liberated, every person who ever sheltered you, I knew about them all. I gave you just enough freedom to make you angry. To give you perspective."

Bonnie trembled. Her lips, her arms. Her hands white-knuckled the chair to stop it, but it was no use.

"But I couldn't have you settling down, growin' roots. That'd ruin you. The wanted posters helped with that. Kept the threat of me alive in your mind. Kept you on the move."

His eyes were dark and victorious and horrible. He took pride in making Bonnie a pawn in his game.

"When you met up with the James kids, I thought about gettin' rid of 'em. Didn't want them ruining my plans for you. But when you both killed those slavers I sent out in the desert—" He spared a glance in my direction. I glared hatefully back at him. "I knew that love hadn't made you weak, like I worried. It woke you up. Made you ruthless."

Her voice was garbled as she asked, "What went wrong? Sixgun had me. But he didn't bring me back. Why not?"

Jones's hand fell from her face, and he stood again, crossing back to his desk, picking up his glass and taking a sip. It was a few moments but felt like an eternity as he paused.

"It was time for you to figure out who the real villain was," he said, shrugging as if handing her over to Zachary Lee was the most obvious thing in the world. "I didn't expect you to get hurt so badly, and I hoped the Ellis boy would've been useful for something, but the longer it was that you hadn't regained your memories . . . I honestly thought I might've lost you for good. If the baby had lived, I think you would've gotten there sooner. After seeing how much you grew after being with the boys, I'm sure motherhood would've made you into something fearsome. I was sorry to hear about what happened."

I growled low in my throat, like a beaten, starving dog facing its first meal in days.

"You don't fuckin' talk about her," Bonnie said through clenched teeth. Tears rolled down her cheeks, hot and angry. "You don't get to do that." Her growling voice matched the fury in my chest.

Jones raised his hands in a gesture of peace, the glass still clasped in one hand. "I tried gettin' my guy to bring you back during that fight, but that didn't go over so well," he said, canting his head to the side in a thoughtful gesture. "When I heard about the pending nuptials, I knew it was time to collect you."

"To what purpose?" Bonnie asked through gritted teeth. "You've been playing a long game, but what's the end goal?"

"I thought that was obvious," he said, his eyebrows dipping in confusion. Like he couldn't believe Bonnie hadn't pieced together whatever was in his fucked-up head. "It's time to take your place. As the first, and only, Hanged Woman."

No.

Bonnie had fought so hard to escape all of this. Her childhood, Jones's torture, her lost memories. Every single day had been a fight, only to end up right back here.

Bonnie let out a hysterical laugh, like the times we'd barely survived death or discovery.

Jones didn't laugh. Neither did I. This wasn't some fever dream. We were here and he was asking Bonnie to join him. To become like him.

"It was always you and me, Bonnie girl. It was always going to be you and me, makin' that bastard pay for what he took from us. Tell me you don't want that. Tell me I'm wrong about you, and I'll let you walk outta here without a second glance. Never to hear from me again."

Bonnie's eyes darted back and forth, as if she were working out a con. I normally loved that expression in her eyes, but now all I felt was cold.

"I say no, and we walk outta here?" she asked, cautious.

"Oh no," he said with a chuckle that made my skin go cold. "*You* walk outta here. The boy is mine. I got him fair and square as part of the spoils of a successful attack. I'm not givin' him back."

We should have known it wouldn't be that easy.

"What could you possibly want with Jesse?" Bonnie asked, her hands loosening their grip on her chair.

"Breeding stock," Jones said simply. "He knocked you up pretty easily, has a good reputation in the fighting circuit. I've started a slave breeding program thanks to a new glowroot distillation. Nasty little drug. Makes the person who drinks it somewhat pliable and very aroused. I could make a lot of money from his offspring. More than regular slaves."

My mouth opened, shock and exhaustion weighing me down heavily. Bonnie touched one of my tied hands, a move that would normally calm me, bring me back to her. This time, my emotions raged inside of me.

This was all my fucking fault.

"And if I agree? What happens to him then?" she asked, her voice shaky.

"Well." Jones sniffed as he sat behind his desk, steepling his fingers and looking over them at us. His calculating gaze fixed on our joined hands for a moment. "You know that every crew member gets a slave once they've been marked. I'm generous enough to give him to you as a welcome home gift." He pressed his lips to his steepled fingers then, silence permeating the room.

There was never going to be a real choice. Just the illusion of one. *This* was the Jones of Bonnie's nightmares.

"So, I'll need to be marked?" she asked.

Like I'd been branded when I went into Lee's service. For her.

"Oh yes," he said without hesitation. "Otherwise, I can't keep you safe here. You know these men. They're brutes. Heathens. And they think you're a traitor. But marked . . . " He gave a slight shrug and let his words fade away.

"They can't touch me without repercussions."

Another long silence stretched, and then she turned to me, her eyes finding my own like gravity. Like the old days in the desert when we'd communicated by glances and hand gestures, a silent conversation ensued between us. *Leave. Leave me here.* I needed her safe. I needed her to know that I couldn't let her do this for me.

The resignation in her gaze made it clear that she'd never do that.

Please, I wanted to say. *Please, go. Stay alive. Find The Kid.*

Bonnie turned from me.

"Okay," she whispered. "Make me a Hanged Woman."

Jones gave a giddy clap. "Wonderful! I knew you'd see things my way. Let's get you on the table for the tattoo. I'll call them in."

"N-now?"

"No time like the present."

He was gone for a moment, a heartbeat, but it was enough that she squeezed my fingers and leaned her forehead against mine.

"Whatever happens, don't speak," she whispered furiously. "He doesn't make threats he doesn't follow through on. Okay? It'll be okay. I'll be okay."

"Bon, *please*—"

My voice cut off abruptly when four men came through the tent flap. One ducked into a back corner past a tarp, another dragged in a tattoo gun, one with a regular gun, and Jones.

One of the men wheeled a metal table with straps attached from behind the tarp. She squeezed my fingers so hard they ached. Jones waved her forward, and she stood. Resigned. Like a criminal destined for the noose.

Shakily, she crossed to it, climbed on top, and lay down. Jones methodically strapped her in, her head the last strap to fasten.

It took every ounce of willpower not to bark out, to fight against my bindings, to beat the fuck out of every single one of them for touching her.

The buzzing started, and she squeezed her eyes closed. Her wrists and ankles and torso were also strapped down, making it impossible to move even if she wanted to.

When the buzzing stopped, Jones loomed over her, staring intently at the tattoo marring her neck. He nodded in approval and gave a flippant wave of his hand. Two of the men left, leaving only the one with the gun.

"Are you ready for your punishment?" Jones asked sweetly.

"Punishment?" Bonnie squeaked and thrashed against the binding. "You didn't say anything about—"

"You know the rules. No one leaves. I may have anticipated your escape, but you still made the decision. I can't let that go without consequences, now can I?" He held his palms open like it was out of his hands. I pulled against my bindings as she thrashed harder, her legs frantic and breaths coming out in sharp bursts. "It's okay," Jones cooed comfortingly. "I know how much you like the water."

Do you know what waterboarding is? Bonnie had asked me once. It was the early days of our travel, when we were still learning to trust one another. *It's drowning on dry land.*

"No!" Bonnie gasped. Panic flooded my chest at her animalistic response.

Brought to the brink of death, over and over and over again.

"No, please! Please don't." She whimpered. She begged. She cried as he unfolded a piece of black fabric.

Useless. Helpless. Powerless. I was a fucking joke to think I could protect her.

"Oh," Jones said as he loomed over her. "Before either of you get any funny ideas about escape or calling for aid, it's probably best you know that even if you did somehow get out of the city, you'd have nowhere to go."

Jones turned his eyes on me. "My men burned Fort Hood to the ground."

What?

He dropped the cloth over Bonnie's face, his eyes blazing in triumph as he nodded to his guard.

Fort Hood was home. The only home that made sense. I always just knew we would go back there after New Orleans.

The guard lifted a bucket and began pouring it directly onto Bonnie's face. She choked, fighting against her bindings. The guard stopped after a moment. She stilled, gasping for air. Jones nodded again. More water. Bonnie's body jerked. Another pause. Water. Eventually, she went still.

You were never going to be able to save her, a little voice in my head said. *Bonnie can't be saved.*

BONNIE

BLINDING LIGHT ASSAULTED ME, and my throat burned as it expelled excess water from my lungs, my chest aching, my body exhausted. How long had it been? A few minutes or days? I couldn't tell. Time was immaterial. All that mattered was that I was still alive. Not the myriad of ways I'd embarrassed myself. The pathetic ways I'd begged or screamed during the burning, choking torture.

The straps that'd held me down fell away, my eyes still adjusting to the light. My exhausted body was hauled unceremoniously off the table, and I nearly collapsed to the floor. Someone barked orders that I couldn't comprehend, and someone else dragged me, half on my feet and stumbling on legs that wouldn't support me.

The arms around me were strong and cruel, a familiar voice in my ear as I kept moving. Jesse was somewhere beside me, if the gruff voice could be trusted.

"It's been a long time, Bonnie," the voice said as I slowly found my bearings. Mud, tents, my vision wobbling, my legs shaking like a new colt's. Then a familiar face sneered down at me lasciviously. *Oh fuck*, I thought, trying to regain more strength in my legs so I could extricate myself from him. I tried to remember our past, but all that I could summon was one night filled with regret, shame, and naked skin.

"I remember what your mouth can do," he said, loudly enough that someone behind us laughed.

"What?" I asked, half-serious as I tried to regain my footing. "Hurt your feelings? Because it can still do that."

He shoved me, harder than was necessary, through the flaps of a tent until I fell onto a wooden slatted floor, barely catching myself on my hands and knees. Jesse, still bound by his hands, came after. And I couldn't even pretend to have the energy to get up, choosing instead to slump back onto my ass.

The tent was nicer than most, proving Jones's claims about wanting me to be part of the crew might not have been total bullshit. Wooden floor, rickety double bed, even a cordoned-off area for a washroom with a shower. It was a luxury only given to those that had *earned* their place, even if the shower was nothing more than a tank on the top of the tent that needed to be replenished every few days. The water was only ever slightly warmer than tepid.

A loud thud stole my attention as two Hanged Men dropped a familiar trunk on the floor. "A present from Jones," one of them said before they left us alone. Just Jesse and me and the trunk.

My chest tightened past the point of breathing. My heart pounded so hard I felt it beating erratically in my neck. All I could see or hear or feel was that fucking trunk. Jesse spoke to me, his arms moving back and forth in my peripheral vision, but I couldn't hear him. Not really.

An indeterminable amount of time later, his hands were on me, and I realized he must've found something sharp to saw the ropes off his wrists. But the touch of his hands on my skin was too much. Too real. I flinched away and he settled on his knees, eyes roaming over me in a panic that I couldn't look at. Ducking my head to avert my eyes, I held my hands up, palms outstretched to stop him from touching me again.

"Bon, let me look at it," he said, his voice just a little too frantic to be considered gentle. His hands found me again, pulling me closer, trying to reassure himself that I was alright. But I wasn't.

My hands shook as I peeled his fingers away from my skin. "Stop," I whispered, so low I couldn't even hear my own voice. He was unde-terred, his fingers burying in my hair, pushing it out of the way, turning my face to look at my neck. God, I felt sick. The side of my neck *where that tattoo was*. Where I was marked forever.

"Stop it," I said louder, trying to pull out of his arms, away from his warm hands that made me remember this wasn't a nightmare. This was real. I was really here. My skin was cold, clammy . . . no, not clammy. *Wet.* And I was back in this place that I thought I'd escaped so long ago.

"I don't think it'll get infected, but—"

Whatever he said next didn't register. My mind spiraled, and my chest felt like it would cave in. I couldn't breathe, and dark spots crowded my vision. I was going to throw up. Fuck, it felt like I was going to die.

"Stop it!" I shouted, my voice too loud to my own ears. "Stop touching me!" I jerked out of his arms and slapped his hands away, my back slamming into the trunk and forcing a whimper from the back of my throat. "Just . . . " I swallowed hard, embarrassed at my outburst. "Just give me a minute."

The concern in his blue eyes deepened, turning dark like storm clouds. I closed my eyes and thought of my hysteria in Lee's house. Savannah had always known how to ground me. What had she done?

"In two . . . three . . . four . . . " I breathed until my heart slowed, exhaling just the same. Cracking my eyes open, I looked around at the place, trying to find things that were familiar. "Brown tent. Ugly quilt. Wooden floor. Angry Jesse. *Fuckin'* trunk."

Okay, while the sarcastic quip seemed funny at the moment, it didn't do anything to make me feel better. Nor did it alleviate the tension strung tight between us, like a wire ready to snap.

"I'm not angry," Jesse said, eyebrows furrowed. "I'm worried."

"I just get *overwhelmed* sometimes," I said, the thrumming panic and crushing weight on my chest easing. "Savannah taught me how to manage when it got bad."

Silence.

There was too much unsaid between us. Too many accusations that sat on the tips of our tongues. Too many fights we'd tiptoed around. Neither one of us knew where to begin. But I couldn't sit here like this or I'd fall apart, and if I let myself fall apart . . . I didn't know if I'd be able to put myself back together again. Instead, the cold, wet fabric of the dress that clung to my skin annoyed me.

I hadn't showered in a long time, and I desperately wanted to get out of these clothes. Unlatching the trunk before I had time to rethink my decision, I flung it open to find clothes, trinkets from my childhood, and even weapons. It seemed that Jones was serious about me being an equal once I was marked. Not that it made me trust him.

Pulling out some sleep clothes, I stood shakily and retreated to the washroom. Before I could disappear behind the tarp, Jesse asked, "What happened on the inside of this?"

I spared a glance over my shoulder, devoid of emotion as he traced the deep grooves on the inside of the trunk. He swung his gaze to me, expectant.

"I did."

Once inside the washroom, I stripped quickly. I found a bar of soap and a wash rag and then turned the lever on the makeshift shower. The slow trickle of frigid water ran over me as I scrubbed my skin so hard, it was red and stinging. After sliding into the thin sleep shorts and shirt, I thought I would feel better. Like everything wasn't as hopeless as it seemed. But when I pushed the tarp aside and looked at Jesse, that sliver of optimism faded.

He sat on the edge of the bed, his shoulders hunched, face in his hands. Once, I thought he was infallible. That he could stand tall in the face of anything as long as it meant standing beside me. Looking at him now, seeing how low I'd brought him, my heart ached in ways I hadn't realized it could.

Padding toward him on bare feet, I sat gingerly on the stiff mattress, leaning back on my hands and sighing in resignation. There was no more avoiding this.

"This is all my fault," he said, looking at me for my reaction. I nodded softly.

"Yeah," I agreed quietly. "It is."

"I'm trying to apologize," he said, voice tight. I shrugged, earning an annoyed scowl.

"I don't lie to you," I told him. "Which, *apparently*, only makes one of us." He turned toward me fully, sitting straighter, his jaw tight. "If you wanted to be with a woman who fed you pretty white lies to stroke your ego, you chose poorly."

"You don't have to be so blunt all the damn time," he replied, his voice sharper than before. Not that I could blame him. We both knew this fight was coming, but feeling the turn in the air was physically painful. I hated it, but I couldn't keep quiet any longer. I'd already done that for so long it felt impossible to open up.

"Tell me," I asked as calmly as I could. "What do you expect me to do? You want reassurance that we aren't totally fucked? Should I pretend that things between us are fine and dandy? That you haven't hurt me? Broken promises? *Lied* to me, repeatedly?"

"We wouldn't be totally fucked if you'd just stayed with Mickey," he said, running his hands through his hair. "Do you want me to apologize for trying to keep you safe? Because I can't do that, Bonnie. I can't."

I chuckled softly, the sound sad and a little mean. "Of course you can't," I agreed, standing and pacing in front of the bed to calm my rising frustration. "Why would you apologize for breaking a promise to me, or putting your life in danger, or taking away my choice?"

"I broke a promise," he said, standing to stare me down, his voice rising. "I know how you feel about that, but it isn't the worst thing in the world. You don't understand what it was like for me. *Three years*, Bon. Three *fucking* years. I didn't know if you were dead. Being tortured every day like you were on that table. I scoured the **country**, losing my goddamned mind, and when I found you . . . I almost lost you again. Every single day in that house when you didn't remember me, I was living on a knife's edge, terrified I'd only found you to watch you walk away. Don't you get it? Losing you again is my greatest fear. I *won't* apologize for trying to keep you alive. I don't *care* what happens to me—"

"I care!" I snapped. Then, after a shaky breath, I tried again. "I care what happens to you." This was it. The moment I needed to find my strength and be brave enough to say the things I'd been holding back. The words burned in my throat, threatening to come out in a rush. "That's exactly how I felt when you were kneeling in that square with a gun to the back of your head." My eyes grew hot, and I swallowed hard. "Like I would die right there beside you. Like the whole world would end if *anything* happened to you."

He reached for me, but I held my hands up to keep him back. He couldn't touch me right now. If he touched me, I'd fold. My bravery would shatter like warped glass. And I didn't know if I could find the courage to say these things again.

"But not giving me a choice isn't love, Jesse, it's *control*." Simmering silence, the kind that threatened to break, filled the air between us, hot and destructive.

"You broke my heart," I admitted. My voice caught on the words, and I tried to clear my throat and blink away the tears. "First with your lies as Audrey. Then again, when you took away my *choice*. You're angry that I put myself in danger, but Jesse . . . you did the same thing to me. Why is it noble when you do it and *stupid* when I do?"

His face was hard, his ears turning red. "Because the last time *you* did it, I was left with the consequences, and I can't do it again!" He didn't realize he was shouting now. "You made the decision in Fort Hood to give yourself up and you didn't have to remember the agony of what happened next. *I did.* I lived with it. Every single fucking day."

My breath caught in my throat. His words were raw. Fort Hood was such a long time ago. We were just two idiot kids, making shit up as we went along, neither of us knowing what we were doing. But he was right.

"I'm sorry," I said sincerely. "Not for forgetting and not suffering alongside you; I can't apologize for something I had no control over." His heaving breaths slowed. "I won't apologize for the decision I made either."

He rolled his eyes, crossing his arms over his chest. "You do realize an apology requires you to take *some* kind of personal accountability, right?"

"I was getting to that," I snapped. I inhaled deeply and tried to say what I meant again, even though this part had always been the hardest for me. "I don't think either of us would have made a different decision in that situation. Not with The Kid on the line like that. *But*"—I stressed the last word so he knew I wasn't finished—"I am sorry that I didn't give you time to come to terms with it. I'm sorry I didn't let you be a *part* of that decision. That I cut you out of it."

His posture didn't change, but his body loosened at my words. It wasn't just lip service either. I meant it. Yet, even though I could admit my part, it didn't change all the recent issues.

"But for someone who was hurt by being cut out of a decision, your actions lately seem pretty hypocritical to me."

"H-hypocritcal?" he choked out incredulously. "Me? A hypocrite. You just apologized for giving yourself up to the Hanged Men three years ago, yet you did again last week. Seems pretty *hypocritical* to me."

I tried to keep my voice even, calm, but it was no use. The dam inside of me cracked open with all the small hurts. "You said you would support me, with the ledger. Do you remember that?" I asked, my voice turning cold. "But at every turn, you undermined me or worked in direct opposition of me instead of *with me*. You didn't include me in the decision to beat the shit out of Lucas and get sent to the Slavers' Parade, did you?"

This time he scrubbed his hands over his face, eyes rolling. "The ledger again?" His voice rose once more, and it felt like it had during those long days in the desert when we'd scream and hurt each other out of fear and mistrust. "I already apologized for that!"

"No," I said, slicing my hand in the air between us. "We both apologized, but we never *talked* about it. We buried it. We pretended we were okay because we were both hoping to work through our shit on the road. And don't tell me you didn't feel that too."

"We could have worked through all this shit on the road the last week, if you'd bothered to talk to me," he snapped back.

"One," I said, holding up a finger to indicate my first point. "The only thing that would've accomplished is giving the Hanged Men, and Jones by default, ammunition to use against us. That's what they do. They pull at perceived weaknesses like threads." His jaw clenched. "And two"—I held up a second finger—"you wouldn't have liked *any* of the things I wanted to say to you in that wagon."

"I don't like how this conversation is going right now, either."

"Admit it!" I shouted, slapping my hands to my sides. "You never liked my plan for the ledger, you had no intention of helping me with it, and every time you reassured me and I thought we came to an understanding, you *lied!*" He marched forward then, his long legs eating up the distance between us.

"Yeah," he admitted with a sarcastic nod. "I *hated* that plan. Which I made more than clear. And if you'd *listened* to me, we wouldn't have been in New Orleans. We'd be safe right now. But *no*, it's Bonnie's way or the highway. You never even considered leaving when I asked. That wasn't very *inclusive* decision-making, was it?"

His height, though towering over me, didn't intimidate me in the slightest. In fact, I stepped nearer to him, tipping my chin and standing on my toes to get closer, a sneer curling over my mouth.

"Yeah, instead we'd be in Fort Hood. Nothing but piles of ashes."

His face went white, eyes wide, and then I realized what I'd said. What I'd implied. *Like your parents.* I blanched, backing away again. Horrified by my own callousness. I hadn't meant it. Not like that.

"Real fucking nice, Bonnie," he said, voice tight.

"I didn't mean it like that," I replied defensively. "I'm sorry. It came out wrong." I twisted my hands together. Shame tempered my anger, turning it from a blaze to a smolder. Instead of backing down or running away, I took a steadying breath and laced his fingers with mine. The friction of his skin sent a wave of calm through me.

"What I meant," I said, redirecting the conversation, "is that I know what it's like to want to run away. Probably better than you, actually." I gave him a small smile. He didn't smile back, but the tension around his eyes eased slightly.

"I *did* consider it," I admitted quietly. "A lot."

His fingers flexed against mine and squeezed tighter, like he wanted to hold onto me. We stood still for a few long heartbeats, until Jesse was brave enough to break the tentative peace.

"Why didn't you tell me that?"

"Because it wasn't the right decision for *me*," I answered honestly. "And because . . . if I'm honest, I'm not good at being open or talking about my feelings. But I can try to do better. I can tell you that Lee took a lot from me, and the one thought I couldn't live with was him taking my future with you. My persistence about the ledger wasn't some grand revenge plot, not really. It was about making sure you and The Kid and Will and Savannah could find that measure of peace I've wanted for you all this time."

He shuffled closer, his chest pressed against me, his arm wrapped loosely around my waist to keep me in place. I swallowed, because I wasn't done. Not yet. And I feared this rift might be too big to stitch back together this time.

"But every time I asked you to trust me, to support me, to be in it with me . . . you didn't. And you weren't. You left me alone while I fought for our future together, sometimes *against* you." His Adam's apple bobbed, the only indication that what I said affected him. "After all this, all the broken promises, all the lies . . . where do we go from here?"

"You keep saying that I lied to you." He looked down at me, squeezing my hand like he was afraid to let go. "But I *had* to lie. Everything between us was real. I just had to hold some things back. You know that, and it's not fair to punish me for desperate measures taken in a shitty situation." I bit my bottom lip to keep it from trembling.

"I'm not mad that you had to lie about your name, or our past. I understand," I explained, blinking back hot tears. "But you took it too far."

His eyebrows furrowed, and even though I saw the desperate words hanging on the tip of his tongue, he didn't speak them. He gave me the space I needed to tell him what was so hard for me to say.

"Y-you proposed to me."

His face slackened, his eyes growing soft and apologetic.

"I know why you thought you had to, I was being a stubborn ass about Lucas and—" I was rambling now. "And it was an impossible situation, but you never even apologized after I remembered everything and we *never* talked about it and—"

He cupped my cheeks, tilting my chin so that I met his gaze. "Oh Bon," he breathed against my mouth. "God, I fucked this up so bad."

I blinked harder at what could only be confirmation. That I'd been his mark and my stupid heart had been too foolish to see through the charade. It hurt. It hurt so much to feel this *stupid* and naive and girlish.

"That wasn't a lie," he said, pressing his forehead against mine as the tears I'd been holding back fell.

"Wh-what?" I asked shakily, sniffling.

"It wasn't a lie."

"It wasn't?" I asked again, needing more than that. More of an explanation. I wiped the back of my hand over one cheek, begging him silently to say it again. To explain.

"Of course not." He pressed his lips to my temple and breathed me in deep. "I wanted to get on one knee when I saw you in the library, a book in your hands, sunlight in your hair, alive, and *mine*. Even if you didn't remember it."

"Oh."

What a stupid thing to say. Of all the ways I'd imagined this conversation going, I never imagined he would say something as wildly, wonderfully romantic as that. And how were you supposed to respond to the most romantic thing you'd ever heard?

He smiled then.

"That you thought it was a lie means I've had my head farther up my ass than I thought," he said, the little smile falling into a frown. "I'm sorry."

"For having your head up your ass?" I asked, teasing him. His small smile returned.

"Among many other things, it seems," he breathed out, expelling a gust of air from his lungs.

"So . . ." I said. He focused intently on my face. "You *meant* to propose to me while we were naked in bed?"

That comment earned a chuckle. "No, smartass," he said, looping his arm around my waist again. "Honestly, I imagined it a thousand different ways. I got a ring for you forever ago. Promised myself that once I found you, I'd make you my wife and then no one could take you from me again. But . . . when I had you there with me, in my arms, laughing and talking, I was happier than I'd been since losing you, and I couldn't imagine spending another day apart."

I beamed up at him. Romance wasn't usually in the cards for us. We'd been too busy with defying death and fighting each other. But this was a side of Jesse I could get *very* used to.

"I just blurted it out," he concluded, shaking his head at himself. "Like an idiot."

"*My* idiot," I corrected him.

"*Your* idiot," he agreed. "I really am sorry." He swiped the tears from my cheek. "I made decisions out of fear, and they weren't fair to you."

I nodded softly, my mind whirring at the turn in conversation. "Do you still want to marry me?"

He sighed. "Bon, I'm trying to apologize."

"Yeah, I got that." I waved a hand to dismiss the concern. "Do you still want to marry me?"

"I mean . . . " he said incredulously. "I'm beginning to rethink it if I can't even apologize—" I glared at him until he shut up and gave a loud chuckle. He pulled me closer, his arm tugging my body into his, and ducked to brush the faintest hint of a kiss on my lips. "Yes, you insane woman, I still want to marry you."

"Then do it."

There was silence for a moment. "Alright. As soon as we get back to The Kid, we can—"

"No," I cut him off again. "Right now."

His confusion only deepened. I was tired of putting my life on hold and being apart from each other. I was tired of not being with the man I loved every day and knowing that we *chose* to spend our lives together. No matter how hard or terrible the days were, I wanted them all with him beside me.

"I don't understand," he admitted.

"Marry me *right now*, Jesse James."

"But we don't have anyone here, and The Kid has your ring, and I haven't showered and—"

"I don't care," I said swiftly. "I don't care about any of that. Well . . . I kind of care about the shower. But I already planned a huge wedding, and it was *awful*. All we need to be married is to make vows to each other and say we're married. I'm ready to do that. Right here. Right now. I don't care if my whole life was some elaborate lie that Jones used to manipulate me. I don't care if we're in one of the worst places and situations in the world. All I care about is spending the rest of my life with you."

Jesse stilled for a long time, his face that unreadable poker mask. Then he squared his shoulders as if readying for battle. "Let me think about it while I shower," he answered, stealing my breath and forcing my heart to plummet to my ankles.

"Really?" I asked, incredulous and questioning. A large part of me never thought he would be anything but wildly enthusiastic. Doubt crept in, louder than my surety from before.

"I need to shower either way," he said, gifting me a crooked smile. "I'm not marrying you smelling like this, Bon. I'm not a complete heathen."

It wasn't exactly an acceptance. As he disappeared into the washroom, my nerves flared to life. Returning to the trunk, I sorted through the clothes, finding that some effort had been made to think of Jesse. Although the clothes were worn thin, or repaired several times over, and it seemed that either they would be entirely too small or hang off of him like the rags they were.

I sorted them, folding the pieces that might fit into a pile. My hand brushed against something cold, and I pulled out a chain of rusty paperclips and twisted wires, baubles of shiny rocks, bottlecaps, and even a small seashell hanging from it. I smiled softly, remembering how a ten-year-old Will had presented it to me as an apology gift after making a nasty comment about my mom.

I remembered him, tall and lanky even back then, like maybe he'd never fully grow into his limbs. While we were robbed of our childhood, there were still some beautiful memories I'd overlooked.

I wondered if I'd ever get to see him again. Any of them. Or if those fleeting memories were all I had left to cling to.

CHAPTER THIRTY-EIGHT

JESSE

THIS WASN'T THE WAY things were supposed to happen. I'd had an image in my mind of what marrying Bonnie would look like, and it wasn't covered in filth and fearing for our lives. It was supposed to be somewhere beautiful, surrounded by our friends and family. At the very least, I should have a ring to give her.

Even as I scrubbed my skin raw beneath the frigid spray, I cursed myself. Bonnie deserved more than this place. More than a shotgun back alley wedding. I wanted to celebrate us, not hide away in this tent.

I raked my fingernails over my scalp, working the bar of soap to give myself a minute to think. I'd wanted nothing more than to call Bonnie my wife for the last three years. I'd be an idiot to deny her this. She didn't care about the normal traditions that came with a wedding. Then again, when were any of us ever considered normal?

The knob squeaked as I turned the water off and grabbed a threadbare towel. I swiped most of the water from my skin and ran it through my hair, then wrapped it around my hips. My gaze caught on the soiled clothes on the floor, disgust making the decision to leave them there an easy one.

As I rounded the partition, I found Bonnie kneeling before the trunk, a small smile perched on her lips as she stared at a chain made of what looked like paperclips and other rusty wires.

"What's got you smiling like that?" I asked, tentative and gentle. Wanting to know what could make her let down her guard in a place like this.

408

Bonnie lifted the chain in her hand for me to see, her smile widening.

"Will," she said, her eyes growing wistful. "He made this for me when we were little."

I brushed her hair behind one ear. Then her blue eyes caught on my bare chest, the color of them darkening as she took me in. A bolt of heat licked through me. Even in the damndest of circumstances, all it took from her was one look to make me hard. After a moment, she turned back to the trunk. I noted the stack of clothes on the floor beside it.

"Did you really make those marks?" I asked curiously as I grabbed them and stepped back. I dressed quickly, the tattered clothes scratchy against my skin. It was better than having to walk around this camp naked, I supposed.

"Jones didn't like it when I cried," Bonnie said as I crouched beside her.

"So he . . . locked you in there?" I asked, reaching my hand out to run my fingertips along the deep grooves. It would've taken a considerable amount of force to gouge these. It was incomprehensible that a child could have done it.

Bonnie only nodded, the weight of her past forcing her shoulders to slump. She reminded me of the child at the Slavers' Parade, turning inward from her trauma.

My heart tightened painfully in my chest. I never wanted to see her revert back to that little girl. Bonnie was strong, endlessly kind, and a fighter. I just had to remind her of that. I knew exactly how to do that.

"Let's do it," I said quietly. "Let's get married."

Her eyes widened, and the blue of them deepened. Had she really thought I could deny her? I took her hand and tugged gently, pulling her onto her feet until we faced one another.

The night was warm; the tent stuffy with the absence of a breeze. It wasn't like the nights in the open desert, but close enough that I could almost feel it, almost see the stars above us standing in as our witnesses.

I cupped her face and pressed my forehead to hers, inhaling her scent, her warmth, her love.

"I've always asked you who you are when we were like this, because sometimes you forget. But I've never forgotten. I've always known exactly who you are." At my words, her breath hitched. "You're the woman who bested me. Who could've killed me, but didn't. Because you saw The Kid, and instead of running away, you saved us. You're infuriating and intoxicating and impossible to ignore." A smile crossed my mouth, a genuine one, as her eyes met mine.

"You like to put all these labels on yourself: outlaw, runaway slave, socialite. But none of those things are you. It's hard to describe, but you're the way I felt when we jumped on that train together. When we leapt from the cliff. When we raced in the desert. You're life distilled into something so beautiful sometimes it hurts to look at."

Bonnie's eyes grew glassy. She nodded, squeezing my fingers tight.

"What you are is so much more complicated. You're a survivor, but that's only because you had to be. A warrior, but only because people see your strength and can't help but be drawn in. A woman who knows herself, truly knows herself and isn't afraid to be exactly that. Undiluted.

"But deep inside, you've always been my wife. The woman I want to build a family with. To raise my children, because to see you with kids, Bon, it's . . . " My voice caught in my throat. Bonnie's fingers found the front of my shirt and dug in, clenching the fabric like she could pull me closer. Into me. Until we were the same person and completely indistinguishable from each other.

I thought of Emma then, of the child we'd been robbed of. Bonnie had been broken by her loss. I knew that. But I also knew the deep well of loyalty and love inside of her. She would've done anything to save her. If Emma had lived, Bonnie would have devoted her entire life to her care and protection. That was the woman I was marrying.

"I promise to give that to you," I said thickly, my words sticking in my throat. "A family. One that defends you and uplifts you and inspires you. I promise that I'll never take you for granted again. No more lies. Not between us. I'll give you anything you want in this world. I'll break it apart with my bare hands if you want. Just never stop loving me. And please don't ever leave me again."

My chest heaved, my vision wobbling with tears as I spoke.

"What you'll do now is promise to be mine forever. Take my name. And build a life with me. Because if you don't, I won't survive it. You're everything I didn't know I needed, and everything I dreamt about all at once. Please say you'll be my wife."

I held my breath as tears flowed down Bonnie's cheeks, her happiness shining brightly in her smile. She nodded furiously, choking out a soft, "I will."

I swiped the salt tracks from her face as she tried to breathe through the swell of emotion. With trembling lips, she covered my hands.

"I always thought hope was cruel," she said. "I'd been abused so often, I craved the taste of it. The familiarity. To hope for anything different knowing it would never happen was the worst thing I could imagine. It made me hard. Cold. I killed my heart because I thought it was only good for hurting me. I used people, and I dismissed them when they got sentimental. Then I saw you in Vegas—"

My head lifted at her words. We'd spoken about Vegas a few times. She'd explained her reasons for making me her mark, but none of them had ever rung quite true before.

"You were looking at the tables, eyes wide, taking in everything around you like it was a gift. I couldn't remember the last time I'd looked at the world around me with anything other than suspicion and disdain."

Bonnie's gaze dropped at the admission. I squeezed her hands tight.

"That wasn't when I fell in love with you though," she said softly. "It was that night by the campfire. When I asked you why you lied for me."

Why'd you do it? Why'd you lie for me back there?

"Do you remember what you said?" she asked. I nodded. Back then, there was no hesitation for me.

Because it was the right thing to do.

"It was the first time I'd ever heard something so honest. No ulterior motives. No quid pro quo. Just you, doing the right thing, because that's who *you* are. Anytime I'm in trouble, you're always right by my side, standing tall in the face of anything that comes my way. And—" She sniffled and wiped her cheeks with her sleeve. "I didn't do anything to deserve it." Her voice broke on the words. It was rare for Bonnie to sound so small. My heart clenched tight; I desperately wanted to take away her pain.

"Bon," I whispered against her mouth, unsure what I could say to comfort her. I just knew that I wanted to.

"You didn't let me push you away," she said, shaking. "You stayed."

A whimper clawed from her throat, and I crushed her against my chest, unable to restrain myself from holding her together to keep her from falling apart, the way we always did. She inhaled deeply as I held her, relaxing against my chest.

"I promise that all your enemies will be mine," she said after a long moment. "I promise that I'll be worthy of your name and your family. I promise that no matter what we do or where we go, it's together. Because we should always be together. Me and you, united, standing tall against whatever comes our way. And I promise that from this day until the stars have fallen from the sky and the world crumbles at our feet, I am yours. I'm not going anywhere."

We were both crying now, wiping at errant tears between sniffles and smiles of joy and adoration. Bonnie tugged the chain around her neck until it snapped and then took the ring off of it. She brought it slowly to my left hand.

"Will you be my husband?" she asked as she slid my father's ring on my finger. The ring I'd given her moments before we'd been wrenched apart. My father had worn that ring every single day. Now she returned it to me, not a broken boy out of his depth, but a husband.

Those five words sent my heart soaring in my chest. This was everything I had ever dreamed of, and now that I had it, I would never give it up again.

"Yes," I said gruffly, before crashing my mouth against hers in a punishing, claiming kiss. We were desperate. Her fingers raked through my hair, and I hoisted her into my arms. In seconds, we'd crossed the room, and I lowered her to the mattress. I covered her, settled over her. Then we peeled our clothes away until we were skin to skin, chests heaving, eyes mapping each other.

Though nothing had changed between us, this felt new. When she looked at me, her eyes sliding over my jawline, there was a trust in her gaze that I'd been missing. It was like seeing her again for the first time. And although we'd been together like this many times, this felt different.

I mapped her skin, her scars, drawing little pictures along her flesh. My lips teased and tasted, my teeth grazing her body in a tantalizing threat of pleasure.

"I shouldn't feel like this," I breathed against her collarbone.

From beneath lazy, hooded eyes, she asked, "Like what?"

"Happier than I've ever been." It was the truth, whole and bare. "It feels wrong to be happy in this place."

Bonnie flipped me onto my back and straddled my hips, her thighs splayed wide. She stared down at me with a conviction mirroring my own and said, "This place and these people don't get to have our happiness, not today."

Then she kissed me deep, until I grew demanding beneath her. She made me beg for once. As she slid down onto me, taking me deep into her body, something in my heart shifted into place. This is where I was always meant to be. We stayed there, in that dirty tent, on the lumpy mattress, promising to love each other forever with our words and our bodies and our hearts. All day and all night, neither of us ready to face the world outside.

So, we didn't. Not yet.

CHAPTER THIRTY-NINE

SAVANNAH

WE'D RIDDEN ALMOST STRAIGHT through from Acadiana for days, stopping only an hour or two at a time to give our horde small breaks to rest. If it had been up to Will, he'd have never stopped. In the quiet moments, when no one else watched him, I saw his fingers twitch, how his body remained strung tight like a bowstring. He put on a show for me, pretending to rest by covering his face with his hat. His hands gave him away every time.

Before sunrise on the fourth day, tension snapped into Will so hard I thought he'd squeeze me to death in front of him. I rested a hand over his, turning to look at him in my periphery.

"We're close, aren't we?" I asked. He only nodded as he slowed his stallion, the others following suit behind us.

Will met Mickey's gaze as we neared the edge of a tree line. Beyond lay an open waste, the muddy ground lined with tracks from horses and wagons. Against the darkened sky, I spied a massive wall. My heart stuttered at the sight. I knew what the plans were. I didn't like that I would be hanging back while Will and the others rode off into battle, but it was the only way for him to do what needed to be done.

At least I wasn't the only one getting left behind. Gabriela had already put together a group of us to make preparations. We'd worked on our horses during the ride to make bandages and scour through extra supplies that might be needed to take care of our soldiers.

I found Will and Mickey talking in low voices with the undesirable woman, Moira. She stalked off not long after, taking two dozen of her

414

people with her. They blended into the darkness as they passed the tree line. Will met my gaze, and I lifted my eyebrows in silent question. He offered me a quick nod. He was okay. Or as okay as he could be.

As the sun climbed high above the eastern horizon, Gabriela and I had neatly organized our supplies. We went from one group to the next, double-checking that those going in were properly armed and would know where to go if injured. We passed out rations from Acadiana. I was grateful that, however begrudgingly, Elena had given us her full support and added a hundred bodies to our cause.

The Kid and Billy had set up a makeshift range. They took turns flicking knives at a wanted poster pinned to a tree trunk. As I looked closer, I realized I recognized that face. To their dismay, I snatched it from the tree, shaking my head incredulously.

WANTED DEAD: William Wayne Ellis. The Beast of the Bridge. Armed & Highly Dangerous. Do not approach. Execute on sight. 1000 Gold Bits.

His likeness was damn near perfect, though it didn't capture the little things I loved about him, like the shape of his bottom lip.

"Where did this come from?" I asked The Kid. He shrugged.

"There was a whole stack of 'em in that mall," Billy offered. He seemed sweet, even if he and The Kid bickered for hours on end.

"Thanks," I remarked, turning on my heel to search for Will.

It took nearly an hour of asking around before I spied him standing with Mickey near the tree line. Afternoon light slanted through the trees, highlighting the lighter strands of his normally dark hair. He gripped his hat, staring out across the wastes. I touched his back, trailing my fingers around to his side as I moved into his line of sight.

"Look what I found," I said, handing over the poster.

Mickey snorted in amusement as he read it. "Think these came from Jones?"

Will shrugged as I took it back. "It doesn't matter."

Movement from down the tree line captured his attention. Moira's gaze flicked from Will to Mickey to me. "My people are getting into place. How will we know who they are?"

The silver flecks in Will's eyes danced as he looked at me. He pressed a swift kiss to my mouth, then crossed to his stallion. He rifled through one of the saddlebags until he came back with a half-crumpled stack of worn paper.

"Here," he said to Moira, flipping through the pages as he passed them over. "This is Bonnie." Sure enough, her face was plastered to the front of a wanted poster, though the words had faded and the page was half ripped. "This is Jesse." A fight poster, I realized. He handed her the rest of the stack. "Give these to your people."

Moira nodded thoughtfully, gazing toward the badlands. "It's your turn now," she said before disappearing.

This was it. We'd kept our people far back from the tree line, ensured our fires were prepped but not lit so the Hanged Men didn't see smoke. Moira's people would infiltrate the city through their secret spots, but they couldn't do it while the guards watched. Will and the rest would show themselves to the guards at the gate and distract them until the undesirables sent out their signal.

Will turned to me, gripping my arm hard as he pulled me out of earshot, not far from his stallion. He studied me, his gaze sliding along my face and brows tight in concern.

"Savvy, I—"

"Hey, this isn't goodbye," I said. I had every faith in him. We hadn't come this far to fail, I believed that down to my soul.

"I know, but—"

"Why are you looking at me like you're saying goodbye?"

"Would you shut up?" he asked, releasing a breathy chuckle. I snapped my mouth shut. He tucked one of my wayward curls behind my ear and then brushed his calloused thumb along my jawline. "*If* things go south—" I opened my mouth to argue, but he fixed me with a hard stare. "If *anything* happens, I need you to get Gabi and run. You see that horse?" He pointed to a white mare, who grazed about ten feet from Will's stallion. She wore a shiny saddle. My brows pinched together. "She's yours. Take her and run."

"You . . . got me a *horse?*"

"Of course," he said.

"When?" Because when did he have time?

"In Acadiana. That's not—"

"You mean for the last four days, I could have been riding by myself?"

"I wanted you to ride with me. That's not important. What is important is that you are *safe*. No matter what happens, do you hear me?"

A lump formed in my throat. I nodded.

"Promise me, Savvy." The desperate edge to his voice made my chest tighten. I cupped his cheeks and pulled him to me for a deep kiss. I pressed our foreheads together and nodded.

"I promise," I said, meeting his gaze. "I need you to promise me something, too." I cleared my throat, my fingers errantly playing with the hair at the back of his neck.

"Anything," he breathed.

"You will *not* die on me," I whispered. "Not anytime soon, you hear me?"

Instead of speaking, Will kissed me hard, wrapping himself around me. When I'd cooked for him in Acadiana, something had changed, even if he didn't realize it or couldn't voice it. I loved him more now than I'd ever thought I could love a person, and if—no, *when*—we got out of this, I would tell him. Because I wanted him to know that he was loved, that he was mine, and I never wanted to spend a day without him again.

A whistle signaled through the trees and broke us apart.

"I'll see you soon," I whispered, then retreated from him, walking in Gabriela's direction, but never taking my eyes from him. He stared after me for a long moment, before the shifting troops caught his attention and he mounted his stallion. I sighed as I stood beside Gabriela, hugging myself as I watched Will guide his stallion away.

The front line would be a distraction to give Moira and her people time to get in. It could be hours or it could be days before this was over.

"They're going to be fine," I said to myself. Gabriela wrapped an arm around my shoulders and tugged me to her side.

"Mickey knows what he's doing," she said confidently. "He won't let anything happen to Will."

I prayed to whatever God was listening that she was right.

CHAPTER FORTY

JESSE

ONCE UPON A TIME, nothing thrilled me like a raving crowd. Their cheers for destruction and domination filled my spirit, gave me wings, helped me through each agonizing day. I'd never needed to be the center of attention, but when lights blinded me and the deafening crowd shouted '*Montana!*', pride filled my chest and made those long days without Bonnie bearable.

In New Orleans, my matches were a means to an end: keep up the facade to get Bonnie back.

"Kill him!"

"Break his back!"

"Chop his head off!"

Tent City was *nothing* like other cities. Heat sizzled from the massive tent roof and from the pulsing crowd that lined the fighting ring.

The sun had barely risen on our third day in Tent City when a Hanged Man barged in and yanked me from the only peace Bonnie and I had known since being thrown in the back of that wagon in New Orleans. Though Jones hadn't kept me chained like the other slaves, I was very much at his disposal.

A fist crashed against my cheekbone, sending a stark jolt of pain through my face.

"Cy-clops! Cy-clops! Cy-clops!" the crowd cheered.

Before I could recover from the blow, my opponent kicked my lower back, sending me sprawling onto the floor of the ring. Light blinded me, the crowd deafened me, but I felt none of that pride I had before, none of that hope.

Now there was only pain.

Cyclops was my fourth opponent today? Maybe fifth. It could have been the tenth and I wouldn't know it. I'd been thrown into the ring early this morning, and the marathon of fights hadn't stopped. With each new opponent, the crowd had grown, money exchanged hands, and the people grew more feral.

A Hanged Man ducked his head beneath the bottom rung of the ring and spit in my face. My muscles quaked as I tried to push myself back up. I'd held my own against my prior opponents, but exhaustion was taking hold of me. How many more would I have to fight? Or would Cyclops be my demise?

A shadow loomed over me as I curled my fingers, bracing myself for the blow.

Bang!

The bulky, one-eyed man crashed to the mat. Though Cyclops's eye was no more. The bullet had gone directly through his head. The raucous crowd stilled, staring in abject horror until one side parted, the people giving the source of the shot a wide berth.

There she was: her curtain of dark hair covered half her face; in her right hand, smoke unfurled from the barrel of her gun, and her blue eyes glowed with rage. *This* was the woman I'd fallen in love with, the one who said fuck it and took what was hers, the one who fought for me and with me, the one I'd taken for granted too long. In all her ferocity and glory.

"Oh, you fucked up," I said to the spectators, grinning a bloody, toothy smile as I shoved to my knees. "That's my *wife*."

Bonnie fired another shot, this one striking the referee in the corner of the ring. He fell backwards, flipping over the top of the ropes and landing with a wet smack on the floor.

"I don't believe *this* is what Jones meant by *conditioning*," she growled, her voice reminding me of that night in Roswell, when we'd heard the low growl of that crater beast beyond that chain link fence.

The crowd shifted again, many putting more space between them and Bonnie's gun. She sauntered forward, shoulders straight, head held high. "Who did this?"

I settled back on my heels, unable to hide my satisfied grin. Watching her intimidate this rowdy crowd made my cock twinge. I probably should have worried about how hot this was, but I definitely wasn't.

Beyond the crowd, across the tent, I spied Jones standing to the side, watching the scene unfold in silence.

"What? Did you all forget how to fuckin' speak?" Bonnie climbed into the ring and crossed to my side, her attention never wavering from the crowd. "Either someone starts talkin' or I start shooting until none of you fuckers walk out of here."

"Your traitorous ass has been back three days and you think you own the place," one Hanged Man said, separating himself from the crowd. There was a familiarity in the way he looked at her, his eyes trailing her form from head to toe.

Bonnie pointed her gun at him.

"You think because Jones put that mark on your neck it makes you one of us?" His hand hovered over his holstered gun. A couple of others shouted agreement but ducked their heads quickly.

"No," she said, her confidence radiating. "It makes me better."

Another shot rang out. Blood spurted from the man's lower leg and he crashed to one knee. He reached for his gun, but Bonnie fired again, grazing his hand. He hissed in pain but shoved to stand on his good leg in defiance.

"How'd you get your mark, Malone?" she asked, sneering at him. "Killin' the sheriff of a small town?" She fired again, this time hitting his good leg and bringing him back to his knees with a cry. "I was here before there *were* Hanged Men. I *built* this crew. I taught you how to run cons, you stupid son of a bitch." She smiled then, her blue eyes devoid of emotion, her teeth bared like a feral beast.

"Sixgun was *never* the monster here." Her gaze darted quickly, assessing the room, before settling back on the man. "It was always me. Jones just finally gave me permission to make you bleed when I wanted to."

With one final shot, he crumpled to the ground, a bullet hole directly between his eyes.

"Who's next?" Bonnie called, lifting her eyebrows, her gun steady in her hand.

The tension reached a fever pitch. She studied the crowd, watching, waiting, her body coiled tight and begging for an excuse to snap.

People started slinking away from the back of the crowd. The silence broke as they departed, most averting their gazes from the ring. Then, above the slowly growing din of the spectators dispersing, there was a long, slow clapping sound.

Jones eyed Bonnie with something resembling pride. He bared his teeth in an approximation of his smile, but his dark eyes were cold and calculating as ever. The moment he turned around, my wife finally allowed her attention to find me.

"Come on," she rasped as the room emptied. She gripped my upper arm to help me to my feet. The cool indifference faded from her gaze, warmth returning as she searched my features, her eyes trailing along my bare arms and blood-covered chest. "Are you okay?"

I nodded. "Are you?"

"Not here," Bonnie said, her gaze sweeping the area. "Can you walk by yourself? Because you can't lean on me in front of them."

"Yes," I said, a lump in my throat. I might have a slight limp, but most of my wounds were superficial. My head spun a little as we climbed from the ring. Maybe I'd lost more blood than I realized.

I understood it. The con. Making these people believe that she was one of them. But I'd be lying if I said I was okay with it. We'd only been here three days, and already the edges of my sanity were fracturing.

Bonnie shoved through the entry and into the larger tent. I followed a step behind, keeping my eyes downcast. Because I was her slave. These people expected me to dwarf myself in front of them, in front of *her*. The crowd parted to give her a wide berth, her rampage in the fighting arena having already reached the masses.

Some eyed her with suspicion, but most of them turned their noses away and ignored her. She'd told me stories of this place, these people, but I never understood it until now.

I ignored the pain in my left leg and shifted my weight more to my right so I could keep up with her swift pace through the dirt road toward our tent. On a sharp inhale, pain jolted up my side. Had I broken a rib? It was all such a blur.

The moment I followed Bonnie inside the flap of our tent, she clutched her belly and collapsed to her knees, heaving and gasping for air as the contents of her stomach emptied onto the floor. I knelt beside her, rubbing my hand gently up and down her back.

"How bad was it?" I asked, gently brushing her loose hair behind her ear.

She only shook her head and gagged, then vomited more. I rose slowly and found a small water pitcher. After pouring her a glass, I settled beside her once more, rubbing her back and offering the water. She dry heaved but caught herself, her chest expanding with the effort. Her already pale skin held a sickly pallor. I helped her settle back on her ankles, then lifted the glass to her lips. She took a sip, swished it in her mouth, then spit it out violently. Her blue eyes turned glassy, and her eyebrows furrowed as she shook her head.

"Jesse, we have to do *something*," she said desperately, gripping my wrist. "We won't survive this."

"What did he make you do?" I asked quietly.

"The next level of my *training*," she said, swallowing thickly and clutching her belly once more. "I took a man apart piece by piece, kept him alive through it all. He didn't . . . stop screaming the entire time. He's making me his monster." Her fingers found mine, and she gripped tight. It was only then I noticed the blood crusting her fingernails, the splatters on her shirt.

Bonnie was right. If it was this bad after only three days, we'd be dead before a week passed. Up to now, we'd tried to find a rhythm, never looking too far ahead, hoping that Will and Mickey and the others would find us, would save us.

We had to save ourselves.

"You're right." I cradled her cheek and brushed my thumb along her jawline. "We don't know how long it'll take the others to get here. So what do we do?"

"We kill him." My heart plummeted. I had murdered people, sure, but that was in self-defense. I'd never actively plotted to take a life, but as I stared into the eyes of the woman I loved, Bonnie *had*. She'd been left little choice growing up. Now, she needed me to be the man I promised. "It's the only choice. We can't escape while he's alive. So, we kill him and find a way out before anyone knows he's gone."

Once upon a time, I'd vowed that if I ever met Phillip Jones, I'd end his life. Maybe that was the declaration of a stupid kid who thought he was invincible.

I'd made myself that promise, I'd made Bonnie that promise, and if that was what it took for us to survive, so be it.

"We kill Jones," I said. Her features shifted, her determination faltering for only a moment. She worried her bottom lip between her teeth, her gaze shifting. "What is it?"

"If we do this, if we can't escape, we're dead." She stared up at me, her confliction evident in the lines around her eyes, the set of her mouth.

I appreciated her candor. If we attacked and Jones survived, we had no chance in hell of escape. But if we did nothing, we'd die just the same. I tugged her toward me, kissing her for a long, charged moment. When I pulled back, I nodded, my eyes scouring her features, committing her plump lips, her worried eyes, her little nose to memory.

"Together," I vowed. "Whether we live or we die."

"Together," she echoed.

While Bonnie strapped as many weapons to her body as she could, I found a thick t-shirt and a fresh-ish pair of jeans. I laced my boots, the air heavy with foreboding. Not between us, but surrounding us. This was the only way to see The Kid again. The only way to see Will and Savannah. Mickey and Gabriela. For a long time, I'd lived because they needed me. But we needed them, too. Life without our friends and family, without the joys to combat the lows, wasn't worth it.

So I would live for them. *We* would live for them and for each other.

Bonnie stood tall over her trunk, passing me a large carving knife. I strapped it to my belt. "We'll scout out where he's at right now and then find a way to get him alone, well, as alone as Jones ever is. He'll always have a guard or two nearby, so I need you to disarm and dispose of them while I take out Jones."

Concern lined my face. "Are you sure?"

"Yeah," she said, though there was an edge of doubt in her voice. "Yes." The word came out firmer. "It was always him and me."

I pulled her close and pressed my forehead to hers, drinking her in for what could be the final time if we didn't succeed. We stood on the edge of this cliff, and we would take that leap together.

"If the worst happens—"

"No," I said. "No, that's not possible." I kissed her swiftly, and then we separated, both knowing we could no longer delay the inevitable.

"Stay close," she murmured before tossing open the flap to the tent. Anxiety ripped up from my belly, surging through my extremities. I'd kept my eyes down for the most part in the camp, but now, I allowed myself to look.

To see hungry faces huddled around campfires, shackled slaves that turned their gazes away when I looked at them. To see Hanged Men playing cards and pulling a knife on their opponent when they lost. To see row after row of tents. Stealth was key, so I focused instead on Bonnie as she marched toward the big tent.

Once inside, we moved, sidestepping anyone who got in our way. I scoped out the room, searching for any sign of Jones. When I didn't see his flash of hair or cigar smoke, I turned back to Bonnie. She tipped her head toward one of the side exits. I followed her silently, ducking beneath a tent flap.

Heavy cigar smoke filled my lungs. Around a circular table sat half a dozen men holding cards and sipping liquor from crystal glasses. Jones sat opposite the door, his dark eyes finding Bonnie. He looked back at the cards in his hand, then laid them down face up.

"I do believe I won this round," Jones said as he leaned over the table to rake the pot toward him.

"We need to talk," Bonnie barked.

The men stilled, their attention shifting to Bonnie and then to Jones. He leaned back in his chair, studying her for a long moment. He put his cigar between his lips, taking in a lazy puff of smoke. A glint of curiosity filled his dark eyes. Then he rose from his seat, clutching a half empty glass in one hand and his cigar in the other.

"Excuse me, boys," he said, though the words were cold, flat. "I'll be back later for that watch." He pointed at one of the men, who chuckled beneath their breath.

Jones nodded at the two guards that had been stationed just inside the entrance, then brushed past us. Bonnie turned to follow him, and I followed her, the guards hot on my heels. I kept my eyes low, my fingers twitching as I itched to stab the men behind me.

The crowds parted as they noticed Jones in their path, reverence in their faces as he passed. They gave us little more than a curious gaze before returning to their debauchery. I thought of The Kid. *Our* Kid. If we didn't make it out of here, at least he had Mickey and Will. They would take care of him. They would have to take care of each other.

A small cord of hope pulled tight deep inside of me. If we *did* make it out of here, I'd never leave The Kid again, whether or not he liked it.

A posted guard opened the flap to Jones's area of the main tent. The man passed through the entryway, and we followed, taking a left turn to where Jones had brought us that first night. The table he'd held Bonnie down on remained, red dripping off of one side.

Jones took his time sipping from his glass and refilling it before he leaned against the front edge of his desk. "What is it, Bonnie girl?"

Bonnie didn't waver. She kept her back straight and chin lifted as she said, "I want to talk about Mom."

He blinked in response, the only sign that she'd done something unexpected. "What about her?"

"I know you're my uncle," she said, her voice clear, strong. "You've never treated me like family, though. Did you hate her that much?"

"Your mother was a foolish girl with stars in her eyes, something I've heard you inherited." His gaze flicked to me before back to Bonnie. "So I'm your blood. What does it matter?"

"Liar," she accused. "If that's how you really felt about her, you wouldn't have done all this to get to Lee. I'm here. I'm with you. But she was my mother and I deserve to know why you're doing all this. So, I'll ask again. Why?"

His eyes flicked to the men in the room, darker than before. He set his glass and his cigar down to cross his arms over his chest defensively. Bonnie was getting to him.

"She was everything I said. Foolish. Full of lofty dreams that would never come true. But," he said with a weary sigh. "She was also my little sister. There were times we only had each other. Growing up, she took care of me, and I took care of her. Call it a character flaw, but I feel *sentimental* about her."

"Even after all these years?"

"Yes. Always."

A guard stormed in. He paid us no attention as he approached Jones. "We have a problem, boss."

Jones just stared at the man. "And that is?"

The guard glanced at Bonnie, then gripped his gun a little tighter. "It's the forces out of New Orleans. They're outside the gates."

Will and Mickey had made it. Relief coursed through my veins like ice, chilling my tense body.

"Pull from the gate, cover the normal places," Jones said to the man. "You know the drill."

As the man disappeared, my gaze met Bonnie's. This was it. I swallowed hard as she nodded. The guards, having relaxed while Jones and Bonnie were speaking, stared blankly around the room, as if news of troops outside the gates were normal. As if there were no chance it could be taken. And maybe it couldn't. Maybe this was all one big foolish dream.

Their complacence gave me an opening. Bonnie lurched toward Jones as I unsheathed my knife and darted toward the guards. My speed caught them by surprise. I swept the legs from beneath one, then popped up to stab the other in his eye. He careened backwards, wailing as he dropped his gun and staggered through the tent flap.

Glass crashed as Bonnie knocked Jones onto his back on his desk. The first guard recovered as I snatched the gun from the ground. His finger went to the trigger, but before he could fire off a shot, I smacked the black metal in my hands to his temple.

Bonnie crowded above Jones, knife in hand. He blocked her blow with his wrist, so she used her other hand to add leverage to the one holding the knife, straining as she used her entire body to force it down.

The guard I'd smacked recovered and ducked, trying to use his weight to take me down, but it didn't work. I'd planted my feet well enough that I caught him, grunting with the effort it took to lift him over my shoulder. He crashed to the ground. I smashed the heel of my boot into his face, then kicked his gun out of reach.

A muffled curse from Bonnie grabbed my attention. With his free hand, Jones had retrieved Selene from his holster and leveled it with her face. Bonnie's knife clattered to the desk as she tried to snatch Selene. Jones laughed blatantly, as though he'd been waiting for some action and he was more than happy to let her think she had a chance. She clutched his wrist, shoving it upward to point the gun away.

Bang!

If she'd been a half second slower, the bullet would have gone through her head rather than the canvas wall of the tent.

Shouts sounded from outside. Jones used his weight to toss Bonnie off of him. I jerked toward them, but he leveled Selene in my face. I froze. His dark eyes scrutinized me more in a second than he had before, as if seeing me fight back wasn't surprising but was ballsy in a way he hadn't anticipated.

Keeping Selene leveled on me, Jones loomed over Bonnie as she tried to regain her footing. A rush of voices and shouts grew nearer. We'd be overrun in moments if we didn't get out *now*.

Jones placed his boot on Bonnie's throat, carefully shifting his weight to restrict her windpipe.

"Run!" she said. My gaze went to her face as she shoved at his boot fruitlessly. "Jesse, *RUN!*"

Our eyes met. How could I leave her here? Jones pressed harder against her throat, and then I saw it in her eyes: *get help. Get out, find help, save me.*

Light flashed off of a large knife as Bonnie snatched it from her side and stabbed it into Jones's calf. He staggered, a half step, lowering Selene. Boots shuffled closer. I glanced over my shoulder as the shouting grew louder.

With one final glance at Bonnie, I yanked my knife from that first guard's eye and sprinted to the side wall of the tent. I stabbed my blade through the canvas, using every ounce of my strength to rip a giant hole in the fabric. Fresh evening air spilled in as I ripped the canvas enough to create an opening I could fit through.

Find Will. Find Mickey. Find The Kid. Kill Phillip fucking Jones and get Bonnie out alive.

Pain sliced down my shins. Fucking barbed wire. I tilted forward, diving over the barbed wire that surrounded the base of the tent. The shouting grew louder as I ripped my jeans to free myself. Jones barked orders from the rip in the tent. I sprinted as fast as I could, trying to remember exactly where the gate was. I'd gotten so turned around in the last few days.

"There he is!" A shot pinged the dirt at my feet. I didn't have time to strategize. I needed to move *now.*

I ran as fast as my feet would go, ducking behind a large tent. I paused, allowing myself one deep breath. The wall loomed large to my right. My pursuers passed, their voices and stomping fading as they searched for me elsewhere. If I followed the wall, maybe I could find a way out, a way to get to my friends.

"*Montana,*" a voice whisper-hissed from behind the next tent.

My wobbly vision cleared as someone slunk from the shadows. A woman with hunched shoulders and a bandaged hand beckoned to me from beneath her hood. I glanced over my shoulder, keeping low as I crossed the space between the tents.

"Who are you?" I asked. The woman let her hood fall back.

"Moira. The Beast sent me," she said. She motioned to an opening at the bottom of the wall, covered in chain link that had been fashioned to blend with the rest of the wall.

Holy shit.

"This way."

I paused, glancing back at the large tent in the center of camp. I wasn't leaving Bonnie here. She'd told me to run. So I would get help and burn this fucking place down until there were no Hanged Men left.

CHAPTER FORTY-ONE

BONNIE

THE PROMISE IN JESSE'S eyes as he escaped carried me through what came next. Jones's boot on my neck had nearly crushed my windpipe, until more guards rushed in. He limped away, barking at them to incapacitate me. Clearly that meant to beat me within an inch of my life. One man hauled me upright, while hands scoured my body, weapons falling from their hiding places. A fist slammed against my jaw, and through the blast of pain, I tasted coppery blood in my mouth.

My back slammed into the floor, boots coming down on me in rapid succession. I barely had time to cry out as a vicious kick to my side made it hard to breathe. Then someone stomped on my ankle, and a *snap* forced my breath to volley out in an inhuman scream. Pain. And more pain. Tears wet my face. And it didn't matter how hard I tried to fight, there was always more, tearing into me and making a mockery of any strength I possessed.

"Strap her to the table!" Jones shouted. The floor disappeared, and I was wrenched upright, my head spinning, my shoulder socket aching from the angle. The metal of the sticky table groaned as they flung me down on top of it. I tried to struggle, but there were too many hands, too many people pressing me down and tightening the straps until they bit into my skin.

When Jones appeared, I shook so hard that the straps were making a beautiful tinkling sound. He unbuttoned the top two buttons of his shirt and rolled up his sleeves as he barreled forward, eyes wild with rare, violent delight.

431

I stopped fighting against my bindings. There was no point now.

I didn't wonder what he would do first. If he would retrieve a blade of some kind or a pair of pliers off the wall. I thought of the man I'd killed here earlier, how he'd begged for the sweet relief of death. That's what would happen to me. I'd break. I knew I would break. But when I closed my eyes tight, I saw Jesse. The silent promise in his gaze. The promise of help on the way. *He made it out.* He had to have made it out. He had to be alive. Because I couldn't imagine a world that he wasn't in. Like a mantra, I repeated it in my head to convince myself he was still alive. That he would come for me. Like he always did. Across the miles and years, he'd never given up on me, and I wouldn't give up on him now.

I tried to empty my mind, tried to divorce myself from my body the way I'd learned on countless cons over the years. Jones approached slowly, barking an order that I didn't listen to. He slapped me hard, the stinging blow forcing me to open my eyes. He leaned over me, his face filling my vision as familiar to me as the faded ridges on Selene.

Even through the fearful tears wobbling in my vision, I saw him clearly now. This man who raised me to be a weapon, a tool, not a person. The apathy in his eyes damned me, devoid of the sentiment he proclaimed to have for my mother. He would rip me apart and not feel an ounce of guilt.

"You are my biggest disappointment," he said. The words stung. Was it because I'd grown up with him, and all I wanted was a sliver of humanity from him? Or was it because, despite the years of torture and oppression, he was still the only father I'd ever really known?

Fear pulsed with every beat of my heart. This was my every nightmare come to life, and Jesse wasn't here to make it go away with his strength. I still felt the burning, gasping darkness from when I'd been drowned on this table days ago. It was that fear, chilling me deep down, that made me say, "And you're mine."

Jones raised an inquisitive eyebrow, long fingers coming together in front of his lips as he waited for the crewmen to gather the supplies he needed to torture me. It hurt when I breathed in, and my ankle throbbed so hard it made black spots appear in my vision.

"My mother would be ashamed of you," I told him as tears slipped over my temples. Jones's eyes screwed up in pain, something I'd *never* seen before. My words rocked through him like a physical blow.

"She was the only person who *ever* understood me," he said viciously, teeth bared. But in the depths of his dark eyes, I glimpsed a well of grief that I understood. My chin wobbled. I wanted to beg. Beg him for my life. For mercy. But I saw it mapped out there. His revenge that had eaten up any humanity he'd ever had. There would be no reprieve for me.

One of the crewmen handed him a black piece of fabric. More tears slipped over my temples, and I wanted to tell him that he was wrong. That I understood him. I understood what he'd become, because I almost had, too. But I didn't have the chance as the fabric plunged my world into blackness.

Then came the water.

A trickle to wet the fabric, clinging to my face, cutting off the air and sticking firmly to my skin. Then the water kept coming, faster, until it filled my mouth and my mind shattered.

"What'll it be, farm boy?" Jesse stared so deeply into me that I couldn't breathe. His blue eyes flickered with the light of the campfire before he leaned forward and pressed his lips to mine for the very first time. And it felt right. It felt like forever. It felt like everything I'd ever been missing.

All I could feel was the desperation of fighting for air and being unable to drag it into my lungs. It filled my mouth, crowded the fabric into my nostrils. My body bucked. Broken bones didn't stop me from straining every muscle, arching my back, wrenching my arms at my sides until my wrists felt like they'd come apart.

"When we find Mom and Pop, you should stay with us!" The Kid's bright expression flooded my mind. "Jesse and Pop won't let Sixgun hurt you. Mom's gonna like you a lot; she always talks about how she wished there were more girls around, and you can sing while Pop plays the piano and—"

There was no clever trick to outsmart the water. It was everywhere and nowhere all at once. My lungs threatened to burst, and the water clawed at the back of my throat, the burning of lungs that couldn't expand. Choking and gasping and straining until I found the precipice of something permanent and dark.

"I forgive you," I said to Will, who looked up at me, incredulous. Unbelieving. Looking like my childhood best friend again. The way he did the day I first met him. Dark curls a mess on his head, unbrushed and unkempt. Distrusting and dirty-faced. But with this forgiveness we got to start again, and he wrapped me in his arms.

The fabric disappeared, and I expelled the water violently, until it was all I could do to drag in sweet air, whimpering between the jagged gulps of oxygen. They twisted the piece of fabric, wringing the water out, and before I could protest, they covered my face again, the world going dark a second time.

"Find things you remember." Savannah's voice filled my mind, anchoring me in the darkness. "You're safe."

It lasted for minutes, years, millennia. Nothing but me and the frantic fight to survive. Each time felt longer than the last, with shorter recovery between. My body was spent, exhaustion weighing me down until I felt too heavy to move anymore. Until that frantic fight lessened with every session.

Each time, I found a memory to hold onto, a piece of those I loved who I had to keep fighting for. Each time I thought I couldn't hang on, they were with me. In the dark and the pain. Holding me together. Keeping me from giving up. My life had been filled with so much pain that I hadn't stopped to look at the beautiful parts. I gathered them now, like pearls on a string, desperate to hold on and never let go.

"I've always asked you who you are when we were like this, because sometimes you forget. But, I've never forgotten. I've always known exactly who you are . . . You're life distilled into something so beautiful sometimes it hurts to look at . . . you've always been my wife."

And Jesse was always there. Even as it got harder to cough the water out, my throat ravaged like I'd swallowed broken glass, he was there with me. Holding my hand and staring over the cliff into the darkness below.

I thought I heard the blast of gunfire in the distance, but it could have been my ears popping or my bones cracking. Darkness surrounded me now, only this time, it didn't scare me anymore. This time I welcomed it. I thought of the lake. The Kid's laughter echoing on the summer breeze, joyful and liberating. My mind went to how Jesse's lips had felt, slicking against mine beneath the heat of the summer sun, how easily he'd dragged me against him in the cool water. As if he knew, even then, that we fit together perfectly. Like the jagged pieces in a stained-glass window. Because together we were *beautiful.*

My lungs burned worse this time, the water in my throat forced down too far for me to choke back anymore. And my body was tired. I was so tired.

Bonnie, you have to stay—

My heart ached as Jesse's words echoed through my mind. I was trying. I was trying *so hard.* I wanted to see all the beautiful promises of our life together come true. The family I'd always wanted. One that we made *together.* The way we'd done everything.

At least until now.

This part, as my body convulsed on the table and the fabric stayed firmly in place, this I would do alone. *Emma.* Her name was a prayer, a tether. Memories flashed: singing softly to her as she grew strong beneath my heart, furious little kicks in the middle of the night against my ribs, how tiny her fingers had been the night she was born, tufts of blonde hair and long eyelashes that fanned dark against her perfectly round cheeks.

I gagged against the onslaught of the water, but with one last weak shake of my head, my lungs forced themselves open, and I breathed the water in. Deep.

I heard a child's laughter, a girl, and I felt my mother's hands in my hair, soothing me as if saying it was okay to stop now. To slip away. But it wasn't my time yet.

I made a promise! I shouted in my mind. I made a promise. And I kept my promises. I wouldn't stop fighting. Not yet. *Please, not yet.* The light from beyond the fabric dimmed, but I wasn't done fighting.

I'm sorry, Jesse, I'm so sor—

CHAPTER FORTY-TWO

WILL

I COULDN'T SMOKE WHILE I was on patrol. The end of my cigarette in the fading light wouldn't really be a beacon like it would once night fell, but it was a bad example for the others. My saddle creaked as I rode down the line, assessing the men who were also astride horses. Tips of hats and nods of quiet respect as we got reports for the last few hours that the undesirables had done it. They'd made their way into the city, infiltrated the wall. Had begun quietly killing some of the guards near the gate.

Mickey remained by my side, stoic and silent, a steady presence that kept me from going absolutely insane. His hand stayed on his gun the whole time, like he was ready at any moment for the fighting to begin.

I could feel it in the air; the approach of battle stung astringent in my nostrils. It smelled like sweat and fear, tasted like blood. The undesirables had snuck into the badlands early this morning, digging trenches under the cover of darkness, adding a few nasty surprises for the Hanged Men if they tried to meet us on the flat land. We'd had eyes and guns on us since we'd come out of the trees.

That's right, motherfuckers, look at us, I thought to myself. My stallion tossed his head, hooves prancing and ears twitching in a way that had my entire body tensing. He sensed something. Some disturbance that I couldn't yet discern. Yanking the reins toward the wall, I raked my eyes along it, refusing to blink.

A shout rose from near the gate. I rode a few steps closer, still not seeing what was happening.

"What do you see?" Mickey asked, but I didn't answer him. Nothing. There was nothing yet. Then, I caught it. Movement as two small figures emerged from the base of the wall. Moira's red hair caught the fading light and the other . . .

Guns popped, dust flying around them as they ran toward us. I didn't think. I didn't wait. Digging my heels into my stallion's sides, he shot forward like lightning.

"Will!" Mickey called after me.

"It's Jesse!"

It was all I had time to say as I flattened myself over the back of my stallion. I let him loose on the ground, his legs driving into the muddy earth and speeding faster, faster, faster. The guards on top of the wall converged on them as they ran. More shots. Jesse was fast, but something was wrong with his leg. He struggled to move fast enough, to swerve and avoid the bullets.

He was too far away. Too far. I wasn't going to be quick enough. Moira was close on Jesse's heels, shouting some kind of direction to him. The space between us seemed endless as I raced toward him. My stallion leapt over a trench, and in the brief moment we were airborne, my stomach plummeted to my boots, nearly unseating me at the force of our landing. The gunshots were getting louder, one whizzing by my shoulder. I ducked lower over my saddle and dug my heels in harder, whipping the reins and shouting for him to run *faster.*

Bang!

Red sprayed, and Moira fell, unmoving. She'd been protecting Jesse's back, which was now exposed to the guards. *Twenty feet.* He was *right there.*

"*Jess!*" His name erupted from me in a roar. *Not today, motherfuckers. Not today.*

Fifteen feet. He didn't try to zig-zag anymore, instead sprinting head-on toward me. I wasn't going to fail him. I wasn't going to let him die. I was done losing people I cared about.

If I needed to be a hero, or a beast, or the next fucking apocalypse to keep them safe, I'd do it.

Ten feet. I swung a leg over the saddle as we approached. I leapt, landing hard on my feet, and sprinted. My stallion circled, obscuring us from the gunmen so I could eat up the space between us. Jesse collapsed against my chest. A shot whizzed by my ear, and I had my gun in hand, holding Jesse upright with my other arm. His chest heaved raggedly as he fought for breath, gulping and struggling to speak. I squeezed off three shots, watching bodies tumble from the top of the wall.

My stallion had reached us again. "Get on the horse," I commanded, keeping my eyes trained on the wall for new guards to replace the ones I'd murdered. Jesse clenched my shirt and shook me hard, until I was forced to look at him.

"Bon—Bonnie. They . . . they have Bonnie!" The panic in his eyes flooded me. I didn't have time. No time to assess the state he was in. No time to back down. I nodded solemnly.

"Get on the horse," I demanded more firmly, tilting the brim of my hat down and putting two fingers in my mouth to let out a piercing whistle. It was *now.* Jesse scrambled onto the back of my stallion and I climbed up in front of him. The pounding of hooves shook the ground at our feet. I raised a hand in the air, and with a swift cutting motion downwards, the unholy sound of hundreds of war cries lit the air as our army charged.

Jesse's eyes widened as he saw the force joining us. From the tree line on the left, Hanged Men rushed forward, attempting to stop our progress, but it was useless now. The cavalry already bore down on us at the gate, battering rams made from felled tree trunks in tow. We were taking the fucking gates down, and there weren't enough of them to stop us from doing it. I shot at the men on the wall, keeping them from doing too much damage, suppressing fire until the others could get close enough.

As the cavalry flowed around us, the battering rams drove forward with the force of a stampede. With a metallic shriek, the gates burst open, and we flooded in.

Mickey caught up to us. "You stupid little shit! You could've gotten yourself killed!" he shouted, his face screwed up in worry and anger.

I grinned at him, and he exhaled in relief as he stared between us. "Bonnie?"

"She's still inside," Jesse said, his voice raw and thick with emotion. "We have to hurry. Jones is going to kill her."

Fear, *real* fear, slipped down my spine, chilling me from the inside out. Sparing a quick glance at Mickey, I shrugged at him in apology before spurring my stallion forward through the gate. Guns popped. Our cavalry mowed down the Hanged Men, hooves crushing bodies beneath them. Some of our people on foot had flowed in, teeth bared, faces crimson with the blood of their enemies. Mickey was right behind us as we surged forward, only slowing when I had to kill someone in our way. I handed my empty gun back to Jesse, and he put in a fresh magazine and shoved it back at me.

"Where?!" I shouted over the din of battle.

"The large tent!" he shouted back.

We rushed forward, but there were so many people in front of the tent that it'd turned into a bloodbath. Slaves in chains bashed their manacles against Hanged Men, crushing their skulls, and the swell of bodies was too tight to move.

Attempting to mount a defense at the head of the chaos was Jones, gun in hand. Mickey's eyes locked on him, and he squared his shoulders.

"Go ahead," he said. I caught his attention, worry weighing down my brow. "It's okay, son, we've got unfinished business. Go get Bonnie." He didn't give me the chance to talk him out of it. Instead he clicked his tongue and rode into the fray, intent on facing Jones.

"Around the back!" Jesse shouted, and we changed direction. "I cut an entrance here!" My stallion couldn't make it through the narrow opening, and even though I hated to dismount, we slid from the saddle and Jesse took the lead. There was thick barbed wire and a jagged hole in the canvas. He barreled forward, not caring if his jeans stuck in the wire or he sliced his legs up.

"I'll cover the entrance while you get her," I told him swiftly, my back to him. I kept my eyes on a swivel between the two entrances. He nodded, then disappeared without a word.

CHAPTER FORTY-THREE

JESSE

BETTER PREPARED THIS TIME, I climbed over the barbed wire, desperation clawing up my throat. We'd seen Jones, but that didn't mean Bonnie was safe. I pulled myself through the torn canvas, stumbling as I surveyed the room for my bearings. Desk. Chair. I glanced to my left, in the direction of the torture table.

The room was empty, except for that table, and the still form laying on it. I clenched my jaw. She was sleeping. Just sleeping. I raced across the room.

"Bonnie," I whispered, using my left hand to release one of the straps holding her down. With my other hand, I snatched the towel covering her face, then I shook her shoulder. "Bon." Her head flopped lifelessly back and forth. "Bonnie, come on." My eyes burned as I fought against my instincts. The lack of her chest rising and falling brought hot tears to my eyes.

"No," I murmured, gently turning her face toward mine. She wasn't breathing. She was covered in cuts and other wounds, but her chest remained still. "No. No, he *doesn't* get to take you away from me."

I tipped her head back, trying to remember my lessons from Fort Hood, when Mickey insisted we learn CPR. I looped my fingers together, then shoved my combined palms down on the center of her chest. One, two, three. I counted to fifteen, then leaned down to cover her mouth with mine. Two breaths. Two breaths was all I had to do.

Bonnie's chest inflated, then deflated. It didn't rise again.

Bile rose in my throat as I went back to compressions. Her form wavered in my vision, hot tears spilling unbidden down my cheeks. I tried to focus on counting, on pressing down hard enough to get her heart to start again. Two breaths. Compressions. A blur of emotion, of the life we should have had.

Fuck, I'd have stayed in New Orleans with her as long as it meant she was *alive*.

My compressions grew erratic, no longer steady and sturdy as they should have been.

Someone gripped my shoulder. "Back the fuck off!" My voice broke as I shoved them away and tried to get my compressions back in sync.

"Jesse," Will said, digging his fingers into my forearm. "Jesse, back up." I shook my head, still trying to get her heart pumping.

I didn't hear his groan, or anything he might have said. Will wrapped his arm around my throat and pulled hard, yanking me bodily from the table. My vision wavered as I stumbled, and he slammed his fist to my jaw. I wheeled backward, hitting the ground hard. I coughed, hand going for my throat as I launched myself back to my feet to face him.

Will straddled Bonnie on the table, using his full weight to compress her chest, sweat beading on his brow. I stopped short at the sight, my bottom lip wavering as he leaned down to breathe into her mouth.

I couldn't lose her. I couldn't lose the woman who promised to stand by my side and go through life together. Not after *everything* we'd been through. My life meant nothing if I didn't have Bonnie. My chest tightened as the compressions continued. I staggered back, knees hitting Jones's desk. I caught myself, fingers gripping the mahogany.

I saw red. Without hesitation, I gripped the desk and flipped it over, papers and glass crashing to the dirty floor. I lifted his chair and smashed it against the body of the desk once, twice, a third time, not satisfied until it was in pieces.

With my chest heaving, I started toward them. Will shifted back, his hand balled into a tight fist. He brought it down hard against the center of Bonnie's chest. She jerked. But her chest didn't rise.

My knees gave out. I crashed to the ground, clutching my head, inhuman howls renting from deep inside of me. I needed her like I needed oxygen, like I needed the sun, like I needed The Kid.

Please, I prayed. *Just bring her back. I'll give you whatever you want.*

Movement caught my attention near the jagged opening. My brother stood there, staring at Bonnie, unshed tears in his eyes as he turned to me. He'd never forgive me for this. Bonnie had been the bridge between us, the one to hold us together when all I wanted to do was fall apart. She helped The Kid when he wanted to learn how to shoot. She was kind and gentle, and my mother would have loved her, would have spoiled her even more than she spoiled my brother.

I wasn't the only one who needed Bonnie. We all did, but The Kid more than the rest.

A gurgling sound came from the table. I jumped to my feet, watching as Bonnie coughed. Will scrambled from the table and tipped her on her side, water expelling from deep in her lungs. I didn't dare to hope. It could be some sort of medical fluke.

Deep blue eyes, the depths of which held my entire life, blinked open.

I closed the distance to her, not sure if this was real or if I was imagining it. Or maybe I'd died out in the badlands before Will reached me, and this was where I ended up. With a shaky hand, I reached forward to brush the drenched strands of hair from her face. She choked and gasped for breath, more water coming out.

Will rubbed her back with one hand and kept her steady with the other. The Kid moved to my side, tears flowing freely over his cheeks.

"Bonnie?" I dared to ask.

Those eyes flashed to mine. Icy relief coursed through my veins. I leaned down to her level.

"We lost you," I whispered, brushing her cheek with my thumb. "God, we lost you."

A strangled sob came out of me. She covered my hand with hers, and though she didn't speak, that touch healed something deep in my soul, the pieces that had broken and fractured, the pieces that would have gone with her in death, because I was hers in every definition of the word.

When she could take a deep breath without gasping, Will helped her sit up. I made quick work of the rest of her bindings, and The Kid wrapped Bonnie in a hug, clutching tightly to her. She cried out at the contact. The Kid loosened his grip, and she lifted a shaky hand to plunge her fingers in his hair. Her eyes caught mine above his head. Even as she grimaced, there was a flicker of happiness there.

I moved to them and pressed my lips to her temple, brushing a light kiss to her skin.

"It's over?" Bonnie rasped, the garbled words coming out in a question. She looked up at me with wide eyes.

No, it wasn't over yet, but I didn't tell her that.

"Get her to the med tent," Will said, breaking the moment. "It's on the east side of camp, big tent with a red cross painted on it." I nodded to myself, pulling back from them. "I'll find Mickey and we'll go after Jones if the fucker is still alive."

As much as I wanted to squeeze the life out of that monster, Bonnie needed me. My thirst for vengeance dissipated.

"C'mere, Bon," I said gently, looping one arm around her back and then under her legs. She grimaced and quaked against my chest, biting back cries of pain as I settled her weight in my arms. I held her tighter as we went for the exit, noting her hiss when her ankle flopped awkwardly.

After maneuvering through the barbed wire, I stood face to face with a kid I didn't recognize. He looked at The Kid, then over my shoulder at Will as if waiting for instruction.

"Billy, meet Bonnie and Jesse," Will offered. He shot me a quick glance before darting off in the direction we'd left Mickey.

"Billy?" I said in a voice stronger than I felt and fixed him with a stare. "I need you and The Kid to cover us to the med tent. Can you do that?"

Neither of the teenagers hesitated. Instead, they lifted their guns and readied to pave our pathway to safety.

Chapter Forty-Four

WILL

MY HEART POUNDED IN a staccato rhythm, matching my footfalls as I sprinted toward where I'd last seen Mickey. Adrenaline surged in my veins, making me shakier than I'd like. I'd almost lost them both today. I would never forget Bonnie's unresponsive face, or the sounds of anguish ripped from Jesse. I needed to set eyes on Mickey, needed to know he was safe.

I skidded to a stop as I rounded the corner, the scene before me almost comical. The Hanged Men had been decimated, the crush of bodies from before gone. Instead, there were two old men punching the shit out of each other like they had nothing better to do.

A relieved chuckle bubbled out of my mouth. Mickey threw Jones off of him, but Jones charged in again, sending an elbow towards Mickey's jaw. Relentless, neither of them aware of their surroundings at this point. Marching forward, I muscled between them and pushed Jones off of Mickey while they both labored to breathe normally.

"Enough," I said, but Jones never knew when to quit. He charged forward again, and this time, I kicked him square in the gut, knocking him to the ground, where he glared up at me, wheezing. "I said *enough.*" Mickey leaned his hands on his knees as he fought for air. "Look around," I told Jones, opening my arms wide. "It's over."

Realization dawned on him slowly as he scanned the area and noted the lack of chaos. He dropped his head back for a few long moments. Jones rose slowly to his feet, slapping the dust off his jeans as he surveyed the city he'd built, now empty and quiet.

449

"Huh," he said, his shoulders relaxing as if a great weight had lifted. Mickey's eyes never left him, like he was afraid the moment he did something even worse might happen.

Jones laughed. He laughed and laughed and laughed, until an edge of hysteria crept into the sound and water pooled in his eyes. Mickey stood upright then, watching in silence.

"How the fuck did you manage to do this, Mick?" he asked.

"I didn't," Mickey admitted, putting a hand on my shoulder in acknowledgment. I glanced at him and found pride in his eyes. Pride in *me*. In what I'd done here. In following through and not failing the people I loved.

Jones's dark eyes drank me in, from head to toe, nodding softly. "I always underestimated you, didn't I, Ellis?" he asked with a shake of his head.

Mickey walked forward, cautiously, and I almost saw an echo of the young men they'd been. The friends they'd once been a long time ago. From the corner of my eye, I saw wagons coming in, the people from base camp with medical supplies to tend to the wounded. A familiar head of curls and bright whiskey eyes caught my attention. With a quick nod to Mickey, I jogged over, Savvy and Gabi unloading crates until they caught sight of me.

"Will!" Savvy cried, jumping down and launching into my arms. Lips crashing hard against mine. As good as it felt to have her in my arms, I didn't have time to lose myself in her. Not yet.

Putting an inch between us, I looked between them both and said, "Go to the med tent, east side of the camp."

Gabi stood from her seat, clutching her belly, her face going white. "Is it . . . ?"

"Bonnie," I said, taking a step away. "Mickey and I are dealing with Jones, then we'll meet you. Go." I kissed Savvy on the top of her head before returning to Mickey. As I approached this time, Mickey and Jones were just talking.

"You failed her," Jones accused. "You failed her, and you failed her daughter, and you failed *me*."

Anger pulsed in my chest. He was talking about Bonnie's mom. The woman Mickey loved and mourned. The one whose loss nearly wrecked him. Mickey hung his head, nodding softly, his voice a garbled mess when he said, "Yeah, I did."

"No," I said, offended for him. I wouldn't tolerate this bullshit.

"Will—" Mickey said with a sigh.

"*No,*" I repeated. "Fuck that. *You* failed Bonnie." I pointed an accusatory finger at Jones. "And you failed your sister every single time you beat her daughter. Burned her. Tortured her. *Killed her.*" Mickey's head shot up, eyes wide and panicked. "It's a good thing you underestimate me, or you might have succeeded this time."

Jones smiled, his teeth flashing in the waning light. "That girl can't be killed," he said.

"Well, you did a damn good job of trying, you sick fuck."

Mickey squeezed my shoulder, as if to hold me back. "How do you wanna do this, Phil?" he asked, motioning between us. It was time. Time to take him in. Time for this to finally be over.

"I'm not goin' quietly—"

Bang!

Mickey and I flinched, dropping low and crouching at the deafening shot. Jones staggered on his feet, clutching his side. Not far off, a malnourished girl, barely more than skin and bones, with shackles on her wrists, held a smoking gun before dropping it to the mud. Her eyes went wide and she fled around a corner.

Mickey ran to Jones, dropping to his knees beside him as he fell, dragging him into his lap. Jones's breaths were rapid and shallow. The crimson stain expanded on his shirt.

"Damnit," Mickey said, his hands bloody as he held his old friend. "It didn't have to be like this."

"Yes," Jones said, his words more labored than before. "Yes, it did. Mick, listen—" He gripped the front of Mickey's shirt in his fist. "Lee can't go unchecked—"

"You and your *goddamned revenge* is what got us into this in the first place—"

"Shut up and *listen*. Lee went to Montana. He's the one who got Anna and Jeff. He wants . . . " I crowded in close, trying to catch every strangled word. "He wants what they hid."

"Hid?" Mickey asked, clearly confused.

"There's a silo under the barn in Montana," Jones said. His hand grew weak and dropped from where it clutched Mickey's shirt. "He can't get them, Mick."

"Can't get what?" Mickey asked.

"The bombs."

Holy fuck! My mind went blank and my vision went white. Bombs. Nuclear bombs. That was what Jesse's parents hid in Montana, what Lee sent my father to retrieve. Why burning down a whole town meant nothing in comparison. Because whoever possessed the bombs would effectively rule the world. Who could ever stand against you when you had the apocalypse at your fingertips? My hands plunged into my hair and pulled hard at my scalp.

"Hey, Mick," Jones said, almost a whisper now, his eyes glassy.

"Yeah, Phil, I'm here," Mickey replied.

"I'm always gettin' to Emma faster than you, huh?" he said with a chuckle so quiet I barely heard it.

"Asshole," Mickey said, his breath catching as Phillip Jones died, bleeding out in the mud. After a long moment, Mickey settled Jones on the ground and started to stand. As soon as he found his feet, he stumbled. I caught him by the arm.

"Careful," I said, letting him go. He tried to walk forward, and his legs almost buckled beneath him. "Woah." I caught him again and slung one of his arms around my shoulder. "Are you okay?"

Mickey shook his head back and forth as if trying to shake himself awake. "Yeah," he said, but he didn't sound too sure. Fear clenched my heart.

"Mickey," I said, scouring his body until my eyes landed on a dark spot on the front of his shirt. I pressed on it, eliciting a hiss of pain. "You're hurt."

"It's just a scratch," he murmured, trying to pull his arm from my shoulders. I didn't allow him to let me go.

"Well, we'll find out in the med tent," I said, guiding him along.

"There's no need for that," he protested. "I'm fine. I should be helping out here—"

"We're going to the med tent. Everyone else is there, too. Don't be such a stubborn prick."

"Who died and made you king?" Mickey grumbled.

I arched a brow at him and replied flatly, "Jones."

He smacked me on the chest, and I snorted.

"What? Too soon?"

Together we passed groups of undesirables and our people, picking locks on slave manacles and sorting through the dead Hanged Men on the ground. A few tents still smoldered, having been set ablaze during the battle. The tent came into view, and we stumbled in together, Mickey complaining the entire way. There were a few cots and shelves with basic supplies in the corner. It was smaller and less equipped than I remembered, but I'd been gone a long time and knew more about medicine now.

Gabriela rushed forward as I sat Mickey on the cot next to Bonnie's, where my friends gathered, either sitting on stools or standing nearby.

"Mickey," Gabi gushed, touching his bloody face.

"It's nothing, love," he said, kissing her softly. "Just Will fussing over me."

"It's not *nothing*," I retorted. "But he insists it's just a scratch."

"It *is* a scratch. I just got a little poke when I was fighting with Jones."

Jesse's eyes rose from Bonnie to me for the first time, and we locked eyes solemnly before I nodded.

"It's done." He sighed in relief, bringing Bonnie's hand to his lips and kissing her knuckles.

"Alright, old man," I said, pulling out a bottle of distilled alcohol and some gauze and pulling a stitch kit from the shelves too for good measure, in case his *scratch* needed a stitch or two. "Let me see it."

Rolling his eyes, Mickey untucked his shirt with a grunt, his fingers undoing the buttons and letting the fabric fall away. The half-grin on my lips fell. My face was numb. There was a buzzing sound in my ears, high-pitched and tinny. I shook my head as I stared at his abdomen. The wound itself was small, barely bleeding now. But the placement, the angle, the bruising under his skin that spread out from it . . .

Every book I'd ever read filtered through my mind. I was wrong. I wasn't a doctor, so what the fuck did I know? Putting down my supplies, I pressed on an area of his abdomen to feel for—

"Fuck!" Mickey swore. My hands lowered, trembling so hard I didn't think I could hold anything. My mind was blank. It had to be blank. Because the alternative was . . .

Without a word, I strode to the shelves, blinking rapidly as wetness dripped off my chin. My nose began to run, and my eyes burned so much that I couldn't read the labels. I pulled a crate down and rifled through it. It didn't have what I needed, so I dropped it with a bang and I pulled another one down, my hands shaking even harder than before.

"Will?" Gabriela asked carefully. I didn't speak. Didn't turn around. I just pulled another crate down. My hands weren't working right. They *weren't working right.* I sucked in a sharp breath to stave off a hysterical sob. Throwing the damn crate to the floor, I grabbed another one, pulled out a drawer, faster and faster. More and more frantically.

"Will," Gabriela repeated, more apprehensively. She covered my hands with hers to still them. I dragged my sleeve over my eyes before I turned to face them. Silence.

I couldn't look at Mickey. More tears welled in my eyes, wobbling at my lash line, my lips trembling as I fought the gravel in my throat. I glanced at Gabriela.

Even without words, she understood. She inhaled sharply, covering her mouth to muffle a sob. I mopped my face and fisted my shaking hands at my sides before looking at Mickey. My insides turned to ash.

"Y-you're bleeding internally," I explained, my voice gruff and barely intelligible. "Which isn't good." I glanced at my friends then, at Savannah. They all looked at me like I was the answer. That I *should* have the answer. Like I was supposed to fix it. "But you ru-ruptured your appendix." They still stared, and I didn't know if my legs could hold me much longer.

"It's okay," Mickey said, nodding at me. "Just tell me, son."

I crossed to his cot, but I couldn't stand any longer. I lowered to my knees beside him, tears sliding down my cheeks.

"I can't fix it," I admitted. "I can't—I can't . . . I'm so sorry, I *can't fix it.*" I couldn't breathe. *I couldn't breathe.* I buried my head in the edge of his cot, clutching the front of my shirt. It felt like the air had been sucked from the room, like there were stones crushing me from all sides. And it hurt. It hurt so much.

Savannah placed her hand on my shoulder to steady me, breathing slowly with tears in her eyes. Mickey's hand came down on the back of my neck, and he ran his fingers through my hair. I clenched my jaw, but it didn't go away. It just got worse. The pressure, the thin air, the pain. Savannah whispered to me as she wiped my face, but I couldn't hear her.

"Just breathe, Will, just breathe."

I nodded frantically.

"No," Jesse said behind me, firm and demanding. "*No,*" he repeated incredulously. I turned my red, bloodshot eyes to him. "No, you brought Bonnie back." He shook his head. "She was dead and you *brought her back.* You can fix this." He scoffed, his eyes roaming the room to find someone else who believed his words.

Gabriela was at Mickey's other side, crying softly, pressing her lips to his temple while he clung to her.

"You can fix *anything,*" Jesse said, confidence ringing in his tone. Hope and faith in me. That I was the answer. I shook my head, another wave of tears slipping down my face. "You *can,* you haven't even tried!"

Savannah squeezed my shoulder tight, as if to anchor me. I rubbed my sleeve over my face again and stood on shaky feet to face my best friend. Chest heaving raggedly, I managed to say, "I can't. I'm sorry, I *can't.*"

Jesse stepped closer, his own jaw clenched with emotion. Savannah angled herself in front of me, like she would be a shield between us if she had to. Steadying myself, I tried to explain it to him again. In a way he might understand.

"To fix it, I'd need to do surgery—"

"So do the surgery!" he shouted, looking around frantically, like he was begging the universe to give him back the hope he'd regained when I saved Bonnie.

"I can't!" I shouted back. "I don't have what I need and—" He tried to cut me off, but I barreled forward. "I've never done surgery before, and there's not a sterile environment. And there's *nothing* I need here. I looked. I would *try*. I would try *anything*. I swear, Jess, I would do anything. I'm s-sorry. I'm *sorry*." I wavered on my feet.

"Enough!" Mickey shouted.

Everyone's attention snapped to him and Gabriela. Silence fell. Then Mickey leveled his stare at me. I felt the pressure of everyone I loved in this room, watching me, waiting for a miracle I couldn't provide.

"Tell me."

I pulled off my hat and brushed my hair away from my eyes, twisting the brim between my fingers so hard it should have ripped.

"The appendix collects bacteria in your gut," I said, my words wooden as I leaned on the clinical language from my books. Savannah slipped her hand into mine. "So, all that junk inside is leaking into your abdomen. It's going to poison you slowly. Causing infection, fever, and sepsis."

"How will it happen?" Mickey asked, his voice tight. My lip trembled as I imagined it, and I took a moment to steady myself. He needed this. He needed this from me right now, and I needed to be strong enough to give it to him.

"Slowly," I said, talking around the lump in my throat. "Days, if you're lucky. Weeks, if you're not. You'll be sick and in pain and your organs will slowly shut down. Until they just . . . stop working."

Jesse slid to the floor and put his head in his hands. Bonnie and The Kid watched quietly, silent horror on their faces. Gabriela hadn't stopped crying. But Mickey took a shaky breath, glancing around the room at the people here with him, and nodded in resignation.

Then, after a moment of contemplation, he said simply, "Well, we can't have that."

Gabriela sobbed harder, as if she knew something I didn't. Then she nodded, whispering something in his ear that made his face screw up. A choked sound came from his throat as they pressed their foreheads together. He rubbed her jaw with his thumbs, and they breathed together.

"You won't let me die like that," he said, looking at me with tears in his eyes. "Will you, son?"

I didn't think it was possible for my heart to break. I'd tried so hard not to love anyone. Not to care enough that I hurt like this. Not after my mom. Not after sawing at the rope she swung from in our tent. Savannah squeezed my hand and sniffled next to me.

I shook my head in denial. Because he couldn't ask *that* of me. He couldn't do that to me. Not him.

"*Please*," he begged. "Please help me die with dignity."

The numbness that had somewhat protected me to this point dissipated, leaving behind a raw nerve where my heart was. Where all those stupid dreams had taken root. Where every time he'd called me *son* was burned into my memory. Like he meant it. Like he felt as if that was what I could be to him one day. All the words I'd never had the courage to say burned on the tip of my tongue.

But he was asking me to kill him.

To end all of those dreams and all of that hope, to erase him from this world like he hadn't changed me in ways I'd never recover from. Savannah stood taller next to me, but Jesse had raised his head, looking between us with betrayal clear in his blue eyes. The same blue as Mickey's.

"No," he said again, shaking his head in denial. "You can't *do that*."

Mickey motioned to Jesse, and he stood, crossing the room to his uncle's bedside.

"When have I asked anything from you?" He waited for Jesse to respond. But he didn't. He stayed silent. Mickey reached for him, and

Jesse clasped his forearm as if they'd done it a thousand times before. "When you burst into my life, I'd been dead for so long. Not in my body, but in my spirit. Then there you were . . . demanding that I get sober and filling my house with noise, and joy, and *life*. And I'd forgotten about all of it. But Jess," he said, leaning close to his trembling nephew.

"At twenty years old, you already knew what was worth fighting for. You had no lessons to learn from me. You're already more of a man than I'd ever been. I was the one who needed to learn from *you.*"

Jesse sucked in a sharp breath.

"And it's because of you that I have all *this*." He motioned to the room around him, to Gabriela, who steadily mopped her cheeks.

"You're going to be okay," he said. Nodding as if it were a fact. Then he pulled Jesse down into a hard embrace. "Thank you." When Jesse straightened, his eyes were wet and he nodded. "This is what family does, right?" Jesse nodded again, turning away from all of us.

"I never agreed," I said, angry now. "I never said I would do it."

Mickey smiled at me, but I shook my head and backed away, sniffling and running my sleeve over my face again.

"You can't make me."

Mickey just smiled again, silent. And it made me so angry. He didn't *know*. He didn't know what he was to me. He didn't know how this would break me.

"No," he acquiesced. "I can't. But I hope you will. I hope you'll spare me from the pain. Spare Gabi from seeing me . . . like *that.*" He swallowed hard. "And I think I know you well enough to know you'd never let me be remembered that way."

I pulled away from Savannah and paced, needing the frenetic energy of movement to keep myself upright.

"How dare you ask him to do this?" she asked, her voice quiet but cutting. "How dare you?" Mickey looked at her and smiled, tears welling in his eyes. "You know what he's been through. What he's done. How could you?"

I paused in front of the shelves that didn't hold the supplies I needed, sparse and bare as my impotent fury burned to life inside me. Until I couldn't take it. I ripped several crates down, bandages unrolling across the floor as they fell.

"You told me I couldn't take the easy way out!" I pointed at him. "You said I couldn't die!" My breath caught. "You promised me that you'd be here . . . " My voice choked off as I tried to stave back my tears. "You . . . you call me *son*, and you tell me you're my family, and you're full of shit!" I shouted, knocking down another shelf and not caring at all. "Now you want me to *help you* take the easy way out."

Everyone stared at me, but Mickey's blue eyes were all I saw as they wavered with emotion and he almost fell apart.

"Come here."

I hesitated. But how could I deny him?

He motioned me forward, and like I was being pulled, my body moved on its own. "Come *here*," he said, his arms open wide. I fell into them. I wasn't ashamed of it. Every moment was already stolen. He wasn't my dad. No matter how much I wished he was.

"I wish we had time," Mickey said, holding onto me. "I wish I could've had the time to show you that blood doesn't mean family, and it doesn't mean *fate*." He let go of me and, with a shake of my shoulder, he looked down at me with finality.

"But I don't," he said quietly. "All I can tell you right now is"—he squeezed my shoulders—"don't take the easy way out. Love deeply. Take care of each other." His face screwed up then, fresh tears spilling from his eyes. "Take care of Gabi and the baby. Promise me you'll do that." He spared a glance for Gabi, and then his gaze fell back to me. I nodded. Throat tight.

"I promise," I choked out.

"Then I know they'll be okay," he said, smiling as he blinked back more tears. "Because they'll have you."

Taking in a shaking breath, I stood and walked away. A strange sense of calm washed over me. I pulled out a drawer and, after a moment's search, wrapped my hand around a scalpel. Sometimes, this might be what helping people looked like, and if I was going to live up to Mickey's expectations, I needed to be strong enough to handle it.

Mickey was on his side now, the uninjured one, looking at Bonnie and The Kid. "I'm sorry," he told Bonnie. She shook her head, rejecting the apology. "I was young, and stupid, and . . . you could have been *mine*. You should've been. Emma would've wanted that." Bonnie reached between the cots and took his hand.

"Just tell her I love her," Bonnie said, her voice barely audible. "And we'll be even." Mickey chuckled softly and nodded.

Gabriela sat on the cot beside him, and they held each other, his hand resting on her barely swollen belly. I felt shaken again, remembering the baby. The child who would never know their father. The way he'd touched all of us, changed us in ways that were impossible to explain.

Gabi and his child would never want for anything. No matter what they needed, I would be there.

"Anyone who wants to leave," I said, scalpel in hand, "should do so now."

No one moved.

In fact, they all shifted closer. The Kid pulled Bonnie's cot so that she was closer, too. I approached, feeling the tension in the room about to snap like a wire that'd been pulled too taut.

"Will it hurt?" Gabriela asked through her tears. I shook my head.

"Quick little cut," I told them. Smiling sadly at Mickey I said, "It'll feel like a scratch." He chuckled. "Then it'll feel like falling asleep. And we'll be right here. The whole time."

He nodded, squeezing Gabi's hand. I moved forward, and he inhaled sharply with anxiety and nerves. With a flick of my wrist, I sliced his artery and lifted thick gauze to staunch the bleeding so that it wouldn't look too gruesome.

"Look at this," he said, his eyelids drooping. "How did I get this lucky?" He blinked once, marking the faces of each person. Then his eyes fluttered closed. And a few moments later, his chest stopped rising and falling. With trembling hands, I pressed two fingers to his carotid to find his pulse had stopped. He was gone.

He was gone.

I looked at my hands, blood drying thick and settling into the lines of my palms. Like tributaries of the river I thought I'd left behind. I couldn't stop staring. It was tacky, and as I flexed my fingers, the crimson stains didn't move. The scalpel clattered to the floor. All I could feel was the eyes from before, the expectation that I'd fix him. But I hadn't fixed him. He was gone and I couldn't fix him.

He was gone.

Someone wrenched me into their arms. I'd expected Savannah, but these arms were different, bulkier. And it took a moment to realize Jesse had pulled me in, squeezing me as hard as he could. Like if he held me hard enough, the pain we shared would ease. Jesse. My best friend. Who had begged me to save Mickey. *I failed.* I failed them all. I failed myself.

"I'm sorry," I muttered into his shoulder. He just squeezed me harder. "I'm sorry," I repeated, wondering if he'd heard me. He didn't speak. And he didn't let go. "I'm *sorry*," I breathed. "I'm so sorry." I didn't know what was happening. Something inside of me had cracked. "I'm sorry," I said. "I'm sorry." I didn't know who I was saying it to now. "I'm so sorry. I'm sorry, I'm *sorry*, I'm sorry." I couldn't seem to stop saying it. I didn't know how to stop. "I'm sorry."

"Will," Jesse said, his voice thick. "It's okay."

"I'm sorry," I broke against him. "I'm sorry," I whispered.

"I'm sorry, too," Jesse said. Then I cried, gripping the back of his shirt. He didn't let me go. He didn't let me go through it alone. His shoulders shook. And we just stood there. He and I, steady against the hurricane of grief coursing through the room. I wouldn't have been able to withstand it without him.

This was the price, I realized after, when I pulled the sheet, trembling in my hands, up over Mickey's still body to cover his face. This was the price of war. And we were young and stupid if we thought we'd escape unscathed.

Savannah stayed. Constant. Stoic. She never made her grief a burden. Instead, she waited for me. She held onto me. Bonnie clutched Jesse and The Kid, running her fingers through their hair. Gabriela sobbed over the sheet that covered Mickey, muttering sweet nothings in Spanish that he could no longer hear.

And even though we wanted to live in this moment, to hurt and heal with each other, the world outside didn't wait for anyone. They found us. They asked us for more than we could give. But now there was no one else. We weren't kids anymore. None of us.

I stood tall, put aside the devastation of our loss.

Mickey would expect nothing less.

CHAPTER FORTY-FIVE

SAVANNAH

THUNDERHEADS ROLLED IN THE distant sky as a thick, late summer breeze kicked the dust up. A storm brewed to the south. Over the last two days, we worked. We dismantled what was left of the Hanged Men, freed the rest of their slaves, and dealt with our grief the only way we knew: by working through it.

The heavy clouds were rolling in faster than we'd anticipated. We'd hoped for a burial at sunset, but if the storm got here first, there would be no send-off tonight.

I slipped my hand into Will's as we stood over Mickey's pyre. He'd refused to let someone else prepare Mickey for his passage into the great unknown. I stayed by his side the entire time, knowing I couldn't leave him alone. He needed me to be the rock upon which he rested, and I would do it every time.

With red-rimmed eyes, he stared at Mickey's wrapped corpse. Dozens of other pyres lined the dirt where tents once stood. No one left after the battle was won. The remaining Hanged Men even joined us in picking up the pieces. Another group had arrived earlier this afternoon, old friends of Bonnie and Jesse from Flagstaff.

Will kept himself apart from it all, and I was content to be his shadow. I knew what Mickey meant to him. He didn't have to tell me. I just knew from the moment I met the man that he was important, someone Will looked up to.

Wind kicked up the dirt again as someone passed out lit torches. Will leaned forward, as if telling Mickey a secret.

"The first time you called me *son*, I wished you'd been my dad. I imagined it a lot, actually. And I promise that your child will never want for anything, never have you far from their thoughts. Thank you, for saving me from myself."

Jesse approached, lit torch in hand. Bonnie leaned heavily on The Kid as they walked beside him. I spied Gabriela a short distance away, Elena's arm wrapped around her shoulders as they quaked. Will and Jesse's eyes met. With a nod, the latter placed the torch to kindling. I inhaled sharply as fire caught, the flames licking over what remained of our friend.

Hundreds of pyres lit up around us, the smoke filling the air even as the wind washed it away. Will lifted his head, his eyes narrowing slightly at an unlit pyre nearby. He took the torch from Jesse and headed toward it.

I'd helped with preparing her body. I didn't know her well, but Will trusted her with the most important part of our plan, and I would be grateful for her sacrifice. I stood next to him as he stared down at the woman's wrapped form.

"Moira." He paused as if waiting for the wind to reply. "You *hated* me when we first met," he said with a smile. "I don't blame you. I was a piece of shit back then." He took a steadying breath and then stared at her wrapped face, almost like he saw her beyond the linen. "Then you noticed that we were the same. You told me my face may be pretty, but my soul wasn't. And you were right. It wasn't. I was *undesirable* just like you. Just like all of us. The only difference was that you wore your disfigurement with pride. You banded your people together against a common enemy. Gave them a purpose. And in the end, you gave your life for my friend . . . " He sucked in a sharp breath. "Thank you."

Will lowered the torch, taking his time to ensure the fire caught. Once it built high enough, he tossed the torch on top, stepped back, and then wrapped his arm around me, tucking me tight against his side.

I didn't know what lay beyond this place, but whatever it was, I wanted it to be together. I'd kept quiet, never pushing, never making him feel like I needed some display of affection, but as he tucked me against his side, the tension ran out of me.

We'd get through this. Somehow.

Smoke rose high in the sky as we retreated from the coming storm, following close behind Bonnie, Jesse, and The Kid. They'd been given a larger tent, one that allowed the space needed between them and gave Bonnie room to breathe. I squeezed Will as we lingered in the entryway, but he stared inside without emotion.

"What're you waitin' for?" Bonnie asked as Jesse fluffed the pillows behind her back. I glanced at Will. He blinked a couple of times.

"Nothing," I said, then tugged him inside. Jesse set out camp chairs for us. The Kid left to find Billy, I think, leaving the four of us alone. I sat beside Will, and Jesse planted himself on the floor next to Bonnie.

"Some of the men are slaughtering cattle to cook tonight, give everyone a good meal before we disperse," Jesse remarked.

Ah, *this* was something none of us had acknowledged. With Mickey gone and so many dead, what was there left for the rest of us? There were things unresolved in New Orleans, with Lee, but we weren't in any shape to tackle that. Bonnie needed rest. She'd have to go through months of therapy before she could properly walk on her own.

"I can't wait to get back to Flagstaff," Bonnie said, a glimmer in her eyes that I hadn't seen in forever. I offered a half-hearted smile. "Beck and Quanah have already said they've got plenty of room for us."

A lump formed in my throat. When I left New Orleans, it was to get Bonnie and Jesse back. Now that I'd done it, I wasn't sure my destiny lay with them.

"It'll be nice to get away from this shit show," Will said.

I blinked, worrying my bottom lip with my teeth.

"Flagstaff is great, but don't piss off the innkeepers," Jesse said, chuckling as he glanced at Bonnie.

"You wouldn't have pissed off that innkeeper if you hadn't illegally given him Selene for a *shower*," Bonnie teased.

The ease between them made my heart ache. What felt like a long time ago, I'd envied the way Jesse looked at Bonnie. I'd craved it like decadent cake just out of reach.

"I haven't heard *this* story yet," Will said, his shoulders loosening as he leaned forward on his knees.

As they launched into a story about their time in Flagstaff, I stared blankly at the floor. Conflict coiled in my belly. They all seemed set on their paths, and, as if it weren't even a question, Will planned on going with them.

"—Savannah?" Bonnie's voice snapped me to attention. I blinked rapidly, refocusing on the room and my friend, just like she needed. Because my discomfort couldn't be a burden on any of them, not after what they'd lost.

"Yes?"

"You good?" she asked, concern lining her face.

I felt Will's gaze on me then. I offered a fake smile. "Yes. What was the question?"

"Have you ever ridden on a train?" Jesse posed. I shook my head. He launched into another story, this time about playing poker on a train, back before he and Bonnie really got together.

I'd promised myself a long time ago that when I got out of New Orleans, I would head north. I would go back home. I would find my mother. I would face my past head-on. But doing that now meant leaving the people who had become my friends, my family. I glanced at Will. His hands moved animatedly as he talked, sharing a story I didn't hear.

It was strange, being like this with them. Before, I'd always felt included. But now, I felt separate, as though the ground cleaved in two beneath us, taking the three of them far away from me.

Almost as if I didn't . . . belong.

And maybe I didn't. They had years of history, of being in the worst of places, but at least they had each other.

I remembered that little girl who stepped off of a riverboat from St. Louis, clutching a threadbare doll to her chest. That little girl didn't realize her life was changing and not necessarily for the better. I'd been so scared of everything around me. Kind of like now. I'd worn my fear as armor, shielding myself as best as I could for ten years in Lee's house.

My promise to return to St. Louis dissipated once Bonnie and Will came into my life. They became my purpose. I put them first. In the beginning, with taking care of Bonnie, then later, with Will, making sure he wasn't alone. And now, with getting Bonnie and Jesse back.

When did I let my life become everyone else's?

"You ready?" Will asked. Some of the darkness had faded from his eyes. He stood above me, extending a hand. I gripped his fingers, and he pulled me from my seat.

"We'll see you guys at dinner, right?" Bonnie asked. I lifted my gaze to hers. Something shifted in the blue of them.

"Well, *I'm* not turning down a steak dinner," Will remarked. My heart squeezed a little. He'd get through this one way or the other. I offered Bonnie a smile, and then we left their tent.

Lightning zigzagged through the distant clouds, dancing as the storm approached. How they were going to have a cookout when the bottom dropped, I didn't know. For once, it wasn't my plan and it wasn't my problem. I clutched Will's hand, watching people nod at him in reverence or lift a glass in our direction.

By the time we arrived in our tent, my body ached from the tension. I brushed past Will to find some fresh clothes. I needed to wash away the day's exertion, if only to make myself feel better. I rifled through my bag, retrieving a small bottle of shampoo and a bar of soap. There was a communal shower nearby.

"Hey," Will said. I pivoted toward him, forcing the tension from my features.

"Hey," I said back.

Will crossed to me, tugging the stuff from my hands and dropping it onto the haphazardly made bed. I'd tried to leave the room in some semblance of normal before we went off to work this morning. He gripped my hands in his, pulling me with him as he backed toward the bed. He lowered to the mattress and tugged me against him.

He buried his face in my belly, and I tangled my fingers in his hair and leaned down, inhaling the familiar scent of tobacco and salt from his skin. He held me tight against him. With each breath, he relaxed into me. My bottom lip quivered.

What if I went with them to Flagstaff, and this didn't work out? Would I be left for the rest of my life to watch Will return to his old ways? Could I survive it?

"You've been quiet," he murmured against me. I ran my fingernails against his scalp, something I'd learned a while ago that helped him relax.

"It's been a hard few days," I whispered.

Will pulled back, his dark eyes intent on mine. "You're right." He leaned on the mattress, resting on his elbows. "We haven't had time for us."

I nodded, giving a half-hearted shrug. "You needed time for *you*." I cursed myself silently as the word came out too harsh. "I didn't mean it like that." I shook my head. "You needed space after Mickey. I wanted to give you that."

His dark eyes lightened. He nodded and then tugged me down to straddle his lap on the mattress.

"You're amazing," he said, his eyes devouring my features. He tucked a loose curl behind my ear, his hands following a familiar path along my neck, down my shoulder, around my waist. My body reacted to him, as naturally as breathing. I cradled his head in my hands, fighting against the temptation to lose myself in him.

Because losing myself in him was the problem.

I'd never expected this. I'd never worried about letting myself free fall into him, not after that night on the bridge, not after the things he'd said. But now I hesitated, our mouths centimeters apart as I stared into his eyes.

But, Savvy, I can't love you.

Maybe a part of me believed that would change, that if only he'd open his heart to me, he *could* love me. There were times he looked at me and I thought my heart would burst right out of my chest because I knew he felt *something* for me.

Then I remembered Gabriela's story of her and Mickey. How it took ten years. How she'd sacrificed and given so much of herself to a man that she couldn't change, because he had to change *himself*.

Will'd been so locked down in his grief that maybe there just wasn't room for me. I bit back tears that threatened to fill my eyes. I couldn't be Gabriela, holding on to a sliver of something that may never be. I couldn't follow him blindly into the next great adventure, because that wasn't me.

"What's wrong?" he asked, brows furrowing. He leaned back, his hands falling to the mattress at his side.

"Nothing," I whispered. "Nothing's wrong."

He cradled my cheek, brushing his calloused thumb along my jawline. "Then what is it?"

"I love you," I said, tears filling my eyes and spilling onto my cheeks.

Will froze, so still and silent he could've been made of stone. When, after a long moment, he blinked back into consciousness, he stared at me. Another long silence ensued before he shifted me from his lap and stood. His rejection stung, making my cheeks burn.

"What?" His voice was tentative, imploring.

"I love you, and I know you don't love me," I said, the words in a rush. "And you told me that you couldn't love me, and I didn't listen. I loved you anyway." I shook my head and scooted to the edge of the mattress. "I love you, William. And it's because I love you, because you *promised* me that you would let me go, that I have to leave."

"What?" he asked again, dumbfounded. "You want to leave?"

"I've spent ten years of my life being what everyone else needed me to be," I said, swiping at my cheeks. "Lee's lackey, Bonnie's nursemaid, your strength." I bit my bottom lip, afraid to look at him, to see his emotions, because they would influence me. "I have to be what *I* need now. And what I need is to go home."

"Oh," he said, the word falling from his lips without emotion. "Okay."

I couldn't blame him. Because he told me exactly who he was. I nodded to myself, then shoved everything down deep. My strength had to be for *me* now. I gathered my things, packed them in my bag, and headed for the exit, but stopped, eyes shuttering. I shouldn't look back at him. I knew I shouldn't, but I did it anyway.

Will stared at me blankly.

"Be well, William." When he didn't respond, I left him there. I didn't know what the future held for me, but it was time I took it into my own hands. Even if it felt like my chest cleaved in two. Even if I knew I was leaving my heart with him in that tent.

Because home called for me, and home couldn't be William Ellis anymore.

Chapter Forty-Six

BONNIE

A STORM WAS COMING, though, if I were being honest, it was already here. The wind bustled, tossing my hair and bringing with it the metallic taste of electricity. Jesse shifted me in his arms, jostling my bad side. I hissed, and his grip loosened to cradle me more gently.

"You know you don't have to carry me everywhere, right?" I asked, amused. I'd been studying the muscled cords of his neck and shoulder, committing another piece of him to memory. The fleur-de-lis brand stood out starkly against his sun-tanned skin.

"I know," he replied simply. "I want to."

He hadn't left my side since that day in Tent City. Not for a moment. Not when the funeral pyres were being prepared. Not when Beck and Quanah showed up and demanded privacy. He stayed through the teary reunions and the embarrassment of not being able to bathe myself. He watched me sleep, his eyes tracking the steady rise and fall of my chest. And while the constancy of his overprotectiveness grated on my nerves, a part of me never wanted him to stop. So while I might grumble about him carrying me playfully, I also found that spot on his shoulder that I fit so perfectly into and rested my face there as he carried me around the camp.

Will had splinted and bandaged my ankle, but it would need a real cast once we made it back to Flagstaff. Months of physical therapy awaited me, but so did a little recently vacated two-bedroom house. And if Quanah and Beck had their way, it would have flower boxes outside the windows and reclaimed paintings on every wall. A place that was warm and welcoming, a place we could love, even if only for a little while.

He found a covered area near the festivities, yet far enough removed that we weren't forced to socialize with anyone else. Setting me gingerly in a chair, he pressed his lips to my forehead before walking off to fetch one for himself.

The wind gusted again, and I filled my lungs with the petrichor, my skin buzzing in anticipation of the rain. A child's laughter pealed across the open space, and my eyes fell on them. A group of ten or so children, some undesirables, some freed slaves. They played together; two little girls made crowns of braided long grass, and the littler ones played tag. The Kid and his tall friend, Billy, stood off to the side, engaged in conversation but keeping a watchful eye out for them.

Jesse returned, dragging a chair beside mine before sitting. "What're you looking at?" he asked, studying the side of my face.

"Them." I motioned to the children. "Look at them," I whispered. "They're *laughing*."

He faced them, taking in the scene as another child's laugh split the air. The ghost of a smile feathered over his mouth, but it fell again as he sat up straighter.

"Wait," he said, recognition in his eyes. "Isn't that the kid from the Slavers' Parade?" I scanned their faces, finding a boy with dark hair, no older than The Kid was when I'd first met him. He was skinny, but his face wasn't gaunt and haunted like most of them had been in that place. It was hard to remember if it was the same child or not. "He had a sister, the little girl who helped me after I was whipped." He sat forward then, his elbows on his knees, searching the children's faces until he found her playing tag with the others, a braided long grass crown nestled in her hair. "Oh *thank God*." He sighed in relief.

We stayed silent for another long moment, just watching them play. I thought of the laughter I'd heard before everything went dark. How certain I was that it was Emma, waiting for me in whatever lay beyond this life. As another peal of laughter sounded, I wondered if there had been a message in that vision.

"What happens to them now?" I asked Jesse quietly. He sat back, crossing his arms over his chest as he contemplated.

"They go back home, I guess," he answered after a moment. I turned to face him, sorrow marinating deep in my bones.

"Didn't you tell me their mother was shot at the whipping post?" I asked. He met my gaze and nodded softly, swallowing hard. "And The Kid's new friend is an undesirable, right?" He nodded again. "Those kids are abandoned at the fringes when their deformities can't be hidden. Who are they going back to?"

Jesse's eyes tracked behind me once more, following the group of children in this rare moment of joy. He didn't speak. Neither of us had an answer, not really. Instead he reached out and tangled his fingers with mine, bringing the back of my hand to his mouth for a kiss.

"Hmm," he hummed against my skin. "This hand looks a little bare." He grinned, then rose from his seat. "Hey, Kid!"

The Kid glanced at us, suspicion in his eyes until he saw Jesse. He walked over, glancing behind him a couple of times.

"You still got that box?" Jesse asked.

The tense lines of The Kid's face loosened, and a smile slipped across his mouth. He shoved his hand into his pocket and retrieved a small black box. Jesse took it from him and then knelt in front of me. He captured my left hand with his.

"I've been wanting to do this for a *long* time, Mrs. James," he admitted. Then without preamble, he opened the box. A ring glimmered from its velvet resting spot. Jesse pulled it from the box and slid it onto my finger. It fit perfectly. When I lifted my hand to look at it, shock washed warm down my spine. I blinked at the welling emotion in my chest.

There, on my hand, wrapped in wires of silver, was my carved bead from Flagstaff. The one I'd been gifted before Jesse and I danced together the very first time, so blue it was almost black, like the lake we'd found all that time ago.

"It's my bead," I whispered happily, eyes glued to the dainty ring.

"To remember you by," he said gruffly. "And I did, Bonnie. I remembered you. Every day on the road, praying that you would be just in the next town." He kissed the ring on my hand, sighing in contentment. As if a weight had been lifted from his shoulders. "Do you like it?"

I nodded, swallowing around the lump in my throat. "I love it."

Wrenching my gaze from the beautiful ring, I pulled him toward me for a deep kiss. Deep and lingering, mouths open and hearts wild. I was seconds away from begging him to pick me up and bring me to bed when we heard The Kid complaining loudly beside us.

"I told you," he said with a sneer, his friend Billy standing beside him. "You have to get used to *a lot* of kissing."

Billy shook his head, grinning as we broke apart to acknowledge them. "I already told you, I'm not going to Flagstaff," Billy told The Kid, who deflated a little at the news.

"Why not?" Jesse asked, surprising me. Billy's eyes went wide when Jesse spoke, the tips of his ears a little red. He shrugged, his shoulders hiked high.

"I dunno," Billy muttered. "I figured I'd head back to New Orleans. I know the score there."

Jesse nodded, but something was different within him. Changed. I supposed that was true enough of us all after everything.

"Or you could come with us to Flagstaff," Jesse offered.

"W-with you?" Billy's eyes darted between us. We glanced at each other, to see if there was any hesitation. But I saw none.

"Yeah," Jesse said, standing to his full height. "With us."

It was like seeing Will as a child, that insatiable hunger to belong that I never noticed hiding somewhere behind the eyes. Jesse held out his hand and Billy took it eagerly, his eyes still suspicious of his good fortune. When he turned away, The Kid was right there, beaming at him.

"I *told you* that you'd have to get used to the kissing," The Kid teased.

"Who cares about *that*?!" Billy hissed. "*Montana* just asked me to come with him. Your brother is *so cool*!" I chuckled as Jesse sat back in his chair, staring after the two boys who were, for once, not truly bickering. His eyes were wistful, a small smile on his mouth.

"You realize you just doubled our teenager problem," I said once they were out of earshot. Jesse groaned and fixed me with a playful glare.

"It's your fault," he said firmly.

"Me?" I asked, clutching my newly adorned hand over my heart.

"Yes, *you*, with your '*what happens to them now*' speech. You knew I was gonna fold like a deck of cards." He snorted. I batted my lashes at him sweetly and leaned closer. He shook his head furiously, trying to stave off my attempt at coercion.

"You know . . . " I said slowly.

"No," he replied, firm.

"You haven't even heard what I'm going to say yet," I pouted.

"I don't have to. Whatever it is, I *refuse*."

"You remember how many kids you told me you wanted?" I asked, my grin spreading wildly across my face.

"Oh, Bon, *no*," he groaned.

"An even dozen, wasn't it?" I reminded him. "Hear me out." I peeled one of his hands away from his face. "Let's take all the displaced kids to Flagstaff—"

"You *can't* be seriously trying to adopt like forty children, Bonnie. I swear, between you and Will I'm going to have an actual stroke—"

I smacked his arm and rolled my eyes. "Of course not!" I assured him. "But I am suggesting that we take all those kids to Flagstaff. And we help them find families. Try to reunite some of the slave kids with any living relatives they might have left. Help rehabilitate some of the undesirable kids with their deformities. Find places for them so they aren't forgotten."

Jesse was quiet now, contemplative yet again. Then his eyes trailed to the children playing beyond us. He nodded softly and cupped my cheeks in his palms before pressing a firm kiss to my mouth.

"That," he admitted quietly, "I think we can do."

We planned like that for a while, ideas and strategies coming together as inspiration struck. We were going to help them. The children. I think Emma would be proud of us for that. At least, I hoped so.

"What about your father?" Jesse asked.

My shoulders tensed. "What about him?"

"You spent a lot of time reading his ledger. Now we know what he wants." He shuddered. Will had told us about the bombs. Jones revealed to Mickey that *that* was what Anna and Jeff James had hidden in Montana. They died to protect their secret when Sixgun set fire to Jesse's life.

I'd been avoiding thinking beyond returning to Flagstaff, but Jesse was right.

"I think we can't face my father until we have the entire picture," I said.

With a silent nod, Jesse looped his fingers with mine. Understanding passed between us as the wind grew blusterier, and the rumble of distant thunder loomed on the horizon. The clouds were so low and dark as they rolled in that the storm would break any moment.

That was when I saw him. Will, barefoot, with his shirt only half-buttoned, looking for all the world like a lost puppy. Directionless and empty-headed.

"Will!" I called. His head snapped up at my voice, and he blinked a few times before heading over. Jesse tensed beside me, obviously worried for our friend.

"What's going on?" Jesse asked, his eyes searching for any visible damage. A stone settled deep in the pit of my stomach. One that said this damage wasn't the kind that could be healed with a bandage or a stitch.

Will was well and truly *broken*.

He shook his head but didn't speak for a long moment, and when he did, there was no emotion in his words.

"Savannah's gone." He swallowed and nodded as if to remind himself that it was true. "She left me."

No one spoke while Will gathered himself, and then Jesse leaned forward on his knees expectantly but didn't speak.

Irritation built in my chest. "Is this what the two of you do? Sit around and stare at each other when shit goes down? No *wonder* men can't get anything done."

They both stared at me.

"What are you doing here with us if she's out there?" I asked, motioning toward the road that led away from the camp. He shook his head again, refusing to listen to sense.

"She said she loves me, and, like I told her weeks ago, I can't love her," he said, anguished. "I promised her that I'd let her go."

"Oh fuck that," I said vehemently. Jesse peered at me and arched his brow as if to say *hypocrite.* "That wasn't a real promise, it was a back door. An exit strategy in case things started to feel too *real.*"

Will shoved his hands into his pockets and refused to meet my eyes.

"Will," I said, trying to get his attention, but he pointedly ignored me. "Will!"

He still didn't acknowledge me.

"Goddamnit, Will, you've been in love with that girl for years and *everyone* with eyes knows it except for *you*!"

He finally looked at me. "No." He shook his head. "I'm not *capable* of love."

I rolled my eyes, and Jesse snorted derisively before leaning back in his chair.

"No? Not *capable*? Look around you, dipshit." I opened my arms and motioned to the people meandering about with food or lost in conversation. "*You* did all this. And you did it because you love us." I waved a finger between me and Jesse. "You're capable. And you feel it. And you feel it for *Savannah.* Which probably scares the shit out of you, I get it. I've been there." I paused, lowering my voice slightly. "Mickey wouldn't want you to waste a second of your life and miss out on the girl of your dreams. He'd want better for you than that."

Will didn't move. He still just stood there, letting my words sink in. And quite frankly, it wasn't happening fast enough for me.

"Jesse," I said, giving him a nod.

Jesse rose from his seat and smacked the back of Will's head so hard that the sound reverberated. Will glared at him and cocked his fist back to retaliate, but Jesse put his hands up in a gesture of peace.

"She told me to." He pointed at me.

"Do you *always* do what she says?" Will grumbled, rubbing the back of his head. Jesse sighed and wrapped an arm around my shoulders.

"Happy wife, happy life, man."

"Wife?" Will asked, his eyes widening as he marked our rings. "Since when?" Jesse didn't get a chance to answer before Will let out the most frustrated groan I'd ever heard. "You *robbed* me!" he said, pointing an accusing finger at me. "I didn't get to throw a bachelor party!" Jesse chuckled at the stricken look in Will's eyes. You'd have thought I just stole his firstborn child.

"You aren't getting out of this with your charm and wit, Will," I said, not falling for his usual diversions. His easy smile faltered and fell. He looked at Jesse, his fingers twitching.

"What if I'm not good enough?" he asked quietly.

Jesse clapped a hand on his shoulder. "What if you are?" he countered, and they shared a smile that seemed to strengthen something inside of Will that I hadn't ever really seen before. His brows furrowed as he fought with something internally, but just as I was about to start yelling profanities at him for procrastinating, his face relaxed, his expression resigned. As if he'd made a decision he wouldn't be able to take back.

"What are you still doing here with us, dipshit?" I asked.

Instead of a grin, a hopeful smile brightened his face. He backed away as thunder bellowed in the distance and the first drops of rain fell. He ran, the wind whipping over him, feet bare, towards his stallion. A moment later, he soared past us, riding bareback and racing down the storm.

Jesse watched beside me. "Do you think he'll make it?" I asked, and his blue eyes found me, the storm locked inside of them just as violent as the one surrounding us.

"Oh yeah," Jesse said with that conviction that I loved so deeply. "They'll make it."

CHAPTER FORTY-SEVEN

WILL

THE FIRST DROPS OF rain didn't bother me, but as the sky broke apart and the torrent fell, they stung my skin. My stallion flew, not bothered by the crack of the thunder overhead. My hands fisted his mane, my thighs gripping his back without a saddle. I didn't have time. Too much had already passed.

Bonnie was dying in my arms. She was dying, and there wasn't anything I could do about it. Fear churned in my gut. The night was dark and storming, lightning flashing as I crossed the threshold. Then, appearing from within the house, a woman with the brightest eyes I'd ever seen caught and held my gaze.

Savannah hadn't noticed me then, not really, but I'd noticed *her.* That night, I saw her command the room like she was born to do it. That night and every moment after, I'd noticed her. I'd noticed her gentleness and her ferocity. I'd noticed the poetry of her movements and the viciousness of her dismissal. I noticed when she hid herself away from the world and made herself small. I noticed when she allowed herself to be free. Loving Bonnie with her quiet, caring soul and bickering with me when I ruined all her pretty little plans.

The water sluiced down my body as we raced faster into the dark night. *Please,* I begged in my mind, desperate for any sign of her. That she hadn't been swallowed up in the blackness surrounding us. Not her. She'd always been my light. I *had* to find her.

479

My heart raced and broke and died every second. A crack of lightning lit the air across the horizon, and silvery light limned a figure in the distance.

Hope hurt. But Bonnie was right: if I risked nothing, then I'd lose every time.

"Savannah!" I called over the storm, my voice breaking on her name. My stallion didn't need the encouragement of my heels digging into his sides. He ran like we were racing between heaven and hell, the devil on our heels and gaining on us.

I called her name again, but she didn't turn around. Maybe she didn't hear me, or maybe she didn't *want* to. The next time I called for her, she turned, one arm raised to keep the rain from her face. I couldn't make out her expression in the low light, but I tugged hard on my stallion's mane to slow him to a soft canter.

Her expression was a mix of confusion and pinched grief. Not the bright-eyed woman I'd met so long ago. Not the sunlight through whiskey that burned through every part of me. Instead, her eyes were dim and dismissive.

I'd done that to her.

"What are you *doing* here?" she asked, shouting over the wailing wind that ripped at our hair, our clothes.

"You left me!" I shouted back as our horses circled each other.

"You said you'd let me go," she replied. I thought her chin quivered slightly, but it could have been a trick of my eyes. It could have been the storm. It could have been the darkness surrounding us.

I chose to believe that hope wasn't lost.

"I lied!" I shouted so that she could hear me over the rain.

"You don't lie," she countered.

"I thought I didn't," I confirmed, shaken by the admission. "But I did. I lied to you, and I lied to myself. I don't wanna be left behind anymore. And I'm not letting you go."

"You don't have a choice, William. I've made mine. I'm going to St. Louis!"

"I know! I know you have to go back. You have to find your mom." She dropped her arm and let the rain fall unbidden over her face as she stared at me. "So we'll go," I declared. "We'll go and I'll help you find her. And whatever you find, I'll be there to help you deal with it."

Savannah tugged the reins, slowing her horse. She shook her head at me. "Those are pretty words. But you said it yourself, you can't love me. So why delay the inevitable?"

Swinging my leg over the back of my horse, I dropped barefoot into the mud and gripped the reins of her mare. "Get off the fucking horse."

"No."

"Savannah Beauregard, if you don't get off this fuckin' horse I'm going to drag you off it."

She jutted her chin defiantly.

"Alright," I said, jaw tight. "Don't say I didn't warn you." Reaching up to her waist, I gripped her tight and pulled her from the saddle. She slapped my arms and kicked the whole way, though I didn't expect anything less. As soon as her feet hit the ground, she shoved me hard in the chest.

"How dare you!" Her hands balled into fists at her sides.

"I'm not having this conversation on the back of a goddamned horse!" I said, but she wasn't listening. She shoved me again, and her brow was screwed up in a way that made it clear the rain wasn't responsible for all of the wetness on her face now. I tried to grab her hands as she shoved me again, but she twisted away. She was working herself into hysterics now, her whole body taut and furious.

Gripping her shoulders, I shook her once to make her level all that furious beauty at me, until fire flashed in her eyes, lighting her up the way I loved.

"I do love you," I said, tasting rainwater. She shook her head, trying to twist out of my hold once more. "Did you hear me?" I asked, desperate. "I said that I—"

Her palm collided with my jaw, and while the blow didn't hurt much, it did shock me.

"I don't believe you," she said, lips trembling. "I *can't* believe you."

Fair enough. I wouldn't believe me either if the roles were reversed. Panic and desperation clawed up the back of my throat. How did I prove it to her? How did I make her see that I wasn't just saying what she wanted to hear? I screwed my eyes closed and took a deep breath to steady myself before trying again. This time, I decided, I would tell her everything. I wouldn't rush to the end. I'd tell her every wayward thought that'd been battering around in my head so she could *understand* these feelings eating away inside of me.

"You have exactly thirty-six freckles," I told her. She stared at me incredulously, her head shaking back and forth in disbelief.

"Freckles?" she asked, sarcasm dripping from her tone. "You want to talk about—"

"Yes!" I hissed. "Thirty-six. You have thirty-six of them, but only twenty-nine are on your face. My favorite is the one behind your left ear, because I don't know how the hell it got there, and I've spent many sleepless nights thinking of each and every way possible that it wound up in that exact location."

Her mouth snapped shut.

"And you hum while you're baking, which is the only way I can tell that you love it as much as you do because you rarely smile in the kitchen. It's calming for you, like meditation, I think, but you also concentrate so hard sometimes when you work that it's hard to tell. It's the humming and the little smile of satisfaction you have with your cup of victory tea once you're done that tips me off."

"Will, I—"

But I didn't let her finish what she was saying, because I knew it wasn't enough. There was more. There was so much more. I just needed her to know it all before she decided to leave again. I needed to know that I'd done everything I could before she walked out of my life forever.

"Your mother smells like *Opium*, that perfume they use in the brothels. I found the doll you hid from Lee, and I recognized it right away. I bought a vial of that perfume the next day and kept it in my saddlebag, just in case you started to miss her." I stared into the dark clouds, blinking as the rain ran into my eyes before allowing them to fall back to her. "Fuck, none of this is coming out right," I said, pushing my wet hair off of my forehead. "I don't love you because I'm observant.

"I didn't think I was capable of loving anyone," I tried again, searching her eyes for some kind of sign that I was making any sense at all. Because I felt stupid. Stupid, and scared, and small. "Not because I wasn't capable of human emotion, like my father," I explained, a hint of panic lacing my voice at the thought. "But because I didn't think that I was worth enough to love."

The truth of that statement sucked the breath out of my lungs. I dragged air in like it was precious for a long few moments after I said those words. "When I was born, it was as a means to control my mother. Keep her submissive. My life was nothing more than a threat, one my dad used to keep my mother in line," I admitted painfully, the words coming from my lips broken and bloody. "And when I got older, nothing changed. I was a means to an end. For Bonnie. With the Hanged Men. Lee."

I pushed the sopping strands of hair off of my forehead, because it was already dark, and she needed to know that I wasn't hiding anything from her. Not anymore. This was the truth of me. Raw and real and agonizing. Take it or leave it. My eyes watered, but with the rain it didn't matter. I finally let myself just feel it.

"I think I loved you the first night I met you," I told her honestly, biting my bottom lip to stop it from trembling. "But it didn't matter. Because I couldn't be loved *back*. How could I? I wasn't a real person. I wasn't anything more than a tool to be used by other people. I was bad, rotten, fucked up from the start because of my dad. And you are *so fuckin' good*, Savvy, you're as near to perfect as I've ever seen."

My breath shuddered. My chest heaved. My fingers twitched. But I didn't stop. I *couldn't* stop. The truth spilled out of me now like a dam breaking and flooding everything below it. I hadn't known how much I'd held back until right now, in this moment, when my entire life was on the line.

"I stayed away from you after that first night because I was terrified that I'd fuck you up. Ruin you. Make you just as ugly and unlovable as I was. Part of me wanted to. I wanted to *so fuckin' bad*, baby," I said through clenched teeth, desperate to stop the well of emotion that had risen within me but ultimately knowing it was impossible. "If you weren't so poised and elegant and put together, then maybe, *maybe,* there was a chance you could look at me and see someone worthy enough to stand by your side. But I kill people."

I opened my hands in a helpless gesture that made her beautiful brown eyes waver in an emotion that I couldn't name or comprehend. Almost like pity but deeper, it hurt to see her crumple in front of me, like she was familiar with the kind of heartbreak I was confronting her with now.

"And you loved me anyway," I said, wanting to bury my hands in her hair. Wanting to touch her skin. To feel her warmth. Yet knowing, without a shadow of a doubt, that I had no right to. "And when I was ready to give it up," I told her, swallowing hard. "You were there, begging me to stay."

It wasn't just my body shaking anymore. It was my soul. My heart. Whatever threads that strung me together were vibrating with shame, begging me to cut my vocal cords that kept speaking.

"You challenged me to be better," I choked out. "You and Mickey and Jesse."

"William—"

"And because you did, I discovered that I *am* worthy. I'm worth having friends. I'm worth the trouble it takes to have me in your life. I'm strong enough. I'm capable enough. I am *enough*." I rushed to tell her. "And I'm enough for you.

"I love you, Savannah Beauregard," I said, my words rushing hot from my lips. "I'm *in love* with you. I love you when you're perfect and when you aren't. I love you when you're angry and when you're calm. I love your childishness and your maturity. Your confident kindness and your impatient cruelty. I love how thoughtful you are, and how you nag me. I love the fact that you don't trust easily but you've never doubted me. I know I've given you absolutely no reason to, but *mi amor*, please trust me when I say that before you loved me, I didn't exist. You laid your eyes on me, and a new man was born."

I cupped her cheeks, blinking to clear my vision so that I could memorize the fullness of her pillowy mouth and the freckles I'd mapped a thousand times like constellations. If this was the last time I saw her, I wanted it all burned into my mind.

"You gave me your heart," I said, swallowing hard. "And I was careless with it. I hurt you. I hurt us both." I pressed my forehead to hers. "Mine isn't worth much," I admitted. "It's a shriveled, blackened thing. But *Savvy*"—my hands shook—"it's yours. It *always* has been."

"A-are you sure?"

I chuckled softly against her mouth, nodding. "Yes, baby, I'm sure."

"And you really want to go to St. Louis with me? You were so excited about Flagstaff, and Bonnie and Jesse—"

Instead of responding, I kissed her hard. My mouth parted hers and drank the whimper of pleasure she made. She was so sweet, her skin warm against the cold rain, and I crushed her against me. Her hands buried in my hair, pulling me closer. She wrenched her mouth away from mine to suck in a quick breath and asked, "Why didn't you just say all that before?"

Rolling my eyes, I lifted her into my arms and walked her farther away from the horses. "Because you *terrify me*," I said simply. "That wasn't obvious?"

Her lips ran down my throat, and I shuddered, kneeling in the mud. "You know that one pretty speech in the rain isn't going to make up for this, right?" She smiled brightly. I nodded.

"Don't worry," I said, laying her down in the mud. "I plan on making it up to you several times over."

"Will!" she cried out as I started to unbutton her jeans. "Can't we go back to the tent? This weather is awful, and I wanted to come back as soon as I left."

"I like the storm," I told her, cold hands mapping her body. "We met the night of a storm. Besides, everyone else is fucking in the tents.

Where's the fun in that?" She shook her head and pulled me down to kiss her again.

"Life's never going to be boring again, is it?" she asked, staring up at me with eyes so bright they mirrored the stars we couldn't see through the storm. A wicked grin curled on my mouth.

"Never."

Chapter Forty-Eight

JESSE

THE SUN PEEKED OVER the eastern horizon, highlighting the fog that'd rolled in overnight. I sat outside of our tent, watching as the camp came to life around me. There were things to get done today, but my motivation was severely lacking. Maybe it was because our friends were leaving us. I'd never imagined that after we got out of New Orleans, Will and Savannah would go their own way. In my head, it was the four of us, plus The Kid and Billy.

It was selfish of me, but I couldn't be sorry for it.

Will appeared through the fog, carrying a couple of steaming steel mugs. He sat next to me on the rickety bench and offered one of the mugs to me. I took it without a word. For once, we sat silently together, staring out at nothing.

I understood why they had to go to St. Louis. Savannah and Will had already done so much for the two of us, but my chest tightened with how much I'd miss them.

"Are you two packed?" I finally asked.

Will nodded as he sipped his coffee. "Just about. Savvy's saying good-bye to Gabriela and Elena." I snickered at the mention of the latter. Even after everything, Elena still eyed Will with suspicion when we told her our plans.

"Bonnie still sleeping?"

I shook my head and chuckled. "Worse, she's organizing."

Bonnie had gotten up before dawn and employed Billy and The Kid to help her round up the children we'd be bringing with us. Beck and

Quanah were thrilled at the prospect of more kids out in Flagstaff. I was just happy that we didn't have to send them back to New Orleans, to the fringes. They deserved a better life, and I hoped we could give it to them.

"Just sucks that y'all will be so far away," Will said quietly. I nodded.

"The guys from Fort Hood said it's totally gone." The military base we'd found Mickey in hadn't exactly been home, but it'd been close enough. We'd made friends, built community, and Jones took it away with a single order. I cleared my throat and patted Will's shoulder. "It's not forever, you know. We will see you again."

Will only nodded and sipped his coffee. I admired his decision to go with Savannah. As much as I'd miss them, he needed to go out on his own. He needed to figure out what his future looked like, with Savannah.

I only hoped they found what they were looking for in St. Louis.

"Well, you two look like you swallowed something nasty." Savannah approached, dressed in her road gear as she placed her hands on her hips. Will's expression softened, and a smile curled on his mouth. He handed me his empty mug and crossed to her, wrapping his arms around her waist and kissing her senseless. She giggled as he pulled back from her.

My friend really was an idiot to think he didn't love her. He looked younger, lighter. Like he'd been in Fort Hood, full of hope and possibility.

"Where's Bonnie?" Savannah asked. "I looked for her after Gabriela and the Acadiana crew left but couldn't find her."

"Probably barking orders at The Kid and Billy. We found a free wagon yesterday, but it needed a wheel replaced," I said. "How was Gabriela?"

Savannah's mouth turned downward. "As good as she can be."

Grief licked up my spine. I'd asked Gabriela to come with us to Flagstaff. She'd only patted her belly and told me that she needed to be with her godmother, at least for a while. She'd already hung up her assault rifle when she found out she was pregnant. Now, she was going to give herself time to rest, time to grieve. She promised to keep in touch.

I'd wanted to convince her, because we were family too, but Mickey would have told me to shut the hell up and let Gabriela do what she wanted.

"You ready?" Savannah asked Will. He nodded and looped his fingers with her.

I followed after them, leaving the steel cups on the bench. Soon, this place would be empty. At least those cups would be some small indication that we'd once been here.

Over the last day, most of our forces had departed. It still boggled my mind that Will had done this, had brought together people from every walk of life all in the name of saving us and defeating tyranny. As I walked in line with them, I glanced at my friend, admiring the man he had become since the time I put a bullet in his shoulder.

"What?" Will asked as excited voices sounded ahead of us.

I clapped a hand on his shoulder. "Nothing," I said with a smile.

Most of the people who remained were those from Flagstaff. They'd been waiting for us to be ready to leave. In truth, as Bonnie caught sight of Savannah and Will and her eyes dimmed, I didn't think we'd ever be ready.

"I have something for you," Bonnie said, leaning heavily against the wagon. She reached over the side and dug in a bag, then pulled out an old piece of paper. Savannah stood beside her as Bonnie unfurled her old map. I even spied the X I'd marked on the page when I'd told her where Roswell was all that time ago.

"These"—Bonnie pointed to the hand-drawn stars on the map between here and St. Louis—"are safe houses. Tell them I sent you and they'll take you in for the night."

"She doesn't need a safe house, she has me," Will remarked, flashing both of them a grin.

Bonnie rolled her eyes as she offered the map to Savannah. With glassy eyes, the women embraced, gripping each other tight. "You better bring that map back to me," she said, her voice cutting on the words.

"We will," Savannah said, giving Bonnie one final squeeze before turning to hug The Kid.

"You finally got it," Bonnie said to Will. He looked at her curiously. "An apple pie kind of life." He ducked his head, and she pulled him into a tight hug. "Don't fuck it up," she whispered as they broke apart.

One of the men with the Flagstaff group approached, holding something. "Letter for Savannah Beauregard?"

Savannah took it, furrowing her eyebrows as she glanced at Will and then at Bonnie. She ripped the seal on the envelope and unfolded the letter. She let out a gasp, her eyes immediately filling with tears.

"What is it?" Bonnie asked.

"Etty," Savannah said, her breath catching. "She's alive."

Will warmed at the news. "I had no doubts. She hasn't gotten to hit me with her rolling pin yet." He turned to me and extended his forearm. I gripped it tight, then yanked him in for a hug.

"Take care of each other," I said to him as we parted. When he looked at me, I once again saw the man he had been when we first made it to Fort Hood, wide-eyed, hopeful, but also a little sad. Who knew back then that William Ellis would become my best friend? "Take care of yourself, too."

"I'll think of you in bed. And even though you won't admit it, you'll think about me, too. I am an *amazing* cuddler. You won't really get a chance to miss me anyway, *hermano*, I plan on writing to you every single day." With a parting wink and one final hug between Bonnie and Savannah, Will wrapped his arm around her shoulder, and they headed for their horses. I watched them for a long moment, until they were nearly out of sight.

Bonnie touched my elbow. I turned to her and wrapped an arm around her, tucking her loosely to my side. Her ribs still hurt if I gripped her too tight. The splint on her ankle did well enough, but from the way she leaned into me, I could tell she was feeling it. I was thankful that most of our journey would be via railcar, but we'd have to take the wagon for the first few days until we reached the nearest stop.

"Hey," she said in a low voice, tipping her chin to my left.

The Kid stood apart from the others. He had a length of rope in his hands as he stared across the wide, empty city, tying and untying the same knot. I'd thought he'd be happy to head to Flagstaff, but the tense set of his shoulders told me something was wrong.

"I've got him," I murmured before pressing my lips to Bonnie's forehead. I helped her sit on the end of the wagon, then crossed through the mud to my brother. He didn't see me at first, but his eyes shifted across the landscape, his jaw clenching and unclenching. When he caught sight of me, he stopped knotting the rope.

"Are you almost ready?" I asked, tucking my hands into my jeans pocket.

The Kid glanced out across the barren landscape. "What's gonna happen when we leave?"

Something in my chest cracked open. He didn't sound like a surly teenager. Instead, I saw that little boy who overheard me tell Mickey that our parents were dead. Back then, I'd deferred to Bonnie; I didn't know what to do with a kid. But now, I saw every single fear in his eyes, some of which were my fault. I clasped the back of his neck and guided him a little farther off from the others.

The trauma of losing our parents had been bad enough. Then he lost Bonnie and Will. Then me and Mickey as I found every reason to stay away from Fort Hood.

"Well, we'll be in Flagstaff for a while," I said quietly. "But after that—"

"You're going to leave me again."

I stopped, turning to face him fully. My little brother wasn't a child anymore. He'd traveled across the country, became an outlaw. Hell, he stormed a fortress city and survived it all.

"I'm sorry, Kid," I said, my chest tightening. "About so much." I nodded, staring into blue eyes that mirrored mine, that mirrored Mickey's. "I should have known you could handle the truth about Mom and Pop. I shouldn't have left you in Fort Hood when I went to find Bonnie. I should have brought you straight to New Orleans that day outside of the city. I—" I swallowed around the thick emotion in my throat.

"I'm sorry I went back into that house, and I'm sorry that I left you behind." I cupped his face. "Most of all, I'm sorry for not being the brother that you needed."

"But—"

"You had to grow up fast, Kid, *too* fast, and I wasn't there for you." He lifted his chin, and for the first time, I could see the man he would become. Smart like Bonnie, funny like Will, kind like Savannah, and strong like me. "From now on, wherever we go, you go with us."

"You mean it?" he asked, his blue eyes wide with hope.

"I give you my word," I said. "And outlaws always keep their word."

"Number three," The Kid replied, and I nodded.

I wrapped my arm around his shoulder and turned him back toward the wagon, toward Bonnie and Billy and the others who were coming with us.

"After Flagstaff, we're heading to Montana," I said, clutching him tight. "Kid, we're finally going home."

KEEP READING FOR AN EXCLUSIVE PEEK AT

THE THRILLING FINALE TO THE FOOL'S ADVENTURE SERIES

Jess,
Lee is back in New
Orleans. It's time.

Dr. William Wayne Beauregard, Esq., MD,
The Fourth, ~~Breaker of Hearts~~ (Savannah
made me scratch that out), Your best friend.

ACKNOWLEDGMENTS

Chains & Reckoning was, by far, our most challenging book to write. Bonnie, Jesse, Will, and Savannah's journeys were *difficult*, and honestly, we were avoiding saying goodbye to a beloved character. Here's to the literal hours we sobbed while writing death scenes, break-ups, and some of our best work to date. Thank fuck it's finally published.

The Fool's Adventure series as a whole would not be what it is without our amazing readers. Who knew when we published *Guns & Smoke* that we'd find some of the best people in the world?! We love each and every one of our crew members. We can't wait to share the fourth and final book in this series, Blaze & Glory. Thank you for coming on this wild ride with us!

Special thanks to:

Alexandra Ott, for her incredible line editing services.

Nicole York, for her amazing art, photography skills, and friendship.

Michelle & John Cavalier of Cavalier House Books for being the best indie bookstore in the world!

Jonathan Sevier for being our biggest cheerleader, bringer of coffee & snacks, world-class father, and card-carrying member of the 'Under the Ellis Charm' club. Paw Paw Wayne for being our biggest fan and inspiration for the series. And many countless friends, co-workers, and family members for their support and encouragement.

Sign up for our newsletters or follow us on socials to get the latest teasers, exclusive content, and updates!

ALSO BY LAUREN SEVIER

Songs Series
Songs of Autumn
Songs of Winter

The Fool's Adventure Series
Guns & Smoke
Leather & Lace

ABOUT LAUREN SEVIER

Lauren Sevier lives a simple life in small town Central, Louisiana with her family and sweet Border Collie. She's a proud firefighter wife and mother to her miracle son, born through IVF after an eight-year battle with infertility. She works for a non-profit hospital in Cardiology. Writing and being in the service of helping others are her two passions in life.

She started writing song lyrics and poems on the front porch swing of her family home. She and her best friend get most of their inspiration on girl's night, after a glass of wine, or after watching movies from the early 2000's. They have plans to publish many series in the future together. However her passion is derived mostly from being a mother to her adventurous, imaginative, and affectionate son who ceases to amaze her every single day.

For more information, go to www.laurensever.com.

ALSO BY
ABBIE LYNN SMITH

The Fool's Adventure Series
Guns & Smoke
Leather & Lace
Chains & Reckoning

ABOUT
ABBIE LYNN SMITH

Abbie Lynn Smith is an author of romance novels. She holds a Bachelor's degree in theatre, where she learned the art of storytelling. A lifelong resident of southern Louisiana, she is a lover of coffee, naps, and animals.

When not writing, she can be found spending time with her rescue dogs, Klaus and Mama.

Abbie is passionate about mental healthcare and believes that helping others with their own mental health battles is her small way of changing the world. Abbie grew up watching westerns with her grandfather, which partially inspired the setting of her co-authored debut novel, Guns & Smoke.

For more information, go to
www.abbielynnsmith.com